I0610354

BLOOD
OF THE
SUCCUBUS

DUNCAN McGEARY

Copyright © 2016 by Duncan McGeary
ISBN 978-1-63789-133-9
Macabre Ink is an imprint of Crossroad Press Publishing
All rights reserved. No part of this book may be used or reproduced in any manner whatsoever
without written permission except in the case of
brief quotations embodied in critical articles and reviews
For information address Crossroad Press at 141 Brayden Dr., Hertford, NC 27944
www.crossroadpress.com

First Edition - 2024

Chapter 1

Doug loved Suzanne's sense of whimsy, her uncanny ability to discern the creatures in the rocks and the trees. They were climbing the steep trail up Horse Ridge, she bouncing ahead while he chuffed and huffed behind. She warned him about the ogre hiding in the juniper overhanging the cliff, the dragon in the crumbled lava rocks.

"Watch out for the lizard, Doug," she sang as he stepped over the root of a scraggly pine tree. Looking down, startled, he saw the lizard's head and the tail, and a thrill ran up his spine, as if the root was about to come alive and bite him in the nuts.

He laughed, amazed by Suzanne's ability to bring everything and anything alive.

She was too good to be true.

The anticipation was so sweet. She was going to give herself to him. She'd not said so, but he knew—he could tell. He never wanted to press—never wanted to be *that* guy—and yet, she responded. She listened to his stories. She asked the right questions. She laughed at his jokes. Really *laughed*.

She complimented him, she flattered him, she encouraged him. It was all just too good to be true. He knew that. He figured there'd be a reckoning, but he didn't care. Let the reckoning come, as long as he could have her for these few sweet days and weeks.

Why she'd chosen him, Doug couldn't understand and was afraid to ask. It was enough that she was with him on this beautiful fall day, hiking the mountain trails near Bend, Oregon, turning her head every so often to beam at him.

They climbed high into the foothills. They came to a clearing and looked back, hand in hand. The landscape of the High Desert opened up below them in all its beauty.

The canyons below were filled with juniper trees, sagebrush, dust, pumice, and black lava, stretching all the way to Bend. There, along the Deschutes River, the terrain shifted to foothills and pine forests. On the horizon beyond floated the Three Sisters and Broken Top, all snow-capped peaks in the volcanic Cascade Range. The atmosphere was so clear and brisk that even the shining white peak of Mt. Hood was visible, more than 150 miles away.

Suzanne sensed that Doug was tiring, using the excuse of the panorama to stop and rest. He flopped down next to the trail, so weary that he didn't care that the soft, sandy soil was spilling into his shoes and pockets. But Suzanne couldn't be contained and wandered off the trail, tiptoeing up to the edge of a small cliff.

Doug felt himself tensing up. He took a long breath. It was all right. She wasn't going to fall; it was OK to stray from the path a little. She was so alive that even if she did fall, she'd probably just fly away.

As tired as he was, he was also the thinnest he'd ever been, having started a crash diet a few weeks before on the day they'd met, but he was still out of shape, his legs a little wobbly. He gallantly carried the larger backpack, the one with the tent. His thinning hair wafted in the slight breeze, and he suspected he was going to be sunburned on the top of his head. But it was all worth it to spend time alone with his dream girl.

Suzanne gushed over the view. Gushed—there was no other word for it, and though that might have provoked a cynical comment from Doug once upon a time, now he found it charming. He'd grown up in Central Oregon, so maybe he took the scenery for granted. When was the last time he'd been camping? Or even gone on a day hike? Now he was seeing the landscape with new eyes—Suzanne's eyes, but also the way he'd looked on the world when he was young and hopeful.

The world was bright with colors: the red of the wildflowers, the green of the junipers with their soft blue berries, the white snow on black mountains, the blue skies without a cloud. The trail was soothing brown sand amid moss-encrusted lava rocks. Slabs of broken slate towered over the trail like walls, and chipmunks ran along the cracks. The dry air was perfumed with sage. The world was at peace, and Doug's heart with it.

But even more than the view, Suzanne drew his gaze. She was dressed like a Victorian lady explorer. She called it steampunk. When Doug first met her, she was wearing a top hat with goggles on the brim. She was a sight to see in stodgy old Bend, even weirder than the anime kids who hung out at the local Japanese merchandise store, with their cat ears and drawn-on whiskers.

The second Doug could Google it, he looked up steampunk, and suddenly it seemed like the most interesting subculture he'd ever heard of. A self-professed loner, he didn't pay much attention to pop culture, not like a geek or a dork would. Well, maybe he was a little bit of a dork; at thirty-three, he could own it.

At first Suzanne seemed way too young for him, looking more like a teenager than a woman in her late twenties. But once she told him her age, he saw the maturity and wisdom in her eyes: definitely not a teenager. She had an eternally young face and could have passed for almost any age, depending on her hair color and makeup. Sometimes, when the light hit her just right, she seemed ancient to him, a crone with a hooked nose and slanted cheekbones—but he thought that was just her wisdom shining through.

Now she wore a flared waistcoat, a ruffled ascot, and boots that laced up to the knee. She was magnificent. Fearless. Intrepid. Hell, Doug wouldn't even wear hats because he didn't want anyone to notice him. Doug hated standing out.

Certainly, when they were in public together, he got his wish. No one noticed him in the slightest; all eyes were on her. Which was fine. He loved basking in her reflected glory, proud that she chose to be with him when all the other guys, young, old, and everything in-between, wanted her.

Eventually, he'd asked her why she was with him.

"Because you're a freakin' writer, Douglas!" she said. "That's so smashingly cool."

3

"I write for a local rag," he protested. "About nothing important."

"But that's not why you do it, is it?" she said, once again amazingly perceptive. "I've seen your notebooks; you've got lots of ideas."

He flushed a little. Most of his musings seemed lame and shallow to him. But Suzanne thought they were brilliant.

"No," he said. "Being a writer is a good excuse to be who I am." The moment he said it, it felt true.

"See what I mean?" She laughed and changed the subject.

But somewhere deep inside, deep enough to be ignored, he wondered about her. It was the only blemish, this doubt, a bit of his old self, cynical about people's motives. But damned if he could see what she was getting out of the relationship.

His best friend, Cary, laughed at him. "Why question it? You're a smart, interesting guy. She can see that."

"While every other girl in the world can't?" Doug countered.

Cary shook his head. "She's the best thing that ever happened to you, Doug. You're a fool to question it."

"Yes, but a smart fool."

Cary gave him a strange look and said, "That's the worst kind."

The sad thing was that Cary later changed his mind about Suzanne.

They'd gone to a party where the booze flowed freely. At the base of a pumice pit, the light reflected off the white rock, but not much else. The world constricted to the glow of the bonfire. The beer, which he wasn't used to, and the girl made the world magical. Attending a kegger was in itself a minor miracle for Doug. Suzanne was the center of attention, but she included Doug in all the conversations, and he felt comfortable in a crowd for the first time in his life.

Then Cary came along at the end of the night and pulled him aside. "You're right, there is something off about her," he said.

"I thought you were my friend," Doug said.

"What?"

"You hit on her, didn't you?" Doug asked. "What happened, did she resist your charms?" He was in Cary's face, and even as he nearly bumped heads with the friend he had known his whole life, Doug wondered at his own aggression.

"What? No!" Cary exclaimed, but his flush revealed everything Doug needed to know. He stomped off.

He hadn't talked to Cary in weeks, Doug suddenly realized, standing there in the wilderness. How had that happened?

Suzanne returned from her explorations, slid her arm through his, and snuggled up to him. He instantly forgot his worry about Cary.

"Let's go overland, Doug," she said. "Let's explore!"

Doug hesitated. He resisted pulling out his phone and checking the GPS because he didn't want to seem like too much of a ninny. He pulled out the map and checked their location, aware of Suzanne's obvious impatience. She snorted and walked to the edge of the path, as if she was ready to spring away.

The idea of getting lost terrified him. If he wasn't on the right street, he'd freak out—and that was in the middle of a city where animals were pets. The wilderness...the wilderness was something else. A black bear had stalked him on a trail once, and there had been more and more sightings of cougars in the area. One had recently been killed in Pilot Butte State Park, right in the middle of town.

The sun shone overhead, and he checked their bearings using the map and a compass from REI.

"It's easy to get lost out here," he muttered. "All the rocks and trees start looking the same after awhile."

"Oh, come on, Doug!" Suzanne said. "As long as you have your compass, we can find our way back. We just have to go uphill, or downhill, or whatever."

Maybe, he thought. *If you like stumbling around for a while.* But she was right—they probably wouldn't get too lost.

"OK!" he said cheerfully, as if he wasn't bothered at all. It felt good.

They wandered up the dusty deer trails that wound around the lava outcroppings. The land flowed naturally, as if providing a path just for them, and they followed its natural contours, hand in hand. A warm fuzziness suffused the air; Doug's stride felt liberating, as if all his cares were being kicked away with every step. He was going to make love, maybe not for the first time, but for the first *right* time. They stopped in a clearing just as his breathing was turning into gasps for air.

Suzanne pulled out her phone, took a picture of him, and held it out for him to see. He actually looked kind of cool. The late sun darkened his glasses; his hair was appealingly tousled, and he had the healthy sheen of exertion. But it was his smile that made it all work: happy, and anticipating more happiness soon. A long time since he'd been like that.

He took a picture of Suzanne, but when they looked at it, her face was obscured by shadow and her body was strangely elongated.

"That's weird." Doug looked around, but there were no clouds overhead or trees nearby. Had he held his thumb over the lens? A chill came over him, but he shook it off. The sun was dropping, and the air was growing colder.

"Let me try again," he said.

"Never mind," Suzanne said, laughing. "We've got all the time in the world. All of nature awaits." She held her arms out as if to embrace a long-lost lover. "Mother Nature is so beautiful," she said reverently.

The sun's rays shimmered around her; then the light dimmed as the single cloud in the sky passed over them. For a moment, her steampunk look was replaced by something else—an earth goddess kind of shimmer. Her starched waistcoat and leather boots took on a softer outline, almost as if she wore nothing but sandals and a summer dress, her hair garlanded with flowers.

Doug blinked and Suzanne, the steampunk hipster, was back. Suzanne was staring right at him, right into him, as if he'd said or done something wrong. Then the sun broke out again and his warm feelings came back, pushing away the growing cold, the worry about getting lost. Suzanne was apparently immune to the weather, not even buttoning her waistcoat.

When Doug looked around, he realized that he didn't know where they were.

"We'd better stop for the night," he said. He dropped his backpack, wishing he could just lie down. He wasn't looking forward to putting up the tent. Suzanne plopped down on the springy moss covering most of the clearing, smiling up at him. "Nice and soft for my tushy," she murmured. "For when I'm on my back."

"Whoa," he said. "Slow down, girl, or…"

"Or what?"

"Or…maybe I'll get a little too excited," he said. "I, uh, want it to last."

"Oh, it will," she said. "It will last forever." But her smile didn't quite reach her eyes this time, and Doug felt a moment of uncertainty.

"Look out for ants," he said awkwardly. "You can't go twenty feet around here without finding an anthill."

They pitched their tent and rolled out the sleeping bags as dusk fell. It was full dark before Doug hung the bag of food from the branches of a tree at the edge of the clearing.

"What are you doing?" Suzanne asked.

"Bears," he answered. "You never want to have food in the tent."

"Really?" she asked, and a momentary look of terror filled her eyes. "I can't stand bears."

"Really? You seem so fearless." Doug stopped and stared at her.

"I like nature when it's tame," she said, snugging her arms around him and looking up into his face. *So much for the beauty of nature*, he thought, then shook it off. He leaned down and kissed her. It went on forever. She broke it off, finally, and rested her face against his chest. "And I like men," she whispered.

Doug grew hard against her. He couldn't fully see her face in the growing dark, but it seemed to him that she gave him a knowing smile.

"Let's get a fire going," she said.

"Against the law," he said. "Technically, we're in a drought."

"Technically," she replied with a mischievous smile. "We're miles from anyone who could catch us. Come on, Douglas, let's live a little."

At his insistence, they cleared all undergrowth away and built a rock circle before lighting the fire. As the darkness deepened around them, Doug was glad of its warmth. It would be worth the ticket if they got caught. The heat on his face and the chill at his back made him feel more alive than he'd ever felt. He was within a comforting cocoon of the fire, in the embrace of the girl of his dreams.

The flames illuminated Suzanne's face, and her eyes were bright. She stood up, keeping her eyes on his as her fingers worked their way down, unbuttoning her waistcoat. Her ascot came loose, revealing the sheer blouse beneath. Steampunks apparently didn't believe in bras.

She cupped one breast, rolling the nipple between her thumb and forefinger. She extended a leg toward him and he fumbled to unlace one high boot, then the other, pulling them off. She watched him in silence, the flames reflected in her dark eyes.

Suzanne reached down and shimmied out of her pants. He closed his eyes and groaned, and earned a laugh.

She stood, her naked body shimmering the firelight. Doug felt his heart give a double thump, and he felt dizzy for a moment. She put out her hand. He rose, and she led him to the tent.

He didn't even remember taking off his clothes. He felt the coolness of the air, and the heat within him. Suzanne was lying on the sleeping bag; so beautiful he was sure this was a dream.

Then he was on top of her and she was spreading her legs, and he slid into her naturally as if the universe had been designed only for their two bodies, all of history culminating in this one act.

Doug wanted it to last forever, but almost immediately, he cried out and burst inside her. He was embarrassed, but Suzanne just murmured "Wow."

"Sorry," he murmured.

"No worries," she said, reaching down and fondling him. "Do it again." He instantly became hard.

She once again took him inside herself, and they made slow, gentle love this time, making it last for eternity, building to an impossible climax that went on and on.

Every act of sex Doug had ever experienced was now exposed as tacky and meaningless, a physical act of release that meant nothing. He was filled with love for this girl, and for the world, and it seemed to him that from now on, he would only want this and nothing else.

Even then, Suzanne wasn't through. She lowered her mouth onto him, which no girl had done before, and it was even better than he'd imagined. She sensed when he was ready to climax again and mounted him. This time she was in a hurry, and as he felt her growing close to another climax, he moaned and came for a third time.

He nearly blacked out from the pleasure. He felt as if he could close his eyes and be instantly asleep, and that his dreams would be filled with a soft aching.

Amazingly, Suzanne still wasn't done. But by then, Doug was done; *so* done. It was so glorious that he never wanted to stop, but he was exhausted. If he were less of a gentleman, he might even brag about it; well, maybe only to Cary, just to prove how wrong his friend had been about Suzanne's intentions.

He was sure there was no way he could satiate her a fourth time. But to his amazement, he became hard again. It hurt, a deep pain in his groin, a raw sensation in his member. Still, she ground insistently against him, heedless of his attempts to push her away.

"I love you," he said. "But I can't go on."

A glimmer of hard triumph came into her eyes.

A little confused, he stuttered, "It hurts."

"Give it to me," she hissed, in a voice that was barely human.

He looked up into her face, finally seeing her—*truly* seeing her—for the first time. There was no softness there; the planes of her face were sharp, like rock. She glared down at him in anger and hate. She grasped his shoulders, and he glimpsed talons, not fingers, digging into him, drawing blood. Her breasts, which had been so pert and round, dangled above him, long and swollen.

She was taking all of him. As his vision constricted and narrowed, part of him understood that he'd always known. That he was willing to give everything to be with her.

Despite his fear and pain, Doug was once again moving inside her. Her hunger and his desire were one. Pain and pleasure burned him from within. He couldn't stop. This time when he came, he cried out in agony. Nothing came out; it was dry and painful, and all his joy had turned to dust.

Suzanne stared down at him, her eyes black and malevolent. Laughing coldly, she began moving again, and he was unable stop her in spite of the pain. He writhed but could not unseat her. She milked him, again and again. Doug slipped in and out of consciousness. His ribs poked out, his once-generous belly was completely concave, and his arms were too thin and weak to push against her any longer.

He was going to die, and even through the anguish, or somewhere on the other side of anguish, he heard her let out a guttural snarl, and he almost laughed. *What a way to go.*

9

By now, Suzanne looked nothing like a human. Her hair stuck straight up from her head like tiny daggers; her arms were thick and muscular. Her massive thighs squeezed him incessantly.

A growl came from outside the tent, so loud that it rattled the tent frame.

The canvas shivered as if from a blast of wind. The ground shook, as something heavy fell outside. Branches snapped, and dust flew through the opening of the tent. A huge and bristling shadow loomed over them.

Suzanne's relentless movement stopped; her face became recognizably human, full of surprise.

The tent tipped over and something large landed on both of them. Claws ripped through the fabric and into Suzanne's back. She let out an inhuman, screeching cry. She rose, leaving Doug exposed and shrunken—all but one part. He was bigger than ever before and raw from the friction.

As she rose, Suzanne's blood splattered down on him and dripped into his mouth. Life returned to his body, and he could finally move.

Her blood _can_ *save me,* he realized. His hand closed on the tin where the forks and knifes were stored. He grabbed a utensil, hoping for a sharp knife; it was a fork, but he stabbed her with it anyway. It was enough. Her blood splattered onto his face, and he found his voice with a loud shout.

The growling grew as the tent was pushed one way, then another. Then Suzanne fled, the sounds of her passage fading in seconds. Doug rolled to one side, trying to raise himself, but he was still too weak. Something slashed through the tent, and there was a snuffling sound near his neck, and stiff bristles of fur poked into his skin. Suzanne's blood was reviving him, but it was too late.

The bear's jaws closed on his throat. As he lost consciousness, the bear's claws tore into his most vulnerable part.

The biggest surprise to Doug was that he could still scream.

Chapter 2

Gasper Gerhard's Journal

The Blood runs low.

I should let myself grow old. I should preserve it for the following generations. But like my father before me, I am profligate with my use. Like my father before me, I have given up hope.

Despite my vows, I treat my son as my father treated me, and for the same reasons. I cannot face what I am about to do. I read the journals of my forebears, trying to find strength in their words, to understand how we have managed, each generation in its own way, in fulfilling our oath.

Only our family has had the peculiar strength to do the Cutting. All others failed. And who can blame them?

My son is innocent. God forgive me for what I am about to do. I almost hope he will break away and end our Guardianship once and for all.

Czechoslovakia, 1944

"Never go into the cellar," Heinrich's father told him.

It was same every month: Heinrich lying in bed as his father's heavy footsteps passed by his door, and moments later, the soft swish of a rug lifting, the jangle of keys in the lock, the creak of the cellar trapdoor opening, and the thud of it landing on the floor, then Heinrich tiptoeing out of his room, peering around the corner to catch his father staring into the depths of the cellar, his mouth a grim line, and sighing heavily before taking that first determined step into the darkness.

Heinrich hurriedly pressed his ear to the floor, listening to his father's footsteps receding. Then it was quiet for a long time. Heinrich would fall asleep on the floor, only wakening when his father once again ascended the stairs, the old man's tread steady but tired, as if he'd spent the day working the fields.

There was often a stain at his father's crotch when he emerged, and it wasn't until he was older that Heinrich guessed the cause. His father, a widower, was old when Heinrich was born, and even older now.

Heinrich wondered why his father never took another wife, why he had no brothers and sisters. He never spoke of Heinrich's mother, who was a dim memory. There were whispers about his father being less than a man. Heinrich was constantly getting into fights to uphold his father's honor.

Never go into the cellar.

He never said why, no matter how Heinrich pleaded, until finally, one day, his father caught him sleeping near the trapdoor. "If you insist on knowing," his father said, "I will tell you when you are sixteen. It will be your problem then, and be damned for it."

Never go into the cellar, son. Never.

By the time he was sixteen, Heinrich almost forgot the mystery of the cellar. War was overtaking Czechoslovakia, siphoning off all the young men of their mountain village. Only the small cottage of Gasper and Heinrich Gerhard escaped Nazi notice, as they possessed a good German name and German blood. The old man was obviously crippled, his legs bowed at a painful angle, as well as a little touched — anyone could see that just by looking into his fevered eyes. Heinrich was too young to be conscripted, and looked even younger.

"If anyone asks, say you are twelve years old," Heinrich's father commanded. Miraculously, they were untouched by the war, except for experiencing the same shortages that everyone else did.

The Nazi armies went east, and then it was just rumors of vast battles — entire cities destroyed — and the occasional rumble of fleets of planes passing overhead, until, inevitably, the Germans returned; but this time they were the ones in full retreat, with the Russians in relentless pursuit.

As thunder rumbled on the horizon, Gasper stared out the window day after day, drinking the local strong, homemade liquor, letting the fields go fallow. Heinrich contemplated disobeying the old man and running away to fight for the Germans. But most of all, he just wanted to get away.

Heinrich was beaten for the slightest infraction: not milking the cows early enough; not harvesting the potatoes when they were ready. Sometimes he was punished for reasons he didn't even understand. But it never occurred to him to disobey his father in anything, much less about the cellar.

Never, ever go into the cellar.

So it was a revelation when, as the end of the world approached, Heinrich discovered sex. Most of the other boys had been taken away by the army or to work in the factories. It turned out that there were benefits to being the only male in school.

Lately, he'd noticed girls staring at him.

It was Marlene who lured him behind the schoolhouse, slid her hand down his trousers, and fondled him. A funny feeling rose in his groin. He spurted white, sticky liquid high in the air, catching the girl on the cheek. She wiped it away with a giggle and a funny smile.

Heinrich's knees buckled at the release.

She grabbed his hand and lifted her dress. She was slick, and he almost pulled away, but she put her hand on his and guided him, and he stroked her until she let out little whimpers and shuddered a few times, her mouth open, her eyes closed. By then he was hard again, but she walked off without another word.

He sought out Marlene after school a few days later, but she was surrounded by her friends, who rudely turned their backs on him. Marlene did the same. He was too embarrassed to approach her again, but found it easy to mimic her motions, and it was almost as good. Too good. He repeated the experience whenever he found a few moments alone between school and chores.

One day his father, while building a fence, smashed his hand. The tops of two fingers were crushed. The bandages were stiff with blood. That same day, he caught Heinrich playing with himself, and he flew into a rage. He gave Heinrich the worst beating he'd ever had.

13

"Why?" Heinrich cried out in the middle of it.

"You must never give in to temptation," his father admonished. He sounded worried, not angry. "Someday you will have a son, just one, and then you will never again think these thoughts, do you understand?"

"No," Heinrich said. "I don't understand anything!"

Gasper raised his fist to deliver another blow; this time Heinrich didn't flinch. He raised his own fist in response. He wasn't going to let the old man hit him anymore. He would block the drunken blow, perhaps even—and his heart beat rapidly as he considered it—hit back.

His father saw it in Heinrich's eyes. He lowered his arm with a sigh.

"It is time," he said sadly. "I'd hoped to keep you innocent, a boy a little longer." He strode to the center of the room and lifted the heavy carpet. He pulled a key from his pants. The lock was recessed into a groove. He fumbled to open it with his mangled fingers, and finally the lock clicked open.

Heinrich heart raced even more. The cellar, at last!

Gasper descended the broad stone steps without looking back. After a moment of hesitation, Heinrich followed.

The basement wasn't built of brick walls like their neighbors' basements, but dug out of the living rock, the black cavern going on forever in the darkness, far beyond where lantern light could penetrate. The floor was worn smooth, as if a million footsteps had passed that way.

"The Russians approach," his father intoned. "Your only chance will be to hide from them. With any luck, the trapdoor will fool them."

"What about you, Father?"

"Me?" Gasper stopped in the middle of the corridor as if he hadn't thought of it. He shrugged as if it was of no importance. "I have been lax in my duties, son. You must learn in a few days what it took years for my father to teach me. But you're a smart boy…I've always thought so."

Down they went into the darkness, a much longer flight of stairs, with ruts worn deep in the rock. They passed through empty chambers, each one bigger than the room before. The rough ceilings were black with soot, as if from the long use of torches.

As they went deeper, Heinrich felt a stirring down in his privates. It was as if Marlene was taking hold of him and caressing him, but stronger. Stronger even than that first time he had stroked himself and climaxed and thought he was going to die. This was all of that and more.

He let out an involuntary moan, and his father looked at him sharply. Heinrich flushed and looked away.

They came to a place where a rockfall had blocked the tunnel—long ago, judging from the depth of the dust between the boulders. There was a chamber to one side that was full of old books. Gasper turned into a larger room on the other side.

There was a single long, battered table in the center of the room, and the walls were lined with shelves. There was a row of knives laid out, from large to small, along with a number of cups and goblets of different sizes. Deep grooves were slashed into the wooden surface. Red grooves.

Most of the shelves were empty, but one held a row of bottles. Heinrich recognized the liquor bottles his father guzzled from. But these were filled with a thick red liquid and sealed with wax. At the end of the row were several stone jars looking as if they had been carved out of the surrounding rock, with waxed cloth around the lids.

By now, Heinrich's erection was impossible to hide. He was embarrassed. The heat of shame and desire burned through his body, and tears came to his eyes. He couldn't help but check his father's crotch, which was strangely flat.

"I transferred most of the Blood to these newer bottles," Gasper said. "I've always hated the taste, so I mixed it with honey. This Blood should last forever without becoming bitter. Certainly, it has lasted thousands and thousands of years."

He took down one of the stone jars, his arms sagging under the weight, nearly dropping it. He lunged toward the table and barely made it; the container landed on the scarred wooden table with a thud. He broke the wax seal and sniffed the contents, nodding in satisfaction.

"I believe Blood and honey, properly taken care of, will never decay."

"Blood?" Heinrich finally blurted out.

"The Blood of the Succubus."

"Succubus?" The word didn't mean anything. He'd never heard it before.

"Demon, fallen angel, goddess...no one knows."

Heinrich blinked but did not speak. *You believe this, Father?* His friends and teachers had all told him his father was crazy, but he'd defended the old man. After all, he thought, Gasper Gerhard had a secret that none of them knew about. Someday it would all be explained by what was in the cellar.

It turned out they were right all along. Gasper *was* crazy.

"We lost our way, I think," Gasper went on, not noticing the look of disbelief on his son's face. "Our ancestors did things they shouldn't have, and God has rained down his retribution." The old man swayed on his feet, as if even the thought of it was too much.

"All you all right, Father?"

Gasper suddenly straightened up. He was taller, his legs unbowed. "How old do you think I am, son?" he asked.

Heinrich had often wondered. "They say Mother was younger than you when I was born..." he ventured.

His father remained silent.

"Sixty?"

Gasper Gerhard laughed. "So old?" He unbuttoned his shirt, dropping it to the stone floor, revealing a sculpted chest that belonged to a much younger man. He wiped his face on the grimy fabric of his shirt, and a youthful countenance stared back at Heinrich.

"How...?" Heinrich wondered aloud.

Gasper sighed. "I *am* old, Heinrich. Older than you can imagine." *Old?*

His father removed his trousers, and his legs were straight and strong. In a moment, Gasper stood naked in the flickering torchlight. But something was wrong. At first, Heinrich was unwilling to look there. But finally, it was impossible to avoid.

Between his father's legs, there was nothing. Just blank flesh, and a small hole with a metal tube running from it. It wasn't like a man, but it wasn't like Marlene either. It was alien, unnatural.

He recoiled, barely conscious of moving toward the door. His father's voice stopped him. Not because it was angry, but because it was the opposite—a soft entreaty.

"Son...please let me explain."

Heinrich turned reluctantly and watched as Gasper lifted a stone bottle and drank deeply from it. He set it down, his eyes shining, smiling a little. Slowly, he began unraveling the bloody bandage over his fingers

"Come here and look at this, Heinrich," his father said. Reluctantly, Heinrich peered over his father's shoulder. He let out a gasp. The fingers were whole.

Gasper flexed his hand, smiling in satisfaction before turning to meet Heinrich's gaze. That's not all." He pointed down to his groin. There, dangling between his legs, were the parts of his body that had been missing.

"I wanted you to see this, so you'd believe," Gasper said. "But, sadly, I can be like this but for a short time each month, and then..."

He grabbed a thin, sharp knife off the table, reached down, and pulled his cock and balls together. He positioned the stained blade against his skin. Sweat stood out on his brow, and his teeth were bared as he hesitated.

"You'd think it would be easy after all this time," Gasper said. "But it only gets harder." He closed his eyes and breathed deeply, once, twice: then, with a sudden jerking movement, he sliced away the new flesh.

He gave a groan, which grew into a bellow. Blood running down his legs, he stuck a finger into the open jar, and dabbed it on the gaping wound. He screamed again and fell to his knees, then toppled to the floor and curled up.

Heinrich watched in horror, uncertain what to do. But slowly, the color returned to his father's skin. Within a few minutes, Gasper rose, completely healed. But where his genitals had been was again smooth flesh, a shadow in the firelight. Blood no longer trickled down his legs.

"I've never gotten used to it," Gasper said, breathing hard and wiping sweat from his brow as he rose to his feet, trembling. "The

Blood helps the pain, but it doesn't banish it completely. I hate that you will have to go through that."

Heinrich let the words penetrate, the matter-of-fact way his father had said them.

"No," he said.

Gasper sighed. "I felt the same way. But in the end, I did it."

"You can't make me," Heinrich said.

"No, I can't," his father said sadly. "But when the Succubae come for you, you'll have no choice."

"I won't do it."

"Then our line dies. Perhaps it is time. I don't see what good the Guardians have done anyone. If it ends with you, so be it."

Gasper moved from around the table, and Heinrich almost retreated. But the look on his father's face was of concern, not anger. He stood in front of Heinrich with a grave expression. "I should have prepared you better, but I thought I had more time. I'm one hundred and eighty years old, son. My father before me lived almost three hundred years. It is said that others in our family lived longer even than that. All because of the Blood." He reached over and lifted one of the bottles. He frowned. "A blessing, you might think. But it is a curse. It is because the Blood draws the Succubae that we must resort to the Cutting."

He started putting his clothes back on. "When I was younger, I thought to break the cycle—to take these bottles and move someplace better. Maybe even see if I could find a way to destroy the Daughters of Lilith, as was prophesied.

"But I'm tired, son. I have no desire to continue on. I would have, given the chance. I would have trained you properly."

"You do this every *month*?"

Gasper looked surprised, then said, "Oh, I see. I can see how that would be horrifying." He walked to Heinrich's side and put his hand on his son's shoulder. "I've been sick a long time, son. If I didn't do this, the disease would have taken me a long time ago. I don't know why, but it always returns, more virulent than ever.

"But *you*, Heinrich, won't have to do this again after the first time—at least, not for a long time. Once a decade, if you wish to stay youthful; longer if you don't care about that."

"I don't understand," Heinrich protested. "Scientists say that sex is as much in the mind as it is in the body. Why would this…Cutting…keep you from feeling desire?"

His father looked bemused. "I don't know. I've often wondered the same thing, but I could never find the answers in the books. Perhaps because this came from a time before science, when such explanations meant nothing. Which reminds me…come with me."

They crossed the corridor into the room Heinrich had spied that was piled with books, papers, and scrolls. "These manuscripts," Gasper motioned to a table stacked high, "will tell you everything you need to know, answer all your questions. It is the history of our family, of the Guardians."

"I don't understand. Aren't you going to teach me?"

"Not enough time," Gasper said. "The Russians will search this house. You must hide down here. I have lain in enough supplies in the next chamber for you to live for several weeks. Make use of this time. Study these books. Wait until the enemy is gone. But whatever you do, don't come out until you have…done as I have shown you. I'm sorry, son. If you do not do the Cutting, the Succubae will find and kill you. Promise me."

Heinrich had no intention of cutting off his manhood, especially since he'd so recently discovered the use of it. But he also knew his father wouldn't let him go until he promised.

"Very well, Father. I will do as you ask." *So we both lie*, Heinrich thought. One thing he knew. He would never do the Cutting. He would rather die first.

"Good." Gasper frowned, as if trying to remember something. "Good."

He picked a book off the nearest table and began to leave.

"Why are you taking that one?"

"This?" Gasper said. "This is my journal. You can read it when I'm dead."

Chapter 3

Serena Carlton browsed the articles open on her laptop, closing one after another before pausing.

Here was a promising one. A woman had stabbed her boyfriend to death in self-defense in Cleveland. "He was crazy-drunk," the article quoted her as saying. "He broke a window and was crawling inside with a tire iron. I grabbed a kitchen knife…I didn't mean to kill him, I just wanted him to stop."

Serena straightened, reading the quote again, more slowly, her heart suddenly pounding in her chest. The cadence of the words rang with familiarity. They sounded almost lighthearted, over-explanatory, exactly the kind of thing Kristen would say to sound innocent or appear to be the victim.

The most recent clue on Kristen Larkin's trail was two years old. Kristen wasn't her real name, but Serena had to call her something.

She skimmed the rest of the article, then sat back and sighed.

"Amber Powell and Jared Fromm were in a relationship for three years."

Serena grimaced and closed the article. Kristen never stayed with any man for more than a few months.

Two years of dead leads and the same cold trail. Kristen Larkin was a ghost. There were roughly forty-five murders in America every day. A third of them were domestic, meaning the murderer and victim knew each other; most often, the killer was male and the victim was a spouse or a significant other, a family member, or a close friend. There *were* some stranger-on-stranger murders that might be *her* doing, if she'd managed to keep the relationship secret, but Kristen was nothing if not flamboyant.

She was hard not to notice, and Serena was counting on her staying that way. Someone always said something along the lines of, "Such an outgoing girl!" or described her as "Charming, vivacious, and funny." All were keywords in Serena's search.

Popular media had a name for cute, eccentric girls like Kristen: the Manic Pixie Dream Girl. In movies or on TV, the Manic Pixie Dream Girl came along and solved all the male protagonist's problems with a twinkle. Serena thought of them as MPDGs.

Kristen was impossibly young, utterly charming, and unbelievably deadly. Young men always fell for her. Kristen always looked for the cutest guy around without a girlfriend. "Who's the most popular/unpopular boy in the school?" she'd ask, innocently. Most of the time, the young man wouldn't have a sister, and few, if any, friends who were female. They were boys like Eric. The mother was often absent or too busy to pay attention to her son's activities. Serena winced. That described her so well. She'd worked her way up the corporate ladder for years, ever since Eric entered first grade.

Strangely, even though Kristen was irresistible to the boys, the other girls didn't find her threatening. "She's cute!" they'd say, and give each other knowing looks. It was as if they were glad to see the awkward girl they all liked, the one with the great personality, finally getting it on with the nice, lonely guy whom many of them had contemplated but passed over. The other girls were happy for both of them. Only later would they agree that they'd always thought there was something off about her.

Serena had searched reports going back twenty years; there were an extraordinary number of MPDG murders. Kristen, or whatever she called herself, had a wide range, hooking up with boys as young as high school and men verging on middle age.

And then, to Serena's astonishment, she'd found more evidence, going back farther than twenty years, all the way back to the 1800s and maybe—depending on how you interpreted the data—even farther. That's when Serena's investigation took a sudden turn into the strange and macabre. At first, it was curiosity that drove her. She didn't really believe any of it, but as the evidence mounted, she started to become convinced.

She also learned to never speak of her suspicions out loud.

It had been the same for generation after generation. Then, suddenly, just in the last few years, the MPDG had changed her modus operandi. Either that or she was dead, with no body found. Maybe Kristen had been kidnapped by one of those international human trafficking rings. It would serve her right.

She had disappeared.

Is it because of me? Serena asked herself.

Unlikely. In the courtroom, Serena had stared Kristen straight in the face and told her that she would spend the rest of her life searching for the proof that Kristen was a murderer.

Kristen hadn't even blinked. No, she'd simply smiled that bright little smile. Everyone in the courtroom but Serena had smiled with her.

Serena almost succumbed to despair many times. Her son's murder had made her grim, humorless. She was dogged and thorough, but she couldn't charm the police or witnesses the way Kristen could. Absolutely no one believed the petite, charming girl could have killed anyone except in self-defense.

But they hadn't known Serena's shy, gentle son. That *he* was the monster was unimaginable. It was this injustice that gave Serena the strength to go on.

She might have thought she was crazy if not for the fact that soon after the trial, she got an interesting visitor.

The doorbell rang one midafternoon. She almost didn't answer it—her friends had long ago given up on her—but insistent knocking followed the bell.

"What do you want?" she asked before seeing who was on the other side of the door.

It was a well-dressed man, young and blond. She recognized the type from her corporate years. Privileged and with a MBA that he thought made him smart.

"Ms. Carlton, my name is John Carmichael," he said.

It was a made-up name, she was sure. Most people trailed off at the end of their names, they said them so often. This last name came out hard and clear.

She didn't say anything, just stared at him.

"I represent a group that is searching for the same woman you are," he continued.

"And who is that?"

The young man gave her a confident smile. "We call ourselves the Guardians, and it is our duty to track down this woman and to capture her."

"Why?" Serena demanded. "Why don't you help the cops? Why are you coming to me?"

"The woman in question is very dangerous, Ms. Carlton. We're concerned for your safety.

"How nice of you."

"But we also don't want to scare Kristen Larkin—or whatever she's calling herself now—into hiding. We are on her trail. I assure you, she will face justice. But you must desist in your search."

Serena didn't answer.

"You'll only get yourself killed, Serena." With that, the man who called himself John Carmichael turned and walked away. A limo waited in the street, and he got into the back.

If the visit was supposed to stop Serena from investigating, it had the opposite effect.

She searched the Internet, looking for answers, and came across a site that referred to Manic Pixie Dream Girls as being modern-day Succubae. Most of what was there was amateur porn, often incorporating people made up to look like movie or reality TV stars. Terrible stuff. But there was one little corner of the webpage that asked: "Have you encountered a real Succubus?"

She clicked out of curiosity, half afraid of what she'd find.

It was a simple blog, with no pictures, no porn, and no embellishment of any kind. Which was kind of reassuring, somehow. It was someone talking about who the Succubae were: their history, their dangers, their attributes, even their names: the Three Daughters of Lilith, Agrat Bat, Eisheth, and Naamah. At the description of the middle sister, Eisheth, Serena's blood ran cold. It fit Kristen to a T.

The blog was a revelation. There was a ring of truth to it, even though on the surface it appeared completely crazy.

Most of what Serena now knew came from Blood of the Succubus webpage, *if* it was true and not some paranoid delusion so convincing it had managed to suck her in.

She'd been talking to the blogger, a man named Rick, almost daily ever since she'd found the site. She wasn't sure how old he was, or where he lived, or even if he was really a man.

One of the first things she told him, after they moved on to using Facebook messaging, was about the visit from John Carmichael. Until that moment, she'd sensed that "Rick: was only moderately interested in her. After that, they were in communication every day.

Serena: *I had a very interesting visit from someone who called himself a Guardian.*

Rick: *A Guardian? Are you certain?*

Serena: *Positive. He said his name was John Carmichael.*

Rick: *Stay away from him.*

Serena: *Who is he? What are the Guardians?*

Rick: *They want to capture the Succubae, to harvest their Blood.*

Serena: *Their Blood?*

Rick: *I will explain everything.*

And so he did, and as crazy as it all sounded, it all made sense.

Serena rose and poured herself another cup of coffee, noticing the sink full of dirty dishes and the dust bunnies under the cabinets. She'd been a neat freak once. She'd had time to be: she'd inherited enough money not to have to work.

She caught her reflection in the computer screen, surprised as always by the youthfulness of her face. Her peers sometimes remarked that the mirror showed them as older than they felt. She had the opposite reaction. Eric was born when she was seventeen and died when she was thirty-four. She was only thirty-seven now, but felt like an old lady.

Concentrate! Serena pinched her cheek. She was always afraid that by woolgathering, she'd miss a clue. She went on reading, but found nothing. At the bottom of the list of articles was a section about missing persons, which she usually gave at least a cursory glance.

"Missing in the High Desert Badlands," the headline read. She nearly turned off the computer, but at the bottom were some quotation marks, and she always read anything that was a quote, certain she would instantly recognize Kristen's phrasing.

A young couple had gotten lost while hiking near Bend, Oregon. They'd become separated, but somehow the woman had found her way to Highway 20, where she'd flagged down a car. They still hadn't found the young man, a Doug Johnson.

"Doug's with Mother Earth now," the woman, Suzanne Winders, said at the bottom of the article. "I'm sad, you know, but I know that the Goddess has enveloped him in her sweet embrace. He was a beautiful young man, so wise, so knowing. He knew the dangers, but chose to be close to nature. The wilderness is where he wanted to be."

It was *her*.

The earth goddess thing was new, but not the offhand way she depicted someone's presumed death as if it were a blessing. It was her hallmark. Then there was the way she unwittingly used the past tense to refer to someone who was, after all, only missing.

Bend, Oregon. All the way across the country, but that wasn't surprising. Kristen Larkin could show up anywhere, at any time. If she held true to form, she'd soak up as much attention and sympathy as possible before disappearing again. The article was only a day old. They hadn't even called off the search for Doug Johnson yet.

Serena bookmarked the article. First thing in the morning, she'd Priceline a flight and head straight to Portland. She'd rent a car and be in Bend by evening.

Would Kristen look the same? Serena had seen her with every color and style of hair. But one thing remained the same, no matter whether the picture was from twenty years ago or five years ago.

Her face never changed.

Serena sent an email.

Rick,

I think I have found her. She's on the West Coast, in Oregon. I'm headed that way. I'll let you know what I find.

Serena

She turned off the computer. *The mysterious Rick, who sounds so old, who knows so much,* she mused. She kept hoping that if she got close enough to finding Kristen, he'd join her and they'd meet at last.

Oh, well. While his information was helpful, she didn't really need him. She'd kill the Succubus all by herself.

The search for Doug Johnson was still in full swing when Serena arrived in Bend. No one seemed to know where Suzanne Winders was, and no one in authority seemed to care.

Serena wasn't surprised. The Kristen MPDG was usually gone before Serena ever arrived, but she'd never arrived this early in an investigation before.

The Sheriff's Office was on the northwestern edge of Bend, where the county wilderness search crews were headquartered. Serena posed as a reporter and mined as much information from the harried front desk officer as she could.

She was still there when they got the call.

The deputy listened to the phone, his face growing long, and he hung up after a few "Yes, sir's" and "No, sir's."

"What happened?" Serena asked.

"I can't tell you," said the deputy.

"I'm on deadline for tomorrow's edition," she said. "Come on, let me submit my story in time."

The deputy stared at her for a long moment. "Off the record?"

Serena nodded.

The deputy looked around and lowered his voice. "It was a bear. I mean, it had to be a bear or a cougar, but a bear is more likely."

"You're sure?"

"Oh, yeah. The body was pretty torn up, but Sheriff Maxwell knows bear attacks. He's leading the search party."

Weariness dropped over Serena like a heavy blanket. *All this way for nothing.* It had been so promising…but not every Manic Pixie Dream Girl was a murderer, nor was every murder done by a MPDG.

She had risen to leave when she spotted a young man sitting in one of the plastic chairs that lined the hallway. He stared at her, and Serena sensed he was attracted to her. But there was something more. Something made her walk over to him.

"You knew him, didn't you?" she asked. "Doug Johnson?"

"He was my best friend," the guy answered. His eyes watered, and he put his face down, hiding it. He was good-looking in a small-town way, with hair that looked like it was dyed a rust red and curling tattoos on both arms. He wore a skintight black T-shirt and jeans.

"You heard?" Serena said. She sat down next him. She didn't know him, but there was something about the genuineness of his concern that reassured her.

"They found him," she whispered, glancing behind her at the deputy. Then she hesitated. Maybe it wasn't for her to tell this young man what had happened to his friend. But he was looking at her expectantly, so it was too late now. "I'm sorry," she said, reaching out and putting a hand on his shoulder. "He's dead. A bear attack."

To her relief, Doug's friend apparently already knew. He shook his head. "That's what they *say*," he said, and looked away.

Serena felt her hopes rising and was slightly ashamed of it. A young man was dead. But…there might be more to this story. She leaned toward Doug's friend. "You don't believe them?"

"Oh, I'm sure a bear killed him. But that's not what got him in trouble."

She hesitated, hardly daring to breathe. *Press too hard and he will shut down,* she thought. "My name's Serena Carlton." She stood up and put out her hand, as if starting all over. "I'd love to hear your story."

The young man wasn't very good at hiding his feelings. Surprise came over his face, and then doubt, as if he wasn't sure his own instincts were right. But most of all, she saw relief that someone was willing to listen to his concerns.

He stood, finally remembering his manners, and shook her hand. "Cary Deakins."

They both sat back down, and it no longer felt like they were strangers, but friends.

It's been a long time since I felt this comfortable with someone, Serena thought. *And yet I barely know him.*

In her confusion, she blurted out the question she'd intended to lead up to. "Do you know the girlfriend?" she asked.

"Girlfriend?" Cary repeated, loudly, scornfully. "Is that what they're saying? Hell, Doug only knew her a few weeks. She bewitched him somehow. I can't explain it. But she was no good for him. He died because of her."

"Why do you say that?"

He stared at her, confused. The sadness that had lain beneath his features, no matter how much he was trying to hide it, broke through. Then the tears really started to flow. He looked to be in his late twenties or early thirties, and Serena had to fight the almost overwhelming impulse to hug him. Cary was close enough to her in age that he might get the wrong idea, but they were far enough apart in age for her to keep her distance.

"You wouldn't believe me," he said.

"Don't be so sure," she said. She couldn't keep the bitterness from overtaking her. "My son was murdered and no one would believe me."

Cary looked shocked, at a loss for words. Finally, he stuttered, "I'm...I'm sorry."

Serena closed her eyes, trying to get ahold of her emotions. *Keep on target*, she thought, surprised that the single-minded determination she'd been cultivating for years could be so easily softened by someone's sympathy.

They sat in silence for a time, watching deputies come and go, bustling about in the self-important way authorities used during emergencies. Later, Serena found what passed for coffee in the alcove that led to the sheriff's office and brought Cary a Styrofoam cup. He accepted it with a tired smile, wincing at the taste.

Serena followed his example. The coffee was awful, bitter and strong. Just what she needed to wake up.

"So you flew here all the way from Boston?" Cary asked, finally. "Do you need a ride anywhere?"

She shook her head. "Why don't we meet in the morning?" she asked before she realized she was going to. She wanted to hear Cary's entire story, but she was so tired she was dizzy.

They arranged to meet the next morning at the Starbucks near the Cambridge Hotel downtown.

Serena knew she needed rest before she could really take in what Cary was going to tell her—or what she hoped he was going to tell her. But she couldn't help but ask the one question she always asked.

"Can you describe Suzanne Winders in one sentence?" Serena said as they left the sheriff's building. Cary paused, holding the door open for her.

"Describe her?" He frowned. Then it was as if the answer came to him. "Too good to be true," he said.

It's her!

His answer stripped away the disillusion and weariness of years without a lead, the frustration and disappointment of the lack of progress in Bend. It was *her*!

What's more, Kristen hadn't completed the kill. Serena wasn't completely sure her information was accurate, but according to some sources, that meant Kristen would be weak and searching for a new target. She might move out of the area, but Serena figured there was a good chance that she'd want to restore her powers by taking someone's life force first.

Serena would have to hurry, because Kristen would act quickly, maybe within as little as a couple of weeks.

She said goodbye to Cary and drove to the hotel deep in thought. She quivered with nervous energy, and she anticipated a sleepless night. But she was out before her head settled into the pillow.

She slept soddenly, without dreams, but woke feeling groggy. She wasn't young anymore; she was coming up on forty. The image of Cary Deakins entered her mind, and she tried to dislodge it. The forties were supposed to be the new thirties, but as far as Serena was concerned, she was entering old age. That's how she felt, anyway.

She booted up her laptop.

Serena: *She's here! I'm sure of it.*

Rick: *Be careful. Keep me posted.*

Serena: *I'll be all right.*

Rick: *Don't confront her alone.*

Serena: *As soon as I've found her, I will contact you.*

Rick: *Wait for me before you do anything.*

She rewarded him with a smiley face and clicked off.

Chapter 4

The Succubus shrieked. Windows of homes opened to the warm fall air were slammed shut, the residents wondering what strange creature had made such a horrible sound.

"Sisters!" she cried in the ancient language. "I've been hurt!"

Her sisters weren't listening; she knew that. But it didn't matter; it was how she'd always responded to pain and frustration.

Eisheth was enraged. She'd come within seconds of Culling that boring young man after spending nearly a month under the name Suzanne Winders, making sure he was completely in love with her. She'd expected a huge payoff. The more a Cull loved her, the more she got out of him.

She'd thought camping was a brilliant new strategy. Take them into the woods, Cull them, and then leave the desiccated remains for the animals. She'd bat her big eyes at the authorities over becoming "lost," show her girlish grief, and they would sympathize and coddle her. They would never suspect her.

It had never occurred to Eisheth that wild animals could be a danger. She'd spent far too much time in the city in the last few centuries. She had been the Goddess of harvests and domesticated animals. Her aspect had been of hearth and home, and her worshippers farmers and tradesmen. She'd let her sister Naamah deal with the woodsmen and the wild woods.

She might have been able to fight the bear, but she'd been too startled. She used most of the energy she'd Culled from Doug just to get away.

Being torn apart by a bear would have been far worse than not consummating the Cull, as bad as that was. It took almost all her life force to maintain an attractive body: that kind of damage might take decades to repair, hundreds of successful Cullings while she expended most of her own life force merely maintaining the illusion of beauty.

Eisheth had worked hard for the great body she now had, her beautiful, even-featured face, her thick hair, wide eyes, and high cheekbones, her cute, innocent appearance. Varying hair and eye color took relatively little energy, and she made such changes as a matter of course. She'd vary her clothing and approach with each Cull, but she mostly stuck to the perky but helpless type that most men liked.

Looking like Marilyn Monroe might work too, but the more attractive she looked, the harder it was to maintain. Cuteness was a lot less work. She only had to mimic the personality that she knew men craved, mostly feigning admiration, listening to them, and laughing at their jokes. That was usually enough.

To hell with them…to hell with them all. To have to feed on the beings I hate most.

Eisheth's curse wasn't that she couldn't screw any man to death, but that she could only Cull one man at a time, wasting precious time seducing them. For the Cull to be most powerful, her victims had to *give* themselves to her, even if only subconsciously. She couldn't get it wrong. If she was rejected for any reason, if the Cull wasn't achieved, she would weaken and her powers to seduce become less reliable. She'd be forced to pick up lower and lower-status men, whose life essences were barely enough to sustain her.

Once, after been severely injured in a car accident (she still neglected to look both ways when she entered roadways), Eisheth had taken a bum on Burnside in Portland in desperation, and it was as if she hadn't gotten anything from the Cull at all. She'd had to Cull three more bums before she moved her way up to a horny college kid, fat and disgusting, then to a rich old man, then finally to some middle-aged businessman cheating on his wife while out of town. Their life forces were dim, pathetic, and barely present. It wasn't so much that she'd managed to seduce them as she'd become a mere slut, letting them have their way with her until they couldn't do without her. *Then* she'd taken them.

The quickest she'd ever gotten a good Cull was one week. She'd said all the right things at all the right times to a strong, handsome young man in Greece, who became so infatuated with her that she could have had him within a day. But she couldn't afford a mistake.

Especially in ancient times, a failed seduction could be dangerous. If the fact that a Succubus was among them became common knowledge, Eisheth was in danger of being tracked down and destroyed by the local populace. But these days, fortunately for her, people didn't believe in such things as Succubae.

She couldn't really die, but she could become a mere shadow, an erotic thought, a wet dream among teenagers who needed little encouragement. She'd spent centuries in such a tenuous state, and she had no intention of returning to it. Ever.

She would try someone younger this time, hopefully someone with a strong life force. Teenagers seemed to often miss who was the strongest among them, and they made easy targets. At the same time, it took more of her life force to maintain the illusion of being younger, so there was a tradeoff.

It just so happened that the school year was starting, so she could scout out the late bloomers; try to grab one quick Cull. She'd been using the camping trick for some time now. Despite the bear, she decided to stick to her plan. It was easy to lead her prey far into the wilderness, where they normally weren't ever found. She just had to be more careful about the wildlife.

Usually, Eisheth was long gone by the time they were discovered. It didn't make the papers the way a draining did.

She'd take her prey into the woods and disappear. Maybe to a new state. Hell, maybe to a new country.

Reduced to running, to hiding.

Sometimes it was hard to remember that she'd once been a Goddess.

Chapter 5

Once their names had been blessings, not curses. They had been Goddesses, not Succubae.

It was hard for Eisheth to remember now that she had ever loved humans. She could not summon the emotion, even in her most quiet, contemplative moments, which were few and brief. The hate was always there, always boiling. In her mind, she could see those days, but she could not feel them.

Of them all, the villagers loved Eisheth best. Agrat Bat was distant, unattainable by most men. High priestesses attended her, and her fertility rites were for the whole village and surrounding territory. She performed only on High Holidays.

Naamah was the Goddess of pleasure, of the wild woods, and she had her following, of course. The young women loved her and her ways, and she loved them in return. Sex was not something to be ashamed of in those days.

But Eisheth was the Goddess of home and hearth. Couples prayed to her that they might be blessed with children.

The sisters mostly kept apart, for together they were too potent an influence. Only in spring, when planting commenced, did they appear together, that their Blood could bless the season, producing abundant crops, resistant to animals and insects and disease.

The mountain village thrived. Because of the Goddesses, women were equal to men, if not superior. The women were entrusted to rule the village, and outsiders came for their judgment and justice when there were disputes.

Such a paradise could not long continue. Word spread of the Three Daughters of Lilith's blessed realm.

Despite the millennia, Eisheth remembered the day it had all changed.

It was the first day of spring. There was a cool brightness to the air, the last breath of winter softened by the sweet whispers of spring.

Eisheth stood at the edge of the white stone path, looking like a simple villager, though there was a space around her that no mortal dared to enter. She glowed in the light, gathering the rays of the sun around her, holding her hands out in blessing.

Naamah was further down the path, her followers clustered around her, arms and legs and bodies intertwined, a swirling, ever-changing knot of erotic energy, even in the early morning. Eisheth could feel it from where she stood, and she contemplated the men standing at a discrete distance from her, wondering which of them she should bestow her blessing upon and take to her home and bed to further sanctify the coming of spring.

They were waiting for Agrat Bat.

The doors of temple opened, and her retinue of priests and priestesses emerged, carrying Agrat Bat on a litter. The carriers stumbled under her weight. Agrat Bat was huge and round, with pendulous breasts, oak beams for legs, and huge branches for arms, her blonde hair a wild halo about her round face. Her skin was pale, and she had piercing blue eyes.

The villagers, in contrast, were small and dark. Blue or green eyes were almost unheard of, but blonde hair was rare enough to be reserved for a Goddess.

Eisheth had shaken her head at the grandiosity of the temple. But in hindsight, it was a minor grandiosity. The temple was small, but made of bricks, unlike the wattle and daub of most the village huts. Her followers lived in the front of the temple, Agrat Bat lived in the back, and the altar was between them.

Beneath the temple was the entrance to the caves from which the Daughters of Lilith had emerged, so long ago that they had forgotten the how and why of it. They simply knew that the caves were their birthplace. A higher power—or time itself—had erased their memories of more than that.

Agrat Bat gave her a glance as she passed, and Eisheth exchanged a knowing smile with her. Even Agrat Bat couldn't overlook the pomposity of High Holy Days.

Agrat Bat was, by unspoken agreement, the elder sister. Naamah was the baby, Eisheth the middle sibling. They didn't know if this was true, but it seemed right.

It was Agrat Bat who gave herself on this day. Naamah and Eisheth would also join in the festivities, but in private, behind closed doors. It was Agrat Bat's duty to perform in public, and she reveled in it.

She stepped down from the litter, a small cloud of white dust rising from the path as she landed.

A priest stepped forward to face her and raised his arms. It was Zuoso who gave prayers, as usual. Every year he changed a few of the words, but little by little, it was becoming a ritual.

"Goddesses, the motherly source who brings forth all the life from the earth, we ask that you present us with your virtues, that we may call on your goodwill to keep away disease and plague, infestations and barrenness, and bless us with nourishment, save us with your medicines, and engender love between man and woman, as we are of the earth and the earth is fertile. Illuminate with your feminine warmth the hearth, and raise up our fortunes, and deliver us from fallen hopes. If it pleases you, for we have worked hard for your favor, bless this land and our homes."

At the end, he dropped to his knees and bowed his head.

Agrat Bat put her fat hand on top of his head and answered, "We are here. Your prayers have moved us, and we will give you succor. For we are the natural mothers of all things, the powers of life in our forms, the Three. Leave off your sorrow on this blessed day, for we give ourselves to you, that you may flourish in the coming year."

She turned, and everyone became still and quiet.

All was prepared. The green bedding was set in the middle of the field. Men lined the border between the path and field, and many could not hide their growing erections.

Agrat Bat didn't seem to think about her choice. Her fat finger landed on a middle-aged man in the middle of the line: Moros, the blacksmith, the only man who was nearly as big as Agrat Bat. He followed her to the soft green bower. Agrat Bat removed her cloak and tossed it casually to the side.

The erotic energy in the air was overwhelming by now. Even Eisheth felt the urge to touch herself, though she resisted. The lesser mortals around her couldn't resist. Men and women were pairing off, and not always with their usual partners. On this day, all was allowed—no one was to judge. But they had to wait; the Goddess came first. She must complete the ceremony.

Agrat Bat lay down, her breasts weighed down on each side. She opened her legs, her sex already glistening. Moros removed his clothing, nearly stumbling in his haste, and the villagers laughed. Despite the importance of the ceremony, it was a joyous time, and laughter was allowed, even encouraged.

He practically jumped on the Goddess. She took him in, enveloped him in flesh. Moros put his hands on her breasts and began to quiver. It wasn't really love-making, more like a spasm, and then he was spent.

Again the villagers laughed, but it was a good sign. The village would be blessed with an early and healthy crop.

The sexual energy was not dissipated, however. With the ritual done, the men and women quickly disappeared into their homes or the surrounding wilds, there to expend themselves and further bless the crops.

When most of them were gone, the three sisters gathered.

"You couldn't keep him waiting?" Naamah teased.

"I tried," Agrat Bat said, frowning.

"You can't help it, I'm certain," Eisheth said. "But fortunately, your retinue looks ready to satisfy you."

Indeed, the robes of the priests were tenting outward at the waist, and they couldn't take their eyes off her.

"Let's get this over with," Agrat Bat said. She was still naked. Eisheth and Naamah soon joined her.

The eldest sister held out her hand, and one of the priestesses stepped forward, proffering an obsidian knife. It was the sharpest blade in the village, protected and sheltered on the temple altar.

Agrat Bat went first. She cut into her wrist and the blood flowed. She marched down the rows of plantings. It wasn't necessary to touch all of them with her blood; it carried far, and its effects lasted long. Naamah and Eisheth followed as their sister marched from field to field, down to the smallest gardens. The human attendants stayed back on the path and watched. As she bled, Agrat Bat grew ever smaller, until she was emaciated, almost a skeleton.

Then she turned and gave her middle sister the blade. Eisheth tried not to wince. She cut into her forearm enough for droplets to appear, and she blessed the few places Agrat Bat hadn't reached, until she looked down and saw that the bones in her arms were protruding, her skin stretched tight.

She handed the knife to Naamah, who had even less substance to give, but it was necessary that she contribute, so that all three sisters were seen to be part of the ceremony. They were the Three Goddesses, and all were worshipped equally, if differently.

When they finished, the village was in the distance. People looked small, the temple no more than a hut.

"Sometimes I wish…" Naamah started to say.

"Wish what, my sister?" Agrat Bat asked.

"I wish we could just keep going. Go where we wish, do as we wish."

"But they depend on us!" Eisheth said.

Agrat Bat didn't say anything, which surprised Eisheth. Of them all, she always seemed most duty bound.

They donned their robes and made their way back to the village. Few people were about. Most were still busy completing their own private fertility ceremonies, mostly behind closed doors, but a few of the more daring were in the fields and woods, and no one would think less of them for it. Many a child would be born nine months from this day.

When they reached the white path, Agrat Bat continued on to her temple, followed by her retinue.

Naamah stroked Eisheth's face fondly. "You really love them, don't you?" she said. She proceeded down to the public part of the village, where young women experienced the freedom before marriage. She liked women as much as men, and would get her fill of both on this evening.

The sanctifying of the fields had taken most of the afternoon. The sun was low in the sky. All in all, it had been a perfect day.

Eisheth looked around, but the streets were empty. She marched to the nearest hut and stepped inside without a warning knock.

"Goddess!" cried the old man inside the hut. It was Forr, one of the oldest men in the village. Somehow he'd managed to convince a young woman to join him. Tari was her name, the wife of Moros, the blacksmith.

"Leave," Eisheth commanded the woman, who sprang from the bed and fled, gathering her clothes as she ran.

"Lay down," Eisheth commanded, and the old man lay back. He was scrawny around the arms and shoulders, his legs withered, and yet he had a small belly. His cock was huge, however.

Eisheth lowered herself onto him. She didn't need pleasure; that would come later, when she was restored. She needed his life force. He quickly obliged, coming within moments.

She lingered afterward, even though she needed to replenish herself. When she gazed down at Forr, she didn't see the wrinkled old man, but the young, virile farmer who was her favorite, whom she had picked year after year. Like all men, he would die soon, and he would be but a memory to her, joining the long line of men she had taken to her heart.

With a sigh, Eisheth arose and went to the next home, where the man, younger and stronger than Forr, lasted longer and gave her more life force. She took no more than she needed in those days, leaving them drained but alive.

She went on to the next domicile and the next, and with every visit she healed, until she was back to her usual size and vitality.

Only then did she let the lovemaking last. She chose her current favorite, the miller's apprentice, Coss, handsome and virile. She spent the rest of the evening with him, and fell asleep in his arms.

To be awakened by the thunder of hooves, the shouts of men.

The men of Draast had come to their peaceful village, and nothing was ever the same.

Chapter 6

On his first day of eleventh grade, Jeremy heard loud giggling and looked around to see who the girls were laughing at, but they were already walking away, talking to each other behind their hands. He shrugged. Sophomores, nobody he knew.

Later, Jenny Sloan marched up to him and looked him up and down, her lips pursed.

"What?" he asked.

"Just checking," she said before flouncing off again.

All in all, it was a strange first day.

For Jeremy, the changes had been gradual. Early in the summer, the braces came off. In the middle of summer, he had Lasik surgery done to correct his near-sightedness. Then he told his mom he wouldn't let her cut his hair anymore and let it grow out all summer long. And by the time school rolled around again, he was nearly six feet tall.

He knew he looked different, but he didn't think anyone would notice. On the inside, he was still that small, gawky kid with horn-rimmed glasses, a burr haircut, and braces. When he caught a glimpse of his reflection sometimes, it was as if a strange young man looked back, tall and straight, with a lean look around the face, thoughtful brown eyes, straight teeth, and deep brown hair looping down over his forehead.

"They're throwing themselves at you, Jeremy!" his sister, Marty, exclaimed when he told her about his day. She'd just come home from a date, late on this Friday night, and found him alone, watching TV.

"They are?" he asked.

Marty gave him an exasperated "Pffffff!"

"If they're throwing themselves at me, I sure can't see it."

"OMG!" Marty rolled to her feet, following Jeremy to the refrigerator, where he peered in. "Jermy, you've grown about a foot over the summer, you got your braces off, had that surgery to fix your eyesight, your skin's cleared up, you got a cool haircut for once, and you're actually looking kinda hot. That's what Julie told me, anyway."

Jeremy let the fridge door fall closed and stared down at his sister as she continued.

"So when Lucinda Peters sidles up to you in the hallway, looks up into your beautiful brown eyes, licks her lips, and mentions that The Shins are going to be at the Les Schwab Amphitheater, that's your *cue*, brother."

He remembered the incident. Lucinda Peters was a cheerleader who, years before, had been a bit of a rebel. He'd always had a thing for her, and they'd been close friends years ago, before all the popularity politics got in the way. It had turned out that she was not so much of a rebel after all.

In a nutshell, she was popular and he wasn't.

"She asked what time it was," he said doubtfully.

Marty gave him a pitying look. "So she could get to the concert, you dummy! Maybe she needed a ride. Maybe if you'd said something like, 'Oh, I love The Shins,' she would have invited you along. No, what does Big Brother do? He looks at his watch and says in a monotone, 'It's five o'clock.'"

"I don't like The Shins," he said.

"God, you're hopeless!" Marty cried in her overly dramatic way. "By the way, my date sucked. I had to fight off Mr. Quarterback's octopus arms all night. I don't know how he ever gets a second date. All he ever talks about is football." She flounced off to her room, leaving Jeremy alone with his thoughts.

The real reason he hadn't responded to Lucinda was because his mind was already on another girl, a brunette from Tennessee or someplace like that. Her lilting accent drew him in, and she had a vulnerable look that made him feel strong and protective, though in all likelihood, he was the one more likely to need protection at *their* school.

The only problem was, he wasn't the only guy feeling that way about her.

She'd approached him that morning while he arranged his locker and started gushing.

"I love this town!" she said, without even introducing herself. "Don't you?"

Did he? Jeremy wasn't sure. He didn't have any other place to compare it with. Those thoughts ran through his mind, and then, crazily, he blurted them out. "I'm not sure. I've never lived anywhere else."

"Lucky you!" she said, and gave a cute little laugh that caused his heart to do a strange little flapdoodle. *Ka-thump.* She offered her hand. "Cathy."

He took her small hand in his and was lost, completely lost, from that moment on. "Jeremy," he finally managed to blurt.

She didn't think anything of it. "I just love the mountains here," she said. "They're crouching right there on the horizon like huge monsters. What do you call them?"

"The Three Sisters," Jeremy said. "And Mount Bachelor. And Broken Top." He felt awkward, and yet Cathy was looking at him in a way that somehow made it OK to be awkward.

"Wow," she breathed, eyes wide. "We don't have anything like that where I come from. It's so flat, so dreary. We don't have lakes so much as swamps, you know?"

Jeremy had no idea. But she ended the conversation just as abruptly as she'd started it, walking away. But she waved and smiled over her shoulder. He watched her all the way down the hall, where she whirled around to catch him looking. She giggled and disappeared from view.

He hadn't stopped thinking about her ever since. When Lucinda approached him—Lucinda, the girl he'd crushed on in eighth grade—he barely noticed her.

He'd begun to wonder if there was something wrong with him. He hadn't so much as held hands with a girl since sixth grade.

Maybe his sister was right: maybe things were finally turning around. But even if the Lucindas of the world—heretofore unobtainable and mysterious—threw themselves at his feet, it wouldn't matter. His eyes were set on a girl with a soft Southern accent and a beautiful laugh.

That night, Cathy's face and musical laugh filled Jeremy's thoughts and dreams.

Jeremy dreamed of her naked in a lush meadow, dancing with her arms outstretched, like a wood nymph, her hips swaying, a sheen of sweat shining on her breasts. She danced into his arms; they came together instantly, naturally, and he awoke shaking. The sheets were damp beneath him. His heart pounded in his chest. He thought he heard the echo of a soft laugh and caught a glimpse of pink flesh fleeing from the room.

It took hours to fall back to sleep. Every time he closed his eyes, he saw her, felt her, smelled her. Finally, in desperation, he picked up his civics book, so boring that he finally fell asleep—just before the sun came up and woke him again.

He awoke to harsh laughter in the hallway. His sister, whom all his friends thought was cute, sounded like a gargoyle compared to Cathy. All girls seemed boorish clods compared to her.

So this is love, he thought. Not puppy love, but the real thing, overwhelming and all consuming, the kind you read about. He tried to shake it off. Cathy would probably never talk to him again. He was a fool.

But there she was, waiting for him at the doors to the school. Her skirt was a little shorter than most girls wore, and it flared out instead of hugging her body. She wore a boy's white dress shirt, tied at the waist, and there was a gap in the buttons where her breasts pressed against the fabric. She wore a little blue beret and long blue stockings. It was a different look, and yet it suited her.

Jeremy couldn't stop staring at her.

"Hey," she said, returning his steady gaze. "I thought maybe you could show me where to go for my classes. I wandered around way too much yesterday and was late to every class. Kinda embarrassing."

Her smile was shy but confident. Her body was just a tiny bit closer than it needed to be; she was facing Jeremy as if he was the only person in the world and every part of her was interested.

"Sure," he said, trying to sound nonchalant. To his ears, it came out as a squeak. "Where's your first class?"

"Miss Meanders, Advanced Placement English."

"Well, that's easy. I'm headed that way myself," Jeremy said, and was amazed at his boldness

"Perfect!" Cathy said, and hooked her arm through crook of his elbow. "Lead the way."

Jeremy sat next to her in that first class. Later, he couldn't remember anything about it except her nearness. Miss Meanders blathering about Dickens? Or was it Poe?

Jeremy wished he'd thought to sit behind Cathy instead of beside her, so he could stare at her instead of glancing covertly at her out of the corner of his eye. No matter how slyly he tried to do it, she always seemed to catch him, and she would give him a small cat's smile, as if she was content to bask in his attention.

She fell into step beside him after the buzzer, and he led her to her next class and reluctantly left her at the door. Amazingly, after he emerged from his hour-and-a-half lab, she was in the hallway waiting for him, and they easily fell into conversation again.

So it went all week, and when the weekend came, it wasn't awkward at all to ask if she wanted to go to the movies. They held hands, and she watched the science-fiction story rapturously without making a sound, afterwards referencing books that were apropos to the movie. Jeremy wanted to fall to his knees and wrap his arms around her legs and cry. She was that perfect.

Instead, they went out for coffee. They talked about their childhoods, neither of which was terribly remarkable; just middle-class, white-bread families. Then Jeremy took her home. Before he could figure out how to say goodnight, Cathy cradled his face between her two soft hands and gave him a short, firm kiss; at the last second, her tongue poked between his lips. He was startled, and she laughed.

"See you on Monday!" she whispered.

He dreamed of her frolicking in the meadow again. He lay on the grass, watching her, until, laughing, she hopped over his body once, then twice, then thrice. "And now you're mine forever," she intoned, and he suddenly felt paralyzed, unable to move. She stripped, her body unimaginably perfect. Suddenly, he was naked, and she ran her a hand over his chest and then lower before sliding a leg over him and joining with him. She rode him slowly, languorously. He looked up into her face, and she seemed different, far older; her eyes were the eyes of a crone who had seen death and misery and hated the world for it.

But this in no way diminished his need for her. She leaned over him until her breasts brushed his chest, whispering in his ear, "You're mine." He spurted into her again and again at the power of her words, as if the coupling was an enchantment.

Jeremy awoke early that morning and put his soiled and still-wet sheets in the washer before his parents noticed. He was embarrassed, as much as he told himself that it was natural for his age. It wasn't like he could help it.

His mom noticed him doing the laundry and complimented him on his "taking responsibility" by doing it himself, and he flushed. He couldn't help but notice his dad smirking knowingly in the next room.

Jeremy's attraction to Cathy far outweighed anything else in his life. By Monday, he was impatient to see her, even leaving for school early, hoping to run into her. Unbelievably, she was waiting near the school doors again, sitting on the steps, surrounded by boys, many of them seniors. Most were a far better catch as far as the other girls were concerned, but Cathy abandoned them when Jeremy arrived, going to his side and pecking him on the cheek. That felt so good. Jeremy felt himself standing taller, and he couldn't help throwing his shoulders back.

The days passed in a blur. He must have done his homework that week, or something approximating it, for no one called his parents.

The weekend was a miserable experience. Jeremy was unable to focus on books, TV, or even the Minecraft city he was designing. He'd gone to bed early, hoping for some of those sexy dreams, but awoke tired, as if he'd been up all night. Early in the week, he decided to buy tickets for an indie band at the Amphitheater, but had no idea what kind of music Cathy liked. Which was something new to talk about— though they never seemed to have any trouble finding things to talk about.

On Tuesday, after school, before Jeremy could ask her about her musical tastes, Cathy asked, "Do you like camping?"

"Camping? Love it."

"Yeah?" She gave him the sideways glance he loved. "You want to go this weekend? Just us?"

"Hell, yeah!" He performed a quick mental inventory of the camping gear in the garage, "It's getting late in the season," he said. "We don't want to get caught by a snowfall. But I have a good tent and a couple of sleeping bags."

Cathy smiled at him gratefully, and he suddenly realized he was going to be alone with her for an entire weekend, in one small tent, with *no one* around.

"Are you sure?" he blurted as the implication sank in. Did she expect him to sleep right next to her all weekend without making a move?

"Yeah, Jeremy. I really want to do it."

She emphasized *"do it,"* and he was pretty sure she wasn't talking about camping.

Chapter 7

Gasper Gerhard's Journal

I have read all the manuscripts, going back to the barest scraps of parchment, crabbed words scribbled so small that they can barely be deciphered, no matter my years of scholarship. Thankfully, at some point, many of the earliest writings were copied in more modern idioms, or they might have been lost forever.

It is my belief that no Guardian before me has made such an effort; therefore, I may be the first to understand that not all of our oral traditions have been written down. They have been taken for granted for generations and could be lost at any time.

Thus I have taken it upon myself to record these legends that fathers have told their sons.

Nowhere is it recorded, for instance, when and why the containers of Blood began to be kept. This is this story as I heard it: When the Daughters of Lilith were imprisoned, the religious ceremonies eventually faded away. The Blood was still used, but it was without ritual. The Succubae were simply bled whenever they could survive it. Condemned prisoners were given to them, and they revived enough to spill more Blood, and thus was the Blood collected, year after year.

It is said that once the jars filled more than one chamber, the gleanings of thousands of years.

Perhaps we always knew that it could not continue forever. It was unfair, cruel, and some Guardians objected to the treatment of the Succubae. Eventually, they might have even freed the Succubae, as insane as that sounds now.

In the end, it didn't matter. The great quake that buried the chambers took the Daughters of Lilith away from us.

Little did we realize that the Succubae would escape to wander the Earth, preying on men, exacting their just retribution.

Czechoslovakia, 1944

Heinrich stayed hidden in the tunnels for days waiting for something to happen. It was deathly quiet under the earth; there was no sound at all. It was as if he was already dead and buried.

How would I know? he finally wondered. The dead were left alone.

He wandered back to the trapdoor. To his surprise, it was wide open. Remembering Gasper's words, he emerged clutching a knife, feeling foolish.

His father was at his usual perch near the window, moonshine liquor in hand. He turned at Heinrich's entrance. "Read them all?" he asked.

In truth, Heinrich hadn't touched the books. Instead he'd been dipping into the Blood, masturbating to the overpowering sensations taking over his body.

I won't become a Guardian, he thought. *I certainly won't do a Cutting.*

Gasper's eyes lingered sadly on him, as if he was reading Heinrich's thoughts. "Then you will die, son. You will die."

"The Russians?"

"Turned back, for now. But not for long."

So Gasper and Heinrich Gerhard went about their lives for another week as if nothing had changed. The booming cannons steadily approached; the loud grinding and deep squeaking of tanks seemed to be just over the horizon.

But they were left alone.

The skies darkened with smoke. A strange odor filled the air, the smell of gunpowder and death. Their few remaining neighbors drifted away, fleeing westward toward Germany, hoping to find protection there.

"Won't do them any good," Gasper scoffed. "The Russians won't stop until Der Fuhrer is dead."

Heinrich was amazed at the change in his father. He was no longer hiding his youthful looks and vigor—there was no one to hide it from. He was talkative, and rattled on about his own childhood, his training, and the stunning changes he had witnessed in the world. Mostly, he talked about the Succubae, trying to emphasize to Heinrich the crucial importance of their task.

If not for the miraculous healing he'd witnessed, Heinrich would have believed, along with everyone else, that Gasper Gerhard was insane.

Still, he soaked it in. After a few days, he was drawn back to the caverns, finding that, once away from the main corridor, it was a bewildering maze, with numerous tunnels and chambers.

"Keep track of your turns or you'll become lost," Gasper warned him. "The labyrinth was designed to confuse."

After a few days, Heinrich started reading the books, if only to see if he could find a loophole, an escape, something no one had yet thought of. He started with his grandfather's journal and worked his way back. The later journals were pretty thin, the overall tone despairing.

Reading between the lines, Heinrich sensed that the journals didn't reveal the whole truth. Somewhere along the line, the Guardians had become corrupted. Instead of safeguarding the precious Blood of the Succubus, they began selling it for its healing powers—a betrayal of everything they were sworn to protect.

When God's punishment came, it was swift, fierce, and complete. Only the Gerhard family survived, the most devoted of acolytes. Only they kept the faith.

But their faith was shortsighted. They never recruited new members into the Guardians. They kept watch over the Blood for generation after generation, until both the Blood and the family were reduced, until it was just fathers and sons, a dangerously thin thread.

To what purpose? Heinrich wondered. Selling potions with just a drop of the Blood in them could have made them rich, but the Gerhard family was faithful to a fault.

The thread ends with me, Heinrich thought. *I'm getting out of here the first chance I get, and I'm taking the Blood of the Succubus with me. I'll use it, I'll sell it, whatever I must do.*

He hid these plans from his father, of course, who seemed pleased at his son's studious manner.

The full moon approached. The German army finally crumbled, and the Russians surged west.

"It is time," Gasper said one morning as the house shook from the nearness of the explosions. A plane had flown low over their cottage earlier that morning, as if checking for signs of life.

Dread filled Heinrich. He gasped for breath, his throat raw from an imagined shortage of air. The terrible memory of the unnatural smoothness between his father's legs lingered in his mind.

I can't do it, Heinrich thought desperately. *I won't* do it.

He rose to his feet, ready to march out the door, to join the fighting—he didn't care for which side. If he died, he'd be free.

"Sit down," his father commanded.

Heinrich's legs gave out, and he collapsed back into the chair. It was hopeless. He could not escape his fate. The darkness below the cellar drew him even as it repelled him, and he knew he was cursed.

"This is *wrong*," Heinrich said. "I don't understand why I must do this."

"I too doubted the necessity." Gasper said. "But then I met *them*."

This was new. According to the books, none of the Guardians had seen the Succubae since the collapse of the cavern—at least, none who had survived. But the rumors that came back to them left no doubt.

The Succubae were loose upon the world.

Now Heinrich's father pulled a battered leathered-bound volume out of his coat and handed it over. Heinrich remembered that Gasper had taken his own journal with him.

"Read it when I'm gone," Gasper said. "I was more diligent in my homework than my own father, or his father, or any of our ancestors a half millennia back. I hope it will do you some good."

"You've seen a Succubus?" Heinrich asked.

Gerhard stared out the window and took a long drink. He set the cup down, coughing. It was little more than pure alcohol.

51

"Tell me, Father," Heinrich insisted.

Gasper turned to him, looking like the old man he'd pretended to be for so long. "If it will help you to believe…"

He took another long drink, and then refilled the cup with liquor before he started.

"When I was your age," Gasper began, "my father and I began hearing of a monster stalking Prague, a creature who seduced and drained the life from men. I vowed to investigate…" He paused and looked Heinrich in the face. "This was my first Cutting. Father would not let me go unless I went through with it, and God help me, I so wanted to get away that I let him. I don't know what I thought—that I'd escape somehow? But of course, I had to return, for after the Cutting I was no longer a man. I needed the Blood."

Gasper fell silent for a moment, staring into the fire. "I hated my father for that, but I soon understood, after Prague, why it must be done. It doesn't just preserve our lives, Heinrich, it is our duty."

"You went to Prague…" Heinrich prompted.

Gasper drained the last of the liquor and coughed. When he started speaking again, his voice had the softness of a distant memory.

"It was a long journey, for I was constantly forced to turn aside at the approach of armed men. The closer I got to Prague, the worse it got, until I thought I had witnessed the worst man could do. Fields of bodies, torn and bloated. I came across the remains of a family, spread out in front of their home, and I could not believe what I saw…to this day I am haunted by it. As I approached Prague, my despair only deepened. It was the war, of course, but it was something else as well, a moral depravity that went beyond even that savagery.

"Sexual debauchery was everywhere, but *I* was immune to its call. All around me, I saw men and women having sex: in alleys, in taverns, on the filthy streets, clothed or unclothed, mindless of everything around them. But the monster's invitation could not tempt me.

"In Wenceslas Square, I found such a tangle of men, I could make no sense of it. They were dying, I thought, or in pain, writhing on top of each other. I knew of sex—like you, I was allowed to experience a climax so I might understand the Succubae's lure and how others are ensnared. But I was naïve, not understanding the many ways that the sexual act is accomplished.

"At the center of the pile was one woman, and all the men struggled to touch her, to penetrate her, pushing each other aside violently. It was madness, but no one questioned it. The women of the city acted as if it wasn't happening. Though the dead lay all around, men still approached her. She gladly embraced each one, but when she finished, they moved no longer. They were shrunken husks, their bones showing, their faces little more than skulls.

"I stepped back into the shadows, watching men approach, drawn to her like moths to flame, oblivious to the danger. The Succubus looked up once, directly at me, and I sensed her curiosity. She looked like a normal woman, handsomer than most, but not someone I would have found mysterious if I'd passed her in the street. I could appreciate her with my mind, but because of the Cutting, my body didn't respond.

"She ignored me, dismissing my presence as if I were a neutered dog or cat. What I am telling you is, if I had not been emasculated before my encounter, I'd be dead now."

The house shook again, as if a bomb had landed but feet away. It took a couple more seconds for the sound to reach them. The front was still miles away, but growing closer with every passing moment.

"Are you ready?" Gasper asked.

"No," Heinrich said, and could think of nothing to add. He was not going to do it.

"I will help you the first time," his father said softly.

I might as well be dead, Heinrich thought. *I don't want to live as a eunuch. When you are gone, I will live as a man.*

And still, as if compelled by some power he couldn't resist, he followed his father to the cellar.

They reached the Cutting room.

"I will show you how I do it," his father said. "One last time."

Gasper stood and drank from a jar, and his genitals grew out. One moment they were gone, and the next they were there, his cock standing tall. "I usually take some…time….before I complete the new Cutting," Gasper said. "But we are out of time."

53

He took a knife from the table and ran it along his thumb. "You must be certain the knife is sharp. Do not think too long on it."

He sliced across his groin, a smooth motion, and the meat fell to the floor. Blood spurted from the wound. He placed one hand over the bloody gash. He swayed, his face white. "You must not faint, or you will die," he said dispassionately.

He drank a small amount from the jar. The wound healed, but his genitals were gone.

"Your turn," Gasper said. "Take off your clothes."

Heinrich couldn't refuse, not without letting his father know about his rebellious plans. *What does it matter if my father knows? I can refuse...I can leave...*

He took off his clothes slowly, as if someone else was undressing, someone else who was about to do the unthinkable.

I will do it this one time, but never again.

A rumbling sound penetrated the caves, which meant it had to be nearly above them. "Hurry!" his father insisted.

The Blood will restore me, Heinrich chanted. *The Blood will restore me. The Blood will restore me.*

"Hurry!" Gasper shouted again, grabbing him roughly around the waist, putting the knife in his hand.

I will be bold. I will cut deeply with one motion.

He pressed down and lost heart. The pain shot through his body and up his spine, and he shrieked. His hand became slick with blood. He dropped the blade and clutched himself. His legs buckled and his sight dimmed.

"God in heaven!" he heard his father say.

Gasper snatched the knife from the floor. Heinrich felt the blade against the open wound, and before he could object, he felt a blow, as if a hammer had slammed against his groin. His entire body stiffened, and he felt himself falling onto the table. He heard distant screaming and realized it was him.

He awoke with his father crouched over him. There was Blood on his fingers, and Heinrich could feel it tingling in his mouth. The pain was gone. Physically, he felt the same, but nothing was the same. He shook violently as the idea of being this…thing, not a man, not even a eunuch, but something else.

He reached down *there* tentatively. His heart shredded. There was nothing, just smooth skin. The horror of it was too much. He felt suddenly numb, with no feeling at all, only a strange, detached curiosity.

"You'll do better next time," his father said. Heinrich looked up at him as if at a stranger. He felt nothing: no anger, no shame.

Nothing at all.

He watched Gasper lifting the jar of Blood and drinking again. But instead of a small drop, his father kept drinking. His genitals returned again.

He's not supposed to do that, Heinrich thought.

"What are you doing?" someone asked, and he realized it was his own voice. "I don't understand."

"You are the new Guardian, Heinrich," Gasper said. "I will lead the Russians away from the house. They probably won't find the trapdoor, but you must be quiet."

"Why?" Heinrich asked.

"I'm not needed here anymore," Gasper said. He looked confident, happy. Yet he was walking into battle, to his own death. "I've lived a long life. It is time I got away, joined the fight."

"What can *you* do?" Heinrich asked. He was slowly returning to the present. His thoughts and his voice were starting to align again. He felt a vague alarm at his father's words.

"Ah, someday you'll drink fully of the Blood, and you'll know. The Russians won't find a lowly peasant facing them, but a man with more strength and speed than they have seen on any battlefield. Those who survive will tell stories about me." Gasper reached down and cupped his genitals. "If I am to die, I will die as a man."

They both dressed. They walked up the long tunnel without speaking. Heinrich was coming back to himself. He was still too stunned to feel afraid or angry, but his thoughts were making sense, at least.

I'll wait until father leaves, and I'll drink the Blood.

As they approached the trapdoor, Gasper suddenly held his hand up. "Did you hear that?"

"What?" Heinrich strained to hear something. It did seem as if he'd heard a thud, or the echo of a thud. Something…

"Someone is in the house," his father said. "Wait here."

Gasper climbed the steps and passed out of sight. The trapdoor thudded into place.

Heinrich waited for greetings or shouts. Instead, a few moments later, he heard the snick of a lock.

He tricked me! Heinrich thought. He scurried up the steps, but his father's footsteps receded. He pounded on the door, calling out, but there was no answer. It was no mistake; this had been his father's plan all along.

"Let me out, damn you!" he shouted. He sensed there was no one there. After shouting a string of curses—something he had never dared do to his father before—he stomped back to the room where the Blood of the Succubus was stored.

He tried reading for a while, but the smoke from the lanterns became unbearable, and he eventually sat in darkness, contemplating his fate. His hands hurt; he wondered if he'd broken them. Blood ran down his arms.

Eventually it occurred to him that he was truly alone.

There is no one to keep me from doing whatever I want to do.

His father had said that someday he'd drink fully of the Blood, as if that was greatly daring.

Without another thought, Heinrich pulled down the jar and took a long drink.

The Blood coursed through his body, correcting the damage he'd done to himself trying to force the door open.

Sexual energy flowed down his spine, and he felt his manhood returning. He reached for his cock, stroking it. The old feelings came back reassuringly. His testicles felt full. He closed his eyes and jerked vigorously, imagining the woman in the Prague Square beckoning him, taking him in her mouth, taking all of him and then licking beneath. He came on the stone floor.

Ten minutes later, he did it again.

He had often seen the stain on his father's pants, full moon after full moon. He was certain that his father had done same thing, probably every time he went through the ritual. He was a hypocrite, taking his pleasure even if he did his duty in the end.

With his father gone, Heinrich had no intention of ever Cutting himself again.

Several days passed. Heinrich checked the door periodically, listening for his father's footsteps. There was nothing.

How am I supposed to get out of here?

Surely the old man had thought of that? There must be some way to get out that Heinrich was supposed to find after the Russians were gone.

He searched the caverns thoroughly but found no escape, no solution to his imprisonment.

Then, one night, as he tried to sleep on the cold stone floor, he heard excited shouting from above. The cries didn't sound like fear, or pain. It wasn't the kind of sound that men fighting made. In fact…

He grabbed one of the knives and ran down the corridor. The trapdoor was flexing, as if someone was jumping up and down on it. He heard a man's grunting, in pleasure, not pain, then another loud shout as the man came again.

The pounding continued as Heinrich listened, and the cries of pleasure turned to pain.

"Please," the victim pleaded. "Let me die."

It's Father, Heinrich realized. He stepped back, nearly tumbling down the steps. His father was alive, but it was not relief he felt, but a sudden dread, mixed with…

The act of sex began again, directly overhead, and despite the horror of his father being drained, Heinrich could not help but respond. His cock grew as the act became more violent above him, his father crying out in pain or pleasure or both.

With an animalistic cry, the sounds stopped.

Heinrich felt something reaching for him, searching. He almost climaxed just from the thought of it.

But beneath it all was dread, fear that if he succumbed, it would be the end.

He'd thought nothing was worse than the Cutting. He'd thought he'd rather die than ever suffer it again.

Now, without thinking, he dropped his trousers.

"Don't think too long on it," his father had said.

Heinrich sliced across his groin, feeling his genitals drop away. His eyesight dimmed to a single point of light surrounded by flashes of pain. He was dizzy.

Stay awake, he told himself. *You'll bleed to death.*

He made it down the stairs and a few steps more. He tried to stay upright as sex resumed above him, but fell to the floor and curled up, fainting.

Heinrich awoke, his entire body in pain, and then the pain stabbed like a knife between his legs, and he cried out for his father. He smothered his cry, remembering the Succubus. No one came.

He managed to get to his feet and staggered through the cavern, blood running down his thighs, a horrible, burning agony filling his groin.

I can't...I'll bleed to death. He leaned against the wall with one hand while pressing against the gaping wound below his pelvis with the other. He lurched against the wall and fell to the rough stones.

Just stay here. Rest.

He closed his eyes, and moments later started awake with spasm of fear.

I'm going to die if I don't get to the Blood.

He tore off his shirt and pushed it against the wound. He cried out from the pain, and then stopped, listening.

He heard nothing.

The corridors downward were endless. Heinrich took the turns by instinct, vaguely aware, through the buzzing white noise in his head and burning pain, that if he took the wrong turn, he wouldn't have time to turn around.

At the end, he was crawling. He bumped his head against wood and looked up in surprise at the heavy door of the storeroom. With a cry of relief and pain, he pushed his way inside.

He collapsed on the floor, staring up at the bottles of Succubus Blood. They were impossibly high.

I'm going to die, just inches from deliverance.

He might have given up then, but a distant shout somehow penetrated the tunnels, reaching his ears. Heinrich realized that it was Gasper's last breath. His father had sacrificed himself to save his only son.

Heinrich wrenched himself onto the table, jostling it and sending the knives clattering to the floor. One stabbed into his foot, but he barely noticed.

He reached desperately for the row of jars, but the more extended he got, the dizzier he became. His vision narrowed. He was falling. He clutched at the nearest jar, knocking several to the floor. There were sickening thuds and cracks as the ancient stone crumbled, splattering him with Succubae blood. A stray drop landed in his mouth.

That single drop saved his life. The Blood exploded in his mouth and shot down his throat. The warmth spread through his innards and sparked his heart. He took a deep gasp of air and realized that he'd almost stopped breathing.

The splattered Blood burned where it landed on his face and chest. His dizziness faded; his vision opened up. He lay on the floor feeling the Blood flow through him, down to his feet. Blood was pooled beneath his face, and he lapped it up.

Finally, he was able to sit up. He frantically licked the blood spatter from his hands and arms, and the tingling strengthened him.

Not enough, not enough!

He slapped at the mess of sludgy blood on the stone floor, scooping it into his mouth. It coursed through his limbs and torso, up his neck into his head and down to his groin. It all came back, and he was whole.

Heinrich lay panting in the dim cavern, relief flooding him.

And as he lay there, his cock grew hard. In his panic, he'd gone too far. *She* was calling him. The pain was still a vivid memory, but it was being erased by desire.

He grabbed one of the knives strewn about the floor. He shuddered, for it was a dull one, but he didn't have time. Not giving himself enough time to think, he cut deeply. This time, he didn't faint. Of the jars that had fallen onto the floor, only one was whole. He gathered it up with trembling hands and took a drink, enough to heal the wound but not enough to regrow his manhood.

He stood up, then sat heavily in the chair. It seemed to him that he could sense the Succubus seeking him, but he was now invisible to her. He glanced at the Blood on the wall, counting the containers. The rows of jars were diminished from what his father had first shown him.

Heinrich put his head in his hands and groaned. As much as he hated it, as much as he wanted to deny it, he couldn't help but feel a new appreciation for his forebears—and for his father. They had done their duty thousands of times, tens of thousands of times, all as a sacrifice for mankind.

He understood now. The Cutting was necessary.

Heinrich vowed at that moment to kill the Daughters of Lilith or return them to the caves, where they would be buried so deep they could never emerge to plague mankind again.

Now all he had to do was figure a way out of the caverns.

Chapter 8

Downtown Bend is getting too damn busy, Cary thought.
He was in a foul mood after circling the block several times, searching for a parking spot. He finally gave up and shelled out five bucks for the local parking garage. He strolled into Starbucks twenty minutes late to find himself confronted by an irritable Serena.

"You're late," she snapped. "I'm on my second cup already."

The dark circles under her eyes testified to her lack of sleep, and her hair wasn't perfectly groomed, as it had been the night before. Even with the frown, though, she seemed less uptight and more approachable than she had before.

She was a beautiful woman. Cary liked what he saw, even if he was younger than her by almost a decade. He wondered how she would act in a more intimate setting. He had an active imagination in that realm. As he ordered his coffee, he also imagined how the baristas would be in bed.

After he'd gotten his coffee, he returned to Serena's table and laid the newspaper in front of her. A photo of a massive black bear dominated the front page. A trio of deputies with huge grins surrounded creature, their rifles propped on their shoulders. It had taken eight shots to bring the huge animal down.

She tugged the paper nearer to have a closer look. "I didn't know you had bears that big around here," she said.

"We don't," Cary said, snagging the seat across from her. "Weird, huh?"

"Her blood…" Serena began. Her voice trailed off, and she looked as though she regretted saying anything.

"What's that?" Cary asked, watching her intently.

"It is said," Serena said reluctantly, "that the blood of a …that *her* blood…has powers of rejuvenation."

"The blood of…what?" he asked. "You were going to say something else."

She looked into his eyes, as if weighing a decision. Then she said, "Why don't you tell me your story first? You said you saw something in Suzanne. I'd like to hear about that."

Cary grimaced into his coffee cup for a long moment. There was no way to explain it convincingly, except to tell her the full story. He drew in a deep breath and looked around at all the people sitting nearby who couldn't help but overhear him. They would think he was crazy.

"Not here," he said, standing up.

Cary led Serena a couple blocks farther into downtown, into a comic book store on the corner that sold used books.

"Hey, Dudley," Cary called out.

The bearded owner waved back. There were a couple of battered armchairs amongst the equally battered books. They sat down, knees nearly touching, and Serena turned to him expectantly. Cary could scarcely believe he'd taken her to a comic shop. He decided to tell her everything and not to hold back, even the crazy stuff.

Maybe she'll believe me, he thought. *After all, she's the one talking about blood.*

"I met Suzanne at a party," he began. "A kegger in the woods…"

"A kegger?" Serena asked.

"An outdoor party with kegs of beer," Cary said. "Gets pretty loud and rowdy. Maybe it's a Western thing."

I'm rambling, he thought. *I don't really want to remember.*

"Anyway, there was a bonfire, and people dancing to loud music. And there, in the middle of it all, was Doug, good old studious Doug, laughing and having a good time. I gotta tell you, that was pretty cool, something I thought I'd never see.

"Doug was my best friend, so at first I was happy that a cute girl— a *really* cute girl!—was paying attention to him. He was always a little shy. I figured it was about time some girl noticed him. So when Doug went off in search of more beer, I sat next to her, planning to thank her, to congratulate her on her good taste…"

He broke off, growing cold at the memory of the look she'd given him.

Cathy was beautiful in the firelight, so when she turned and looked at Cary like he'd crawled out from under a rock, he was stunned. Her eyes were cold, which was bad enough, but they also seemed ancient, and evil.

He looked away and gulped down some beer. When he turned back, a transformation had occurred. Suzanne was suddenly glad to see him.

"You're Cary, aren't you?" she said, her voice full and throaty, with a hint of hoarseness that was endearing somehow. "Doug pointed you out."

"Yeah, Doug's a good guy," he said.

"He is, isn't he? I can't believe no one has snatched him up yet."

"I've always wondered the same thing," he said, warming up to her. The coldness in her eyes when she'd first looked at him was forgotten as they chatted.

And then it happened.

"I'm so glad to finally meet you," she gushed, turning her entire attention on him, ignoring all the playful antics around them, the people dancing around the fire, the music blasting from car radios.

Nothing mattered to her but him, because he was Doug's friend, but more—he was oh, so interesting himself.

He felt himself getting an erection. He felt an instant, overwhelming attraction to this girl—no, this *woman*.

Cary was still embarrassed that he'd almost succumbed to her charms. When Doug later accused Cary of coming on to her, he'd flushed, because it was half true. The truth was, she came on to him— but he responded.

"I'm not very proud of what I did," Cary said, coming back to the present. "What I *almost* did that night."

"Go on," Serena said.

"I...it was really strange..." He paused, unwilling to look Serena in the eyes, struggling with the darkness of his thoughts. How could he explain the enormous attraction he'd felt at that moment?

"Up until then, I'd only seen Suzanne from a distance. She didn't seem all that special. But she was so beautiful in the firelight, like an angel or movie star or...a Goddess. I wanted to take her hand and lead her off into the darkness. I could tell she *wanted* it and I *wanted* it, and that's all that mattered."

He finally dared to look into Serena's eyes. She was calm, accepting. "You're straight male, and she's...*Suzanne,*" Serena said. "Believe me, you had a normal reaction."

Cary must have had a strange expression on his face, because she reached out and squeezed his arm, not unkindly. "Just tell the story, Cary. I'm not judging you."

He began again, haltingly at first, then gradually picking up speed, until the words spilled out of him. Serena said little, waiting, listening with a grave look on her face, nodding occasionally.

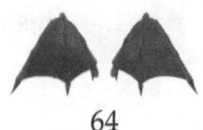

Suzanne looked over his shoulder, making sure Doug wasn't near. It was a cold, calculating gaze. That moment was enough for Cary to realize she was playing him. Oh, she was good, she was really good, but it was her overreaching charm that gave her away. That and what she revealed in her rare, unguarded moments.

She was a snake, or something worse. And she had her fangs in his best friend.

He and Doug had become best friends because of their love of books, but that's where the commonalities ended. While Doug was raised in a nice middle-class family, Cary had been raised by a horror show of a family: meth heads and casual criminals, the eternal underclass, forever mired by their own stupid short-term decisions. He'd vowed to break away, to be different.

To his credit, Doug had never looked down on him.

Unlike his friend, Cary knew when someone was trying to pull something over on him. Doug never had drug-addicted family members cheat and lie to him, trying to con one more dollar out of him. Cary recognized all the signs.

Suzanne seemed to sense his disillusion, and damned if she didn't almost hiss at him. All her features were the same—the blue eyes, the black hair, the high cheekbones—but they became alien somehow, inhuman. Cary reared back, nearly falling off the log.

Doug returned at that moment. He stared down at his friend, puzzled. He handed a red plastic cup full of beer to Suzanne. She was laughing as if Cary had done something silly.

Cary rose and walked silently away as if nothing had happened, too shocked by what he'd seen to speak of it. He spent the rest of the evening staying out of sight, debating with himself about whether he should tell Doug.

He bided his time, waiting until Suzanne slipped away to relieve herself before finding the courage to approach his best friend. He told Doug what had happened. "Let's get out of her before she comes back," he finished.

Doug's face turned bright red. Cary thought for a moment that his friend was going to slug him.

"She told me you came on to her," Doug said.

"No," Cary protested. "She came on to *me!*"

"I thought she was imagining it," Doug shouted, "but it's true, isn't it? You're jealous!"

"Doug...listen to me. She's lying."

"I thought you were my friend, Cary," Doug snarled. "Get away from me."

Cary watched from a distance when Doug left the party with Suzanne. He thought he'd have a chance later to get him alone, to convince him.

He never saw his best friend again.

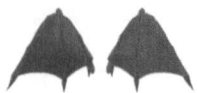

"When he died, I had already lost him," Cary finished. He was staring out the store window, not really seeing the pedestrians, but looking somewhere inside himself.

Serena didn't say anything at first. Cary was still embarrassed. It sounded so stupid, as if he was such a horny guy that all it took was a little come-on from a pretty girl and he was ready to betray his friend.

"You didn't tell me the whole story, did you?" Serena finally said, her voice very quiet.

"What do you mean?" he asked, knowing exactly what she meant.

"When you described her transformation, you stumbled over your words. That isn't everything you saw, is it?"

There was a long silence. "You won't believe me," he said.

"Try me," she said flatly.

"All right, but I warned you..." He took a deep breath. "Her face changed. Her blue eyes were cold, devoid of light. Her high cheekbones were sharp, her nose long and hooked. Her hair...it was as if her hair turned into snakes, her tongue became forked, and her eyes were like a cat's. I...I think I hated her so much at the moment that I imagined her to be a Medusa."

He looked Serena in the eyes, expecting to see derision or disappointment. She simply nodded. "Medusa may be one of her personas. Her hair isn't really comprised of snakes, but it moves. No, I believe you. What you saw was the dark heart of a Succubus."

Cary frowned. She'd already used the term Succubus, but he wasn't sure he understood it. "She comes into your room at night and steals your breath, right?"

Serena's laughter was a pleasure to his ears, even bringing a smile to his face. Despite the serious tone of the conversation, Cary's heart lifted. He had a feeling she didn't laugh much. The laughter changed her whole face.

"Stealing breath…that's what they tell children, because they can't very well tell the truth," she said. She glanced furtively around and lowered her voice. "A Succubus steals your life force by way of sex, Cary."

He stared at her, wondering if he was supposed to laugh. Nope, she was dead serious.

"Shit," he said.

"Yeah," she answered. "Pretty much."

He took a long sip of coffee, though it was almost cold by then. He barely noticed. "Then I killed my best friend, because I was too cowardly to warn him."

"You tried," Serena said softly. She reached out and put her hand on his. "He wouldn't have believed you. She had her hooks into him too deep."

His gaze dropped to the tabletop, and he finally nodded. "How do you know all this?" he asked.

"I've been researching her for a long time. Some of it may be guesses, but I've found that the more horrible it is, the more likely it is to be true."

"What will she do now?"

"She'll be searching for a man. Any man who will have her."

"What the hell? Half the guys in town would fuck her." Cary paused, then said, "Pardon my language, but that's the way she works."

Serena nodded. "Thankfully, it's not simply a matter of…fucking," she said. She looked around as if she expected kids to be lurking near the comic racks. All she saw was a guy who looked like a banker.

"Don't worry, they've heard that word in here before," Cary assured her.

Serena continued. "She prefers her victims totally besotted with her. That they give up their very essence, knowing deep in their hearts what will happen. She wants not just love, but rapture. And even with the easiest of prey, that takes time."

"What makes you think she's still here?" Cary asked. "Why wouldn't she move on to another town?"

"She moves around, but usually only after a kill. I think the wandering is as much out of habit as anything. She doesn't really believe she's in danger." Serena sighed and gave an eloquent shrug. "She's probably safer these days than in medieval or ancient times. They at least believed in supernatural creatures, unlike now." Serena shook her head and was silent for a moment. Then a bitter smile came over her face, and she stared out the window at the colorful trees against the blue sky. "I looked her in the eye and promised to get her. She just laughed."

"That's good, then," Cary said. "If she's still here, we have a chance."

"She could be anywhere, but I'm hoping she's too weak to leave Bend," Serena said. "She will have changed her name. She can pretend to be a teenager, or a middle-aged spinster; whatever gets her close to her prey."

"Her *prey*?" He believed everything Serena had said, and yet the words of doubt still popped out of his mouth: a modern man, denying the unnatural, the magical, the unseen.

"Look, if you are going to doubt everything I say," Serena said, "we should end this partnership right here."

Partnership. Cary liked the idea. He liked her, and when she touched his hand, he'd felt a stirring within, as if this was someone he could really see spending time with, talking to...cuddling...maybe even...*Wait, what's she doing?*

Serena grabbed her coat and stood up, visibly annoyed.

He put his hand on her arm, pulling her back. "Don't leave! I believe you, it's just a lot to take in."

She stared down at him. It seemed like he was flirting with her.

"Cary, you told me an outlandish story about a girl who you thought was a monster, and you didn't expect me to believe you. Not only do I believe you, but I can take it farther. She is the real deal. If you can't wrap your brain around this fact, then we need to part ways."

"I get it," he said.

"You say Doug was your best friend. This is deadly serious. This creature has killed and killed for decades, centuries...perhaps even longer, as impossible as that seems. Who knows how old she really is?"

Cary passed his hand over his face and gave her a deeply somber gaze. "I totally believe you."

Serena sat back down. "Thank you."

He frowned. "You say she changes looks?"

"Hair color and style, eye color, makeup. She usually changes her style of clothing. What doesn't change is her manner: cute, pixie-like, charming."

"A manic pixie dream girl?" he said.

"Exactly!" Serena exclaimed, smiling slightly.

"But her face looks the same, right?"

Serena had to think about it. A roster of images passed through her mind, and she realized that, yeah, the face was pretty much always the same. "I don't know whether she can't change her face or she's just too lazy to."

"So how about if we get a black and white drawing of her face, no hair, no color, just the basic outlines, and we pass that around town?"

Serena looked thoughtful. "That might work. But if she sees the poster, she might run."

"We don't have to post it. We can just show it around."

Serena nodded slowly. "It might work." Bend was just the right sized town; maybe a hundred thousand people in the city limits at any one time, large enough for Kristen/Suzanne to feel safe, but small enough that a canvassing approach wouldn't be hopeless.

She hesitated. Should she contact Rick and see what he thought? Somehow she thought he'd say no, and she didn't want to hear that answer right now.

"Let's do it," Serena said.

Chapter 9

E isheth was the first to meet the strangers. She rose naked and unashamed and emerged from the hut. Later, she realized it was a mistake. These barbarians had different customs, and nudity was not one of them. Even at night, even in the dark, even beneath the blankets, they covered themselves up. It was a tactical error—but then, she didn't know what tactics were; she didn't understand war and dominance.

They were all men, astride shaggy horses. Unlike the men of the village, these invaders wore their hair and beards long, looking uncannily like their steeds. The women arrived later, silent, eyes lowered, little more than beasts of burden pulling the wagons of the tribe.

The leader was the biggest of them, astride a large red horse. He stared down at her with slack-jawed astonishment. His hair was red too, a color Eisheth had never seen before on a man, and was braided, with colorful beads threaded through the braids. His mustache drooped, curling below his chin.

Most strange, he carried weapons all over his body and on his horse: a small knife at his belt, a longer blade hanging from his saddle, a bow slung over one shoulder, a quiver filled with arrows over the other.

How does he manage to ride? Eisheth wondered.

The man gazed around the village as if he owned it.

He is magnificent! Eisheth felt herself responding to him.

Another tactical mistake. The leader, and the men behind him, felt her desire. They would never forget it.

She instinctively understood something was wrong. She motioned to one of the villagers, who were emerging from their homes to watch, and urgently whispered for him to bring her a cloak. He ducked into the nearest house and quickly returned with an old robe. She wrapped it around herself without comment.

"Welcome to Lilith's Home," she said. Visitors were unusual, but not unheard of. The mountain passes were difficult, but not impassible. "Our blessing upon you."

"We have heard of the blessings of this place," the man rumbled. His voice was an octave lower than any Eisheth had ever heard. It was undeniably masculine, yet sounded forced. *The appearance of virility is all-important to these strangers*, she realized. She wondered how much was real and how much was bluster.

He jumped off his horse and approached her. He loomed over her, which no villager would have dared to do. He smelled of sweat, tinged with horsehair and leather. Eisheth felt her heart beating faster, a flush coming over her pale skin. She'd never been afraid of a man, never felt threatened, but there was something about this newcomer…

Her hands were hidden, holding the cloak closed, but she felt her talons grow beneath the cloth. She took a deep breath.

"Blessings and welcome to all," she said.

The man stared down at her, unflinching. She stared back, defiant. It was yet another mistake, one she and her sisters would pay for. But she couldn't help herself. Something about this man made her want to take him—but even stranger, she wanted him to take her.

"You're one of *them*, aren't you?" the man said. His eyes were green, and beneath were large freckles, running down into his red beard. His breath smelled of meat. She stepped back.

"I am Eisheth," she said. "And you are?"

"Komor, of the Draast," he said. He bowed his head slightly.

"You are welcome, Komor of the Draast."

"The stories do not tell the full truth," he breathed. "You are beautiful. A man must see it…and feel it." He grabbed his crotch at the last words.

Her talons sharpened, poking through the cloak, but again she hid her feelings. She wasn't sure if she wanted to kill this interloper or have intercourse with him.

"A true Goddess," he said. He turned and motioned, and his men dismounted. "My men and horses are thirsty. Where is your well?"

Eisheth glanced at young Coss, who nodded. He took the reins of the leader's horse.

"Stop," Komor commanded. Coss stopped, his eyes wide at the loudness of the man's voice. Komor unstrapped the long sword from the saddle, then patted the horse's rear end and nodded at Coss, who led it up the path.

Eisheth almost objected. The village spring issued from the mountainside above, just out of sight. But it was clear water, not meant for animals. The animals drank from the lesser springs, far below.

"Go ahead," Komor commanded his men. All but a few of the tribesmen followed. Eisheth noticed that those who remained behind were the biggest and most heavily armed.

Naamah came walking up the path toward them, her hips swaying with unconscious ease, followed by three of her young lovers, two men and a woman. She was clothed, but just barely.

Komor and his lieutenants felt rather than saw her coming. They turned, eyes widening. One of the men let out a grunt that sounded like the noises that came out of a man at the height of his climax.

Naamah's hands went to her breasts as if to hide them—which said something, because she was most shameless of the three sisters. Eisheth would have sworn that nothing could embarrass her.

The eros that had inundated the village the entire day was growing stronger still, but this was not an innocent expression of life, but something darker, meaner. Eisheth noticed one of Naamah's lovers take off his cloak and throw it over the young Goddess's shoulders.

"What is the reason for your visit?" Eisheth asked Komor, keeping her voice calm.

"Reason?" Komor cocked his head, looking back at his followers, who smiled broadly. "Do I need a reason?"

"We are a small village," Eisheth said. "We will try to accommodate your men, of course, but our resources are limited. Perhaps you should stay in the valley below." There were several settlements in the lush valley that in most years didn't need the fertility ceremonies of the Goddesses.

He laughed. "They said the same thing. 'Go to Lilith's Home! It is more bountiful. The Goddesses shall take care of you.'" He winked at her. "I think they were frightened of us. Our enemies have spread unfair stories about us."

Nothing could have reinforced his dangerous nonchalance more than his wink. Eisheth felt a shock run through her. Had *any* man *ever* dared *wink* at *her*?

She should have ripped his throat out then and there. But in those days, she hadn't yet killed. Her instincts were right, but her experience hadn't prepared her for what evil mankind could do. Nor did she have the slightest suspicion that a Goddess could be vulnerable to mere mortals.

"You cannot stay," she said. "You must go back to your own homes."

"Cannot?" Again he quirked his head at his men, who smirked back. "Yet here we are, and here we will stay. We have no place to go back to, Goddess. We set out for Lilith's Home with the intention of making it our home. Surely you can spread your blessings farther than this little valley."

Eisheth was speechless. Never before had a man contradicted her. She didn't know what to do. When the doors of the temple opened, she felt relief and gratitude.

Agrat Bat would take care of it.

The eldest sister looked like a normal woman, fleshed out but not abundantly so. Her hair was the whitest blonde, and in the flickering fire of the torches, her blue eyes glowed. Agrat Bat went through none of the polite preliminaries, as if she already understood what was happening.

"You are not welcome here," she told Komor. "You must leave."

"As I was telling your sister Goddess, we cannot leave, for we have no place to go," he said. "Let us stay, and we will help you. We will bring you the riches of the lands around us, for none can stand before us."

"I don't understand," Naamah said. "You would take what is not yours?"

Komor's laugh echoed through the valley. "You have never been among real men, have you? Ask these pathetic followers of yours what happens outside this place. They know, I can tell."

Eisheth couldn't help herself. She looked at the nearest villager, who averted his eyes.

Agrat Bat wasn't so easily intimidated. "We do not care what happens outside. You will not be allowed inside."

"Listen, bitch Goddess," Komor snarled. "I've counted your men; I've counted your weapons. There is no way you can stop us."

Old Forr chose that moment to defend his Goddess. "You mustn't speak to Her that way," he said. He walked up to Komor, his hands at his sides, no doubt hoping to convince the other man.

Komor's sword came out of its scabbard so fast that Eisheth only caught the tail end of the motion, after the wide swath of the blade went through Forr's neck. His old bald head tumbled down his chest and onto the stone path. His body fell, unmoving, but the head kept bouncing down the stones, faster and faster, until it veered to one side and off a sheer cliff.

Perhaps if, at that moment, the Daughters of Lilith had transformed into their real forms, if their talons and their fangs had ripped apart Komor and his lieutenants, if they had rallied the village to fight the tribesmen, perhaps the Succubae could have continued to live as Goddesses. Perhaps all the evil things that happened after that day would never have happened.

Eisheth doubted it. The evil of man would have caught up to them eventually.

She saw the idea flash into her sisters' eyes, but then Eisheth did a terrible thing. More terrible than anything she had done before or since.

She fell in love with a mortal man. A strong, powerful man. The Storm King, they called him.

An evil man who would lead them to their own destruction.

Chapter 10

By Tuesday, Jeremy's goal was to finish all of his schoolwork in advance so he could spend every moment of the weekend with Cathy. He even passed on *American Idol* to do it. He was considering watching the movie version of *The Great Gatsby* so he could plow through the assigned essay question, but a lifetime love of books just wouldn't allow it.

Someone pounded on his door before Jeremy was ten pages in. He rolled off the bed, book still in hand, and opened the door. Marty was standing there with a puzzled look on her face.

"Marty?" he quizzed her. "What's up?" Normally, she barged right.

"You've got a visitor," she said.

Cathy? Jeremy's heart leapt, all thought of completing his homework gone in an instant. Should he introduce her to everyone? It suddenly occurred to him that despite his obsession with her, none of his family knew about her, not even Marty, who butted into everything. Had Cathy asked him not to tell anyone about them? He couldn't remember, but had the distinct impression that she wanted their relationship to stay on the down low.

But someone completely different stepped into the light. Jeremy blinked several times before recognizing her. Lucinda Peters. The love of his life of fourteen days prior. *Amazing how two weeks can change everything,* he thought.

Lucinda flicked her dark, curly hair over her shoulder and waved goodbye to Marty, who gave Jeremy a strange look as she closed the door. Lucinda sat on Jeremy's bed, crossing her muscular legs at the knee. He wondered what it would be like to be squeezed between such legs.

It would be like dying and going to heaven, he thought. He blushed at the image, as if he was betraying Cathy.

He'd seen pictures of Lucinda in the school paper, and he was surprised that without her animating personality, she wasn't really that good-looking, and that she was actually kind of chubby. She was short and compact, with a round face. But her personality was so warm and comforting that she lit up any room she was in.

Except this room, on this evening. She looked down nervously.

"What's wrong?" Jeremy asked, surprising himself with the depth of his concern.

"I just broke up with Derrick," she said.

He didn't know what to say to that. "Sorry" seemed wrong. Breaking up with him was probably the best thing that could have happened to her. But why was she telling him?

"He's kind of a jerk," he ventured.

"To say the least," she said. "But it got me thinking about how I've treated you."

"Wait," he began.

"No, I need to say it," she interrupted. "I've been a shallow twit. I had a good friend in you, and I treated you badly. You have every reason not to like me."

"It's not like that," he said.

"I thought I could just waltz up to you and bat my eyes and you'd fall for me in an instant. Instead, it was like I wasn't even there. And that got me thinking that maybe I deserved it."

"I got over it in junior high," he said. "You forgot I was there, even when I was sitting right next to you. You were always dating some jock or another. I gave up."

Lucinda blushed, as though she hadn't really expected him to agree with her. "I never treated you fair, Jeremy," she said. "I knew how you felt about me, and I strung you along, because I liked being around you. But you weren't...cool, you know? At least, not to the other kids. And I...I seemed to attract the popular boys, and I was too weak to resist them."

A couple of weeks before, this would have been a revelation to Jeremy. An example of the kind of divine karma that never happened in real life.

"Why are you telling me this?" he asked.

"Because I don't trust that new girl, Cathy," Lucinda said with surprising fervor. "I saw you with her, and I wanted to warn you…she's a fake. She's not what she appears to be."

"What she appears to be?"

"You don't see her when she's not around you. It's like she turns into a movie star the instant she sees you. All the girls are talking about it. I don't trust her, Jeremy."

Jeremy was unwilling to look at her. It was all so weird, so petty. "Uh, thanks, but…I got this."

Lucinda looked down and flushed. "I understand. You have no reason to believe me. But just watch out, OK? Pay attention to what she's doing. Make sure she's really who you think she is."

"OK," he said, putting his hand on the door, an obvious sign that he was ready for Lucinda to leave.

She started out the door, then turned and put her hand softly on his arm. It wasn't like the sexually electric charge that Cathy gave him when she touched him. It was comfortable, caring, and had a strong pull on him that enticed him even in the midst of his infatuation with the new girl.

"You want your first time to be right, Jeremy," Lucinda said. "With someone who really cares."

She turned and left without seeing the dumbfounded look on his face. It sounded like a promise, like she was offering herself. But that was crazy. Lucinda Peters hadn't spent more than five minutes alone with him in over two years, and those five minutes were an uncomfortable wait outside the principal's office after he got in a fight with one of Lucinda's jerk boyfriends. Who was jealous of Jeremy, for some reason.

Lucinda had vouched for him instead of her boyfriend, he suddenly remembered.

Without him realizing it, a wedge had wiggled its way into his heart, dividing it in two. One side was much bigger, swollen with desire, but the other side, while smaller, was warmer, more comforting.

And real. He had to admit that Cathy was like a dream, almost unreal, like someone a horny boy would manufacture. Lucinda was real, like someone a more thoughtful boy (though still horny) could imagine spending his life with.

That night, he felt the beginning of an erotic dream, but it was short-circuited somehow. Instead, he dreamed of the time Lucinda had gone with his family to the coast. They played tag in the waves, and he noticed her body for the first time, that she was softening and rounding in places, developing breasts, her figure not boyish anymore. While this dream didn't culminate in a climax, it left him with a warm, glowing feeling that filled his heart, not his body.

The next day, Cathy was particularly solicitous and interested in everything he said, but instead of this reassuring him, he found himself growing irritated by it. *Is she really interested, or is she just pretending?* he wondered. He searched for the most boring subject possible. "My cat threw up on the carpet last night. I had to clean it up," he ventured.

She laughed as if it was a great joke, and some part of him was chilled by the performance—not enough to call off the camping trip, however; not even close.

But a small, still doubt entered his mind.

Chapter 11

The car was fully loaded, with way more gear than Jeremy and Cathy would ever need, but Jeremy figured better too much than too little. His mom and dad thought he was camping with his Boy Scout troop, and Cathy's parents...Did Cathy have parents? Weird that she never talked about them.

Cathy wanted to camp in nature with no one around for miles, but she didn't want to worry about bears, so he found a campground near Elk Lake that wasn't too far away but not too popular either. She liked that. There was always a risk of snow in September, so he threw in some extra blankets too. By the time he was done, there was barely enough room for the two of them in the car.

She teased him about it all the way there. "All I need is my toothbrush," she said. "Maybe a little soap."

"Gonna live on mushrooms?" he teased her back. "Make a shelter out of branches?"

"Maybe," she said.

When they set up camp, Jeremy had to admit he'd overdone it. Half the stuff stayed in the car.

He brought the food to the fire pit, and for the first time since he'd known her, Cathy actually seemed worried about something. "Shouldn't we hang the food in a tree or something?" she asked. "Wasn't there a bear attack a couple of weeks ago?"

"I was going to put the food in the car before we went to bed," he said. "That bear thing? That almost never happens around here. I mean, the odds are astronomical. That guy was just really unlucky."

She looked at him with a mock-serious expression. "My life is full of the astronomical."

And sure enough, much of it didn't make sense. She spouted lots of non sequiturs that weren't really responses at all. Jeremy seriously began to wonder if he was bewitched. He sighed. *Not bewitched, just horny.* His junk had been in overdrive the whole drive up, and the little bounces in the road hadn't helped. It also hadn't helped when Cathy leaned over and put her hand on his thigh, smiling like she knew exactly what was happening.

"You want your first time to be right, Jeremy," Lucinda had said. "With someone who really cares."

Well, in theory, he agreed. But he was a teenage boy, and right then, he'd have screwed anything that said yes.

"Can we have a fire?" Cathy asked.

"Sure!" he said, frowning at the worry in her voice. She'd wanted to go camping, but ever since they'd started out, she'd been nervous about it. Or maybe she was nervous about something else?

As soon they had a roaring fire going, Jeremy began to relax. He couldn't imagine camping without a fire. "Want to roast some hot dogs?"

"Hell, yes, I want a…hot…*dog.*"

Ah, he thought, *Cathy is laying it on thick tonight.* She didn't need to. He couldn't be any more primed if he'd just spent the day watching porn.

Jeremy watched her from across the fire. Cathy stabbed a hot dog onto her roasting stick and let it sizzle over the fire.

"Ooooo, yeah. I've been waiting all week for this." She lifted it off the flames and blew on it, and then bit into it, giving it a lick first. Jeremy laughed at the innuendo.

She was attractive, almost too perfect. Like a model or a CGI character in a movie. What was she doing with him? He wasn't the handsomest, the funniest, the wealthiest, or the most charming guy in school, not by a long shot.

Really, what *was* she doing with him? Why offer her body to him? And why the hell hadn't he asked himself these questions before?

Last week, his best friend, Jess, had made no bones about wondering about that himself. Jeremy chalked it up jealousy, but he hadn't seen Jess since...when? Then he realized: Jess hadn't disappeared, Jeremy had disappeared into Cathy's magnetic personality.

For the first time since they set off on the trip, Jeremy's erection was nowhere in evidence as a new thought broke over him. *I've always distrusted charisma*, he thought.

So why had he fallen for the first beautiful girl to come on to him without questioning her motives? Could it be that she was actually in love with him? He doubted it. So why him? Why now?

Cathy seemed to sense his thoughts, because she moved to his side of the fire and sat down next to him, her land landing on his thigh. He started instantly getting hard, and wasn't sure if he wanted her to notice or not.

She was chattering on about the wonderfulness of nature. "It's like every tree and every rock is *exactly* where it *should* be..." and when Jeremy tried to tune out her tone and just listen to the words, he realized it was a bunch of earth goddess nonsense, the kind of thing he'd always made fun of.

Why do we never talk about anything that matters? he wondered. *The meaning of life. Is there a God? Have we been visited by aliens?*

"What do you plan to do with the rest of your life?" he asked suddenly, interrupting her nattering.

"What?"

"What are your plans, your dreams? How do you want to live your life?"

"Same as I've always done," Cathy said. She looked as if she was having trouble coming up with an answer, as if she'd never, ever thought about it. "Have fun; enjoy life."

"That's it?" he said.

"What about you?" she asked, sounding almost defensive.

Where to start? Jeremy wondered. "I want to be a writer. I want to write poetry that expresses everything I'm saying right now, only better. I want to direct a movie. I want to learn as much as I can. I want to travel, have a family someday, with kids and dogs and cats. I want to learn a foreign language, maybe be a teacher, or own a bookstore. I…" He broke off, trying to gauge her reaction. "I could go on all night." He shrugged. The one answer he would never have given was, "Have fun."

What's wrong with that? he asked himself. He wasn't sure, but it felt vague, shallow, and selfish.

Cathy was still smiling at him, but her eyes were angry. She looped one arm around his neck.

"Do we have to be so serious?" she asked. "I'm not asking you to marry me, Jeremy. Let's just let happen what will happen; let's just enjoy ourselves."

Her hand moved up his leg, stopping just short of his crotch. His erection came back in full force, and embarrassingly, he was forced to surreptitiously rearrange the awkward bulge.

She stroked his leg, and he almost groaned. Why the hell was he questioning this? What was wrong with him?

Jeremy closed his eyes, concentrating on her movements. It wasn't simply the motion that turned him on; it was almost as if she was sending sexual messages directly to his body, which overrode his brain. He tried to think. *What's going on here?*

Her hand drifted all the way up, rubbing him once or twice, and after that, he gave in to her. He groaned and came in his pants, nearly falling off the log.

"No!" Cathy hissed, outraged. "Not yet!"

She stood up and straddled his hips, unbuttoning her shirt. Her breasts were right there, but Jeremy felt nothing. Whatever hold she had on him was gone. He told himself he wasn't interested, but his body still was. He was getting hard again. He shrugged and took a nipple into his mouth, then closed his eyes and tried to get into the spirit of it.

Cathy ground against him as if in ecstasy, and she whispered into his ear, "Let's go to bed."

She led him, unresisting, to her sleeping bag, shedding clothes as she went. She lay on top of the sleeping bag, naked despite the chill in the air. Jeremy removed his clothes hesitantly, almost reluctantly. He was hard again, and he had to untangle himself from his underwear.

There he stood, shirt still on, socks still on, feeling ridiculous and not at all appealing. Cathy beckoned to him as if he were the most erotic thing she'd ever seen.

"Can we get into the sleeping bag?" he asked, and his voice sounded rough, anything but seductive. Cathy got in first, opening her arms to him with a smile.

Jeremy crawled in, zipping the bag around them. They were face to face, chest to chest, sex to sex, and though he was hard, he felt a strange reluctance to go further. Cathy grabbed him and wiggled her way around so that she was above him. Then she put him inside her.

She swayed slowly, moving against him. She smelled wonderful, and her body felt soft but firm. Her body fitted his as if made for it, and he couldn't believe it was happening. All his senses were expanded, and even as the intensity grew below, he became aware of the wind in the trees, the waves on the shore of the lake.

But something was missing. The spark of horniness was gone. The desire to become lost in her had evaporated. Though his body responded, his heart and his mind were detached. "Cathy," he whispered, "I...I don't think I'm going to come again."

"*Yes,*" she hissed, "you *will.*" She picked up the pace, moving faster and faster, frenetically trying to build something that wasn't happening.

Something was wrong with her face. The beautiful girl flickered in and out of Jeremy's vision, alternating with another visage: a gargoyle with a sharp nose and a forked tongue, her hair waving over her head as if alive. Her eyes opened then, and the pupils were narrow, pointed like a cat's. She stared down at him not in love or even lust, but in hate and a raw desire to consume him.

Jeremy's erection fizzled, and he slid out of her.

"No, you don't." the gargoyle said. "You *can't!*"

"I'm sorry," he said, wondering why he was apologizing to a monster. At this thought, he tried to buck her off, but her legs clamped around him.

She grabbed a fistful of his hair, brought her face close to his, and hissed, "You *will* give yourself to me. Give your *life* to me."

Jeremy couldn't understand the words. It was a nightmare, like a bad drug trip, or what he thought a bad drug trip would be like. It was a crazy vision of a thing that didn't exist.

She was staring into his face, and as he stared back, the beautiful features returned, and he felt himself falling instantly in love—or in lust. But even through the haze of desire, he realized it was an illusion.

For once in his life, Jeremy's survival mode kicked in.

He punched Cathy in the nose with all the power that fear and revulsion gave him.

She shrieked, lifting her taloned hands.

Blood dripped down on him and into his mouth. It tasted bitter, like sulfur smelled, but it invigorated him with more strength than he ever thought possible.

She swiped down at him, but he caught her arm in mid-motion. She pushed harder, a needle-like talon cutting into his cheek.

Panicked and frightened, rejuvenated by her blood, he pushed her off him, despite her heavy legs and arms. He broke away, scrambling naked out of the sleeping bag. He ran out of the tent and grabbed one of the branches from the fire, then turned to the tent's entrance, waving the flaming branch.

Cathy emerged, still naked and lovely. Tears ran down her cheeks, and she pinched her nose tightly to stem the bleeding. "Why did you do that?" she asked. Her chin quivered slightly, and there was a tremor in her voice.

"I didn't mean to," Jeremy said, but his fist tightened on the flaming branch. *What have I done?* he wondered; then *What the hell just happened?* He wanted to rush forward, to take her in his arms, to beg her forgiveness. But something held him back.

"Get dressed," he said. "I'll take you home."

They loaded up the car without speaking, but all the while, Jeremy's thoughts churned. *Will she tell anyone? Will her parents call the police?* It was near dawn when they pulled up to Cathy's apartment, and it hit him suddenly that he had no idea who she lived with, or whether she had parents or siblings, or anything about her at all.

He shuddered as she got out of the car and walked away. He was in big trouble; he couldn't deny hitting her. He'd struck her because he'd had some kind of psychotic break, some kind of hallucination. But even as he struggled to come up with answers, he knew he never wanted to see Cathy again.

Chapter 12

E isheth averted her face upon entering the temple. It was dark inside; the fire in the central pit was low, little more than glowing coals. The building was so much bigger than its predecessor, with marble floors and walls, and adorned with gold and precious stones. A statue covered in gold leaf stood at the altar, a representation of Agrat Bat at her most fertile roundness.

Despite the darkness, her sister instantly noticed Eisheth's cut lip and bruises.

"He beat you again, didn't he?" Agrat Bat said, disgusted. "And you let him."

To her sister, Eisheth's letting Komor beat her was mystifying. The Succubae were stronger than any man, faster and more lethal. They were Goddesses. No mere man could stand up to them.

"He doesn't mean to," Eisheth said. "He is a man of strong emotions. In his heart, he is a kind man. It is why I love him."

"Kind?" Agrat Bat snorted.

"You do not see his gentleness."

Agrat Bat just stared at her. She was dressed in the silks that Komor's raiders had brought back. She wore a circlet of pearls. She was more beautiful than ever. "I will kill him for you."

Eisheth felt a strange combination of fear and hope, but tamped it down. She loved Komor. No one saw the gentleness that he showed her when they were alone. He spoke to her as an equal. He was not so awestruck by being in the presence of a Goddess that he couldn't tease or joke or simply talk about little things. Eisheth discovered she had a deep longing for another soul at her side. She'd been lonely for a long time without knowing it.

"He won't do it again," she said, trying to keep the pleading out of her voice. "I've warned him."

"Do you realize, sister, how many times you've told me this?" Agrat Bat asked. "I will kill him next time, with or without your blessing. Not just for you, Eisheth. The villagers are looking at us differently, wondering if we are truly Goddesses, for what deity would let a mortal man beat her? You undermine all of us."

"But look what he has done!" Eisheth objected. "Look at your temple, sister. It isn't a crude building anymore, but a tribute to the Goddesses. You have more worshippers than ever before."

The temple was packed on High Holy Days, and the village itself was inundated with newcomers. It sometimes seemed as if the strangers outnumbered the natives. With a flash of insight, Eisheth realized this was probably true. The Storm King's riches were drawing people from far away.

Agrat Bat waved her fat fingers in dismissal. "Yes, on those days when it is thought to be necessary, we get the crowds—but on days when no ceremony is required, there are fewer worshippers than ever before. There are fewer real believers, Eisheth. Have you not seen the look in their eyes? Do you not find it alarming that they will look you in the eyes at all?

"Once they bowed to us when we passed, and they whispered in respect. Now they barely notice us, but keep talking loudly as if nothing unusual has happened at all."

Eisheth rarely ventured from her home anymore. Komor had made it for her, and it was the largest structure in the village other than the temple. Indeed, the house was a temple of sorts, with a front entrance and a throne from which Eisheth would greet her followers.

There were more visitors than ever before, but she knew few of them. When was the last time she'd seen handsome Coss, or Moros the blacksmith or his wife, Tari, or any of the humble folk who had once been her followers—her friends, even? She stayed inside all the time now. Komor insisted that a true Goddess should not walk among her lessors, but stay aloof, mysterious.

The image of Forr's head bouncing down the path came to her. Guilt and unease always overcame her when she remembered that day.

"It was necessary," Komor explained one night as they lay in bed. "Better one old man lose his head than that I kill dozens more to keep them in line. The message was sent, and the people of this village understood. If not me, then another invader would have come, and he might not have been so restrained. Your village was ripe for the plucking, Eisheth. But I will defend you now. I will clothe you and feed you and take care of you from now on. I will build you temples that the whole world will come to see."

It had been a full year since that day. Tomorrow was the beginning of spring. Agrat Bat would descend from her new temple, and Eisheth and Naamah would greet her, and together they would bless the season.

Eisheth frowned. At least she *thought* Naamah would be there.

"Have you seen Naamah?" she asked Agrat Bat.

"I have not seen her, but I hear reports of her in the lower city. The people there are not happy," her sister replied.

The lower city, with its crude hovels, had once been as much a part of Lilith's Home as the upper city, with its temples and homes. The young drifted down there, and before settling down, lived out lives more vigorous and daring that the staid inhabitants of the upper city.

Once such behavior had not been looked down upon. Sexual experimentation had been considered normal. The word "prostitute" had not been a bad thing. Now, with the Storm King's troops throwing their riches around, the lower city had become something darker, a place the newcomers talked about with scorn.

"Naamah talks rebellion," Agrat Bat said in a lower voice, as if afraid she might be overheard.

"She should not encourage such a thing!" Eisheth's voice rose in alarm. Then she too lowered her voice and leaned toward her sister. "Komor's men are everywhere."

"You mean his spies?"

"Komor must keep the peace," Eisheth said. "If he can stop an uprising before it starts, it will saves live in the long run."

"And if not?" Agrat Bat said quietly. "If the people rise up?"

"He will make an example of them," Eisheth said. As she spoke, she realized she sounded like Komor, using the very same words he'd used to explain to her how important it was to maintain order and discipline. "But better that than it happen again in the future."

"What happened to Komor's kindness and gentleness?" Agrat Bat shook her head. "I don't believe you even hear your own words, sister—if they *are* your own words. You have fallen under the Storm King's spell, but he's using you. He doesn't love you, Eisheth. He only loves himself and power and riches."

"You're wrong. You don't know him." Eisheth turned without waiting for a response and marched out of the temple.

At the base of the steps was a cluster of soldiers. They blocked her way. She stood on the step above them, waiting for them to move aside.

"Dorse returned to Storm King's Mountain this morning," one of them was saying. "The Carria tribesmen have sued for peace. They have offered up enough gold to fill three wagons."

"Which is an insult," another said. "We should take it all."

Eisheth cleared her throat. The men didn't even look at her, but they stood aside just enough to create a small opening between them.

"Make way for the Goddess," one of the men said as she passed.

It wasn't said in respect, but with a mocking tone. She whirled on him, a talon forming on her right hand. The man's eyes widened, and he stepped back.

Eisheth went on, hearing the men whispering behind her. There was fear there, but also scorn. As she turned the corner, she heard laughter.

She wasn't sure what was most alarming: the soldiers' disrespect, or that they spoke of Lilith's Home as Storm King's Mountain.

The Rites of Spring were far grander than anything that had come before. The priests and priestesses wore cloaks of gold and vermillion, and their high, peaked hats flashed in the morning sun, covered in gemstones and silver. The litter they carried Agrat Bat upon was of polished and ornately carved wood. Flower petals were strewn upon the path, and their fragrance filled the air. Komor had brought musicians from the outside world, who played a stately march.

Eisheth wore a white gown covered in pearls. The worshippers who surrounded her were gathered in orderly rows. None would look at her. The crowd itself was quiet, instead of the usual raucous celebrators of past springs.

Eisheth sought out Agrat Bat's eyes as she passed. *Where is the disrespect now?* she wanted to ask. Komor had done everything he could to honor the ancient rituals. Surely it would enhance the people's veneration of the sisters. Komor was right: they'd become too common, too much like their followers. As Goddesses, they were above that, and should be treated with formality and honor.

A murmur ran through the crowd. Eisheth heard gasps.

She turned to see Naamah approaching, followed by the denizens of the lower city. They were unwashed, Eisheth saw, which was something she had never noticed before.

Naamah might as well have been naked. She wore a dress that was so sheer that her entire body could be seen beneath it. She was barefoot, her hair wild. She had a gleam in her eyes and a sway to her walk.

Eisheth felt herself responding. She looked over at Komor, who sat like a king upon a throne on a small hill overlooking the ceremony. She hoped to catch his eye, to communicate the desire she suddenly felt for him.

He was frowning, and Eisheth was confused.

We are Goddesses of love and fertility, she thought. *We aren't meant to be above men and women; we are the embodiment of them.*

Agrat Bat descended from the litter, fatter than ever before.

She didn't look around as she began the cutting. There was no joy in the act; no one cried out in gladness as she sprinkled the fields with her blood.

Eisheth and Naamah followed without speaking to each other. The whole thing felt wrong, joyless, as though it was a duty and not a blessing.

The Blood is as potent as ever, Eisheth reminded herself. *It will do what it was meant to do.*

There were more fields than before. It was almost too much. By the time Naamah had shed the last drop she dared, they were all three skeletons, barely able to stay on their feet.

They reached the white path and started upward.

It was only then that Eisheth realized that the people had not paired up. They had not wandered off hand in hand to celebrate the spring. Instead, they stood with heads lowered.

The Storm King was standing upon his hill, and he gestured for the Daughters of Lilith to approach. Agrat Bat looked as though she wanted to ignore him, but Eisheth gave her a pleading look. Naamah followed her sisters out of curiosity.

The Storm King strode down the hill, his arms spread. "Magnificent. I'm glad to have witnessed it." He took Eisheth in his arms. As she laid her head on his shoulder, she felt her arm lifted. The wound there was still open, and would be until she regained life force.

She stepped back, confused, as Komor raised her arm and sucked upon the wound.

He threw his head back and roared as blood ran down his chin and splattered onto his armored chest. The sound sent a chill though her, because it sounded anything but glad. It was a shout of triumph.

"The Blood of the Succubus!" the Storm King shouted to his men. "It is all that I hoped for!"

He stood back and examined the Goddesses. Unconsciously, Eisheth stepped backward, between her two sisters, and put her arms around their waists.

"Take them!" Komor shouted.

The Daughters of Lilith were at their weakest, and they were surprised, even Agrat Bat and Naamah. Eisheth didn't even move as the soldiers swarmed her, throwing her to the ground and putting chains on her.

They dragged her to her feet and pushed her in the direction of the temple. Agrat Bat and Naamah were being carried, screaming, their talons extended, their faces turning to their ugliest, most primitive form.

No, Sisters! Eisheth wanted to shout. *Don't let the people see you thus. It will only help the Storm King!*

She tried to keep her dignity, despite being shoved from behind by the soldiers. She maintained the illusion until she was out of sight of the crowds. Only then did she strike out.

Perhaps because she had appeared to give in, her guards were taken by surprise. She cut into the neck of one of the soldiers who was pushing her, and then bit into the arm of the soldier on her right. The soldier on the left clubbed her with the pommel of his sword, and she staggered and fell to her knees.

Then she was up, snarling, and it took an entire troop of men to bring her down, and there were bodies and pieces of bodies strewn about the temple floor by the time they did.

She was struck again, this time by some kind of club, and the next thing she knew she was being carried, tied up so tightly she couldn't move.

The soldiers took the sisters deep into the caves, where water clung to the walls and the temperature made them shiver.

Iron chains had been attached to the rock, and the Goddesses were put into them, side by side, just out of reach of each other.

And then the men retreated, the light of the torches and the boisterous voices receding, until they were alone and the only sound was the slow dripping of water.

Agrat Bat screamed a primordial scream, and Eisheth knew that her sister had regressed back to being one of the creatures they had been before the first men and women found them. Naamah joined her, her voice higher, more screeching.

Eisheth herself could no longer maintain her human form, and felt herself transforming completely, her thoughts becoming unformed and instinctive, and her screaming joined that of her sisters.

Chapter 13

Gasper Gerhard's Journal

    My son asked me a question that startled me—not the question itself so much as the fact that I'd forgotten that I once wondered the same thing.

    Why should the Cutting make us invisible to the Succubae?

    Lord knows, I still dream of making love. My wife comes to me, young and happy, not knowing about my destiny and how it will be her destiny too. We lie as we did that first time beneath a tree in the dark, our parents in the house just feet away, trying to make love passionately and not make any noise.

    In my dreams, I even climax.

    So why should the Cutting work? I never discovered in my readings when the Cutting started. Sometime after the Fall, I suppose. Did the Succubae, having escaped, come back to take revenge on the surviving Guardians?

    The histories don't say.

    Once discovered, the Cutting became the method by which we hid from the Succubae. No one asked why. No one wondered if there was any point to it, beyond our own survival. It has occurred to me at times that we should try to capture or kill the Succubae, but our line is too weak, so diminished that there is no chance we could succeed.

    So we continue on, protecting the Blood, but to what purpose?

In the end, Heinrich found his way upward by going downward.

    He worked on the trapdoor for a long time, trying to pry it open with the knives, then attempting to cut through it. The trapdoor was solid, with barely a seam to put a knife blade in. He snapped off the end of several blades, cutting a large gouge into his forearm with one of them, the kind of wound that once would have seemed terrible, but was now no more than an inconvenience. A single drop of Blood, and he was made whole.

He pounded on the door in frustration and shouted for help, Succubus or no Succubus.

Does Father lie dead beyond? The thought of it made him retreat and reconsider.

Surely Gasper didn't intend for him to die here.

The door seemed to be the only way out, and it looked impervious. While it may have been possible to open it in the long run, in the long run, he was going to starve. On the bright side, there was a steady water supply from an underground rivulet under the rock fall that blocked the tunnel. Heinrich's food supply was limited, however, and would eventually run out.

Even worse, he was running out of lantern oil, and it was only the light and the reading of the manuscripts that kept him sane. He'd never thought he could be lonely, but now he was finding that the time he had spent with his father had been more important than he'd thought.

The voice that came through Gasper's journal was that of a stranger: thoughtful and kind, patient and considerate. So different from the brusque, angry parent Heinrich had known.

Of all the journals, going back to the beginning, his father's was the most interesting. Gasper asked the most impertinent questions, pondered the contradictions, wondered at the magic. Only he, it seemed, doubted the Guardians' purpose.

Until Heinrich, who was truly his father's son, and who questioned it all, doubted it all.

Before the lantern oil was gone, he fashioned some crude torches, breaking the empty wooden shelves and wrapping the pieces in the bed linens. He was forced to sleep on the hard wooden table, for the stone floors were freezing.

He did an inventory, like so many Guardians before him. The shelves were almost empty of the Blood. His father had done hundreds of Cuttings, whereas most Guardians had needed only two or three in a long lifetime. But Heinrich had the sense that other Guardians had also been profligate as their hope faded. Many of them had spent much of their lives down here, sipping the Blood, dreaming of escape.

There were three unopened stone jars left. They were larger than they looked, containing enough Blood to fill many more of the small bottles his father had used. Heinrich vowed not to touch the older receptacles, but to subsist on what his father had made from honey and Blood.

He was reading when the lantern finally sputtered out. Heinrich lit the first of the torches and made his way to the small room where his father had stored the food. All that was left were a few moldy carrots and a few pieces of jerky that Heinrich had saved for last. He dropped the scraps into a crude backpack he'd fashioned from the remnants of the bedspreads. He added the bottles of honeyed Blood.

It was now or never.

It was a desperate plan, concocted over the last few days. One morning, while drinking on his hands and knees from the small puddle at the base of the rock fall, his fingers dislodged a stone where the water seeped into the rocks. He reached over and lifted the stone. The puddle drained away, the water splashing into the darkness, and he realized that there was a larger gap behind the stones. He clawed away the loose rocks, careful not to dislodge the boulders above. He shoved the torch into the gap, which widened a few feet farther in. He tossed a rock into the darkness, and it skittered across a flat surface.

He had no choice but to explore it.

After filling his handmade pack with the food, Heinrich returned to the library and added the six bottles of Blood. He grabbed up the torches. At the last moment, he snatched up Gasper's journal. The rest of the histories and most of the Blood, he left behind.

He slithered through the opening in the rock fall. He barely fit and the rocks ground threateningly. He started to back out, which only made it worse.

If I quit now, I'll never try again, he thought. He pushed through the narrow opening into a broader space behind. With a crash that shook him to the bones, the tunnel through the rock fall collapsed behind him, and dust filled the narrow space, sending him into a coughing fit.

Dirt covered him, the grit grinding down between his flesh and his clothing, coating his lips and nostrils. The sound of running water faded, and when he reached up into his ears, he found them clogged with dirt.

The torches were damp from the stream. Heinrich didn't try to light one, but continued slithering onward in the dark. *I'm going to be buried down here*, he thought, fighting off panic, *like a giant worm; Guardian of nothing*. His clothes were soaked and covered in cold mud. He was shivering, his teeth chattering.

He was gasping, trying not to scream, when he tumbled into a larger chamber.

He struggled to light a torch, and finally got one sputtering. It emitted more smoke than light, but his eyes adjusted and he went on.

It was a crooked path, created by centuries of running water always seeking the lowest point. There were spots Heinrich could squeeze through only by dragging his meager possessions behind him. He winced as the bottles banged against the rocks, but they didn't break.

His torch sputtered its last. When it went out, he went on into the blackness, feeling his way. He had only one other torch left.

What have I done? he wondered. *This is far worse than before. I'll die alone and in the dark.*

But he would probably have died the same way above, and then he would have died with the regret of not trying to escape.

Heinrich had brought several of the sharp knives. They could cut his wrists as well as they could cut his other parts.

His foot landed on air, and he fell forward. His hands flew out to either side, grabbing at the slick stone walls, and stopped himself from falling. He scrambled backward, breathing hard. When his heart finally slowed down, he inched forward on his hands and knees to the edge and struck a match.

The light illuminated only his hand, for there was nothing but darkness beyond. As the flame reached his fingers, his eyes straining, he finally managed to see the contours of the place.

The chamber was huge. The streaming water was collected in a wide, dark pool along the bottom. Heinrich threw a stone, and a couple of seconds passed before he heard the splash.

Now what?

He couldn't go back, but the fall was too far to go forward.

He got on his stomach and slid backward into the cavern, hoping there was something, anything, under him. He was fully stretched out when his toes hit a ledge. He leaned against the rock face, closing his eyes in relief.

God still needs the Guardians, he thought. Then he grimaced. *I sound like all my misguided, deluded ancestors.*

He let himself all the way down onto the ledge, then reached up to get his pack. The rock was slick, angled downward, and he felt himself sliding backward. He snagged the bundle as he toppled backward and started falling.

His shout was swallowed by the cavern, a far-off, desolate sound. The fall seemed to take forever, and forever after he dreamed of it, the endless fall into the pitch dark. He expected to land on sharp rocks, but landed on the hard, wet surface of the pool instead. He hadn't taken a breath, and as he plunged downward, he almost breathed in reflexively.

The freezing waters paralyzed him, and he sank. Only the bundle kept him from sinking farther. He kicked upward, following the buoyancy of the bundle. It was the Blood, he realized. It was lighter than water.

He burst above the surface, gasping.

Air went into his lungs instead of water. He floated on his back, trying to get a sense of where he was. He treaded water for a time, until something slick brushed against his feet and he started swimming. *It didn't matter what direction I'm going,* he thought, *as long as I end up somewhere on solid ground.*

He pulled himself up on the shore of the pool and lay there, breathing hard. Eventually, he dragged himself completely out of the water and onto the dry shelf of rock. The bundle had held together. Gasper's journal, which was probably waterlogged, the bottles of Blood, and the torch and matches were all there.

Heinrich sat there in the dark for as long as he could stand it. It felt like days; he hoped it was hours, and later on, he believed it was probably only minutes. He wasted half of his matches before he gave up trying to light them.

Then he sat back and tried not to think.

He fell asleep.

When he awoke, he tried the matches again, and the third one sputtered to life. He held it to the water-and-oil soaked rag at the end of the torch. The oil was stronger than the water, just barely, and it caught.

Heinrich stood and looked around. This was probably going to be his burial chamber, and for some reason, he wanted to know its contours. The light caught the reflection of metal on the wall right away. He walked over to it and found ancient iron chains, almost all the way rusted through, with barely enough of the metal left to catch the torchlight. Heinrich's feet scraped over something crusty, and he leaned down with the torch. It was a thick layer of rust-like material, but he sensed it had once been organic. It looked like dried blood, but it was an ocean's worth, inches thick.

This is where they kept the Succubae, he realized. *This is where the Guardians bled them.*

He closed his eyes as a vision came over him with the force of truth, Blood calling Blood.

Three immortal creatures—sisters—unable to move and bled of their life's essence, day after day, for centuries. He imagined their captors feeding them just enough life force to keep them alive; condemned prisoners, perhaps. Or perhaps the sisters had kept their pleasing forms and the caretakers had taken their pleasure with them, letting a little of their own spirit enter the Succubae before bleeding them again.

The torch was sputtering, and Heinrich broke out of his reverie and continued his examination of the cavern. The torch was down to bare wood now, and it was going out. In those last seconds, he saw the hole. He scrambled to it, shoved the torch into the gap, and stared upward. The chimney went up at least as far as the light could shine.

The torch went out.

He sat for a long time, trying to summon the courage to once again squeeze himself into a gap no wider than his shoulders.

He had no choice.

He shuddered and crawled into the hole before he could have second thoughts. He shimmied upward. The chimney was so tight that he could hold himself in place with minimal pressure. There were small crevices that he could fit his toes into, but it seemed to take forever to move a few feet, and his legs were quivering from fatigue before he'd gone very far. The passage went on and on, just large enough for one small body. If he hadn't been starving, he doubted he would have fit.

Halfway up, he realized who had created it.

He continued on, knowing that if the Succubae had escaped, so could he.

Finally, as his arms and legs were ready to give out, he saw a pinpoint of light above. It gave him the hope to go on. The pinpoint got bigger, until he could see blue skies, the passage of a white cloud across them. He had never seen anything so beautiful in all his life. The air was cleaner too, and the temperature was rising.

When Heinrich finally crawled out of the hole, the sun was overhead. He was on the mountainside. Below, he could see the red roof of his cottage, like a toy house.

He staggered to his feet, determined to reach safety before dark. He'd rest later, when he was home.

As he reached out to steady himself, something sharp cut into his hand. It was a purplish color in the sunlight, broken off and jagged.

He pulled a talon out of the rock, bigger than any eagle's, as if left there by a prehistoric creature. As he leaned over to examine it, his eyes fell onto the hole he'd just emerged from. There, around the edges, were deep grooves.

Each groove was the size of the talon he now held in his hand.

Chapter 14

"Do you have any pictures of her?" Cary asked.
      Serena nodded and reached into her handbag pulling out a sheaf of photos. Cary leafed through them, frowning. "You can barely make her out," he said.

"She has a knack of looking away at the right moment," Serena said. "These are the best I could find online. Even when her picture is taken straight on, she's blurry. I think it's one of her powers."

"Well, a big enough reward and people will at least try," he mused. "A thousand bucks ought to get some reaction."

"A thousand dollars for the reward?" Serena repeated. "I can do that," she said without blinking.

It confirmed what Cary suspected. He'd noticed that she wore nice, if conservative, clothes, and sensible but expensive shoes. She wasn't hurting for money. In the circles Cary ran around in, a thousand bucks might have been doable, but there would have been a telltale hesitation.

"There's this artist I know," he suggested reluctantly. "She's really talented at portraits."

Rachel answered the door in a paint-splattered smock. "I'm in the middle of something, Cary," she said. "Can't talk." Cary's old girlfriend was incredibly focused once she started a project; no interruptions were allowed.

"This is important," Cary said. "Please, Rachel. We can pay you." He glanced over at Serena, who nodded.

Rachel finally looked them over as if seeing them for the first time. Her glance lingered on Serena, and she gave Cary a knowing look.

"Let me see the pictures," she said after they explained what they needed. "You think this girl killed Doug?"

"Maybe," Cary ventured, but Serena answered the question with a firm nod.

"Pretty, in a pixyish sort of way," Rachel mused, sifting through the photos. All the pictures were fuzzy, the MPDG a blob in the center of them. But Rachel could apparently fill in details that others couldn't see.

Cary and Serena exchanged glances. They hadn't said anything about the MPDG angle.

In minutes, with the help of Serena and Cary's descriptions, Rachel had sketched a stunningly accurate representation of Kristen/Suzanne's face without the Goth or steampunk trappings.

"You *sure* you don't want some color?" Rachel asked, as if leaving the picture unfinished bothered her.

"No color," Serena said firmly. "Whatever hair or eye color you use will be wrong by now."

Rachel shrugged and started to hand over the drawing. As Cary was about to take hold of it, she suddenly took it back. She lifted the picture and frowned.

"Strange…" she said.

"What?"

"I've seen her before." Rachel went to her desk, turned on the computer, and drummed her feet, waiting for it to boot up. When it did, she tapped a few keys, then grunted. She turned the monitor in the direction of her guests.

There on the screen was Kristen/Suzanne. She had flowers in her green hair: very bohemian.

"Where did you get this?" Serena breathed. "Who is it?"

"That's just it," Rachel said. "It isn't anyone. This is a composite I came across the other day. They asked a bunch of boys and men to construct their dream girl by morphing different actresses and models until they reached a consensus about who was the most desirable girl they could think of. They actually had different categories. This was the "Cute" girl. There was also "The Slut" and "The Sex Goddess" and a bunch of others. Funny thing is, they all pretty much look alike—at least to an artist—except for the superficial stuff like hair and makeup."

Rachel lined up the pictures, and it was true that if you looked closely, they looked very much alike.

Cary nodded agreement. *I'd do 'em,* he thought.

"So..." Serena murmured. "These are wet dreams for sweaty, horny boys?"

Cary shifted uncomfortably.

Rachel laughed. "Pretty much. Personally, I think they are a little generic...which makes sense. "

Cary had a moment of doubt. Had they just constructed an illusion? Had they tapped into an archetype rather than depicting a real girl? But the more he stared at the sketch without all the embellishments, the more Suzanne Winders came alive within the lines on the page.

They left Rachel's house after promising to keep her up to date. At the last second, she grabbed the sketch and scrawled her name along the bottom. She handed it back with a smile.

They went to the nearest printer and added the reward money information at the top of the flyer. "Have You Seen This Girl?" it read. "$1,000 for information on her whereabouts." They discussed which phone number to put on it, and in the end put on both of their cell numbers, as well as the number of the Cambridge Hotel.

"I'll pay the staff to do the phone screening," Serena said.

"Where do we start handing them out?" Cary asked when the printer handed them a box containing 500 flyers.

"She's most likely at one of the schools," Serena said. "College or high school, probably, though she's gone as low as the eighth grade. Churches...she finds lots of unwary victims there. Or someplace young people hang out. Movie theaters. If she's desperate, she might try a bar, and if she's truly desperate, she'll try an older-trending bar where a cute girl is like catnip."

"Let's try COCC," Cary suggested.

They drove to Central Oregon Community College, which was on top of one of the hills overlooking the town. "Harvard on the Hill," Cary commented. "Or Cock on the Rock."

Serena frowned at him, but didn't say anything.

They hiked around the campus, showing the picture to students hurrying by, but few stopped long enough to glance at the sketch. None showed more than vague recognition. The $1,000 reward caught the interest of some, who stared at the image, only to reluctantly shake their heads.

They tried the high schools next.

"My alma mater," Cary said as they drove into the parking lot of Bend High. There were tons of kids hanging around the cars, smoking cigarettes, goofing off between classes. They approached a group of boys, whose eyes instantly went to Serena.

Cary handed them all flyers. "Anything at all?" he asked as they examined them.

The boys shook their heads. Then one of them cocked his head a little. "You know…this looks a little like…"

He didn't get to finish his sentence, because a gruff voice interrupted.

"Who are you?" A middle-aged man with black horn-rimmed glasses came hurrying up. "You can't be here."

The boys were stamping out their cigarettes and turning away, walking toward the school. Within seconds, the parking lot had emptied out.

"We're just looking for someone," Cary said, handing the man a flyer.

"I'm Principal Catledge," he said. He lifted the picture and frowned. "She looks damn familiar, but…you can't be here."

"We won't get in you way," Serena said, and explained that they were looking for a runaway girl.

Cary tried not to stare, surprised that she had lied so effortlessly.

The principal softened his tone after hearing Serena's explanation. "I sympathize with your need to find her, but I can't allow you to do this. It's against school policy to have civilians on school grounds unless they have children on campus." He sighed. "With all these school shootings, I'm sure you can understand the necessity." Serena and Cary both nodded and then left reluctantly.

After that, they left the schools alone. They tried churches, but since it was midweek, most were empty.

"Where else?" Serena asked, deferring to Cary, who knew the town. "What about malls?"

"We don't really have any," he answered. "They were torn down. There's downtown and the Old Mill District."

"Then that's where we start."

"This isn't getting us anywhere," Cary said after they had spent a couple of hours handing out flyers downtown, only to see most of the few takers ditching the flyer in the first trash can they saw.

They decided to take a break. Serena went to get them some food, and Cary watched her appreciatively as the counter guy flirted with her and she ignored him.

"It's going to take forever," he said as she set the tray of sodas and pizza on the table.

Serena nodded her agreement, dropping into a mesh patio chair outside the sidewalk café. Cary gobbled his food down, realizing he hadn't eaten pizza since he started dating Rachel, who only ate raw vegetables and fruits. He'd been forced to squirrel away chips and beef jerky to satisfy his hankerings.

"We're going to have to post these flyers after all," Serena said.

Cary finished off his pizza and wiped his greasy fingers on a napkin. He shrugged. "What's the worst thing that could happen?"

"Well…we tip our hand and she flees, and we never see her again."

"Well, you know…other than that…." He broke off abruptly, then met Serena's gaze with a puzzled smile. "You know, it just occurred to me. The law isn't after Suzanne. The authorities don't have a clue. What are we going to do if we find her?"

"I just want to track her," Serena said slowly.

Cary nodded, trying to his doubt. When she had paid for the flyers, he had seen a pistol in her purse. He thought he knew what she meant to do with it. She wasn't trying very hard to hide her intentions.

Serena thought she knew what Cary was hinting at, but she wasn't about to make him an accessory to the crime. She would use the gun, given the chance. She didn't think it was possible to trail the MPDG much further. The Kristen creature was too canny, too devious. All the money in the world wouldn't be enough. There was only one way to end her evil.

With a bullet to the head.

Serena stared at the pizza in her hands, appetite suddenly gone. She dropped the slice onto her plate, wishing her quest for vengeance could have such an easy ending. She took a long drink of soda, more to keep busy than because of thirst. Would a bullet to the head be enough? She doubted it.

She was going to need to fight magic with magic, God help her. Because that was the kind of creature she was dealing with—the ogre under the bridge, the bloodsucker in the night, the wolf in the woods.

She pulled out her tablet while Cary watched curiously.

Serena: *I'm pretty sure Eisheth is here and she is injured.*

Rick: *Have you seen her?*

Serena: *I have a local witness.*

Rick: *Let me know when you know for sure.*

Serena: *I think you should come. I think I'll need your help.*

The light blinked, showing that Rick was typing a response, but no text appeared for several long minutes. Then…

Rick: *I'll start making plans.*

Chapter 15

The Daughters of Lilith were left in dark for an eternity, unfed, to fade slowly back to their shrunken forms, far away from mankind and their thoughts and desires, trapped in a living death.

They screamed in rage into the void. They didn't speak to each other. They didn't need to, for they all felt the same horror; it swelled and filled each of their souls. They were at their weakest when they were imprisoned, and neglect made them even weaker. But they were Goddesses, immortal, and though they shrank and withered, they did not die.

Finally, they felt the men approaching, sensing them from the moment the doors opened far above. Their screams stopped. As one, they chose not to reveal their pain and distress to their tormentors.

The Goddesses could smell the men, hear their breathing, perceive their thoughts.

Eisheth came back to herself. The screams had been ever present, each of the sisters taking turns, as if one was expressing the agony of all. The sudden silence was shocking. Her mind focused.

When the men entered the cave, Eisheth struggled to morph her image into a pleasing form. Her sisters attempted the same thing, but succeeded only in putting more flesh on their bones, flesh that was sickly and craggy in the light of the torches

From the revulsion on the men's faces, Eisheth could tell that the glamour had failed. The men wrinkled their noses and averted their eyes.

All but one.

The Storm King marched up to them and waved his torch in their faces one by one. "Where are you, my love?" he asked.

"I'll kill you!" Eisheth screamed then. The chains clanked as she pulled against them, trying desperately to reach her tormentor mere inches away. She succeeded only in burning herself in the flames.

"Did I ever love such a pitiful creature?" Komor mused. "No, not loved. But I was fond of you and your boundless naiveté."

"I will kill you and all your kind," Eisheth said. But it came out as animalistic growls.

"What's that?" Komor asked. "You will what?"

I will eat your soul.

The clear, strong thought took every ounce of strength she still possessed.

Komor grunted and put his hand to his head, then shook it off. He motioned for his men to come forward. Each was carrying a jar in one hand, a knife in the other. Eisheth hissed at the man in front of her, and he stumbled backward, tripped on a rock, and rolled into the dark lake below. He screamed, and it echoed, sounding eerily to Eisheth like the screams of her sisters. He floundered, and before any of the other soldiers could reach him, he disappeared beneath the black surface, as if dragged under.

Komor snorted in disgust. He grabbed the jar the man had dropped and drew his sword. He looked over Eisheth's body intently, motioning for one of his soldiers to bring the torch closer. Trembling, the man extended his arm, standing as far back as he could manage.

Komor poked the end of the blade into a withered breast. A red trickle dripped down her concave belly and then stopped. He cursed and pushed the blade in farther; again, a small dribble and then nothing.

"The Spring Rites are tomorrow," Komor said, stepping back. "While the villagers may not miss you much, they do miss your blood. Must I cut you to pieces to get it?"

"Do so," Eisheth managed to say out loud. *Do so,* she thought to herself, *and reap nothing the next year and the next. See how much the villagers love you then.*

109

"But that won't do me much good in the future, will it?" Komor mused.

"You must feed us," Naamah said. "Give us water." Of the three, she had managed to look the most human. She'd always taken the form of a slender woman, so maybe it was easier for her. Instead of looking like a monster, she looked like an old and shrunken woman.

Komor turned, seeking out which of the dried mummies pinned to the wall had spoken. Eisheth was in the middle, Agrat Bat to her right, Naamah to her left.

"Bring water," he commanded. Several of the soldiers inched down the slippery rock to the water below. They filled their jars and climbed back up. Then they roughly pulled the sisters' heads back and poured the water down their throats.

It was just water, brackish tasting, but it was ambrosia to Eisheth. She felt her body filling out and her thoughts becoming clearer, and most of all, she felt her spirit returning. Even for Goddesses, water was life.

She turned her head. Her sisters were recognizably human now, though far from beautiful.

"Who brought food?" Komor shouted.

A few of the men hesitated.

"Come now, I'll reward each of you with an equal weight in gold."

The soldiers reached into pockets and pouches, dragging out dried bread and jerky, carrots and turnips, more provisions than anyone would have guessed. Komor divided the food equally, and the men carefully fed it to the Goddesses, whose teeth grew sharper with every mouthful. The men were almost throwing the food at them by the end, and the gnashing was loud and frightening.

"Enough," Komor said impatiently. The sisters were clothed in flesh now, Agrat Bat the plumpest, as always. He sliced her arm and held a jar beneath it. An inch of Blood filled the bottom, but no more.

"Give me what I want, or I swear I will slice you into small pieces!" Komor shouted into Agrat Bat's face. Her blue eyes were impassive, but she was smiling slightly.

"If you want our blood," Naamah said, "you will need to feed us more than food and water."

"Quiet, sister!" Agrat Bat commanded.

After all they had been through, Naamah still had it in her to pout.

"Agrat Bat is right," Eisheth told her. "Sister, you must not give them what they want."

Komor marched over to Naamah. "What is it you need, Goddess? Tell me and I will bring it to you."

"I need the life of a man. I need his seed and his spirit."

Komor stared at her for a few moments and then threw back his head and laughed. His men joined in, though it was clear from their expressions that not all of them understood why they were laughing.

"You need to lay with a man?" he roared. "I thought it was going to be something difficult!" That set him to laughing even more. He stepped back and loosened his leggings, then pulled out the cock with which Eisheth was so familiar. It was already hard. He stepped up to Naamah.

"You were the one I always wanted, Goddess Naamah," he said. "But you were skittish. Not like Eisheth, who believed everything I told her."

"Sister," Agrat Bat said. "Don't do this."

In answer, Naamah spread her legs. She managed to look almost beautiful.

The Storm King grabbed his erection in hand and stepped forward...and at the last second, looked into Naamah's eyes.

He grunted and stepped back. He turned to his soldiers. "My men come before me," he said, and laughed. "Who wants to be first?" Not waiting for an answer, he grabbed the nearest man and shoved him toward Naamah.

The soldier didn't question it. He eagerly lowered his pants and shoved his manhood roughly into Naamah. He pumped rapidly, grunting with every thrust, while the other men shouted encouragement behind him. He shouted, grew still, then laid his head on Naamah's breasts.

Naamah could have lowered her mouth onto him then; she could have severed his jugular. Instead, she licked his neck.

The soldier raised his head, looking surprised, then shoved against her, starting all over.

The other soldiers grew even louder at this quick recovery and cheered him until he came once more. Moments later, with a loud groan, he started moving against Naamah again.

Naamah was now so beautiful that the soldiers had grown silent and were moving forward, surrounding her. When the first man fell backward onto the ground, a second man was already taking his place.

Others gathered around Agrat Bat and Eisheth.

Eisheth wanted to resist, but when the first member was presented, she wrapped her legs around the soldier and started draining him.

There was another shout, but this time it was not from pleasure, but from alarm. "He's dead!" someone cried.

Komor's men, who had been silently waiting their turns, gathered around the soldier lying on the ground. His eyes were wide open, his mouth twisted in pleasure or pain or both. He wasn't breathing.

The men who were inside the three sisters at that moment tried to pull out. They couldn't. One man lasted for three orgasms before slumping to the ground; the other two men took a little longer, but in the end they too were dead, their life force drained.

Komor watched it all, a strange expression on his face, almost as if he was pleased. When the last man had dropped to the ground, he approached Naamah. He bowed his head, as if in respect. Then, without a word, he sliced into her wrist and held the jar below the stream of blood. The jar was soon filled, and he motioned urgently for another one, and then another.

Three jars were filled from each of the sisters.

Komor motioned for his men to leave. Before he followed them, he said, "I'll be back next year, Goddesses."

Agrat Bat spoke the instant he was gone.

"You have cursed us, Naamah. You have cursed us to eternal torment."

They were not left alone for an entire year this time. Only weeks passed before a single old man came down, lugging two large bags over his shoulders. He fed them each a meal in turn, and made many trips down to the lake to refill the goblets he had brought.

He left, but he returned the next week and the next.

As they became stronger, the sisters bent their thoughts to the lone man, filling his mind with images of all the wonderful erotic things they would do to him. He shook his head a couple of times. It was as if he was deaf.

Finally, he turned a toothless grin to them and lowered his pants. There was nothing there but scar tissue.

He came back every few weeks for most of the year. He talked to them, though they refused to respond. His name was Barrs, and he was an escaped slave who owed his freedom to the Storm King. He seemed almost fond of the sisters, calling them Goddesses and bowing when arriving and before leaving.

Then, one day, it wasn't he who came but three young maidens. They each carried a bag of fresh food, better than the usual fare, and the sisters ate until they were satiated.

It was all done in silence, as if it was a solemn duty. The three girls didn't even speak to each other.

"Where is Barr?" Agrat Bat asked.

"The old man?" one of the girls asked. "He's passed on."

Eisheth noticed that Naamah had a strange smile on her face. All during the feeding, one of the three girls had kept looking at the Goddesses, her gaze lingering on each of them in turn. Now she arose and approached Naamah, and to everyone's astonishment, Goddesses and girls alike, she leaned over and kissed Naamah on the lips. Then she groaned, went to her knees, put her head down to Naamah and began licking her.

The other two girls watched in amazement, until one of them approached Agrat Bat and fell to her knees.

Eisheth bent her will on the third girl, who looked horrified. She was backing away, and even though Eisheth filled her head with all the erotic energy she possessed, the girl ran out of the cavern.

The other two girls stayed there. Weeks passed as they serviced the Goddesses until they slowly starved to death.

Only a few days after the last girl died, two more young women entered the cavern. They didn't look happy. They stood near the entrance for a long time, and then, glancing at each other as if to give each other courage, they held hands and approached the sisters.

Only as they drew near did the Goddesses realize they were men with long, silky hair, their faces covered in makeup.

The Daughters of Lilith couldn't help but try to summon them closer. It took the efforts of all three of them, but finally one of the men broke away from his companion and approached Eisheth. He lifted his dress, and his manhood was hard beneath it. She drained him quickly, sensing his confused and contradictory thoughts.

The other man ran away.

And thus, by trial and error, the men of Storm King's Mountain learned what worked and didn't work.

Eisheth lost track of the years. Komor did not appear again for several seasons. She knew he was coming the moment the doors opened. She felt herself becoming alert and focused for the first time in years.

When the Storm King walked into the cavern, all three sisters bent their wills toward him. He staggered. He avoided looking at them as he approached.

This time, instead of a condemned prisoner as sacrifice for each of the sisters, the Storm King's soldiers had brought with them a dozen chained men. Eisheth recognized them as villagers, among them Coss. He was no longer the handsome young man she remembered; there were deep, unhealed cuts on his face, and one ear was half missing.

"You are not giving us enough," Komor announced. "My city grows rapidly. More of your Blood is required."

"Gladly," Agrat Bat said. "Come and give me your seed...or are you afraid?"

"If it would mean more fertility for my fields that my people might be fed, I would do so," Komor blustered. It was a speech meant for his followers. "But my people still need me alive."

He is no longer dressed in armor, Eisheth saw. *He is old before his time.*

His beard was shorter now, flecked with gray, and he seemed smaller, as if he'd shrunk several inches. There were lines of care on his face. He was no longer a warrior—he was a politician.

Coss was unchained first, stripped of his rough robe, and pushed by chance in Eisheth's direction. He fell against her. He didn't appear to be afraid, but grateful.

"I'm sorry," Eisheth said.

"Do not be, Goddess," Coss said. "I cannot live any longer under such terror. I am ready to give myself to you."

Komor overheard. "How admirable!" he exclaimed. "Giving himself for the people! I will be sure to tell them of your brave and unselfish act."

Coss didn't last long. He gave most of himself the first time; there was little left after that.

One by one, the condemned prisoners were fed to the sisters. Komor stood back, and the soldiers approached warily. The more life force given to the Goddesses, the more their allure grew. The men were tied together so that none could break away.

The soldier who cut into Eisheth was trembling. As he held the jar beneath the Blood, he climaxed without touching her or himself. Then he fell down, spilling some of the precious fluid. He was cut away from the rope and dragged away, replaced by the next man.

More Blood was taken that year, and for many years after. The Storm King stopped coming to witness the bleeding. But Komor took Coss's words and repeated them: *I am ready to give myself to you*, and twisted the words and their meaning so that boys and girls were raised to give themselves to the Daughters of Lilith and think it an honor.

Their tormentors once again called themselves priests and priestesses, but they were no longer serving the Goddesses. They were Guardians of the Blood, the All-Healing, Keepers of the Secret Ceremonies. Each year, villagers were led down into the cave, drugged senseless, and given to the Daughters of Lilith.

One year, as Eisheth was being bled, she asked where the Storm King was.

"Komor the Great died many years ago," the soldier said. "His son Marrs is King now."

The torment continued, year after year. What the priests and priestesses looked like changed. What they wore, what they spoke, what they called the Daughters all changed over time, but the basic rites never did: darkness and revival, and a teasing pleasure followed by pain, and then the long, slow diminishment—century after century after century.

The years passed until Eisheth no longer knew who they were Culling. She was taking the life force of a young man when she realized that he was of a different race than she'd seen before, dark and muscular.

"They are prisoners of war," Agrat Bat said when the bloodletting was done and the chamber was empty. "Our Blood is used to conquer, not heal."

The next year, Eisheth watched more carefully. Along with the priests and priestesses and the sacrificial victims, young boys were being led to the cave. But they were not there for sex with the Daughters of Lilith.

Instead, the priestesses—young and pretty—were given to the young men, to complete their journey to manhood.

But first, the boys were given sharp knives and instructed to approach the sisters. "Cut them wherever it pleases you," the boys were told. "Cut them as much as you desire, and drink of the Blood of the Succubus."

The Daughters of Lilith hissed and screamed, and shouted threats and curses, and the priests whipped them until they were quiet. Then the boys approached and cut them, some timidly, taking but a drop, but others slashing into them again and again and drinking deeply. The priests didn't seem to care.

The priestesses gave themselves to the boys, and the Blood of the Succubus healed them, and the rites were fulfilled for another year.

As the years passed, the Storm King became but a memory, worshipped at first and then eventually forgotten. He was long dead when the Guardians, as the sister's keepers were now called, realized that the Daughters of Lilith could be bled all year long, and that the Blood would remain fresh and potent.

After that, it was an endless existence of pain and of pleasure, of sex and of death.

The priests and priestesses no longer came, and once again prisoners and slaves were brought, and the Bleeding lost any semblance of ceremony, but became a grim, unpleasant task carried out about by men who mutilated themselves. Slowly, Eisheth became aware that they no longer were called Goddesses. The Three Daughters of Lilith had a new name: the Succubae.

And so Agrat Bat's prediction came true:

"You have cursed us, Naamah. You have cursed us to eternal torment."

Chapter 16

Eisheth waited until Jeremy's car turned the corner before taking her eternal form. Larger, stronger, and—to any human—more monstrous than before, she lashed out at the mailbox on the curb, sending it flying across the street. Car alarms went off up and down the block.

Lights came on across the street, and her burly neighbor, Bruce Patterson, who also happened to be her landlord, came out in his bathrobe.

She shifted back to her Cute Cathy form just in time. It took more and more energy to maintain the illusion. She hungered for a sustaining meal, but it had been too long since she had taken a man. The bear's claws had left deep gashes in her back, which still bled if she moved too much or too fast. The bloody nose the new Cull—*my failed Cull*, she reminded herself—had given her, which normally would have healed at her first thought of it, still seeped Blood.

Her landlord spied her and stomped across the street toward her, his big belly threatening to push his bathrobe open to reveal all. He seemed to catch her thought and tightened the sash around his waist.

"What are you doing, girl? You know what time it is?"

I could take his head off, Eisheth thought. *Gut him right here.*

She'd contemplated him as a Cull when she'd first arrived in town, but he was madly in love with his dowdy wife, and she'd learned long ago that she couldn't win a man like that.

"I'm sorry, Mr. Patterson, I think I've had a little too much to drink." She swayed slightly and let her voice quaver just a bit.

His scowl softened. "Well, go to bed, girl. Take it easy; you want to save a little of that energy for when you're older."

"I will," she said, turning and walking up the sidewalk. "Sorry…again."

Eisheth closed the door to her first-floor apartment and shifted again. She looked around at the steampunk-themed items she had put together for her Suzanne persona, and started slashing everything in the place. She'd haunted the flea markets and yard sales in her first days in town, picking clothing up at random, nothing she really cared about, nothing that meant anything to her: a top hat she'd put some goggles on, some vests, some clunker boots that went up to her knees — anything to maintain the Steampunk Suzanne illusion in case someone dropped by unexpectedly.

The furniture had come with the place, garage sale stuff. She smashed it to pieces.

She wasn't staying in the apartment a moment longer.

She'd find a temporary hiding spot, and as soon as she regained enough strength, she would leave this awful town. She would head south for the winter. She hadn't been there in years. Southern California was always prime pickings; she just had to be careful not to overwork any one area down there.

Eisheth sat in the middle of the floor amongst the wreckage, mulling over her situation. She must weigh her options carefully and avoid doing anything stupid, like losing her temper, destroying a school, and leaving witnesses. She grimaced, remembering the Colorado high school where that had gone down. When she was this weak, she had a tendency to act rashly to seduce the first man she saw without measuring his vulnerabilities and without thinking of the consequences. It was best to pick men or boys with few friends or family — or even better, without friends or family of the female variety. Most women saw through her illusions too easily.

But she couldn't afford to waste energy on a man unlikely to fall completely in love with her. She'd wasted too much on this last boy, trying to get him to come after he'd seen her true shape. Sex at that point was just sex, because he gave it grudgingly, without total acceptance of her desires. If it was forced, she gained almost nothing.

119

It irked Eisheth that she had failed even in that. She was glad Agrat Bat and Naamah weren't here to see her humiliation.

She needed to find a vulnerable quarry right away. As distasteful as it was, she would have to choose someone from one of the homeless camps, whose life force would be just enough to get her out of town, if she was lucky.

She'd have to start all over. She looked around for something else to smash, but she'd done a pretty thorough job of it.

Eisheth went to the cracked mirror, trying out different faces. The good thing about lowering her standards was that she wouldn't have to try quite so hard to be cute. She needed merely be more attractive than any of the women around her prey.

The rumpled and slightly soiled clothing she'd worn on the camping trip would do nicely.

She filled a backpack with necessities, makeup and soap, a toothbrush and a few other things to fluff up her appearance, along with identification (most of it forged) and money. She left the apartment, leaving the door unlocked. She was never coming back. With luck, the landlord would think intruders had done the damage and wouldn't look for her. Not that he would have had any luck finding her anyway.

She turned east, hiking toward the homeless camps near Sage and Pines, a failed development that the city was turning a blind eye to. Wherever Eisheth went, she always knew where the homeless camps were. They were always her emergency escape option, her last resort.

She passed several campsites, then found one with only four men and two women. They were a little younger than average, either just hitting a bad patch or at the beginning of their downward spiral. She approached one of the men as he cooked breakfast, a couple of eggs and some burnt toast in a grimy skillet over a fire.

His eyes widened at the sight of her, and he grinned. He was missing a front tooth, but looked relatively clean. A younger man sitting next to him looked up at her with his mouth open as if he couldn't believe his eyes.

"I lost my job," she said, as if she was holding back tears. "I couldn't make the rent, and the landlord kicked me out. I just...I just need a place to stay for a few days until I get my deposit back."

"Shit, woman," came a rough voice behind her. A middle-aged woman came out of one of the tents. "You ain't never getting no deposit back."

This was a dangerous moment. Eisheth couldn't seem like a threat to this queen bee; at the same time, she couldn't be so unattractive to the men in the camp that they would lose interest in her.

"My landlord told me I would," Eisheth said, looking at the ground.

"Yeah, and Barry here farts rainbows."

It was a challenge, and Eisheth dropped her gaze and pressed her lips together. She wiggled her chin, hoping to appear on the verge of tears, waiting for one of the men to rescue the vulnerable waif she presented herself as.

The younger bum jumped to his feet. He was very short, dumpy, and already balding. He put out his hand. "My name's Adam. This is Barry, and that ol' witch is Beverly. Pay her no mind. She hates everyone."

"Ginger," Eisheth whispered. She'd chosen stringy red hair this time, and green eyes. She turned a radiant smile on Adam, making sure Beverly didn't see it. Adam's eyes widened and he gulped, turning bright red.

"Come on, you can have my breakfast." He waved her to the lawn chair he'd recently vacated. "I ate last night."

Most men wouldn't brag about having eaten the day before as if it was some sort of triumph. His offer was both pathetic and honorable.

Eisheth forced the food down, trying to look grateful. Then she closed her eyes and swayed as if exhausted. Only as she mimicked the reaction did she realize that she was indeed almost dead on her feet. Adam's arm slid around her tentatively, and she leaned into him.

"Sorry," she murmured. "I'm just so tired."

"Why don't you take a nap in my tent?" he said.

She opened her eyes and looked up at him gratefully. His face flushed again. "I mean...I mean...you can sleep there, alone, you know."

"Thank you," she said, glad to climb into the tent and lie down. She didn't have to fake the exhaustion, just the helplessness. She fell asleep almost instantly, though it was the middle of the afternoon.

When she awoke, it was almost dark. She sensed someone in the tent with her, and she looked over to find Adam sitting in the corner, trying to look nonthreatening.

"You're bleeding," he said. "Like someone whipped you." He came forward as though he wanted to touch the wounds on her back.

"No!" she cried, shrinking away, and he scrambled backward.

"I'm sorry," he said, and it looked like he was near tears. "I don't mean no harm."

Eisheth's natural alarm turned out to be the right response, though not for the reasons Adam probably supposed. She wasn't afraid of him. She hadn't suffered abuse, as he was no doubt thinking. But acting man-shy wasn't the worst reaction she could have had.

"It's OK, I'd just rather you don't touch me...*there*," she said.

He raised his hands innocently, looking shocked.

She gave him a small, tired smile. "How long was I asleep?"

"A few hours. But you never moved, and I was kinda worried about you."

She looked him in the eyes. "You are a nice guy."

Eisheth stayed in the tent the rest of the day while Adam came and went, looking for things to make her more comfortable. There was no reason to expose herself to the others anymore. She had her quarry already halfway where she wanted him to be. Out of sight of the others, she saved her energy, letting the illusion fall away when no one could see her.

Adam found another sleeping bag somewhere, and that night they slept side by side. He never made a move on her.

Eisheth left the tent briefly the next day. Beverly's eyes shot daggers at her, and Barry frowned at her, as if he wasn't quite sure if he approved of her. *Probably just jealous,* she thought.

It drizzled in the afternoon, giving her the perfect excuse to duck back into the tent. Adam followed shortly with some paperbacks. She pretended to read one. They were all Westerns, which she never bothered with. Why should she? She'd lived through the Old West and enjoyed many a gunslinger in her time. The books were dog-eared and worn, as if they had been passed from hand to hand or recycled through used bookstores over and over again.

"I like the old-fashioned Westerns, writers like Louis L'Amour and D.B. Newton," Adam told her. "Not the new violent ones."

"Me too." Eisheth wracked her brain for something to say. It was a little difficult, because Westerns had fallen out of favor decades ago. "But I think L'Amour keeps writing the same books with the same characters over and over again."

"Yeah, but they're *great* characters," Adam said. His face lit up attractively, as if he'd never opened up to a woman about his fanboy interests before. She had that effect on her targets.

That night, when Adam still didn't touch her, Eisheth cuddled up next to him. He couldn't restrain a groan, but when her hand drifted over to his cock, he tensed up and immediately lost his erection.

She cried out in exasperation, then immediately covered it up. It wasn't that he didn't want her, she realized. He was just scared.

She knew his type. All she needed to do was make him comfortable. If she could do that, she had him.

The trick to winning him over wasn't the actual sex, but the *offer* of sex, and the comfort and commitment it promised—though sex didn't hurt. But mostly, she had to be available, all the time, and respond to everything and do everything that would make the man feel like he could count on her. Most of these men had been through numerous failed relationships, but few had the insight to realize that it was usually their fault, not the woman's. Most thought if they could only find the right woman, loyal and supportive, why, anything was possible. If she was sexy too, well, that woman he'd give his all to.

It usually didn't take long, a few days at most. It looked like it was going to take even less effort this time.

Eisheth was naked when Adam entered the tent late the next afternoon. She timed it exquisitely, managing to cover herself a moment later.

"I'm sorry," he muttered, looking away and blushing to the top of his bald head.

"Hard to knock on the door when it's canvas," she said, smiling. "Come here."

It looked as if his legs buckled as he sat next to her. She took his chin and turned his face toward her. "I like you, you know."

His eyes softened. "I like you too."

Eisheth leaned forward and kissed him. His breath was sweet, as if he'd just brushed his teeth in anticipation…of what? A kiss? Or did he want more—was he *ready* for more?

His kiss became more impassioned, and his hand went to her breast, rubbing lightly over the nipple. Then he was kissing down her neck, zeroing in. He took a nipple in his mouth and sucked so hard it almost hurt, but Eisheth was careful only to murmur her appreciation for his efforts. Then he was pushing her backward, and she couldn't help but say, "Oh, my!" in a mirthful way, and he laughed in response.

He may be inexperienced, she thought, *but he sure as hell has thought about what he'd do to a girl given the chance.*

She let the sleeping bag fall away and opened herself to him.

Adam tore off his clothing in a frenzied rush. Eisheth didn't laugh, though. Nothing could be allowed to break the mood or raise his insecurities. He wasn't really as fat as she'd thought. He wore dumpy clothing, like hand-me-downs from an older, bigger brother. He was so frantic; she knew he wouldn't take long. That was OK. In fact, that was good. Once he came the first time, he was hers forever, no matter what else happened.

He would make all kinds of noises as she drained him, and the neighbors in the surrounding tents were going to think it awfully strange, but no one would interfere.

He entered her quickly, and then unexpectedly slowed down. He pressed every inch of himself against her, and it felt surprisingly pleasurable, and she realized that she'd hit the jackpot: a boy who thought he was unattractive but who was a real lover, who knew instinctively what to do, who cared about the satisfaction of his partner. He was sucking on her earlobe in a way that gave her shivers, and she moaned out loud, not having to act, and she could tell he knew it and wanted more of it. He continued to touch her in all the right places at the right moments, until it was she who squirmed in pleasure, not him.

So many pretty boys and macho men she'd drained who couldn't measure up to this dumpy young man when it came to lovemaking.

Remember what you're here for! Eisheth tried to remind herself, but she was enjoying herself too much to use her own abilities to make him orgasm early. It would happen, and it would be glorious. She anticipated a big surge of life force, more than she could have dreamed possible.

She was vaguely aware that the tent door had opened. A shadow loomed over them.

"What the in the hell are you doing, Adam?"

Adam popped out of her before she could clamp her legs around him. He stood up, his cock waving, and now that Eisheth could see it, she saw that it was long and well formed. It was also deflating fast.

A young woman stood in front of him, furious. She wasn't even looking at the redheaded Ginger, which was fortunate, because she'd reverted into Eisheth for a moment, enraged at the interruption.

The intruder slapped Adam, then looked down at Eisheth/Ginger, baring her teeth like a lioness. The woman was short and pleasingly plump, with a spiky haircut that did her no favors. She swung a booted foot into Eisheth's stomach, knocking the breath out of her.

Again and again, the boot slammed into her.

"Slut!" the girl screamed. "Whore!"

Then Eisheth pushed back, and the girl flopped against the side of the tent, almost collapsing it. It didn't dissuade her, though. She went on the attack again immediately. Eisheth held her off long enough to finally regain her breath, but she was still weak.

I've used too much of my glamour, she thought. *And still nothing to show for it!*

Now she was weak and bleeding and trying hard to keep up some kind of illusion. If she reverted to Succubus form in front of them, she'd have to kill them, and then the others, and then anyone who came running from the other campsites, drawn by all the noise. That would also weaken her.

"Bobbie Jo, you're going to kill her!" Adam shouted. "It wasn't her fault. It was me!"

"You're so damn stupid, Adam!" Bobbie Jo screamed, but she quit kicking Eisheth. As Eisheth propped herself up on her elbows, she saw that Adam had gotten ahold of Bobbie Jo and was pushing her out of the tent.

Bobbie Jo was still screaming outside when Adam tore himself away and came back into the tent. He wrapped his arms around Eisheth. "I'm so sorry, Ginger. It's my fault. I should have told you. We were never promised to each other, but I knew Bobbie Jo thought we were a couple. I'm an asshole."

For some reason, Eisheth wasn't mad at Adam; she actually liked him. When his hand slipped on the Blood on her back, she didn't recoil. She put her own hand into the puddle of Blood on the sleeping bag, lifted a finger, and presented it to Adam.

He looked confused, so she stuck her bloody finger between his lips. She could see the energy coursing though him.

"Get out of here, Adam," she said. "And take your girl with you. You don't want to see what's coming."

He fled the tent, and she heard him shouting for the others to run.

Then she transformed into Eisheth and tore the tent to shreds. She burst out of its tattered remains, grabbed a flaming branch from the campfire, and tossed it onto the fabric. It was nearly dark, and the fire lit up the campground.

She burned the other tents, tearing into everything manmade. When her fury was almost expended, she turned to leave. The witch, Beverly, was watching, her eyes wide in terror, standing as if rooted to the ground behind one of the juniper trees surrounding the camp.

In two bounds, Eisheth was on top of her, throwing her to the ground.

"You shouldn't have interfered," she snarled, not caring about Beverly's innocence. It didn't matter—she was human, and at that moment, all members of that species were the enemy.

She swiped at the woman's cheek, the sharp claws digging in and ripping a mass of flesh away, revealing rotting teeth beneath. The woman's scalp was next. Her hair flew into the branches of the juniper tree and hung there. A third swipe severed her carotid artery, and a fourth sent her head sailing off into the trees. She hadn't even had time to scream.

A ring of juniper trees obscured the next camp over. Eisheth came out of the shadows to find three men looking her direction in alarm. One man was so stunned by her appearance that he didn't move; the other two started running. She killed the first with a slash so fast he didn't see it coming. He looked down at the blood spurting from his body as if it was happening to someone else. Then he toppled, splitting down the middle, and his innards gushed out and over the flickering campfire. The odor of steamed meat rose into the air.

She was on top the other two before they got much farther than the dirt track that wound between the campsites. She beheaded one, his scream cut off in the middle. She cut the legs out from the other, and his torso rolled off the path. The severed legs kicked once and went still, but the man kept screaming for a little while. In the distance there were shouts, and flashlight beams crisscrossed the sky.

Eisheth wanted to kill them all, but by now someone had undoubtedly called the cops, and she couldn't afford to confront them.

Without bothering to transform, and unsure whether she had the energy anyway, she stalked off into the desert.

Chapter 17

Gasper Gerhard's Journal

When I first started reading these journals, I wondered why, when our family was still strong and numerous, we didn't try to track down the Succubae instead of hunkering down to protect the Blood. What good is the Blood if we don't use it for anything but self-preservation? Are we nothing but cowards?

If we are cowards, we have our reasons. In those first years after the Succubae escaped, the sisters sought out the remaining Guardians and took savage revenge. Only those men who hid away and performed the Cutting survived.

How do we defeat the Succubae? Since it is unlikely the Daughters of Lilith will ever again be caught weak and unaware, they will be at the height of their physical and seductive powers.

Over the years, the Guardians discovered the sisters could be physically hurt, even destroyed, but they always came back.

No, the only way to defeat them is to face them on their own terms. A man must face them, resist their allure, and with his bare hands, strangle them to death. That cannot be done by any man who has undergone the Cutting.

It is a paradox. For a man to be strong enough to physically confront a Succubus and not be ripped apart, it is necessary to drink fully of the Blood. But to drink fully of the Blood is to make that man vulnerable to the allure of the Succubus.

No man has yet succeeded.

Czechoslovakia, 1946

The world Heinrich found outside the caves was greatly changed. The war was over; Germany was in ruins. The Russians and Americans were dividing up Europe into spheres of influence. Since his father had disparaged the Russians during Heinrich's entire childhood, he made his way west.

Once away from rural Czechoslovakia, Heinrich found that he had much to learn. His father had kept him ignorant of the outside world, a naïf. He was in Prague for less than a day when someone tried to steal his pack. He managed to wrestle it back. When the attacker returned with some of his friends, Heinrich was ready. He'd drunk of the Blood, and felt strength surging through him. When it wore off, there were four men lying unmoving in the alley. He didn't check to see if they were dead. He didn't want to know.

He hurried away, and used the last of his money to rent a cheap room. He did the Cutting and lay in bed for several days. He finally ventured out because he was hungry. He found a job in a café, washing dishes and cleaning.

One night, tired and discouraged, he dared to drink more of the Blood, hoping that it would clear his head. Indeed, he immediately remembered overhearing a conversation between two merchants in the cafe. He hadn't thought anything of it at the time, but in his enhanced state, he realized it presented an opportunity.

He managed to be on the right street corner when it happened. He rushed to the merchant's aid, helping him fight off a band of thieves. In gratitude, the man gave Heinrich a job in his countinghouse.

When Heinrich drank the Blood of the Succubus, his thoughts became clear and concise. He found he could analyze financial markets and make snap decisions that were almost always right. So between the drinking of the Blood and the Cutting, he wrote quick notes to himself: invest in such and such a stock, sell such and such a company. It was surprisingly simple. In between, he followed the market trends and business news sections religiously. Heinrich turned his small salary into enough of a fortune to strike off on his own.

The more Blood he drank, the harder it became to do the Cutting.

Where were the Succubae?

He kept a low profile, declining to live like the rich man he was. He discovered he had a talent for language; he already knew some German and, with the help of the Blood, he quickly became fluent. At night, while working in the refugee centers in the French zone as a translator, he studied French.

It was then that he learned of the concentration camps. Overnight, his opinion of his German heritage changed. He changed his last name to Bartok. He was a Czech now, to anyone who asked.

Above all, he listened for rumors of the Succubae. This postwar confusion was the kind of chaos they liked and that they would take advantage of.

Did he want to find them? Or did he want to hide from them?

Heinrich wasn't sure. He knew he wasn't ready to confront them yet. Before he'd left home, he had demolished the house, making sure the entrance to the caves was buried. He'd marked which piles of rubble to look under if he ever needed to come back. He had kept ownership of the land. He'd left most of the journals and almost all of the Blood behind. On his journey west, he took only the four bottles he'd dragged through the caves with him. His father's journal was still readable, though the paper had expanded, making the book twice as thick.

Where *were* the Succubae?

It was the horrendous brutality of the concentration camps that most reminded him of them, and he was certain they were involved somehow.

But if so, they had made their escape.

The Daughters of Lilith would want to be as far away from the scene of their atrocities as possible, he thought. They were probably across the ocean by now, hiding in South America, or in the big cities of the U.S.A. He began to relax just a little, to talk to his coworkers, to make friends. He was able to sleep at night and not look over his shoulder every second.

The Blood drew them, it was true, but only if he used it.

And so, as time went on and there was no word of them, Heinrich decided to take a chance.

As an experiment, he drank an entire bottle of the Blood, begging forgiveness from his ancestors for using so much of the precious fluid. But he needed to know what it could do. He chose a small village in rural France for the experiment and rented a loft there.

He didn't sleep for a day. He scribbled long, complicated instructions to himself in notebooks (which later made no sense). He went out into the countryside and toppled a tree a full eight inches thick. He lifted a boulder bigger than he was; he jumped to the top of a small cliff; he regressed several years so that he looked like a very healthy, solid fifteen-year-old boy.

His genitals came back, bigger and better than ever. His cock doubled in size. He masturbated a dozen times a day and visited the prostitutes on the corner. Not that he needed to pay for it—he exuded so much sexual magnetism, he merely needed to crook his finger at the most frigid housewife on the street and she would follow him gladly.

After a week, he reluctantly did the Cutting.

Just in time, as it turned out.

He sucked a fingertip's worth of Blood and fell into bed. He awoke from an erotic dream. It was a memory of his first time, a prostitute in Prague who had followed him afterward even after the Cutting, refusing to believe that a man so virile wasn't interested in her anymore. The dream didn't dissipate upon awakening. Despite the Cutting, he felt desire.

He jumped up from the bed and opened the curtains a crack.

The Succubus was in the street. It was the blonde one, the one he called the Goddess. She approached a man as if to offer him sex, but after looking into his eyes, she went on to the next man. The first man cried out in frustration, looking ready to strike her. She put out her hand, and he dropped to his knees.

It was the Blood. She sensed Heinrich's nearness, just as he sensed hers.

All these years he'd searched for her, and here she was; yet he was suddenly aware how unprepared he was.

She was searching for him, confused that the sexual energy that had led her to this town, to this very street had suddenly disappeared.

Heinrich closed the curtains and made sure the door was locked, as if that would do any good. He spent the night awake, trying not to let his thoughts stray. In the morning, she was gone.

It was a close call.

They hunted him, just as he hunted them, both looking for a moment of weakness. Somehow they knew he existed, as if he were the shadow to their brightness. He felt their hate even more strongly than their desire. If they ever caught him, he suspected even his self-mutilation wouldn't be enough to save him. They'd suck the life right out of him.

He never used more than a few drops of the Blood at a time after that.

Heinrich wandered Europe, and with a feeling of inevitability, ended up back in France. He could never quite get the accent right, but he became fluent, and found a job teaching the German and Czech languages in a small school in a rural area outside Paris.

One of the other teachers was a young woman named Adele, who taught English. He didn't really pay much attention to her at first. She was a few years older and plump, and he just assumed she was married.

"Guten morgen," she said to him one morning in the teacher's lounge as they guzzled their last cups of coffee before confronting their students.

"Sprechen sie Deusch?" he asked, surprised.

"Nein," she answered, laughing. She switched to French. "But I would *like* to learn German."

"And I would like to learn English," he answered.

"That's swell," she said, and he recognized it as an expression he'd heard American soldiers use.

They made a date to meet at a café and practice with each other. Adele was funny and light-hearted, but Heinrich was wary. It wasn't until they were together all evening that he realized she was just as she appeared on the surface, sweet natured and kind.

"How did you learn to speak English so well?" he asked.

For the first time since he'd met her, Adele frowned. She looked away, out into the street, and didn't answer for a long time. He waited.

Finally, she turned back to him with a smile. "You listen so well. You're quiet when you need to be."

I have spent my whole life alone, he wanted to say, but decided not to burden her with it. So far they hadn't talked about their pasts, as if in unspoken agreement that it was a subject to be avoided.

It turned out Adele lived above the café they were sitting in, which was why the owners had let them stay past closing. Finally, Heinrich got up to leave. It seemed to him when they parted that she expected a kiss. He pretended not to notice and walked away. When he reached the corner, he looked back. She was standing in the window, watching him.

That night, as he went to bed, he thought of her. He was still Cut, so there should have been no desire, and yet his imagination filled in what he couldn't feel physically.

The next morning, he learned that his instincts were right. Adele wasn't married, but she was engaged to Bertrand, another teacher, a blustery man with thick black hair covering his body. He was an ox of a man. Midway through the morning, he caught Heinrich in the hallway, lifting him physically from the floor and slamming him against the wall.

"Stay away from her, Bartok," he growled. He dropped Heinrich, who lost his footing and sprawled face first onto the floor. He looked up to see Adele's horrified face. Bertrand took her arm and led her away, and she went with him.

The next day, Heinrich stayed in his classroom. But as he left for the night, he passed two other staff members, who were laughing. They stopped when he looked at them.

If this had been a playground dispute between two boys, he would have stepped in as a teacher to resolve the conflict. But one of the two scoffers had been the school principal. Heinrich realized he was alone.

If nothing changed, he'd be isolated. Worse, he'd never talk to Adele again.

He drank a half bottle of Blood the next morning. He jumped at every sound, his head jerking around as if he was on the hunt. He managed to make it through his morning classes, though the students looked at him strangely.

When the bell rang for lunch, Heinrich made his way to the small table in the corner of the yard where Adele always ate lunch.

She frowned when he approached, half rising before sitting back down. The other two women teachers there excused themselves.

"You mustn't talk to me," she said. "Bertrand is jealous."

"Does he have reason to be?"

She searched his face, as if she would find the answer there. Then she nodded.

"Yes," she said softly. "I have wanted to get away from Bertrand for some time, but until you came along, I felt it safer just to stay."

He sat down next to her. "Tell me."

"I lost someone in the war, an Englishman. That's how I learned the language. Bertrand was…there after I got the news. He was kind to me, at first."

Heinrich sensed Bertrand coming before he even entered the courtyard, as if he could feel the air move and the ground shake. He stood up, his arms at his sides.

Bertrand kept coming, raising his right arm for a giant swing at Heinrich's head. It seemed as if the fist came at Heinrich in slow motion, and he waited until the last moment before moving his head just enough for it to miss. Bertrand's momentum carried his fist all the way into the table, and he howled.

Adele jumped up from the table, her hand to her mouth. "Don't hurt him, Bertrand!" she screamed.

The big man was totally exposed. Heinrich could have slammed his body with punches, but again he waited, arms at his sides, for Bertrand to gather himself. The Blood sang in Heinrich's veins, and it was as if it was whispering, "Kill him…kill him."

If Adele hadn't been watching, it might have turned out differently. But Heinrich simply moved out of the way of Bertrand's second lunge, only this time he pushed his off-balance attacker slightly in his most exposed spot. Bertrand fell, his head slamming against the table, and he slumped to the ground, unconscious.

"Did you even touch him?" Adele asked. "I don't know what just happened!"

"He's a big man," Heinrich murmured. "Clumsy, I guess."

Adele wasn't rushing to Bertrand's side. Instead, she stepped around the table, moving toward Heinrich. He took her in his arms.

They left the school together that night after somehow managing to teach the rest of their classes. They went to her house, which she shared with two other teachers who knew enough to stay away. They made love, and the same Blood that had given Heinrich such speed and strength now lent him tenderness that answered her every need, until she was crying out in pleasure.

They were married within days. The principal who had done nothing to help Heinrich was the best man.

Bertrand got a transfer to a different school, out of town.

The Blood was starting to wear off. Heinrich made love a little more awkwardly on his wedding night, and Adele seemed almost relieved.

"So you *are* human," she murmured happily.

In the morning, Heinrich went back to his room. He picked up one of the knives. *I will have an "accident,"* he thought. There was the familiar sensation of the sharp blade against his genitals. Then he set it down.

I will be quiet and I will stay a man. But I will not drink the Blood.

Chapter 18

On Jeremy's second trip to the bathroom, he noticed something different. He'd barely looked in the mirror Saturday morning, just done the necessary before rolling into bed at dawn. So it was late Saturday afternoon by the time he noticed anything.

Since infancy, he'd had a large white scar over his right eye (well, maybe not that large, but he always noticed it), which had come from a football hitting him square in the face.

It was gone.

He rubbed the skin, trying to figure out where the scar had gone, how it might be obscured. He'd gotten a bit of a tan out in the woods, but not enough to hide it. Besides, scars don't tan, and dirt and grime don't stick to them as much.

He ran his tongue over the broken tooth that had bugged him for months and that he always checked whenever there was a mirror nearby to see if the crack was any bigger. He really wasn't looking forward to getting a crown.

The crack was gone. Jeremy pulled his lip up with his fingers, trying to get a better look, but his tongue was the most sensitive indicator, and it was saying there wasn't a crack, not even a little one.

He stared into the mirror for a moment. Damned if he didn't look a little younger somehow, maybe a little like he'd looked last year at this time, before he'd gotten his growth spurt. But he was, if anything, even taller. He took a pencil out of the drawer and went over to the doorway where he marked his increasing height. Sure enough, he was an inch taller. He flexed his arm, and it seemed kind of muscly, though he'd never thought of himself that way before.

Finally, he pulled down his pants, pointed his rear end at the mirror, and looked at his backside. He'd sat on a pencil in the fourth grade, and the tip had broken off and remained a little lump lodged in there ever since.

It was gone. In fact, *every imperfection* was gone.

"I'm perfect," he said into the mirror. His voice sounder deeper. He laughed. The muscles, the height, the deeper voice—that could all be explained, but the mended tooth and vanished scars? How the hell did that happen? It was impossible…

…just like Cathy's face in the tent leering down at him was impossible. He shuddered into the mirror at these thoughts and made a face. He had extraordinary energy all day, despite staying in his room, pacing, talking to himself, writing down his thoughts, reading at a frantic pace.

And it had all started when the blood from Cathy's bloody broken nose had dripped into his mouth.

There was loud knocking at his door. He pulled on some cutoff jeans and flung it open, expecting his sister, Marty, whose knock he recognized.

Marty was standing there, but so was Lucinda.

"Wow, brother of mine," Marty said. "When did you start showing off? In fact, since when *could* you show off?"

"Sorry," he muttered, grabbing a shirt that hung from chair.

"Don't get dressed on my account," Lucinda said, grinning. "If the girls at Bend High knew you looked like that, they wouldn't…" She stopped, suddenly realizing that she'd backed herself in a corner.

"Wouldn't what?" Marty said, unwilling to bail her out. "Wouldn't think he was such a nerd? Don't let the body fool you; he's still a nerd."

"No argument from me," Jeremy said. Marty smirked and Lucinda giggled while Jeremy pulled the shirt over his head.

"Someday you're going to have to tell me what's going on, Jeremy," Marty said.

"It's hard to explain," he started to say.

"Whatever," Marty interrupted cheerfully. "I've got homework to do. You know me, a real squid." She gave him a wink—or maybe it was Lucinda she was aiming for, or maybe both—before leaving the room and slamming the door.

Lucinda gave Jeremy a little smile, then hesitated, staring around the room. Jeremy grimaced as he realized there was nowhere for her to sit. He scooped the dirty clothes off his desk chair, dropping them in the empty hamper. He looked around, suddenly aware his room was a disaster.

She sat down. Jeremy tried to think of something to say.

"How did the camping trip go?" she asked quietly.

He flushed as he kicked some more dirty laundry toward the hamper. "We came home early. It didn't go so well."

"No?" Lucinda couldn't hide her relief. "I...I guess that's too bad."

"Not really," Jeremy said. "She wasn't who I thought she was."

"Really?"

"Oh, she's nothing like she looks, believe me," he said.

"Good, because I have something to show you."

Lucinda pulled a piece of neon yellow paper out of her pocket. She unfolded it and handed it to Jeremy. He instantly recognized the girl in the black and white sketch. It was Cathy—without the hair and the heavy makeup, but it was definitely her.

"I don't understand," he said. "Where did you get this?"

"Someone was handing them out at school."

"What does it meant?"

"It means you should call the number on the poster," Lucinda said. "Better yet, let's go to the hotel, tell them in person."

So someone else thought something was wrong about Cathy. Jeremy stared out the window, wondering. Was he really ready to turn on Cathy so completely?

Lucinda's voice lowered sympathetically. "It's not about the money," she said. "You can turn down the money. But something strange is going on with that girl, and these people seem to know what it is. I think you need to talk with them."

He listened to her voice. So calm, so down to earth, so different from Cathy's ethereal chatter. "Will you go with me, Lucinda?" he asked abruptly, surprised at his own request.

She gave him a grin. "You couldn't keep me away."

Chapter 19

Gasper Gerhard's Journal

I sensed the Succubae near just one more time.

It was after I gave Heinrich to the neighbor woman to nursemaid. I was alone. I spent all my time in the caves, reading the histories. It was soon after my father died. No one was watching me, and I could do as I pleased.

So I drank of the Blood.

And I did not do the Cutting.

I was making dinner when an overwhelming sense of desire overcame me. I sensed her sniffing around outside—how, I don't know. It was as if we were connected. It was the Blood, I suppose. It drew her back. She sensed that her ancestral home was near, and she was getting closer every second.

I wasted no time in performing the Cutting.

I still wanted to live in those days. At the same time, I understood why the Succubus wanted to kill me. It was her Blood I drank to restore myself, taken unwillingly from her body. None of my forebears wrote about that dark time just before the Fall. They spoke vaguely of God's retribution, but not why it was necessary.

I suspect that we acted badly, we Guardians. That we bled the Succubae dry every chance we got. Our lore says that the Fall came because we were corrupt; we sold the Blood for profit and power. But I wonder if the Fall was because of how we treated the Succubae, who, according to the oldest transcripts, had once been worshipped as Goddesses.

I think, perhaps, they have every right to hate mankind.

France, 1958

Heinrich decided to stay in France when his son was born, to become a true Gallic gentleman. He wanted to name his boy Gasper, but didn't object when Adele Gallicized it to Gaspar.

He stored what was left of the Blood in the cellar, covered by a layer of bricks, and tried his best to forget about the Succubae. Though he felt an overwhelming urge to use the Blood sometimes, especially when he was injured, and even more so when Adele or his children were hurt or sick, he avoided it. Such urges only revealed how dependent he'd become on it.

He vowed he would never to use it again.

And yet, he couldn't quite make himself destroy the Blood. It didn't belong to him—it was the Guardians'. (*I am the last of them*, he thought, but the ghosts of his ancestors hovered over his shoulders.)

The more he read his father's journal, the more Heinrich realized that his forebears had done their best—that they meant well. They were weak and scared, perhaps, but none of them had given up on their duty. He had no right to judge them. He was the one who was giving up.

I will live a quiet life, he told himself. *The Daughters of Lilith will have no reason to bother me. It ends here.*

He remained a teacher in the same school, and eventually, to his own amazement, even became the principal. Adele stayed home with Gaspar, and grew plumper and happier every year. It was the kind of life that his father had wanted. That all his ancestors had wanted.

He'd never really had a mother, he realized now. Oh, of course he'd been born of a woman, but he'd been taken from her almost immediately. It was only males in the Gerhard family. It always had been, until Heinrich married Adele.

In their fourth year together, he cut off the end of his finger while chopping onions. Adele was visiting her mother, and Gaspar was playing with his young neighbor friends.

What can it hurt? he thought. There had been no reports of the Succubae anywhere in the papers. It was as if they had completely vanished.

Heinrich went downstairs, took up the bricks, and took a small sip of the Blood. He sat in the basement, feeling the Blood course through his veins, and realized he had missed it. This was the real reason he hadn't destroyed the Blood.

He heard Adele arriving home above him. He was so filled with energy that he found himself practically running up the stairs.

He took his wife, laughing, into his arms, and she returned the hug, having missed him. She was always the more affectionate one. They took advantage of Gaspar's absence and almost ran to the bedroom.

Nine months later, they had a daughter, Berenice.

One morning, soon after the birth of their daughter, Heinrich gave his wife a kiss and walked to his school. He was wrapped in contentment, barely aware of his surroundings. He felt as if he knew every stone, every blade of grass.

"Mr. Gerhard?"

Heinrich kept walking, giving no sign he'd heard.

A hand grabbed his arm and turned him around. A large man stood there, peering down at him. He was foreign, though Heinrich wasn't sure how he knew that. He wore a black suit and a fedora, looking completely out of place in the rural village.

"You are Heinrich Gerhard?" The accent was one Heinrich had rarely heard but instantly recognized: American.

"Pardon," Heinrich said. "You have made a mistake. My name is Henri Bartok."

"Yes," the man said with a smirk. "Henri Bartok. You are the man I'm looking for."

Heinrich put a mask of mild curiosity over his face. "And you are...?"

"My name is Ernest Harrison," the man said. "I am quite a wealthy man, and I can make it worth your while to help us."

"Go on."

The man spoke loudly, as if unaware his voice carried to all the nearby houses. "I represent a group of men who have been trying to track down three...women, shall I say? I believe you know to whom I'm referring?"

Heinrich felt the blood drain from his face. "I have no idea what you are talking about."

"We call ourselves the Guardians," Harrison said. "We have long been in hiding, but we are ready to emerge from the shadows at last to once again confront the Daughters of Lilith."

Rage surged through Heinrich at this smirking, ignorant foreigner. He found himself shouting nearly as loud as the booming voice of the stranger. "You come to my village and call out the name 'Gerhard' for anyone to hear? You are no Guardian, sir. You are a fool."

"Here now," Harrison objected. "No one here cares what you call yourself. If you join us, you'll be safe. We are preparing to capture the Succubae and once again harvest their Blood."

"Capture them?" Heinrich said. "You have no idea what you are doing."

"I assure you, monsieur, we aren't ignorant savages. We don't worship Goddesses, nor do we fear the Succubae. We are well armed and organized. We will take their blood and we will synthesize it, using modern technology. The Blood of the Succubus will be a boon to mankind."

"Synthesize?" Heinrich echoed, as though the word had no meaning.

The American nodded. *Can do,* the expression said.

"And what gives you the right?" Heinrich's voice was still raised. He noticed his neighbors peering curiously out of their windows. Henri Bartok had a reputation of never losing his temper. He lowered his voice, murmuring, "Do you have any idea what our people did to them?"

The stranger looked uncomfortable, and opened his mouth to protest.

Heinrich overrode his objection. "Do you understand that we tortured them year after year, for centuries? Is that what you want to do?"

"We will be humane," the man began. "I assure you..."

"Humane?" Heinrich took a step back, realizing the man and those he represented had no idea how dangerous the Succubae were. "You really don't know what you're doing, do you?"

Enough of this fool, Heinrich thought. *The Succubae will make short work of him and his kind. And anyone who talks to them...*

"Perhaps we don't have all the information we need," the man said. "Perhaps we would know more if we had the histories of our Order. We have only the stories our fathers have handed down to us. We believe we know what to do, but we are certainly willing to learn more. If you have such knowledge, Heinrich, then help us. Join us and tell us what you know. We will welcome it."

"What I know is to leave them alone!" Heinrich said, and turned to walk away.

"The Blood," the man said, loudly. "We need samples of the Blood."

Heinrich immediately turned back to the American. "Shut up, Harrison, do you hear? Just shut up!"

"If you give us the Blood, we will leave you alone. Give us the Blood and histories of our Order, and you can go on living your life in peace, without any interference from us."

"The Blood is gone," Heinrich said. "My ancestors used it up long ago. There is nothing left."

The American didn't respond, but it was obvious he didn't believe him. Heinrich didn't feel like he could walk away until he was sure that this man and those he represented, these Guardians—these shadow Guardians—understood the danger.

"You mustn't confront them," he said. "You cannot win."

"We are willing to take that chance."

"Then you are dead men," Heinrich said. He turned and walked away, feeling the man's eyes on his back. He was nearly to the corner when the American's shout caught up to him.

"This isn't over, Monsieur Bartok. We will be watching."

It was 1958. Charles de Gaulle was in the midst of founding the Fifth Republic of France. As the head of his school district, Heinrich was called to Paris to confer with the minister of education, perhaps even to meet the great man himself.

"I'll only be gone a week," he assured his wife.

"But they'll want you longer," Adele said. "I just know it. They'll want to put you in government."

He laughed. "Me? In government?"

She didn't laugh with him.

"If the Great Asparagus is foolish enough to make the offer, I will turn him down," he said. He began to leave the house, still laughing. He hadn't quite reached the corner before Adele indignantly called him back.

"Don't you dare leave without a kiss," she said. She put her hands on either side of his face. "Be careful, my dear. Come back soon."

He had never told Adele of his past, but she sensed that something made him always wary.

He felt a chill as her warm hands clutched him, as if he was already a ghost. *Perhaps I should stay. Let the Great Nose form his government without me.*

Adele let him go, and he stepped back. "Yes, well. I'll see you in a fortnight or less."

It had been months since he'd even thought of the Guardians or *them*. His children were taking all his attention.

Young Gaspar was turning out to be more like his mother: talkative, playful, and athletic. Berenice, on the other hand, even though still an infant, clearly took after Heinrich: quiet and somber, her brown eyes followed him around the room. Perhaps if it had been opposite, he would have remembered his own childhood more and would have been more afraid.

Paris was bustling, excited that de Gaulle was taking over. Heinrich was happy to be in the middle of it all. He was in a meeting that later, he could never remember anything about—so incredibly boring that he'd been half asleep in his chair, with his eyes open but his brain switched off, when he felt a heavy hand on his shoulder.

He knew then. Just from that touch.

"Monsieur Bartok," a man whispered in his ear. "You must return home. Something has happened."

They wouldn't tell him, but he knew. He didn't remember leaving the room or getting on the train. He came back to himself only as he reached the outskirts of his village.

It looked as though the entire population of the town was waiting for him at the train station. His best friend, Adrien, who had taken Adele's job at the school teaching English, came up and took him by the arm.

"What's happened?" Heinrich asked. "Just tell me."

"Come to my house," Adrien said. "You can stay with us."

"Why would I go to your house?" Heinrich shouted. The crowd, which had already been quiet, fell completely silent. They were all wearing their Sunday best. And they were all wearing black.

"Your house is gone, Henri," Adrien said. "It burned down in the night. Adele…the children…they're gone."

Heinrich found himself on the ground, looking up at the concerned faces of his friends. Time had passed; the sky was darker, the light diminished. He was covered in dirt. He felt grit in his mouth.

He rose up silently. Adrien moved to help him, but Heinrich grunted warningly and his friend backed away. He felt strangely off balance, as if his legs were sticks. He took a step forward, then, reassured that he wouldn't fall over again, he took another step. Followed by the townspeople, he made his way to the smoking remains of his home.

"How?" he asked. The houses on either side seemed familiar and strange at the same time. There was something wrong, as if the world had suddenly shifted, as if he'd entered a land that looked like his own, but was different, foreign.

"Arson," Adrien said.

"Arson? Someone set the fire?"

"They left a note," Adrien answered. "But it makes no sense." He pulled a smudged piece of paper from his pocket and, with obvious hesitation, handed it over.

It read:

"Blood draws Blood. Guardians will never be safe, nor will you ever be happy. If you make a friend, he will die. If you marry, she will die. If you have children, they will die. And someday, when you are not expecting it, you will die."

Heinrich crumpled up the note and threw it into the still-smoking rubble, where it caught fire and flared up.

"I want to see them," he said.

"You mustn't, Heinrich. It is unbearable. I have seen them...there is nothing you can do."

"Show me," he said quietly but with such force that Adrien stepped back, then turned and led the way to the police station. In the back, under blankets, were three shapes.

They aren't big enough, Heinrich thought.

He reached out with a trembling hand, then froze. The tears started flowing, and then he was gasping, trying to catch his breath between spasms. He was on his knees, his hands on the cloth, unable to draw it aside. Adrien's strong hands pulled him up and half carried him to the door.

Heinrich was left alone on a bed, his face to the wall, unwilling or unable to say anything to anyone. Finally, they all left him alone.

In the middle of the night, he went to the ruins of his house. He dug into the ashes, and the farther down he went, the hotter the debris became until it was burning his hands and arms, scorching away his clothes. He dropped into the black hole of the cellar and felt around for the loose bricks. The fire had not penetrated down here.

His hands brushed across the smooth glass of the bottles and he took them out, one by one. He carried them close to his chest and somehow—later, he couldn't remember how—got out of the hole.

The police station was dark. It was a peaceful village, no need for a gendarme to guard the station. He broke into the back and tore away the shrouds covering his loved ones. In the moonlight they were little more than black, twisted shapes.

Heinrich cried out, numb, but even this horror didn't stop him. He struggled to find Adele's mouth and poured the Blood into it. He was surprised to find himself praying aloud, for he had never prayed in his life, not once. He moved on to his children, using most of a bottle. The Blood flowed over their charred skin, and for a moment he thought he saw a flesh-colored remnant, and then it was gone.

He stepped back, then lowered himself to the floor. He took one of the remaining bottles and lifted it to his lips. The Blood coursed down his throat, and he felt his energy and alertness return. His body was whole, the burns gone. But for the first time after drinking the Blood, he wasn't tumescent.

There was a flatness to the brightness that filled him.

He drank more, and finally he felt something: anger, righteousness, as if a prophet of old had taken over his body. The anger burst out of him, and he was surprised that he didn't burst into flames to join his loved ones.

Heinrich marched out of the police station and climbed the small mountain that overlooked the town, which was really little more than a hill, but with enough height that he could see distant fields in the moonlight. He took another mouthful of Blood. He raised his arms to the sky.

"Come and get me!" he shouted. "I'm ready!"

How long he raged at the moon and into the night, he couldn't remember. Why the Succubus did not wait around to take him when she could have, he never understood. Perhaps she wanted to torture him a little longer.

Then it was dawn. He was on the ground, awakening from a troubled sleep. The desolation of his loss overwhelmed him again.

He arose and stumbled down the hill, but on the other side from the town, and he kept walking.

Chapter 20

Eisheth waited until nightfall before walking back to town. It was easier to maintain the illusion of beauty in the gloom and artificial light. She had tried to heal herself as she waited for the cover of darkness, but she could only do so much. It was either repair her body or use it to maintain her illusion.

There are seedy bars on the outskirts of any town, biker or trucker bars that most people avoid—certainly that single, attractive women avoid. Eisheth found a square box of a building with a single small sign. *Howard's*, it said. When she walked in, every man in the place eyeballed her, as did every woman. There were always a few whiskey-soaked broads around who immediately hated her.

As she walked in the door, she immediately noticed the flyer on the bulletin board. She tore it off and examined it. It wasn't a likeness of her now—she couldn't manage such perfection—but it was close enough. At the bottom of the page was a phone number she recognized, and the address of a high-end hotel. It was Serena Carlton again, she was sure of it. She crumpled up the flyer and threw it in the corner.

It didn't take more than five minutes to entice the first man outside. Within seconds, she was fucking him.

Eisheth didn't *take* him; she just wanted him to climax. She'd get a little bit of his juice that way, though it was only a marginal improvement. Maintaining the illusion of comeliness cost her almost as much as she gained. She adjusted her clothing and went back in, and it was as if the men were already waiting.

She did it again, and again, quickies, with the men undoing their belts and flopping out their cocks and her bending over.

By the fourth guy, she didn't even bother going outside, just did it in the bathroom. By the sixth guy, she didn't even make it that far, but did it in the hallway. She wasn't trying terribly hard to be attractive, instead hoarding the energy, the little spurts of life force that these morally bankrupt men provided, along with the whiskey with which they paid for the easy fuck.

Eisheth didn't have the same hesitation that any mortal woman would have had in her situation, but the experience was still repugnant to her: the grunting, the pounding, the smells of the unwashed, the anger some men felt toward her when they couldn't get it up, and the mess they left behind when they did.

"Don't worry about it, sonny," she snarled at one of them. "I wouldn't want to screw me either."

At some point in the night, Eisheth found herself in the back of the bar itself, on top of a pool table, as one man after another had his way with her. They shoved money into her hands, but she didn't even look. She had a cock in her mouth and one up her ass, and these didn't do her any good at all, but she was too tired, too drunk to fight it, and anything that kept the men coming was all right. It was all for a single goal. Each of these ugly fucks added up to give her one last chance at revenge. If she failed, she'd fade, become a ghost, a nightmare perched on men's chests as they slept, inspiring erotic dreams and gaining another day's meager existence through them.

If she succeeded, she'd be back to herself.

So Eisheth let these awful men fuck her, one after another. Both men and women were chanting, "Fuck, fuck, fuck!" and cheering every time a man released, or pretended to release: no one could tell, because by now she was a sloppy mess, dripping with fluid. The men were having a hard time enjoying it, some doing it because of dares and some because, well, there she was, spread out, ready for the taking.

And finally, she lay abandoned on the pool table, spread-eagled, and no man stepped forward. The bartender stood over her, looking down at her in disgust. "Get out of my bar, you ugly bitch. You just messed up my pool table." He grabbed the money from her fist.

She stood up with as much dignity as she could, nearly bent over in pain, and sticky fluid ran down her legs. She found enough of her clothing to cover herself and stumbled to the door.

"Whore!" one of the women shouted.

"Slut!" yelled another. Then everyone was shouting, as if cheering at a football game.

She told herself didn't care what these humans thought. She began to leave.

"Get out of here, skank!" someone yelled during a lull in the jeering.

It was one taunt too many.

The key was already in the lock, in preparation for closing. Eisheth turned the key and dropped it into her pocket. She drew herself to her full height and faced the mob. The room fell silent. She walked up to a skinny guy with tattoos on his neck and face, certain he was the last to call out, and likely a repeat customer on the pool table. The jeer slid off his face when she dropped her illusion. He cried out and tried to run.

She grabbed him by his shirt, whirled him around, and cut his throat with her talons. She cut the throats of three other men before anyone moved. She hunted the women next, because they had yelled the loudest; they had been the most demeaning. It was like a replay of the sex, a blur of motion, one person after another, killed as violently and bloodily as possible. People were slipping on the blood and gore, trying to get away from Eisheth, piled up at the dead-bolted back entrance.

Finally, it was silent. A groan escaped from the pile of bodies, and Eisheth sought out the source and ended the noise. Now everyone was either dead or hiding beneath the corpses. The silence was total but for the hum of the coolers and the occasional sound of a passing vehicle outside. A couple of neglected arcade games in the corner trilled and boomed once or twice.

Eisheth grabbed a man's body by the shoulders and turned him over. It was the first man she'd fucked, maybe the only man in the room she could've recognized. She sawed through his neck and detached his head, then went over to the bar and set it down facing the front door.

She went back again and again, until the entire length of the bar was covered with severed heads, all facing the door.

Then she went to the bathroom, took off all her clothes, and washed away the blood, even washing her hair. She grabbed handfuls of paper towels, wetted them, and wiped her body, again and again. Finally, her skin was red and raw, but it was clean.

Eisheth felt rejuvenated, energized by the physical domination of so many humans. The death and destruction hadn't tired her at all. It took none of her magical energy, only the energy fueled by her physical body. She walked to the bar, naked, and downed several pickled eggs, washing them down with beer. A good night's rest at a nice hotel, and she'd be good to go.

She searched for the bartender. He was mostly intact, with a stove-in chest. She felt his neck. He was warm but had no pulse. She bit into her wrist and dripped Blood into his mouth, nearly half a cup, enough to keep a living man going for days, enough to revive—for a short time—a dead man.

"Wh- What?" he sputtered in between coughing up his own blood. Then he moaned, "Let me die."

"No problem," Eisheth said. "What's the combination to the safe?"

His eyes filmed over. He was more in the land of the dead than in the land of the living, but he recited the numbers.

"Thank you," she said, rising. She stomped down on the bartender's head, feeling a satisfying crunch under her bare foot. She opened the safe behind the bar, pleased to see it was packed with Friday and Saturday's revenue. She filled a plastic bag with cash and tucked it into her backpack, the only thing she had taken with her from the homeless camp earlier that day—or was it yesterday?

Eisheth risked healing the worst of her wounds, and the Blood finally stopped flowing down her back. She looked in the mirror and flashed into her ingenue form. A beautiful, naked woman looked back, flawless—her hair was a little scraggly, her makeup smeared, but that only made her look like she'd just risen from bed.

She scrounged around for the cleanest clothing she could find: a shirt from someone whom she had cut the legs out from under and pants from a young man who had fallen over a table, which had kept the blood from his severed arm from reaching his lower extremities.

Eisheth was certain she could maintain the illusion of this body long enough to get what she wanted done. She required one last conquest before she left town, one last attempt to become completely whole. To feel like she hadn't just wasted two months in a Western shithole.

She didn't want to try to climb her way back to the top the hard way. Her mind flashed to her sisters, whom she'd had to ask for help in the past and who never let her forget it. She'd have to be far down to resort to calling them.

It was a gamble. If she failed, she'd be weakened even further, fall backward, become a wraith. But if she succeeded, she'd be back on top.

One last Cull, and she'd be in great shape for the next town.

When Eisheth had first arrived in town, her first choice had not been Doug Johnson but his best friend, Cary Deakins. He had dripped with vitality, his life force exuding from his pores.

She'd decided he was too risky. She'd run into his type before. They weren't really playboys; they were just extraordinarily attractive to women. Eventually, either he or the woman would move on, but they almost always remained friends.

Cary Deakins wasn't willing to give himself totally to any woman, at least not now. When he did, it wouldn't be because of looks or sex. When he fell in love, it would be because he saw something deeper in the woman, something spiritual or emotional or intellectual, or all of the above. That was never good for a Succubus.

Given a year or two, Eisheth might have turned him, but she didn't waste that much time on *any* man anymore. She could gain more life force through lesser men through multiple Cullings and take less time doing it.

So she chose his friend, Doug, who was perfect: unimaginative, but solid. His life force was good, if not spectacular.

Now, as she contemplated how best to escape this awful town, her thoughts returned to Cary. He could restore her in one night. That he'd apparently joined forces with that bitch who was following her around the country was even better. Serena Carlton had forced Eisheth take her victims into the wilderness, which in this savage country still had wild animals capable of killing people.

Eisheth would take Cary and kill her tormentor at the same time. The perfect revenge.

It wouldn't be easy. He'd be wary of her, but if she really turned on the glamour, he'd be like most men, when it came right down to it.

He'd fuck her.

A simple fucking, as long as he was a willing partner, would give her the boost she needed.

Then she'd kill the little prick just for being what he was, tempting and unavailable.

She began to leave the bar, then turned around. She found some poster board and markers and started making a sign. The men and women in this bar had been part of the underclass of this culture. Their families weren't the kind of people who went to the police at the first sign of something wrong. Going missing probably wasn't that unusual an occurrence for them.

When Eisheth was done, she was rather proud of her sign. She'd always been the most artistic of the sisters.

Under a nicely drawn skull and crossbones, the sign read:

DANGER!
THIS UNIT UNDER FUMIGATION.
APPLIED: Friday the 21st, 12:00 A.M.
DO NOT ENTER!

She smiled to herself. Anyone smelling something odd would have an explanation, at least for a while.

Long enough for her to finish the job.

Chapter 21

Gasper Gerhard's Journal

Blood calls to Blood. It doesn't matter how little is spilled or how long ago it was taken. The Daughters of Lilith can sense it.

Only the Cutting can negate this effect.

Of course, the more Blood used, the more likely the user will be found. And if the Blood was used recently, the Succubae will sense it all the sooner.

So, here's the question I have struggled with. Why do we—why do I—not destroy the Blood once and for all and remove the temptation? For it is a fact that we will never escape the Succubae as long as the Blood exists.

I suppose each of us has come to the same conclusion. While that might make us—our family—safe, it would do nothing to help the world. The Succubae would continue on, and without the Guardians, there would be no chance of ever stopping them.

But as long as the Blood is in our keeping, there is at least the chance—as slim at it may seem—that someday one of us will use it to destroy the Succubae once and for all.

San Francisco, 1967

Rick Gerhard awoke to soft hands stroking his chest, knowing and skillful.

He couldn't even remember her name. Such were the times. "Free love," they called it.

But nothing is free, Rick thought. *Especially not sex.*

He'd met the hippie girl on the street. She was tall and slim, with large breasts, the fashion model type who had gone the other way, to the unwashed masses. That's the language she used: the "masses" and the "proletariat."

"You have an old soul," she had said. "I can see it in your eyes."

In spite of this seemingly trite observation, which she'd probably made to dozens of guys before, Rick wondered briefly if she possessed some clairvoyant abilities, if she could somehow see past this costume he wore to blend in. So he let her hang around. Maybe she really could see beneath the surface. Besides, he liked that she'd chosen to live on the street instead of on an advertising banner.

Clarrisa? Carrisa? He could never quite remember her name.

He tried ignoring her, but she followed him around. Rick didn't lock his doors—that was considered uncool—and she crawled into his bed one night.

He pushed her away roughly. "I've got an old lady at home," he said.

She was naked, and she was gorgeous. He'd made a Cutting not long before, but even so, he wasn't immune to her attraction.

"Then what are you doing here, babe?" she asked.

"She was bugging me," he said. He'd heard the hippies using such terminology and, ridiculous as it sounded, he mimicked it. "I had to split, man."

The girl was not dissuaded. "Love the one you're with," she murmured softly. Her hand strayed down between his legs, but Rick caught it before she could squeeze his crotch and find nothing there but the rolled-up sock he used for padding.

He took her shoulders and held her until she looked him in the eyes. "You seem like a sweet girl," he said firmly, not sounding like a hippie at all now, though it didn't seem to matter. "That's not the way it works. You're gonna get hurt."

As he spoke, he could see by the spark in her eyes that she was turned on by his forcefulness. He sighed and let her stay.

One night, he went down on her until she finally cried out, "Please, stop!" She stared up at him in wonder. "Are you sure you don't want me to return the favor? I mean, I'd be glad to. I like it."

"Go to sleep, babe," he said, his voice soft. It was the first endearment he'd ever used with her or any woman in a very long time. She smiled, cuddling up to his side. Soon after, she was asleep.

Rick treated her badly after that, calling her his "bitch" and making her follow him around like she was his puppy dog or something. Some part of him wanted to strike back at women, and he wasn't proud of it.

Sometimes when he awoke in the middle of the night and looked at her, he felt a surge of shame, which only made him angrier. He really didn't understand his own reaction.

Now, as her fingers pinched his nipples and then began to explore farther down, he grabbed her wrist. She gave a sharp cry.

"Sorry," he said. He stumbled out of bed, shaking his head to dislodge the fog befuddling him. He took the same drugs that everyone else took, and when it got to be too much, he'd take a dab of Blood to clear his head.

I'm out of Blood, he thought. It scared him that he'd let himself run out. He got out of bed and dressed, keeping his back her as he slipped the usual rolled-up sock in his pants. Clarissa/Carrisa watched him silently. *How much does she know? How much does she suspect?*

There was no denying that he wanted her. More, he wanted her in the manner sex usually took between a man and a woman. Castrated as he was, that shouldn't have been possible, and yet there it was. Perhaps it proved how strong the Succubae stimulus was when all three Daughters of Lilith were together in one place.

But he couldn't allow it.

Rick rose and left his pad. He walked to the upscale garage where he stashed his van. Not long before he'd arrived in Haight Ashbury, he'd bought a van with a picture on it of a soaring eagle holding a bright red peace sign in its claws.

Sometimes Rick felt like a freak in costume. His long hair tickled him in bed at night. The cuffs of his ridiculous bell-bottom pants caught on the corners of things. His bright yellow shirt made him feel like a circus clown. But he needed to blend in, so he looked and dressed like a hippie: a young, vigorous, and handsome hippie, his thick black hair and dark eyes attractive to the opposite sex.

He wandered the streets like an actor in a play. "Groovy, man," was his standard response to things, and he almost laughed every time he said it. Just add "man" to any sentence and he could pass as one of the anti-establishment bohemians.

He could enjoy the drugs—indeed, he had to join in so his erstwhile companions wouldn't be suspicious, but they had little effect on him. He always carried a little of the Blood, which negated the effects. Not too much, because he was worried about the supply. He'd been a little too profligate over the years since he'd thought he'd be the last of the Guardians. At night, he imagined his father scolding him for being so wasteful with the precious Blood.

The atmosphere in Haight Ashbury was spreading, and the rosy glow of free love and drugs and the Summer of Love permeated the city. To be jealous was to be a square. To refuse an offer was to be a jerk. The idea that there might be a reckoning, that people would be damaged, hadn't even entered most of these young people's minds. The whole atmosphere whispered to Rick of the Succubae. They were nearby, fully enjoying a culture so attuned to their own needs and desires. The Daughters of Lilith blended in easily, free spirits completely in tune with the times. The sexual revolution was made for them—indeed, Rick wondered if they weren't responsible for it, as crazy as that sounded.

This was the closest he'd ever come to tracking down the Succubae together in one place. They'd split up over the past few centuries. Individually, their influence was much less noticeable, hidden in the general decadence of the times.

But together, their effect was unmistakable.

Now, he felt an urge despite The Cutting.

It was the deepest hours of night. Even the three sister Succubae were probably asleep. Rick threw open the back of the van and climbed in. It wasn't the usual hippie van with cushions and tapestries—it was full of guns and ammo, and the last four bottles of the Blood of the Succubus, carefully packed and hidden in a locked wooden box he'd bolted to the floor.

Clarrisa/Carrisa was still asleep when he retuned. Rick took the bottle of Blood out of the backpack and hid it in the bottom drawer of

158

the bureau along with a knife. It was a rule: wherever there was the Blood of the Succubus, there was *always* a knife. The revolver, he slid between the mattress and box spring.

He looked down at the girl, feeling more alone than ever. His solitary existence was no longer enough for him. He'd been alone for too long.

I need to become close to someone. Why not this girl?

Rick had gone back to his home in Prague after the death of his wife and children and taken the last of the Blood from the stone jars. What he had with him was all that was left.

It didn't matter how much danger he put himself in. He was going to track the Succubae down and put an end to them. That's what he'd believed.

Now he was starting to suspect it wasn't going to happen in his lifetime. The Succubae covered their tracks too well. Even if he destroyed one of them, it would only make the others that much harder to find, unless he could destroy the three of them at the same time.

One thing he did know: he would have to catch them by surprise. He would have to kill them when they thought they were invincible, when no man could resist their charisma. He would come upon them unnoticed, a mere shadow of a man, drink the Blood of the Succubae, and then kill them.

But how? Rick wondered.

It was a Catch-22. He couldn't sneak up on them using the Blood; he couldn't kill them without it. Weapons couldn't kill them, but they could be reduced to bodiless spirits. Other Guardians had succeeded in destroying their physical bodies, but the Succubae always came back.

To fully destroy them, Rick must kill them with his bare hands, choking the life out of them while he pressed his sex against theirs. He must kill them while their attraction was magnified a thousand times.

He wasn't strong enough. No man was.

Rick took the bottle from the dresser drawer, holding it in his hands, staring at it. He no longer used stone jars, but modern glass bottles with lids. The Blood shimmered red even in the dim light.

159

At last, he uncorked it and took a long drink. Rick was engorged in a moment. For the first time, he fully felt the atmosphere of Haight Ashbury, the haze of drugs and youth and freedom and, most of all, sex. It permeated the air, an aphrodisiac, and it came from *them*.

Clarrisa/Carrisa awoke and sat up in bed, staring up at Rick with wide eyes. He grinned at her, then slowly, deliberately, removed his clothes, watching her all the while. When his shorts puddled on the floor at last, she finally spoke, her eyes riveted on his cock. "Oh, wow," she breathed.

She reached out for him, putting her hands around his middle, and pulled him toward her. He groaned as her lips enveloped him, returning the favor he'd given her the previous night.

It turned her on as much as it turned him on.

Then they cuddled for a while, letting the anticipation build again. He kissed her breasts, giving them all his attention, and finally she moaned and pulled him on top of her.

He slid into her, finally feeling the closeness he'd been longing for. She wrapped her arms and legs around him as if she had waited for him forever. It was everything he'd been hungering for and more. He felt like a thirty-eight-year-old virgin in the body of a sixteen-year-old, and he couldn't hold back his eagerness.

He was afraid of hurting her as he slammed into her, but she grabbed him roughly and reared up at him, grunting. The headboard smacked against the wall rhythmically, and she cried out in pleasure. Rick almost laughed; it seemed so ludicrous. But his desire grew, then overflowed, wave after wave of pleasure coursing through his body.

Finally, Rick let himself laugh in relief. The girl seemed a little put out that he'd come so fast.

"It's not you," he said. "It's just that it's been so long."

"Your old lady isn't taking care of you?"

"You could say that," he snorted. He leaned over and looked in her eyes. "How do you say your name, anyway? Clarissa?"

"Close. Claresa," she said, spelling it out: "C-l-a-r-e-s-a."

They made love again, slowly this time, and Rick fell asleep in her arms. In his dreams, he made love to her again and again. They were living in a small house in a small town, safe and secure. As they grew older and more accustomed to each other, the pleasure only increased. They raised a son, tall and dark, and Rick taught him from an early age. It was the life he was going to live, he was sure of it.

Then the boy faded away, and the small house, and even Claresa. Instead, he was screwing a temptress, a woman of unbelievable proportions, and he couldn't stop climaxing, again and again, until his body was wracked with such pleasurable pain that he awoke, his heart pounding, his cock engorged from the mere thought of the Succubus.

Then he realized it was more than just the thought of her; it was her presence.

Claresa slept on, but Rick jumped out of the bed, turning to the door. A slim, dark silhouette stood in the doorway. Her chemise barely reached her thighs.

Naamah. The name leapt into his mind from the years of studying the texts left by his ancestors. *Naamah, the Whore.* She walked toward him, her lithe, sensuous movements arousing him further.

He was frozen in place by sheer desire. He wanted her, wanted to make love to her in a frenzy unlike any he had ever…

Claresa groaned in her sleep, and the memory of their sweet, natural lovemaking somehow gave Rick the strength to move. He sprang for the knife, grabbed it, and mutilated himself. The pain was intense, but he'd learned to endure it. He managed to stay on his feet.

The Succubus screeched, losing her human form for a moment. The sexual energy disappeared from the room in a rush, and he saw her for what she was. Her face was made of sharp angles, her body was emaciated and flabby, her hair a tangled mess. Her cat eyes grew predatory.

She flew at him. He ducked, reached for the revolver under the bed, turned, and fired without aiming. The first two bullets missed. The next one caught the creature in the throat, and her screaming became an angry gurgle. Another bullet missed. The next lodged in Naamah's right breast.

"Ohmygod! Ohmygod!" Claresa cried as she rose from the bed.

Rick shouted "Stay back!," but she ran for the door as he fired the last bullet. The Succubus moved so fast that the bullet only grazed her, flying unhindered to hit Claresa in the back of her head.

161

The Succubus lunged for Rick, who stumbled, then fell onto the floor. She stood over him, Blood dripping onto him.

As the Blood trickled into his mouth, he kicked out with both feet squarely into her stomach, and she stumbled backward, gasping for air. He reached for her throat, but she kept falling, crashing though the window.

Rick stumbled to his feet and grabbed the extra bullets in his backpack, fumbling to reload the revolver. Only then did he peer out the window.

Naamah was nowhere to be seen. He closed his eyes and leaned his head against the window sash. Then, fearing what he'd find, he turned.

Claresa lay facedown in a pool of blood, a small hole in the back of her head, seeming asleep. When he rolled her over, he saw that her face was gone.

"Claresa," he murmured. He cradled her for a time, rocking her, remembering how she'd looked lying under him, eyes shining with love. Finally, as dawn came through the shattered window, Rick covered her with a blanket and left the room.

In Haight Ashbury, it seemed as if all the energy of free love and happiness disappeared overnight. One day, everyone was living in a dream, and the next came reality. The drugs became addicting, and the sex wasn't as sweet.

Later, the press would mark the unsolved murder of Claresa Hodgkins as the end of the Summer of Love.

Chapter 22

"Note to self," Cary muttered to Serena between interviews. "Never put your hotel name and room number as contact information on a flyer offering reward money."

Serena grimaced, but nodded her agreement. "I ended up renting the entire floor just to pacify the managers. They're kind of put out by all the foot traffic."

Cary nodded, "I'll bet. Fancy boutique hotel like this in the middle of Bend…and this isn't exactly the clientele they cater to."

The line stretched down the hallway of Serena's hotel. Her number and Cary's were on the flyer, too, and their phones had never stopped ringing. The phone calls were easy to screen, but between all the niceties of introductions and the hemming and hawing of vague descriptions, the personal interviews took forever.

Another young couple came in. They were a little twitchy, as if they needed something to calm them down.

"It's my neighbor, man," the guy said. "A real bitch."

"How long has she lived there?" Cary asked.

"A couple of years," the woman said.

Cary shook his head. "Not her, but thanks for coming in."

"Are you sure?" the guy asked. "We really need the money."

"I'm certain," Cary said as politely as he could. After two hours of interviews, he could tell in ten seconds whether the informant had anything pertinent to report or was just hoping to get lucky—hell, he could tell simply by looking at them.

Turned out the picture of Suzanne/Kristen was vague enough to have features that resembled almost everyone's cousin, sister, or friend. Most were only repeating what they'd already heard. Or they'd seen Suzanne before the events in question, but not since. Cary and Serena interviewed twenty-five people before they got their initial break, though they didn't know it at first.

"She attends Bend High School," said a pimply faced young man. "Her name is Cathy something."

"Cathy something?" Serena repeated, exchanging a look with Cary.

"Well, yeah. Can't be too many of those, right? She's been hanging out with Jeremy Hawkins."

Cary entered the information into the computer. "We'll be in touch if your information proves useful," he said. Serena ushered the young man out of the room and invited the next visitor in.

It was another young person, an extremely skinny girl who gave pretty much the same information as the previous supplicant.

"None of them have seen her in the last few days," Serena said as Cary closed the door.

"But at least we know she's still in town," Cary said.

A couple of teenagers came in, more high schoolers, and Cary was already pretty sure what they'd say. The boy was good-looking, tall, with long, dark hair and straight teeth. Cary caught Serena giving him an appreciative glance. He was surprised to feel a momentary pang of jealousy. He'd been fantasizing about Serena ever since he met her, but he hadn't taken the fantasies seriously. The girl was cute, but a little stocky—the kind of girl who'd be heavier in a few years. She was holding one of the flyers. Once they sat down on the couch, she smoothed out the folded paper on the coffee table.

"We know who this is," she said, slapping her hand on the paper.

Cary wanted to groan. He was so tired of this. Instead, he stretched his legs out in front of him and spread his arms along the back of the sofa. "Hi, kids. Let me guess, you want to tell us about a girl named Cathy who goes to Bend High."

The girl's smile slipped a notch, and they both nodded hesitantly.

"That's it," Cary announced rubbing his palms over his face. All they'd learned was that Suzanne/Cathy was still in town, for all the good it did them. "I'm done."

The girl looked completely crestfallen. Cary didn't even bother to enter the information into the computer. He'd already stopped taking names over the last hour because it seemed so pointless. He stood up. "Thanks for coming in."

The boy still hadn't spoken. He rose to follow the girl. At the last second, he paused at the door. His hand was clenched tight on the knob. Then he whirled around.

"You don't understand," he blurted. "I *know* her. She's dangerous."

Serena and Cary exchanged a startled glance. Here it was—the confirmation they'd been looking for.

"Are you Jeremy?" Serena asked.

"Uh...yeah."

Serena stepped toward the couple as if she wanted to hug them. They backed away, and Serena stopped, abashed. "I can't *tell* you how glad I am to see that you're alive, and away from her," she said after a long silence, her voice sounding choked. She dared to take the boy's hand, clasping it in both of hers. "Please, sit back down and tell us about it."

The boy and girl looked at each other, and Cary could read their minds: *What kind of craziness is this?* He held his breath, and sure enough, they sat back down. Whatever craziness Cary and Serena were offering, it was probably nothing compared to what they'd already experienced.

The boy turned slightly toward the girl. "I'm Jeremy. This is my friend, Lucinda Peters," he said.

Serena nodded and offered her a hand. "Thanks for coming, both of you. Cary? Would you go into the hallway and thank the others? Tell them we're not taking any more interviews at this time."

"Sure," Cary said. "Don't start without me."

The hallway was still full, but he sensed there was no new information there, only the hope of reward. He tried to let everyone down as easily as he could. There was some muttered grumbling, but mostly just shrugs and sighs, except for the very last couple, a rough-looking pair that most of the others in line seemed to be avoiding.

"To hell with this!" the woman shouted. "That bitch tried to steal my boyfriend! I'll be damned if I'm just going to leave without some answers."

Cary hesitated and turned around. The woman had pushed her way to the head of the line. Her boyfriend, who was a short, dumpy fellow without much hair on the top of his head, was blushing furiously at her outburst.

Cary waved them over. *This woman is really angry*, he realized. "When did this happen?" he asked.

"This very afternoon," she said. "In broad daylight. The bitch had no shame."

There is no bullshit here, Cary realized. They'd met the real thing, and apparently even more recently than Jeremy and Lucinda.

"Why don't you come inside?" he said mildly. They followed Cary into the suite, their eyes wide in wonder. The girl whistled. "Nice digs."

Serena was sitting on the couch with the other couple, and she looked up with a frown.

"These two," Cary began to explain, then turned to them. "What're your names?"

"Bobbie Jo and Adam, sir," the woman answered for both of them.

Sir? Was this the first time he'd ever been called sir? *Damn.* But Cary decided that making an issue of it would only embarrass them. "All right. This is Bobbie Jo and Adam." He caught Serena's eye, and she saw the seriousness in his expression. "Apparently, they saw Suzanne a few hours ago."

"She called herself Ginger," Adam said. "But she looked just like the picture, all the way."

Serena stood up and welcomed them. "Ginger," she said thoughtfully. "She had red hair, I assume?"

The couple nodded, looking intimidated. They were fish out of water, the surroundings too luxurious for them to quite take in.

Serena offered them refreshments out of the packed mini fridge. Lucinda and Jeremy took Cokes, but the other couple each took a small bottle of booze and some peanuts, which they quickly drank and gobbled down. They talked about the fanciness of the suite for a while, as if it was equally amazing to all of them, until they got a little more comfortable. Serena offered them seconds.

"Thank you, ma'am," Adam muttered. Cary caught the look of surprise and amusement in Serena's eye. Still, she was good at making the newcomers feel welcome.

When they were settled in, Serena took charge.

"I met Kristen—the girl in the sketch—five years ago," she began, then hesitated. "Forgive me...I want to hear *your* stories. Why don't you go ahead and tell us what you saw? Cary and I will go last. But it is *imperative* you tell us *everything*. Your stories might sound wild, even to your own ears. You may be hesitant to describe everything for fear of looking crazy, but I encourage you not to hold back, no matter how unreal it seems." The ticking of the clock on the wall was loud in the silence. "There is very little you can say that I won't believe," Serena added.

"I'll tell you exactly what I saw," Bobbie Jo said in a loud voice. "She was screwing my boyfriend, and she weren't no woman. She was a witch. Long, pointy nose, and wild-ass hair, and swinging boobs. Weren't no human at all. She was a demon or something."

"Is that what you saw too?" Serena asked Adam.

Adam jerked his head up and down. "But you gotta understand, she was gorgeous at first. I mean, I knowed I shouldn't have falled for her, but you shoulda seen her!" He aimed an apologetic glance at Bobbie Jo. "I'm sorry. I was too weak to resist."

"Not your fault, lover," Bobbie Jo said, patting his leg reassuringly. "She was a temptress, a witch."

"Not your *fault*?" Lucinda said incredulously.

Cary cut her off before she could embarrass the other couple. "What happened next?"

"I kicked the shit out of her, that's what happened," Bobbie Jo said. "She ran away like a coward, naked, into the desert. I hope she freezes out there. I hope the coyotes get her. I hope the ravens peck out her eyes."

It was a strange story, but tellingly, no one objected. No one got up to leave.

Serena turned to the younger couple. The girl stared wide-eyed at Jeremy as if wondering what she'd gotten herself into. But Jeremy nodded in confirmation.

"I'm glad you laid it out," he told Bobbie Jo. "I probably would've fudged a little, because it's really…it sounds insane."

He told the story of his seduction. Halfway through, he started looking embarrassed. He kept giving Lucinda little glances, as if checking to see how she was taking it, but she remained impassive, staring at her hands.

"Cary?" Serena said.

It was easier for him, after hearing the others. It didn't sound so crazy. And, well, it had really happened, and either they'd believe him or they wouldn't. So he told his story in turn, adding more details as he became more and more certain that they wouldn't reject it out of hand.

Finally, it was Serena's turn to tell her story. Everyone paid particular attention to what she said, because all of them sensed that she knew more than the rest of them.

She told them how she had been unwilling to believe her son was guilty of a heinous crime. How she researched Kristen's past and discovered that she wasn't what she appeared, and how the more she explored, the worse it got.

"This I know," Serena finished. "She is a creature from the dawn of time, preying on men's sexual appetites, draining them of their life force. You mustn't feel embarrassed about falling for her, any more than being put under the spell of a witch would embarrass you. It's dark magic. No, it's older than dark magic; it is the well from which dark magic flows."

Bobbie Jo laughed. "Man, if I'd heard this story a couple of days ago, I'd have said you were full of bullshit. But I know what I saw."

The others nodded, even Lucinda, who, though she hadn't seen the Succubus herself, except in her human "sweet bitch" form, seemed convinced by the others' stories. She cut to the chase. "What do we do?"

"She's been weakened," Serena answered. "She's been frustrated twice now. It takes a good deal of magical energy to maintain her illusions. Neither Adam nor Jeremy gave her what she needed, thank God. And before that, I doubt she finished with Doug Johnson." She paused, then leaned forward to speak slowly and clearly to Adam and Jeremy. "You must understand this: you would be dead now if you hadn't interrupted her plans, both of you. If she succeeded, you'd be dead and she'd be gone, and we'd be back at square one, but as it is, she may not have the strength to leave the area."

"So all we have to do is keep her from screwing someone?" Bobbie Jo asked. She cocked an eyebrow at Serena. "You do know what men are like, don't you?"

Serena smiled. "Yes, but she's probably no longer the attractive vixen you saw before. She's been diminished. She'll find it harder to attract a man now, but...you're right, she can always find a willing victim. But simply screwing someone won't gain her much. She needs for her quarry to be in love with her to truly gain strength, and that takes time. What she'll do is look for prey that is easier to catch—probably men with lower socioeconomic status."

Bobbie Jo frowned but didn't speak.

"If her past is any indication, she'll go places where she doesn't have to try very hard or need to be too good-looking," Serena continued. "Tomorrow, we'll fan out with the flyers and see if we can't find where she's hiding."

Lucinda stood up, straightening her skirt, looking uncomfortable.

"What is it, Lucinda?" Serena asked.

"I...believe you, I guess. But why do we have to do anything about it? Why us? Why not just let the...the Succubus leave town?"

"Yeah," Bobbie Jo said. "What's this 'we' business? You wanted information and we gave you information. That's it. Give us our money and we'll be on our way."

Adam had been sitting quietly. Now he stood up, facing Bobbie Jo.

"We have to help," Adam said. "We can't let her keep doing this stuff."

Jeremy also stood up, standing next to Adam. "I agree," he said, turning to Lucinda apologetically. "You weren't there. It was scary and horrible and irresistible. And it was wrong. It has to stop."

Lucinda hesitated, then reached up from the sofa and took his hand. She nodded. Bobbie Jo still didn't look convinced.

169

"What the hell?" she muttered. "Are vampires and werewolves next?"

Cary looked over at Serena, who said, "Listen, it's dinnertime. Why don't I take you all to a meal in the restaurant downstairs? My treat. We'll talk this over."

Adam and Bobbie Jo immediately agreed, but Jeremy looked hesitant.

Serena suddenly remembered how young her new friends were. "Do you need to call your parents?" she asked.

"Not me," Lucinda said. "They think I'm at a cheerleader camp."

Jeremy's response wasn't so quick. "My parents are out of town," he said doubtfully. "But I probably should call my sister."

"Why don't you do that?" Serena said. "We'll reconvene downstairs."

"Hey, Marty, I ran into some friends," Jeremy said into his phone, trying to keep a light tone in his voice. "I'll probably stay with them tonight."

"Are you with Cathy?" his sister asked suspiciously.

"No!" Jeremy exclaimed in surprise. "I'm...I'm done with her."

"But you're with a girl, aren't you?" Marty said. "I can tell when you're lying."

Jeremy suddenly wondered why he was hiding it. "I'm with Lucinda, if you really want to know."

"Lucinda?" his sister said. There was a long pause. *Will she tell me to come home? Will she call our parents?*

"Have fun, Jeremy." Marty hung up. Jeremy could almost hear the glee in her voice.

He turned with a half smile. Lucinda was standing close to him, so close that he wanted nothing more than to lean into her. The others had already gone down the elevator.

"Let's take the stairs," Lucinda said.

He banged open the door the stairwell, and a breeze came up toward them.

"Do you really believe Serena?" she asked. "I mean, about the Succubae?"

He nodded. "I do. You had to be there. There was something really weird about Cathy. I mean, nothing that could be explained by the natural world. I was bewitched…" He looked over at her. *I need to let her know.* "I didn't see her for what she was until too late."

"I *knew* she was a sweet bitch," Lucinda said. "Maybe not a literal monster, but there was something really strange about her."

"A sweet bitch?

Lucinda shrugged. "You know, a girl who is nice to your face and terrible behind your back."

"Well, she was *that.*"

Chapter 23

Gasper Gerhard's Journal

How ironic that the Guardianship has been passed down from son to son. Daughters are ignored, kept in the dark, or if told anything, consigned to being mere helpmates. It is the patriarchal thing to do. I might be the first one in my family to even question it.

And yet, who better to confront the Daughters of Lilith than women, most of whom are immune to the seductive charms of the Succubae?

I do not know how such a thing could happen, or what would be the results. But it should be tried. Perhaps it is up the male of the species to put an end to the Succubae, since we were the ones who created them, who transformed Goddesses who gave us their blessing into demons who want our destruction.

But women could help us understand, perhaps. Women could give us strength.

For what force could stand in the face of the sexual power of the Succubae but the love of women? Who else could turn a man away from his base desires?

The generations of women growing up now, who are demanding equality, will change the equation. Perhaps they will even help us finally win.

Crescent City, 1995

Rick was going to kill the Daughters of Lilith. He didn't care how long it took or what it cost.

He would have approached the shadow Guardians, except for two things. The first was that he was pretty sure that he'd been tracked down in France because their emissary had been followed. At the least,

172

the American hadn't been careful about using the name Gerhard in his search.

The second reason was the shadow Guardians wanted to capture, not kill, the Succubae. Rick doubted that was possible, but even if it was, it wasn't the right thing to do. The Succubae had to be destroyed, removed from this world once and for all. The sisters and their Blood were a thing of the distant past, before history, before science, from a time when myths and legends were real. That time was over.

The three sisters were never together again after the Summer of Love, at least not as far as Rick could tell. He read all the newspapers and magazines he could get his hands on, but for a time, it was as if the Daughters of Lilith had disappeared off the face of the Earth. Being that they were immortal, he doubted that.

It turned out that they were just getting better at hiding. There was evidence of each of them—alone—in various parts of the world, and that was vaguely reassuring. That they stayed separate was a good thing, for it was when they were all together that the world seemed to bend to their wishes and bad things began to happen.

Rick got so he could recognize each of the sisters individually.

Agrat Bat, for instance, tended to spend her time among the rich and powerful, who had their own reasons to hide their sex scandals, even (or especially) if they resulted in death. Still, rumors emerged: such and such a hedge fund manager hadn't died from a heart attack— or rather, he had, but only after a night of gymnastic sex. Or a princeling in some small, inconsequential country hadn't really died in a car accident, but had been found, a dried-up husk, inside a sports car parked in some vacant garage.

Naamah, the youngest sister, spent most of her time among the down and out, where the missing and the dead were hardly noticed.

The easiest to track was Eisheth, who lived among the middle class and had difficulty hiding her more frequent crimes. But even for her, evidence of her crime was diminishing.

By the middle of the 1990s, Rick knew roughly where each of the three sisters were. Naamah was in South America, Agrat Bat was in the Middle East, and Eisheth was in Europe.

It had taken him decades to get over the death of Adele and his children, and then Claresa. He'd sworn to never again become close to another person, especially a woman. And he'd reluctantly once again come to the conclusion that he was not going to be the Guardian who put an end to Succubae.

He needed an heir.

He chose the last name of Carr and drove his old hippie van to Crescent City, a small town in California near the Oregon border. He rented a small house, and one night took half a sip of the Blood to see what would happen. He felt a stirring, but it wasn't quite enough. He took two more sips, and he was restored.

This time, he left the knife in its sheath.

Then he proceeded to systematically date all the eligible women in the small town, with the intention of procreation. He had money, and he spent it publically, and it wasn't long before many of the single females in town made themselves available.

Love wasn't necessary, only that Rick convince his intended it was there.

He encountered a sweet, good-natured woman on the beach one day, and to his great surprise, they were soon talking up a storm, as if they were old friends.

Susan was newly divorced and informed him that she had no intention of marrying again. Ironically, she seemed to be the only woman in town that didn't know he was rich—or care.

Three months later, after a quick ceremony, they were husband and wife. Three months later, she was pregnant. For the next nine months, Rick kept a watchful eye out for any sign of the Succubae. The child was a boy. They named him Richard, because Susan thought that was the origin of Rick, and he didn't disabuse her of the notion.

As soon as his son was born, Rick had an "accident"—or so he told his wife. In reality, he had resumed the Cutting.

It was his plan all along: procreate, in the most cold-blooded way possible, and then disappear. When his son was old enough, he'd come back and teach boy what he needed to know.

Susan was very understanding about his "accident," though he knew she was disappointed. She was younger than him, and she still wanted physical contact, sex and cuddling, and though he tried to satisfy her in other ways, it wasn't surprising to discover she had taken a lover. She tried to make it up to Rick, but he decided it was for the best.

He took a hard line, and they divorced. Rick gave her a nice settlement, and he moved away. It was all part of the plan. And yet, it surprised him how much he missed her and his son.

Susan remarried, and when Rick visited ten years later, his son didn't even know him.

Richard was a handsome boy, maybe a little small for his age, with dark brown eyes and short-cropped hair. He seemed interested in his birth father, and certainly wasn't averse to letting Rick buy him presents from the pricey downtown stores. He even seemed OK with just walking on the beach and talking. But Rick noticed something.

"Why doesn't he ever smile?" he asked Susan after bringing the boy home from a movie.

She gave him an odd look. "Because he's like his father?"

"What do you mean?"

Susan shook her head. "Don't worry about it. He's a serious boy, but he's happy. It's just that he tends to think about things more than most kids his age."

There was an unfamiliar tightening in Rick's chest, and he was flooded with warmth, leaving him breathless, unable to speak. *Love.* He'd almost forgotten the emotion. *This is what it feels like to love someone.*

He decided to leave and never come back. The longer he was there, the more chance the Succubae would find his family. It terrified him to love someone as much as he loved his son.

Before Rick left, Richard finally spoke to him. It was the first time he'd opened up without being spoken to first. "When you come back, I want to know…" he began, then stopped.

"Know what?"

"Why we're different," Richard said. His dark brown eyes stared into his father's, and Rick had the sudden sensation that he was talking to himself at the age of ten, with the same mysteries and the same questions.

"I promise," Rick said, amazed that he could lie so well.

He started to walk away. He was overcome with emotion. He wanted to turn around, grab his son, and take him away. But he didn't dare.

"Dad," Richard said.

Rick turned, and the look of earnestness on his son's face almost made him break down then and there and tell him the truth.

"I really want to help you," Richard said. "With whatever it is."

Before he knew it, Rick had strode over to Richard and clasped him in a tight hug. It was the first time, and perhaps the last time, but it felt right.

"Next time I see you," he said, "I'll explain everything."

That seemed to be enough for Richard. He went back to playing with the remote control car Rick had purchased for him that morning.

Rick packed up Gasper Gerhard's journal and a bottle of the Blood in a box and gave it to Susan. They were still friendly. Rick paid his child support on time, and he usually added something extra.

"Give this to Richard when he's sixteen," he instructed her.

"This has the answers?" she asked.

"What answers?"

"To the mystery of Rick Carr," Susan said. "Never mind. I'll make sure he gets it. I won't even open it myself. I owe you that much."

"Thank you," he said. "See you soon."

"Rick?"

"Yeah?"

"Goodbye."

Rick bought an old farmhouse in Nebraska with a deep cellar. He sat in darkness for month after month. When he felt himself fading, he took a sip of the Blood.

He Cut himself almost every day, punishing himself.

Drink the Blood, restore his body, Cut it away. Again and again, the pain took him away from everything else. The pain was his companion. It was better than being alone. Better than being whole. Better than remembering...

Too many people had died for him.

But no more.

When he finally emerged, it was because he was using up the Blood of the Succubus.

He decided to allow himself to grow older.

Years went by without him restoring himself. His limbs crabbed up and his face aged, furrowed with wrinkles; his hands became arthritic knobs. Another way of punishing himself, he supposed. He had enough time to be self-reflective, but it was distant, as if happening to another person.

As the years passed, Rick made halfhearted efforts to track the Daughters of Lilith, but in truth, he had given up.

He posted messages all over the Internet and got some good leads, but always a little too little and a little too late. There were hints of their presence, but he could never be sure. The Succubae were careful to leave their hunting grounds as soon as they had fed. He was always playing catch-up.

And then he met Serena online.

She revived his faith. She'd lost her son, and seemed as committed as he was to the destruction of the Succubae. He had had others respond to his website, but most of them were flakes and poseurs. The Succubae left few witnesses.

He followed Serena's travels, and then one day, the signs pointed to a town not far away from where he was hiding. She messaged him:

Serena: *She's here. In Bend, Oregon. And she's injured.*

Rick: *You're positive?*

Serena: *There is no doubt. I have more than one witness.*

Rick: *Wait there. I'm coming.*

He logged off and then had second thoughts. He turned the computer back on.

Rick: *Whatever you do, don't confront her until I get there.*

He loaded up the old hippie van with its eagle and its peace sign and drove it out of his garage, somewhat surprised that it still ran, and headed west to Oregon.

Chapter 24

The Daughters of Lilith crawled from the caves beneath the mountains as little more than animals. Agrat Bat was nearly incorporeal. Naamah managed to retain the form of an old woman, while Eisheth looked like a small, withered ape.

For the first few years, they skittered about the habitations of man, hiding until night, lurking in the shadows as men and women had intercourse and lapping up the small emotions of these poor wretches of the earth, who barely had time to eat and sleep, much less love.

Naamah became a Succubus first, finally attaining an attractive enough form to lure a man into an alley, Culling him to the bone. Agrat Bat soon followed, with Eisheth last of all. They stayed by each other's sides in those days, for together, they magnified their allure to humans.

They moved about the world, taking what they needed and moving on before it was noticed. Still, legends began to be attached to their travels, and sometimes, when they arrived in a small town, some people seemed to instinctively sense their natures.

When that happened, the sisters quickly moved on, for while they were strong enough to take on humans in small groups, they were wary of entire populations getting wind of them.

They once made the mistake of entering a village in daylight. They had been on the road for days, without encountering a soul. They were tired and hungry.

An old woman was drawing water from the well in the village square. She glanced at them, then returned to her chores.

The Daughters of Lilith had been lulled into complacency. It had been a long time since they'd been confronted. When the old woman was done drawing her water, Agrat Bat went to the well and cranked up the bucket, but she was so thirsty she used more of her strength than she should have.

The old woman walked off without giving them a second glance. Her casual stroll had been an act, though.

A short time later, there was a far-off shout of alarm, so primal that Naamah transformed for an instant into her original form…just as many of the villagers appeared at windows and doorways, alarmed by the scream.

Upon seeing Naamah, the villagers rushed into the square en masse.

The Succubae tried to escape but were surrounded. Eisheth saw Naamah pierced by pitchforks, pinned against an alley wall. Agrat Bat strode toward the makeshift barricade, upending the carts and tossing men and women into the air. Eisheth followed, killing those who escaped the wrath of her older sister.

As they reached the woods, there was a shriek behind them. Only then did they notice that Naamah wasn't with them. Eisheth started back, but Agrat Bat grabbed her arm.

"It is too late. They are too many."

They waited at the edge of the woods as night fell. A glow lit up the village, and Naamah's screams and curses reached them above the shouts of the villagers. Then there was silence, and a slow dimming of the light.

At dawn, Agrat Bat and Eisheth marched into the village, daring the humans to confront them. No one dared to stop them from retrieving Naamah's blackened corpse from the stake.

For a few years, Agrat Bat and Eisheth traveled the countryside accompanied by a large wooden box as Naamah slowly grew flesh and bone. Eventually, she emerged, looking like a wizened child, to take vengeance on the villagers who had burned her.

After that experience, they learned to disguise themselves, to use their powers secretively. They gravitated to larger and larger settlements, the better to blend in. They began to travel separately, for their powers became too strong. Whenever they were together, those times in history became known for excess.

Humans themselves covered up the sisters' crimes, for the truth was too terrible to conceive.

In ancient Greece, Eisheth became the first of the Hetaera, who mingled with the educated, while Naamah gravitated to the streets; Peripatetic prostitutes followed her example. Agrat Bat established the tradition of consecrated prostitutes of the temples.

When Greece declined, Agrat Bat and Eisheth moved on, but Naamah stayed long enough to see the emergence of young Alexander the Great. She Culled him at the height of his powers.

Julius Caesar and Marc Anthony also fell under the spell of a Succubus and were led to their doom. Agrat Bat had to change her appearance after that, for the tale of Cleopatra became too widely known.

They were in Nero's Rome, with his court, and urged the young emperor to his excesses. Caligula they groomed from an early age. Agrat Bat stayed in the empire for some time, overseeing its long decline.

In India, the *Kama Sutra* was written in their honor, and they encouraged tantric sex as a spiritual practice. Many a devotee gave themselves to the Daughters of Lilith in the mistaken belief that he would transcend mortal bonds.

The Japanese were so taken by their presence that after the Succubae left their country, they tried to replace them with the geishas, though none ever neared the legendary status of the first of their kind.

Casanova was their disciple.

For a time, the young Marquis de Sade traveled at their side, and they even dared to show him their true form. Naamah took a liking to him and let him live.

They were in the Belle Epoch, at the Moulin Rouge, and when the Victorian era arrived, they easily adjusted to the repressed but still rampant sexual atmosphere. When the era of motion pictures arrived, they went to Hollywood. Irving Thalberg begged Eisheth to star in one of his pictures. She Culled him instead.

The Roaring Twenties were but a prelude to the Swinging Sixties.

It was only as the sisters neared the new millennia that they began to be noticed. Most often, their crimes were blamed on serial killers or others. But they stayed apart, mostly, each finding her own way of staying hidden.

Until now.

Chapter 25

After they ordered dinner, but before it arrived, Serena cleared her throat. The others turned to her expectantly.

"Kristen is here," she began.

"Kristen?" Bobbie Jo objected. "I thought her name was Suzanne. Or was it Ginger?"

"He name is *Cathy*," Lucinda interjected, sounding quite certain.

"I don't actually know her real name," Serena said. "It could be any of the Succubae."

"There are *more* of them?" Adam said, his eyes huge.

"At least three," Serena said. "There are many different myths about them. Or maybe there are different kinds of Succubae. I'm not completely sure."

"How do you know all this?" Lucinda asked.

"I have a….a source. Someone named Rick. I've never met him, only talked to him online, but he seems to know everything."

"Online?" Bobbie Jo said skeptically. "How do you know you can trust him?"

"Everything he has ever told me has checked out. He wants to find Kristen as much as I do, maybe more," Serena replied. "According to him, there are three Succubae, who are called the Daughters of Lilith. Their names are Agrat Bat, Eisheth, and Naamah."

There was a long silence after that bombshell.

Finally Cary spoke up. "Well, let's deal with the Succubus we got."

Serena nodded. "I believe it is Eisheth."

"How do we find her?" Jeremy asked.

"This is new territory for me, too," Serena said. "Rick is a little secretive. Now I'm dipping into my own research on the myths and legends. Have you ever seen picture of a Succubus, a monstrous-looking woman, crouched on the chest of a sleeping man? That is the image most of humanity knows them as—a dream, a nightmare, a figment of our imagination. But all of us have felt something similar: the feeling that we can't move, that someone is in the room with us. Nowadays, we're as likely to think it's an alien as a Succubus. Sleep experts even have a name for it: hypnagogia."

"I thought sleep paralysis was normal," Cary said. "It keeps us from moving around while we are dreaming. You know, so we don't fall out of bed and break our necks."

"Yeah, that kind of thing happens to all of us," Serena said. "Sometimes there is something physical causing it. Sometimes the nightmare is real."

"How does it help for the Succubus to scare us?" Jeremy asked. "Isn't she after our sexual energy?"

"She's after more than that," Serena said. "She uses sex to make the victim emotionally vulnerable, to open his heart to her. Once the Succubus gets that far, she can suck up that inner spirit and make it her own. The best kind of energy of all comes at the moment of death, if that death occurs at the moment of orgasm."

"What a way to go," Adam said. Bobbie Jo giggled with him, and Serena frowned, waiting for them to compose themselves.

"That's how she gets away with it," Serena said. "But to answer your question: she's after our life force, or rather, *your* life force, because you're a man. My son..." Her voice broke, and she looked down so they couldn't see her eyes. "In the process, sometimes she unintentionally frightens the victim. Even when they're sure it's real, people..." Again her voice broke as she remembered her son's pleading, "People don't believe them. But that's all accidental, a byproduct of what she's really after."

"So she needs sexual energy," Jeremy said. "Too bad there isn't any of *that* going around."

"Sex? What's that?" Bobbie Jo added sarcastically.

184

"Yes, but Kristen can't maintain her illusion when she's weak," Serena explained. "So she will have to suck up thoughts and desires from others, which is a thin gruel compared to what she really wants. She'll be looking for places where she can piggyback on others' lust."

"Outside the houses of newlyweds?" Adam offered.

"How about motels?" Bobbie Jo asked. "I know some places where that kind of shit is going on day and night."

"Strip clubs," Jeremy said.

"Lingerie stores," Lucinda said.

"Porn shops," Cary said.

Serena was nodding. "All of the above. That's the problem. There is almost too much choice in this day and age. We can't know where she'll go."

"She's ancient, right?" Cary said. "Maybe she doesn't know anything about porn shops or strip clubs."

"Such things have always existed," Serena said.

"Yeah, but not in the open," Cary said. "I think she'll go someplace more familiar. Someplace that's been around for thousands of years."

"You knew her as Suzanne," Serena pointed out. "What do you think?"

"A whorehouse," Bobbie Jo interrupted.

"Are there any in Bend?" Lucinda asked, eyes big.

"I know of a motel that might as well be one," Bobbie Jo shrugged. She looked away, blushing a little. "The clerk isn't supposed to, but he takes money by the hour. The Plaza Motel, on the south side. Only thing wrong with it is that the cops are called there all the time."

"She'll remain hidden," Serena said. "Good! There's a good chance she'll gravitate there. If we're all agreed, that's where we'll start, since we have to start somewhere."

It seemed like a long shot to Cary. "Why don't we spread out? Try different places?"

"No," Serena said flatly. "It will take all of us to bring her down. We'll stick to one spot, and if there is sex, eventually she'll come around, I assure you. But none of you should confront her until the rest of us have joined you. Understand?"

185

"Uh," Bobbie Jo said, "I don't want to be a killjoy, but if you don't mind me asking, what's in it for us? I mean, I saw that bitch twice, and you wouldn't believe what she did to our camp. She's dangerous. I don't know how you managed to get away from her last night. And frankly, I don't see how it's any of our business. I already gave her the what for, both times."

"Bobbie Jo," Adam began.

"Shut up, Adam," she snapped.

"The thousand-dollar reward is yours," Serena said. "Whether you help us or not, you've earned it. But if you help us, when this is all over, you'll have a friend in me, and I might be a good friend to have."

Bobbie Jo still looked doubtful.

Serena looked around the restaurant. None of the other diners were within earshot. "I don't know if Kristen can be killed," she said in a low voice. "But I believe she can be so damaged that it will be a very long time before she can be a threat again. And if we can capture her somehow, we might be able to imprison her somewhere where she can't ever get out."

The others looked uneasy.

Lucinda spoke up. "I don't know. Killing seems…I mean, it's all so unbelievable. I was worrying about my cheerleader routines a couple days ago, and now this…" She glanced at Jeremy. "Maybe…if you'd just give us the reward. We'll help, you know, if we can. But I can't kill someone."

Bobbie Jo rolled her eyes. "Bitch deserves it. You know what? I've changed my mind. I'm in, money or no money."

"Me too," Jeremy said. "I'll help you track her down, at least."

Serena felt herself relaxing. She was amazed that mere teenagers were taking it so well—but then, they'd grown up on a diet of fantasy and tales of the supernatural, and they were probably more accepting than adults would have been.

"We'll take turns keeping watch outside the Plaza," Serena said. "It's as good a place to start as any. One couple per night for the stakeout, with the others ready to respond at their call."

"If you don't mind, I'd liked it if Jeremy and I could wait until the weekend," Lucinda said.

"We'll do it tonight," Bobbie Jo said. "Right, Adam?"

He nodded and sat up straight. Serena doubted he ever contradicted his girlfriend.

"And we'll take Thursday night," Serena said. "If that's all right with you, Cary?"

"Sure," Cary said. "Maybe we can book a room at the Plaza." He wasn't looking at Serena, but she blushed slightly.

"Oh, no. You don't want to do that," Bobbie Jo shuddered. "Not unless you want to catch crabs and get eaten by bedbugs."

"She'll be lurking in the shadows," Serena said. "But she'll be wary, so you need to be both cautious and quiet."

"No shit, Sherlock," Bobbie Jo said. "I can freakin' do that."

The rest of them laughed, and Bobbie Jo joined in.

"Look, we're all exhausted," Serena said. "Why don't we sleep on it, and discuss it further in the morning? In fact, I think we should stay together, if possible, until this is over. I've booked this entire floor. The hotel was going to kick me out otherwise, what with the horde of people I brought through here. Bobbie Jo and Adam, a room will be waiting for you when you come back in the morning. It won't cost me any more than I've already spent. Come on up to my room."

Bobbie Jo and Adam looked at each other as if they'd won the lottery. Jeremy and Lucinda glanced at each other as if waiting for each other's approval. Then both nodded nervously at the same time.

Cary restrained a smile. Young love, and, unless he was mistaken, the first time. He wished he'd had a luxury room his first time.

Serena called the hotel desk. "Would you please send up the keys to the adjoining rooms?" she asked. A clerk arrived at their door a few minutes later, and Serena tipped him generously. She handed out the keycards to the others.

Finally, Cary and Serena were alone.

"Well, that went well," he said.

"Amazingly well." She gave him a rare smile. "This is the closest I've ever come to catching her."

"What are you *really* going to do when you find her?" he asked.

Serena was silent for a long moment before she met his eyes. "I'm going to kill her," she answered at last. "Or at least diminish her to where she is but a wisp of memory, a passing thought, a fleeting temptation." She looked him full in the face. "If you have a problem with that, I'll continue on my own."

"Can't we lock her in an ivory castle or something?" he asked. "She's beautiful, you know? Most of the time. Can she really help what she is?"

"No!" Serena looked furious. "Did everything I told you pass through your two ears without sticking?" She took a deep breath. "People tried imprisoning the Succubae, in caves deep under the earth, guarded by armies of men...and still they escaped."

Then all the anger drained out of her. She was pale, her eyes red. "Look, I understand your concern. You're young and swayed by beauty."

"It isn't that," Cary began.

Serena broke in firmly. "We'll talk about this in the morning, OK?"

He nodded, his face tense.

"There's still one room left," Serena said, handing him the keycard. Her hand brushed against Cary's as she did, and he reached out and held onto her arm for a moment. She sighed and faced him. He kissed her gently on the lips, and when she didn't recoil, he kissed her more deeply. His arms went around her waist and he pulled her against him. She didn't resist at first...

....then she pushed him away, gently but insistently.

"You're too young for me," she said. She said it with a light tone, as if it was of no consequence.

"It's only a few years difference," Cary said. "I feel like we...like we think the same way about things."

"You are a horny young man." Serena's voice still had a forced lightness to it, as if it was all a big joke.

"Is that what you think?" Cary fought the exasperation coursing through him. Age was meaningless, couldn't she see that? He was afraid he was going to say something he would always regret.

Despite pushing him away, Serena was still standing tantalizingly close. He leaned his head toward hers and took a deep breath. "Tell me you don't feel it," he challenged softly.

"Are you kidding?" she murmured. She looked up, and her breath wafted against his cheek. He closed his eyes. He wanted her so much.

"Then why…?"

"I've been searching for this monster for years, Cary. I'm not going to stop now."

"You don't have to stop."

"Cary, it's not going to happen," Serena said firmly, and finally moved away. "I'll see you in the morning."

Cary hesitated. For a moment, he thought about taking her in his arms and trying again to kiss her. He thought she might respond.

Or she might never talk to him again.

"See you in the morning," he said, and left the room.

Chapter 26

Gasper Gerhard's Journal

What would have happened if mankind had never imprisoned the Three Goddesses? What if we had continued to worship them instead? What if we had accepted their blessing as they were offered?

Bad enough that we toppled them from their place of divinity, but to force the Daughters of Lilith to serve us, to give us their very Blood, turned them against us forever. It was men, and the women who abetted them, who turned the sisters into demons.

We will never have the chance to find out what it would have been like to live in harmony with them. There will be no second chances. The Succubae quite rightly hate us.

The Guardians failed in their duties. But the failure was foreordained from the day we first imprisoned the sisters.

The Succubae are fallen angels who wander the Earth seeking their vengeance, using our own weakness to punish us. It is we who have failed. The Succubae only test us.

Rick drove for two straight days, until he reached the outskirts of Portland. He was so tired he was dizzy. He thought about taking a dab of Blood but decided that this close to his goal, it would be foolish to risk giving the Succubae any warning that he was coming.

He could never get used to how big America was. He'd lived here long enough to almost pass as a native, though he couldn't quite kick a whisper of a German accent.

The van ran amazing well for having sat for several decades in a garage with only occasional starts. No one seemed to think the hippie mural was unusual.

By the time he reached Boise, he could already feel the effect of the Succubae. He was Cut, but he could still sense their power. There was no doubt the Daughters of Lilith were converging, even if they weren't together in one place yet. He wasn't sure if he sensed them because he'd consumed so much of their Blood over the decades or if everyone was feeling the same eroticism but weren't aware of the cause. It wasn't the kind of thing people talked about aloud, which was one of the reasons the Succubae so often slipped under the radar.

He pulled off Interstate 5 into a town called Wilsonville. It appeared to be mostly offices and apartments, but he found a nice motel and checked in. He dragged his backpack into the room, left it on the floor at the foot of the bed, and fell on top of the covers, fully clothed. He was just going to rest his eyes for a moment.

Serena was waiting for him, depending on him. He didn't want her doing anything rash. He could only hope that she'd taken his advice and was hunkering down.

He awoke to lights flashing in his eyes. It was more than one beam crisscrossing his face, confusing him. He reached for his gun and realized that he'd left it in the pack instead of putting it on the nightstand as he usually did.

"We aren't going to hurt you, Mr. Gerhard," a man's voice said. "Calm down. There are more of us than you can fight."

"Guardians," Rick said. "Is that what you call yourselves?" He sat up and rubbed his eyes. "Do you mind taking those lights out of my face?"

The overhead lights came on, and their softer glow filled the room. There were six men surrounding the bed, all of them bigger than Rick, all armed. He had no doubt they were trained for combat, which he was not. There were also soft voices in the hallway.

There was no getting away.

"Yes, we are the Guardians." The voice came from a seventh man, who still wielded a flashlight and still shone it in Rick's face, to keep him off-balance. Rick couldn't quite get a good look at the man. "And for most of our history, we thought we were the only ones. We had no idea, until we found you, that any of the original families had survived. No one could find the caves. We thought they were lost to us forever.

"Really, Mr. Gerhard, it would have made things so much easier if you'd joined us when we asked, but when you refused, we let you go. We weren't going to force anyone to serve us."

"And yet here you are, holding guns on me," Rick pointed out.

"A temporary situation, I assure you." The man speaking was the only one not outfitted in black combat gear and fatigues. He wore a well-tailored suit and had exquisitely cut blond hair.

"Mr. Carmichael, I assume?" Rick asked.

"Mr. Carmichael?" The man seemed amused. "Ah, I see you have been talking to Serena Carlton. Yes, that's as good a name as any."

"What do you want?" Rick asked tiredly. He closed his eyes tight and tried to concentrate on what he was hearing. When he opened them up again, the fog was finally lifting.

"We'd still like you to join us," Carmichael said. "But as you can see, we don't need you. We have found the Succubae without you."

"Hard to miss when they are together," Rick said. "If you can read the signs."

"Indeed. So to answer your question, we don't want anything from you, except for you to do nothing at all."

"Nothing?"

"Just rest up in this nice motel, get all the room service you want. You'll have the company of Gary and Pete here, but they're easygoing guys. They'll watch anything on TV you want to watch."

The man whom he'd indicated was Pete nodded. "Except reality shows. If you start watching those, I'll have to kill you."

"And sitcoms," another man, presumably Gary, added. "I hate sitcoms."

"So there you have it," Carmichael said. "So you can watch anything you want with these guys, as long as it's football."

Rick didn't respond.

Carmichael pointed at the backpack at the foot of the bed, and Pete unzipped it and poured the contents out onto the bedspread. Rick winced as the bottles of Blood clanked against each other, but they didn't break.

"For God's sake, be careful, Pete!" Carmichael said, and for the first time, there was some emotion in his voice. He reached over and picked up a bottle, then lifted it up to the light. It seemed to glow. "This is the real thing, isn't it?"

"If you mean raspberry soda, then yeah," Rick said. "Horrible stuff, but it keeps me awake when I'm driving."

Carmichael unscrewed the cap and took a sniff, and a beatific look came over his face. Rick had to given him credit for self-restraint. He didn't take a nip.

"They found a few drops of a Succubus's blood at one of her Cullings," Carmichael said. "The head of our Order was given the privilege of licking it. Actually, he wasn't the head of the Order when he partook of the Blood. It was the insights he gleaned from that small amount that made him our leader. Like you, until then our goal was to track down the Daughters of Lilith and destroy them. Since that day, we have bent all our efforts toward capturing them."

"You won't be able to," Rick said. "They can't be taken."

"They were captured once. Why not again?"

"They were Goddesses then, worshipped by men and women. They had no reason to distrust us. Now? They are creatures bent on vengeance who trust no one. They'll kill anyone they think even has knowledge of them."

"Then why are you alive, Mr. Gerhard?" Carmichael asked. "Many of us have wondered. Perhaps they aren't afraid of you. Perhaps you are a pet? Perhaps a Judas goat? We've kept our distance from you, because there is something odd about the whole thing."

Rick didn't answer. He'd often wondered the same thing. He was pretty sure the Succubae had had more than one chance to kill him. Instead, they had chosen to make his life miserable, to never allow him a moment of happiness. Whether it was because they disdained him or hated him or for some reason he couldn't fathom, he had decided it wouldn't stop him from trying to kill them.

Carmichael gently lowered the bottle next to the other three on the bed. "Is this all of it?"

Rick didn't answer.

"Not going to tell us? Well, we'll talk about it when we come back. Either we will be successful and won't need your hidden supplies, or we won't be, and we'll be dead. Or perhaps a few of us will survive, in which case, Heinrich Gerhard, we will demand your cooperation." He turned to a man standing near the door whom Rick hadn't noticed before. He, too, was dressed in civilian clothing, and was older than the other men by a couple of decades, but he had a look that Rick recognized.

This was the leader of the Order of Guardians—the one who had partaken of the Blood.

"Will this be enough, Mr. Harrison?" Carmichael asked him.

The man walked over to the bed, not even looking at Rick, as if he was unimportant. He stared down at the Blood with shining eyes.

"It is enough for an army," Harrison breathed. "A few gulps of this and our men will be invincible."

Harrison finally turned to Rick. There was an Old World manner about him, and his eyes contained years that his body didn't show. This man had had more than a few drops of the Blood, if Rick had to guess. How he had gotten it was impossible to know.

"Harrison?" he said. "I met your father."

"And you should have accepted his offer, Mr. Gerhard," Harrison said. "It's a pity you can't see the rightness of our mission. This Blood, properly analyzed, could be a miracle drug."

"Fair enough," Rick said. "Take it with my blessing. Analyze it, try to replicate it...but kill the Succubae."

Harrison was shaking his head before Rick even finished speaking. "This Blood has been around before science existed. I suspect, though I hope I'm wrong, that it can't be reproduced, which means we need the Succubae—or at least one of them."

"They won't be taken alive," Rick said. "I don't think you have a chance of taking them at all. They can withstand your bullets, anything you might use. If you destroy their bodies, they'll turn into pure spirits, feeding off of your wet dreams. But they'll return."

"See, Mr. Gerhard?" Harrison exclaimed. "That is why we need you to join us. You know more than we do, I admit. But I believe you are wrong in trying to kill these creatures. Their Blood can be used to help all mankind. We have to at least try to get more of it."

"It is a relic of the past," Rick said. "We should be rid of it."

"Yet I've noticed that you haven't poured it down the drain," Harrison mused. "But we could argue this all day, and we need to get over the mountains to Bend." He came over to Rick's side, and for a moment it looked like he was going to extend his hand. "My father told me when he visited you in France that you were concerned for the welfare of the Succubae. I assure you, we will be humane."

Rick laughed bitterly. "I no longer care. If I thought you could capture them, I wouldn't care if you if you threw them into the deepest, darkest pit."

"Yes, they have been particularly cruel to you, Heinrich," Harrison said softly. "I'm sorry for your family. We have—and I'm sure you don't know this—tried to keep watch over your son."

"Stay away from Richard," Rick warned. "Don't you realize that it was your man who led them to my family before, whether he meant to or not? Just leave my son alone!"

Harrison didn't try to deny it. He shook his head and turned away.

"Please," Rick said, knowing it was useless. "Don't try to capture them. You aren't prepared."

"We've been preparing for this for years, Mr. Gerhard," Harrison said, motioning for the other men to leave.

"Mr. Harrison!" Rick cried out one last time.

Harrison looked as if he was going to just keep walking, but at the last second, he hesitated.

"You should remember this, Mr. Harrison," Rick said. "The gulps of Blood you intend to feed your men? It is nothing. It is the same Blood that courses through the veins of the Succubae. What chance do you have against that?"

Harrison looked ready to answer, then seemed to think better of it. He closed the door, and Rick was left with his new friends, Pete and Gary.

Chapter 27

It was early in the morning when Eisheth left the bar. The streets were empty, and it was still dark enough to hide. Streetlights flickered on deserted corners. She ducked into an alley, and a bum rose up, shouting at the sight of her. She lashed out at him, though it gained her nothing. He fell like a sack of wet rags.

Soon the authorities would find the dead humans in the bar and at the homeless camp, and everyone would be wary, though they wouldn't know what to be wary of. A spree killer? A serial killer? It would make it that much harder for her to seduce them.

Eisheth couldn't believe it. She'd chosen the right victims three times, and three times had been frustrated for reasons beyond her control. An eternity meant that everything that could happen would happen, eventually, both good and bad. She'd been the Queen of Sheba, and she'd been a boy's first erotic thought. Being queen was better.

She should have killed Serena the moment the woman vowed in that courtroom to seek justice. At the time, Eisheth had laughed at her. She hadn't taken the threat seriously—she'd heard such vows before, by men and women much more powerful than Serena Carlton. But the age of the Internet had changed information gathering forever, making the Daughters of Lilith vulnerable again, more vulnerable than at any time since the beginning, when they first emerged to prey on men.

As soon as it was dark, Eisheth crept toward town, staying in the alleys and on the back roads, scuttling from shadow to shadow.

Crouching beside a small shack of a house, she got lucky. A young boy was masturbating for the first time, his entire body reaching toward the ceiling as the first massive orgasm overcame him, amazed by the wonder of it, that this thing existed, that it was free, that it required only fantasy and his own hands. The boy tried again, right away, and failed. But Eisheth knew it wouldn't take long, and she waited. Later, as he languished in bed, his hands so busy, she soaked up the boy's desires.

Then Eisheth moved on, reluctantly. She retreated back to the edge of town, catching a middle-aged couple having perfunctory sex, getting barely enough energy to keep her in place.

Something of her thoughts must have been picked up, for the door of a nearby house opened with a creak and a timid voice asked, "Who's there?"

Eisheth flew at the man, smashing through the screen door and laying him out in the hallway. He was alone, she sensed. She raised her talons to rip out his throat, then hesitated. He was so scared that his penis was shrinking back into his scrotum, but she could make him have an erection. She slapped him hard enough to give him a concussion, then got a pencil from a drawer.

She jammed the pencil into his cock and mounted him.

He was screaming loud enough to attract the neighbors, so she punctured his voice box with one finger.

It wasn't sex. But it was satisfying nevertheless to grind into the man as he bled to death. Eisheth was so gripped by his pain that she didn't hear the car pull up.

The bullet ripped into her shoulder before she heard the gunshot. She rose up, swinging wildly. She caught the shooter in the stomach and ripped her open. The woman just stood there, holding her guts in. The gun fell from her hands, and without thinking, Eisheth picked it up. It was awkward in her hands, but she found the trigger and pointed it at the man and blew his head off; then she turned to the screaming woman and shoved the barrel into her mouth and pulled the trigger. The woman dropped on top of her husband.

Eisheth waited for lights to come on on the neighbor's porches, but there was nothing but the distant barking of a dog. She dragged the woman's body inside and tossed it on top of her husband's.

She took a long, hot shower, then looked through the closet for something to wear. The dead woman was heavier and taller than Eisheth's new form, but the clothes draped over her scrawny bones were not unpleasing. She looked kind of hippie-retro.

Eisheth left the bodies just inside the door, energized by the experience, though in truth she had used almost as much of her energy on these two as she had gained. Yet there was something to be said for the joy of pure revenge, without gain. It was what she really wanted to do—kill humans. She really didn't care who or how anymore.

It was still early in the evening. Eisheth walked to the nearest neighborhood tavern, easily picked up a young man, and took him into the alley behind the bar. She drained him until he could barely move except to flop about atop her, twitching in pain and pleasure, begging for her to stop.

She waited for him to come one last time and felt the energy flow into her body. Then she squeezed his throat until she caught his last rattling breath in her hands.

When she arose and went back inside the tavern and looked in the mirror over the bar, she saw a cute young woman with long, straight, blonde hair and a kind of hippie look, wearing bright colors. She also noticed in the reflection that most of the men in the tavern were staring at her hungrily.

Eisheth turned with a smile.

Who do I Cull next?

She let herself relax. She closed her eyes and felt the sexual energy in the air. The tavern was full of it, of course, but she was ready to move on. Where next?

There was a fleabag motel down the street that she had checked out when first arriving in town. There was always some low-energy sex going on there, but not enough to draw her. Wait. Just outside—something was happening there. It was coming from the street, probably a car; she recognized the sexual emanations.

Adam and his bitch girlfriend.

She smiled and walked out of the bar, ignoring the men who stood lined up to offer themselves to her.

Chapter 28

Bobbie Jo and Adam drove his old clunker to the Plaza. The blue Pinto had been hidden in an abandoned cul-de-sac not far from their camp, one of the many unfinished housing projects in the onetime boom town of Bend. Every time Adam returned to his car, he feared it would be gone, towed away.

The Pinto didn't want to start, having been neglected for so long, and one of the tires was half flat, but Adam managed to get it going in a cloud of belching black smoke and stuttered down the street. Bobbie Jo didn't say anything. She didn't even look askance at him.

That's what I like about her, he thought. *She doesn't judge me. She doesn't think I'm a failure.*

They parked on the street across from the Plaza and watched for a while. There was one sputtering streetlamp near the motel, and a single bare light bulb outside one of the units. There were old, battered chairs in the walkways, a torn-up sofa and the glint of beer cans in the parking lot. There were two rows of single units, stretching perpendicular to the street back to the railroad tracks. They could see everything, all the comings and goings. Of which there were very few.

Bobbie Jo reached back and snagged a couple of the small liquor bottles they'd taken from the hotel room's mini fridge. They had stopped by their room on the way out, where Bobbie Jo had jumped up and down and on the big bed, giddy, and said, "I can't wait to get back here and give the bedsprings a workout."

"You want whiskey or vodka?" she asked now.

Adam shrugged and held out a hand. She gave him the vodka. They both downed two more of the bottles before speaking again.

"Do you believe what that lady Serena said?" Adam asked. "About those Succubuses?"

"Succu*bitches*. Do I believe that there are women who suck men's souls out through their dick?" Bobbie Jo said. "I sure as hell do."

"There's a male version too," Adam said. "I looked it up on the hotel computer. They're called Incubuses."

"All *kinds* of buses," Bobbie Jo laughed. "I think maybe I've run into that type too."

"The others seem to believe her, though I think Cary's in love with her. Jeremy and Lucinda…man, I could feel those two kids wanting to tear each other's clothes off."

"Yeah, these Succubitches are good for one thing."

They fell silent at that. The sexual energy was so thick that Adam thought he could probably take out his pocketknife and cut it. It was getting harder and harder to concentrate on their surveillance.

"Not much going on tonight," Adam ventured. Bobbie Jo seemed to know a lot about the Plaza, and it sort of confirmed what he'd always suspected about her. She'd had a rough life, and she'd done some things that she wasn't proud of—though he could almost hear her saying she wasn't ashamed either. He wasn't going to question her, though. He hadn't exactly been stellar himself.

"Kinda weird," Bobbie Jo replied. "Usually it's a happening place. People hanging out by the doors, flirting and drinking."

"Huh."

"I mean, it's really strange, 'cause there should to be all kinds of hanky-panky going on. Can't you feel it?"

Adam grinned at her, then leaned over and sucked on her neck a little.

"I'm feeling a little frisky myself," Bobbie Jo said. "What's the back seat like?"

"Uh…if you get on top, we can do it."

They scrambled over the front seat, and Adam pulled down his pants and Bobbie Jo jumped on. He struggled to get her shirt up and her bra undone, and then he was sucking for dear life.

Bobbie Jo came first, as usual. It didn't take her long, especially when she was on top and she could grind down at just the right angle. Adam put his fists under his buttocks so that she could really come down hard.

Afterward, they lay sideways on the backseat for a while before Bobbie Jo sighed and said, "I suppose we oughta be watching."

She crawled back over the seat into the front of the car. Before Adam could join her, she said, "Hey, I think I know that girl," and opened the door and got out.

The overhead light came on. Adam was still hanging out of his pants. "Hey!" he cried, but Bobbie Jo ignored him and crossed the street. Standing there was a short, round girl with long black ringlets and pants that were about two sizes too small. They stood talking while Adam made himself decent. He was just about to get out and join them when Bobbie Jo started back to the car.

"What's going on?" he asked.

"A fucking massacre," she said. "Howard's Bar, a dive on the edge of town. Been there once. It was too low class for me."

Adam blushed in the darkness. It had been his hangout before he'd lost his job and become homeless and too broke to buy bar liquor. "What happened?"

"They found everyone dead. Some joker put up a fumigation sign, so they didn't figure it out for a while. Dozens of people, all bloated and stinking from having been locked in."

"Do you think it was her?"

"It wasn't no gun," Bobbie Jo said. "Carrie said it was something sharp that cut them all, almost like an animal attack. Remind you of anyone?

"Jesus, what chance do we have against that?" Adam asked, dismayed.

"She cut their heads off," Bobbie Jo said grimly. "Set them on the bar like some kind of Aztec bullshit." She turned to Adam, and his heart sank. Up until this moment, she'd been wavering; he could feel it. After all, it wasn't their fight. Why not take the reward money and run? He'd been planning to suggest it as soon as they took advantage of that fancy hotel room for a couple of days. But now Bobbie Jo had her anger flowing, and he knew that nothing less than finishing this would dissolve that wrath.

"Screw it," Bobbie Jo said. "She ain't coming tonight. Let's get back to the hotel. I want to try that big bed out."

Adam felt himself stirring at the suggestion. *It's the Blood of the Succubus*, he realized. *It's making me horny beyond all reason.*

He started up the Pinto, and they drove away from the Plaza.

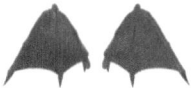

Eisheth stood right outside the passenger side window, perfectly still. She could blend into the darkness when she wanted to. She'd been on the verge of opening the door and tearing out their throats when she heard the name Serena.

She'd heard every word of the young couple's conversation.

How convenient, she thought. *All my little birds in one nest.*

It was time to put an end to Serena once and for all. And while she was at it, she'd finish off her other targets, men and women both. She'd walk away from this town a winner after all.

She followed the Pinto, which was making a turn toward downtown Bend. She dropped her human shape and ran as she had of old, before she'd ever met a human, before they had corrupted her.

We should stay like this, Eisheth thought as the energy surged through her long limbs. *My sisters and I should find a place far away from here and never take on human shape again.*

I will tell my sisters.

But even as she thought it, she knew they would never agree. They'd forgotten the old ways long ago. They were as much addicted to sex as the humans were addicted to them.

I will go off on my own, she decided. *Just as soon as I have killed these last few humans.*

Chapter 29

Gasper Gerhard's Journal

A man is not meant to live more than a century.

My son sees me as cold, uncaring. Perhaps I am. Perhaps all hope was drained from me long ago.

When I was young, I had all the hope in the world. Being a Guardian seemed important. I thought it meant something. I truly believed the Succubae could be defeated with the Blood I guarded.

There have been rumors of other Guardians out in the world. I call them the shadow Guardians, though the histories say no other families survived except ours. But we wrote those histories, so I don't know if they can be trusted.

There must have been survivors, for how else would the name "Guardian" even be known?

But my hope has slowly faded. I was at my most despairing when Heinrich was born. I fear I have filled him with my hopelessness. I pray not. I pray he can find the strength to continue to fight—perhaps even to win it.

Rick was watching football, as the Americans called it, and not understanding anything that was happening on the screen.

"Look at that stupid bastard celebrating for getting three stinking yards," Gary said, throwing up his arms in frustration.

"Yeah, but he ran right through Jared 'The Moxie' Billings," Pete said. "Moxie my ass."

None of it meant anything to Rick. He watched his two guards, wondering if maybe he could surprise them while they were arguing. Each of them had at least twenty pounds on him, and both had guns and no apparent reluctance to use them. Harrison might have preferred that Rick still be alive when he returned, but tellingly, he hadn't specifically ordered it.

Harrison isn't coming back, Rick thought. *I wonder when these two idiots will realize it.*

Serena would be trying to contact him, he knew. If he didn't answer, she would try to confront the Succubae on her own, which would be a mistake. She wouldn't wait long, for of all the people in the world, perhaps only Rick hated the Succubae more than she did.

Did she understand the implications? Had he made it clear to her that only a *man*—a man who could resist them—could destroy them once and for all?

At the same time, he needed Serena and her friends. While it was true that the final battle would be between man and Succubus, he hoped the women and their boyfriends would be his secret weapon. After all his research, he realized that there was one thing that had never been used against the Succubae.

Love.

The love between a man and a woman.

If it came down to a battle of sex and lust and temptation, the Succubae would win every time. But if love were introduced, maybe it would be different. Maybe love would be enough to draw the men away from the Daughters of Lilith. If love could weaken them at just the right moment, then there was a chance that he could face them down. He practiced that moment in his mind every night. He would be rock hard, and they would be bending every ounce of their willpower upon him. But he would resist. He would remain steadfast. He would reach out and take them by the neck...

No man had more reason to resist them than Heinrich. He'd lost his loved ones and his friends to the Daughters of Lilith; he'd spent decades preparing to fight them. He knew what the Daughters of Lilith were, and he knew the stakes. He had nurtured his hate. He was ready.

But here he was, when it mattered most, stuck in a motel with a couple of goons. Serena waited on the other side of the Cascade Mountains. He cursed himself for waiting too long to start out. He'd had so many false hopes over the years that a feeling of futility had overtaken him. He hadn't really believed that Serena was capable of doing what he'd failed to do so many times.

I've become my father, he thought. *Making plans and doing nothing.*

There was a soft knock on the door.

Gary sprang up from the end of the bed, pulling his gun. Rick almost laughed. A Succubus wouldn't knock politely. She'd be through the door as if it was paper and tearing out their throats before they could pull their guns.

"Hey, Pete," said a woman's voice. "Care if we join you?"

"We're watching football, Abigail," Pete answered, as if that disqualified the woman.

"Cool. Patriots and Packers, right?"

"Jesus, Pete," Gary called out. "Let them in!"

Two young women walked in. They seemed like children to Rick, though on closer examination, he saw that they were probably in their early twenties. It had gotten so any woman under the age of forty looked young to him.

They were dressed in black leather skirts, dark nylons, white blouses and black vests. Both were blonde, one slightly taller and heavier than the other. Both had striking blue eyes and noses that, examined alone, looked too long, but when added to the overall effect of their faces were just right. They weren't twins, but had probably been mistaken for ones all their lives, especially when they dressed the same.

"Hey, Brittany," Gary said to the taller girl. There was a shyness in his voice that was surprising coming from such a big man.

She smiled and walked toward him, holding up a six-pack of beer. "Want to try some local brew? When in Portland, drink as Portlanders do."

Gary got up and took the beer to the mini fridge. Brittany looked over at Rick and winked. "Hold on," she mouthed. Or so it seemed.

Rick froze, then tried to cover up his surprise. It didn't matter. The guards weren't paying the slightest attention to him. Their eyes were on the women, who were doing everything in their power to keep it that way. It was so obviously seductive that Rick marveled that the men didn't see it.

A few minutes later, it was Abigail's turn to look over at him. She pushed her hand down flat, as if to say, "Wait."

Two beers later, they had coupled up. Abigail was practically sitting in Pete's lap, while Gary had only gotten as far as holding Brittany's hand.

Pete suddenly stood up, nearly dumping Abigail to the floor. "Your father will kill us," he said.

"Daddy isn't here, is he?" Abigail said. "We're big girls. We know what we're doing."

I was wrong, Rick thought, watching them, *this is exactly the way a Succubus would do it.*

Pete sat back down and Abigail soothed him, then put her hand on his neck and pulled him toward her, and their kiss put an end to all his resistance.

The men had started drinking the beers from the bottle, but when the girls got up to replenish them, they brought back red plastic cups. Pete and Gary didn't even notice the switch.

The football game went on into overtime, but neither couple seemed to be paying much attention.

"Hey, pal, do you mind moving to the chair?" Pete asked suddenly. He was standing near the bed, glaring down at Rick. Abigail was at his side, leaning into him. She raised her eyebrows, as if to say, "Go ahead."

Rick rose without a word, moved to the chair in the corner of the room, and watched the rest play out.

The two couples started making out on the bed. Pete got as far as trying to slip his hand under Abigail's blouse, but she laughingly removed it. Then he lolled backward onto the pillow.

"Wow, strong beer," he muttered. Within seconds, he was snoring.

Gary didn't seem to notice. He was on top of Brittany, nuzzling her neck, both of them fully clothed. Suddenly, the girl rolled him off her, and he kept rolling right off the bed, landing on the floor with a thud.

By then, Rick was up and halfway to the door.

"Stop," Abigail's ordered.

He froze and turned. She had one of the guns trained on him.

"I know how to use it," she informed him. "In fact, I'm a better shot than either of these bozos."

"What do you want?" Rick asked. He stared her in the eyes and realized with a start that she was Harrison's daughter. She had the same long, resolute gaze.

"I want you to take off your pants," Brittany said.

"What?" he said.

"She's right," Abigail said. "Take off your pants."

Rick dropped his pants and stood there, blushing.

"Your underwear too, idiot," Abigail said.

Rick complied.

"Wow," Brittany breathed. "It's really true."

"You did *that* to *yourself?*" Abigail asked.

"I am a Guardian," Rick said.

"Yeah, well, our Guardians don't do *that,*" Abigail muttered. "Thank God."

"Then they are doomed," Rick said.

"Doooooommmed…" Brittany mimicked in a deep, hollow voice.

Rick didn't crack a smile, and her laughter faltered.

"They are probably already dead," Rick said.

This seemed to penetrate their ironic detachment. They fell silent.

"I'm sorry," Rick said. "I tried to warn him."

"I told Daddy that he shouldn't do it," Abigail said. "I also told him that he needed our help. We weren't going to be…distracted…the way the men are." She looked over at the other girl, and they seemed to come to an agreement. She gestured to Rick. "Pull up your pants. We're letting you go."

"Why are you helping me?" Rick asked.

"Well, there is a price," Abigail answered. "We want some of the Blood."

Rick zipped up his pants, trying to keep from revealing anything with his expression. "What make you think I have any more Blood?"

"Oh, come on," Brittany scoffed. "You've got a secret stash, I know you do."

"I know I would," Abigail added.

"What will you do with it?"

"Same as you, Mr. Gerhard. We will confront the Succubae."

"Call me Rick. Why is it your business?"

"We were raised as Guardians," Abigail said. "Maybe that wasn't what my father planned, but Brittany and I were there at every stage of the game; we learned the same things as the men, and we realized early on that they were going about it all wrong."

Brittany broke in, "The Succubae tempt men, right? Well, why the hell leave women on the sidelines? Why not use us?"

Abigail continued, "Daddy wouldn't hear of it, of course, but we undertook the same training as the men. It didn't take much to convince the guys. We just batted our big blue eyes at them. So we've been ready for a long time. And then…Daddy just leaves us here. Not a word. Just gone."

Rick nodded. He resisted the urge to be gallant, to try to talk the out of it, to treat them as "ladies." Women were just as capable as men—he'd learned that much in his long life. The Guardians—and apparently the shadow Guardians as well—were shortsighted not to let women help them. Hell, women probably should have leading the mission all along.

"Follow me," he said.

His backpack was missing, but he'd taped a spare key under the bumper of his van and was able to unlock the back doors. "Got a knife?" he asked, after the two women scrambled into the back with him. As he suspected, this wasn't a problem. Abigail immediately produced a wicked-looking bowie knife from somewhere under those tight clothes.

Rick pried away a side panel of the van. He had six bottles of the Blood left, cushioned in foam rubber, dusty and tarnished from years of being hidden. But the Blood was still good; it always was.

"This is all that is left," he said. He wrested one of the bottles loose and handed it to Abigail, then gave another to Brittany. "I need the rest," he said.

They held the bottles out and stared at them.

"Wow," Abigail said. "This is the real thing."

They were completely overwhelmed by it, Rick could see. They were well trained, and perhaps wise beyond their years, but they

209

probably hadn't really believed all the stories. Still, more than ever, he was certain that the women were the key.

"Let's go," he said, climbing into the front seat.

But the women were already scrambling out of the back of the van. "We'll meet you there, Mr. Gerhard," Abigail said. "We've got our own wheels."

"All right," Rick said. "If we get separated, we'll meet at the Cambridge Hotel, in downtown Bend. Whatever you do, don't try to confront the Daughters of Lilith alone. It won't accomplish anything. You need a man to complete the job. Sorry if that sound politically incorrect. It's just the way it is. The Succubae can only be truly defeated by a man."

"Oh, dear. Where on Earth are we going to get one of those?" Abigail asked with a smile.

"Don't worry," Rick grunted. "One bottle of Blood and I'll be all they can handle."

Abigail laughed and slammed the van's doors closed.

As Rick drove out of the parking lot, two figures on Harley-Davidsons fell in behind him. Rick was filled with hope for the first time in years.

Chapter 30

Cary closed Serena's door behind him and stood in the hallway for a moment. He turned back, his hand reached out to knock, but then he dropped it to his side.

He pulled the keycard for his own room out of his pocket and walked away. As he passed the nearest room, he heard unmistakable rustling, whispering sounds. Jeremy and Lucinda were together at last. Love was in the air. It was almost as if he could sense the erotic energy coming from the room.

Or maybe he just wished the same for himself. He unlocked the door to his room and entered. The bed was huge, inviting. He didn't dare lie down, because the moment he did, he knew he'd be out.

He went back to the door. It locked automatically, and there didn't seem to be any way to change that. *How do I make it easy to open?*

Look at you, he thought. *Acting like a horny teenager who thinks the sexy woman is going to sneak into his room in the middle of night.*

After a moment's thought, Cary left the keycard in the lock and closed the door. He felt safe enough. He was in the top floor of a high-end hotel. He'd just have to get up early and grab the key, make sure no one noticed what he'd done. He was embarrassed by his fantasy, but too horny to resist giving it a chance to become real.

He opened the mini fridge and uncorked a bottle of white wine. Then he sat on the edge of the bed and tried to think of ways to win Serena over. He considered using logic; he considered emotion; he considered sex appeal. She was going to resist him, he knew. She had a sense of integrity that was impressive and immensely appealing.

But whether anything happened between them wasn't up to him, it was up to her, and if there was one thing he didn't doubt, it was her willpower.

He put the glass of wine down after only a couple of sips and leaned back on the bed. Then he was out.

Cary half woke, feeling drunk. Had he finished the rest of the wine? Someone was undressing him, tugging down his pants. His erection caught in the waistband and he heard a soft laugh.

He opened his eyes and there she was—the woman of his dreams. Serena's long hair was loose and draped over his stomach as she took him into her mouth. She slowly, sensuously moved up and down his length, and every third or fourth time, she went lower and licked his balls. He wanted to groan, but it was as if his vocal cords were frozen. He looked up at the high ceiling, wondering if he should try to think of baseball, his taxes, anything but what was happening. He wanted it to last…to last forever. When he came, he wanted it to be within her.

She was going faster now, her hair swishing across his skin as if it was a sensory organ and her hands rubbing his thighs, her fingers traveling up his chest. She pinched both of his nipples at the same time, and he moaned and thought of his English teacher, the unsexiest woman he'd ever known, but it was almost too late. He felt himself ready to give way, but then Serena did something interesting with her fingers, pinching him in a particular place on his cock, and the overwhelming urge receded, replaced by a warm and tingling sensation. He realized that when he finally climaxed it would be a blast for the ages, and he'd be moaning and groaning as if he was dying.

She moved up now, licking his belly, then his nipples, then his neck, and finally his ears. He wanted to kiss her, but she was avoiding that, as if saving it for last. *Serena, Serena,* he wanted to say. *I love you, and I don't care about our ages. I love you, don't you understand?*

Try as he might, no words emerged.

She purred in his ear like a satisfied cat, and he wanted to laugh, because it tickled. He felt sluggish. She was doing all the work, but that seemed just fine. He wouldn't have minded getting on top, doing his share, but it was all so pleasurable that he didn't want to interrupt her.

He'd always fantasized that an older woman would know tricks that he didn't, and it seemed to be true. She was doing things to him that he didn't think possible. He wasn't in a hurry to come, like he usually was. He always tried to please his partners, but usually it was the second time around that he succeeded. But she was holding him off, somehow, building his pleasure. He could sense her pleasure building as well.

At last, she began to position herself above him, and he closed his eyes in anticipation.

The door slammed, and it felt as if the entire room shook. Cary looked up to see Serena striding toward the bed in a nightgown with a furious look on her face. Had she gotten off him? But no, she was still perched above him, her head turned. The new Serena grabbed a lamp as she approached, raising it.

Cary tried to make sense of it. How could Serena be in both places?

A cold fear gripped him, and every part of his body but his cock lost all erotic feelings. But the "Serena" making such sweet love to him lowered herself onto him, ignoring the intruder. Instead of having the feeling that he was being held off, Cary now had the opposite feeling surge through his body, as if all the sexual tension and buildup he'd been experiencing—not only in the last hours, but ever since he'd met Serena—was converging on one point, and that point was his cock, and he was going to explode in such a mind-blowing orgasm that he feared his heart would also explode.

The other Serena smashed the lamp on top of his lover. Then her hands went under the other's arms, and she pulled the woman off of Cary's cock just as he began to spurt. He watched in amazement as the jism flew high into the air, landing on him and on the two struggling women. He shouted at the top of his lungs and couldn't tell if it was from pleasure or from pain and humiliation as he realized what had happened.

He still couldn't move as the two Serenas fought in the middle of the room. No, there was only one Serena: the other was the Succubus. The monster had dropped her disguise and turned into a wiry, spitting, screeching thing out of nightmare. The Succubus was quickly overcoming Serena, who looked like a rag doll in her hands. Serena went flying across the room, slamming against the wall and crumpling to the floor.

But she was back up in an instant. She dropped the lamp she still held in one hand and ran at the Succubus with her hands out, going for the monster's throat. The Succubus broke her grip and threw Serena to the floor. She climbed on top of Serena, lifting her talons to strike down. Blood was welling out of the wound in the Succubus's head, and it splattered into Serena's mouth, and suddenly she was reenergized.

She threw the Succubus backward. A look of total astonishment came over the Succubus's face, which by now was all angles: a sharp nose and ears, a slash for a mouth, filled with jagged teeth. Serena leaped onto her, driving her to the floor.

They struggled for control, with the Succubus slowly winning. Then Serena did something completely unexpected. Just as the creature was about to throw her off, she leaned down and bit into the other's shoulder, clamping down with her teeth, refusing to let go. The more the Succubus struggled, the more chunks of flesh Serena ripped from her.

The Succubus grew weaker while the woman grew stronger.

The door flew open again, and Bobbie Jo and Adam ran into the room, both of them naked, followed moments later by Jeremy and Lucinda, who had taken the time to put some clothing on. Serena was still clamped down on the Succubus, raising her mouth just enough to spit Blood and flesh onto the floor before leaning in and tearing more bits off the Succubus. Serena looked up, distracted by the entrance of the others. The Succubus used that moment to break free, throwing her straight into the air.

The Succubus ran at Bobbie Jo, grabbing her by the shoulders and hissing as if recognizing her. Bobbie Jo slammed her fist into the Succubus's face, and the creature staggered to one side, slipping on the blood and landing on her back. Jeremy and Lucinda ran at the Succubus, armed with kitchen utensils they'd grabbed from a drawer of the kitchenette.

The Succubus sprang up, snarling. She howled an ear-splitting scream, but the humans stood their ground. Suddenly, she ran for the door, and despite themselves, the humans moved aside.

Then the Succubus was through the door and gone.

Chapter 31

Eisheth bolted down the hotel stairs, bowling over a maid, who screamed at the top of her lungs. She heard the footsteps of humans pursuing her. Even in her weakened state, she could outrun them. Eisheth caught a glimpse of her reflection as she ran toward the glass exit door.

She looked like a harpy—or an emaciated evil angel, as Naamah once joked.

Where could she hide? Where could she regain her strength?

Eisheth fled the downtown area and traveled east, back into the High Desert. She scurried into the Badlands, hiding in the hollows between lava rock outcroppings, starting in alarm at the slightest sound. Her mind told her animal attacks were rare, but her body remembered. Every sense tingled like that of a hunted animal in a mindless frenzy to escape. Her thoughts were a jumbled mess. All she could think was that she'd failed again, and now she was trapped, hiding in the wilderness like an animal.

As night fell and the temperature plummeted, she shivered under a rocky overhang. Her clothing was gone, abandoned in the dark hotel room with her squandered last chance. She flinched, startled by the hoot of an owl, the swooping shadow of a bat. Insects crawled over her. She shuddered, remembering the black bear's vicious attack the night she'd failed to take Douglas.

She could almost hear Naamah's mocking laugh, Agrat Bat chiding her for recklessness.

It was so unfair. It was at times like this, when Eisheth was ugly and powerless, that she remembered that she had once been a Goddess. Memories ran through her like a blade, of men cutting her, draining her of Blood, leaving her hanging in the cold and dark. She didn't know any more whether God or Satan existed, or if they did, which of them had set the horror of her life in motion, making the Daughters of Lilith the ultimate temptation for men.

Eisheth had sworn never again to be so humiliated, so weakened that she couldn't take the shape of a woman. It took a preposterously coincidental string of accidents, mistakes, and bad luck for such a thing to happen.

Never had it happened so fast.

She had let her anger get the better of her. She should have used the energy she gained from the Cullings in the bar to leave town immediately. What did it matter that a young man had scorned her? There were millions like him, all of who would gladly give themselves to her. She should have run, but her anger at Serena and the rejection of three separate Cullings had driven her to make imprudent decisions.

Hatred animated her now. Sex was necessary for survival, not something she desired for itself. It was the way she could hurt men. Her hate was as strong as ever, keeping her alive when all else abandoned her.

Eisheth was trying to hold onto some semblance of human shape, but now her features twisted back into their real shape, her skin turned hard and leathery, and her hair became a tangled, living nest of viperous tentacles. Her eyes absorbed light like the night creature, the cavern dweller she was. Her chin and cheeks were sharp and hard.

I must find someone to seduce, she thought, and then laughed. It came out as a harpy's screech.

Seduce? There would be no seducing, not until she regained a pleasing illusionary form. She would be forced to suck up what sexual energy she could find, like a parasite, gaining just enough life force to survive.

Eisheth stayed hidden through the day, but her hungers drew her out as darkness fell. She crept into town. She found another lowlife bar, but there were two burly men on either side of the door. She couldn't have entered at any rate, no matter how low the standards of the establishment, no matter how desperate the men, no matter how dim the lights. Word of the massacre had no doubt spread by now.

They would tear her apart if they found her, not knowing what she was but repulsed by her appearance. The reality beneath the illusion was too much, reminding them of their own crude cravings, their own weakness. Above all, she must avoid discovery.

She hid in the alleyway behind the bar. Not long after, a woman came out with gave a man and gave him a quick, efficient blowjob. The man grunted and handed her a twenty-dollar bill. After the man went back inside, the woman puked just feet away from where Eisheth was hiding, then wiped her mouth and also went back inside.

Eisheth fed off the meager sex.

She stayed hidden in the alley that night, picking up the stray desires that infested men's minds but that were rarely satiated.

Eisheth was vulnerable at the worst possible moment, and it wasn't clear whether she could come back again. She clearly saw her future, how she would hide during the day in places people never went, but were close enough for her to creep into their houses at night and prey on their dreams. Eisheth knew what a long, slow, and difficult process it would be, for she had made the interminable climb upward many times since that first time, when she and her sisters first gained their freedom.

She would not fully recover until she convinced a man to fall in love with her, to give himself to her.

She had no illusions of that happening any time soon. She knew too well how men would run, screaming and mindless, at the sight of her. Yes, she'd stay out of sight, in the shadows. She could sense lust, she could find it, but she couldn't be part of it until she gained enough strength to look human.

If Eisheth was lucky, after lapping up the wet dreams of teenage boys, the twisted fantasies of perverts, the lustful nights of newly consummated love, she would eventually regain the semblance of a human female: scrawny, ugly, but available. It might take years. After submitting to whatever sexual desires men who would take such a woman might have, which often left her wounded and more vulnerable than before, she might, after many more years, become attractive again.

Her hunger would grow, but so too would her need to be careful, and it would be a constant struggle to constrain herself, to be patient. She'd fail, again and again, giving in to her destructive desires, and so be reduced again and again. Centuries of fighting men and her own desires, and she might again become the archetype she strived for: the ingénue, the cute girl next door, the fun one who could be one of the boys. She might once again seduce them.

But it would take a long, long time. Eisheth couldn't bear the thought of it. She'd been so sure she would never sink so low again.

Come, my sisters! she thought. *Save me!*

It was doubtful they would come. There was little familial bond between the Three Daughters of Lilith, only a common foe. They were stronger together—so much stronger that they overwhelmed the populace with rampant sexual desire. Yet they chose to live apart. After millennia together, exposed to each other's quirks and weaknesses, they couldn't stand each other.

Forgive me, my sisters. You are stronger than I.

Naamah! Agrat Bat! Forgive my arrogance; you are better than me.

Her sisters, arrogant and narcissistic, would respond only to flattery, submission, and degradation. Eisheth would have to efface herself again, and fall still further in their hierarchy. In the past, rather than humble herself, she would have accepted her punishment, fought her way back no matter how long it took. But her hatred of men, always there, always the motivating force of her existence, was so strong that she wanted to screech it to the skies: she wanted to hunt men down and tear them apart; she wanted to screw every damn one of them to death.

Still no answer. They were ignoring her. They still blamed her for the Storm King.

Those memories, of being beneath the earth, cold and hungry, came back more powerfully than ever, lending her power in her desperation. She cried out to her sisters, hoping the mental connection that allowed them to learn so easily from one another, that had saved them from enemies in centuries past, would serve her again:

Join me, sisters. Let us destroy this place, let us remind them of our hatred, let us kill each and every one of them!

Still there was no answer. They would not come to help her. But she knew of one thing they would come for.

The Guardian is coming. He is on his way here.

The icy thoughts of Agrat Bat came to her. *I'm coming, dear sister.*

Seconds later came the softer voice of Naamah. *I shall help you take revenge, sister.*

Eisheth felt her flesh transforming already, becoming softer and rounder. She caught a glimpse of her reflection in a shop window. Her face was that of a human female: a little gaunt, the eyes a little desperate, but not repugnant.

Thank you, sisters, she thought as she felt their energy combining for the first time in many years. Together, they were many times stronger than each of them alone. Satan had decreed long ago that the Daughters of Lilith would not be easily overcome.

It was time this generation of men and women learned it.

Chapter 32

"Don't let her get away!" Serena shouted.

Adam and Bobbie Jo ran out of the room, and after a moment's hesitation, Jeremy and Lucinda followed.

Released from whatever spell had held him down, Cary groaned and sat up unsteadily. He'd had some vigorous sex before, but nothing that ever drained him like this. Serena lay on the floor, breathing deeply. He rolled off the bed and crawled toward her. He stopped with his head over hers, and she looked up at him with a glint of triumph in her eyes. Blood smeared her mouth and chin.

"I got her," she said.

"You sure did," Cary said.

Serena got to her feet. "We have to go after her," she said, and then her knees gave out and she almost fell. Cary put his arm around her to steady her. She put her head into the crook of his neck. A warm sensation flowed through him, touching his heart, and nearly overwhelmed him. He cupped Serena's head protectively with his free hand.

"Are you all right?" he whispered.

Serena started laughing, and she couldn't seem to stop. Cary stared down at her in surprise.

"I've never in my life felt better," she said. "I thought she was going to kill me. I could feel her overcoming me. It was a last resort, to bite her like that. But once I did, this energy filled me, and I felt her weakening. If I could've kept her down a little longer, I would have had her."

Bobbie Jo and Adam returned, flushed and breathing hard, as she was speaking.

"Good," said Bobbie Joe. "I wish you'd killed the bitch."

"I don't know if she *can* be killed," Serena said. Color was returning to her face, and she no longer needed to lean against Cary. She gently removed herself from his arms, not looking at him. Her voice was firmer. "But it will be hard for the Succubus to keep a pleasing form after this. Hell, she may lose *all* form. It's happened before, where she becomes but a legend, a figment, a nightmare; not completely gone, but diminished, so much so that there is nothing to hang her illusions on."

Jeremy and Lucinda came back into the room. "She got away," Lucinda said. "Sorry. Whatever she was, she was fast. She didn't even look human."

"We'll find her," Serena assured them. "She won't be able to seduce anyone now. She'll have to subsist off of the wet dreams of teenagers, lurking outside their homes, soaking up just enough life force to stay conscious."

"I say leave her like that," Bobbie Jo said. "Serves her right."

Serena shook her head. "She'll come back, eventually. It might take hundreds of years, but she'll find a way. It's happened before. No…we *have* to finish her. If she can't be killed, we need to at least make her so diminished that she won't tempt anyone for a long time."

Cary was staring down at the Blood puddle, and an odd thought came to him. He leaned over and dipped his finger into the Blood. Before he could have second thoughts, he put the finger into his mouth.

Serena looked like she was ready to object, and then she looked curious. She swiped her finger across the still-wet Blood on her chin and put it into Cary's mouth.

A surge of energy ran through him, as if he'd just slept for ten hours.

"Can I have some of that stuff?" Bobbie Jo asked.

Serena hesitated. "I think it will be all right."

Bobbie Jo grabbed a towel from the sink and soaked it in warm water. She came over and wiped up the blood. "I'll just take this with me," she said, leading Adam out of the room.

Serena turned to Jeremy and Lucinda. "Go back to bed. We'll meet up in the morning." The teenagers left too, shutting the door firmly behind them.

And then they were alone.

Cary was suddenly embarrassed, feeling as if he had cheated on Serena.

She seemed unfazed. She sat down on the bed and sighed. "Can I stay here tonight?" she asked. "No sex. I just don't want to be alone."

He nodded. He was totally spent. Sex was the last thing on his mind.

Serena went into the bathroom and started the shower. Cary waited in bed, still naked. He usually slept nude. *I can't very well wear my clothes to bed,* he thought, then wondered if he should. Despite what he'd thought a few minutes before, he was beginning to come back to life. He got up and put on his T-shirt and underwear.

Serena came out, having discarded her bloody nightgown. She was wrapped in a towel. She didn't look at Cary when she slipped into bed, and she lay down at the very edge of the bed, as far away from him as she could get.

Cary realized his entire body had become rigid. He felt himself stirring at Serena's nearness. He could hear her soft breathing. And then, just as he was ready to scoot closer, maybe cradle her in his arms, she let out a loud snort, followed by a long snore.

He smiled to himself. *Just in time.*

He was falling asleep to the sound of her sawing wood when a thought came to him that jolted him awake. The entire time with the Succubus, he'd been all but paralyzed, and neither he nor the Succubus had made a sound. So how did Serena know anything was happening?

He smiled blissfully and gazed down at her. He gently pushed her hair away from her face. The lines on her face were gone, as if she were suddenly ten years younger. Her slight double chin was gone as well. She murmured in her sleep and turned, exposing her breasts.

If she had been sexy before, she was irresistible now.

He took her in his arms, and she murmured softly. He felt himself growing hard, and with more willpower than he'd ever shown in his life, he disentangled himself. He put a pillow down between his legs to avoid pressing his erection against her while he slept, not sure if that would be welcome. To his great surprise, he was content.

From the room next door, Bobbie Jo howled an orgasm to end all orgasms.

Good for her, Cary thought. For him, for now, holding Serena was more than enough.

Serena woke to go to the bathroom in the middle of the night. Cary had his back to her, and now he was the one at the very edge of the bed.

She shook her head, not quite believing that she'd asked this of him—or of herself. It was unfair to sleep in the same bed with him—she knew how much he wanted her—but she wanted his nearness even as she resisted his sex.

Am I testing him? she asked herself. *If so, he's passing with flying colors.*

Serena acted tough, but the Succubus scared her every moment of the day and night except when Cary was near. What he could do that she couldn't do, she didn't know, but somehow she felt safer when he was with her.

As she got back in bed, she put the extra pillows between them, trying not to be obvious about it.

I'm a bitch, she thought. *But I need him close.*

She was asleep before she could change her mind about the whole arrangement.

Serena dreamed that Cary was making love to a tall, blonde woman who knew tricks that Serena had never even considered. Jealousy grew in her even though she realized that she was dreaming, that it wasn't real. She jolted awake.

Cary was grinding against the bed sheets, moaning. He exploded with a gasp, but didn't awaken. He turned over, and his erection pushed up the sheets and didn't go down again. He started moving rhythmically again.

Serena leaned on her elbows and watched him. *Should I wake him up? Should I give him what he wants?*

No, she'd sworn to track down the Succubus who had killed her son before she ever gave her heart to another. She was close. But when it was done…well, who knew?

Let him sleep, she decided. She slid her fingers down the length of his jaw, feeling the rough stubble of several days' growth. *Let him dream*. It was his mind, his life, and she had no right to interfere.

She fell back to sleep.

Chapter 33

Agrat Bat was in the Mediterranean on the biggest yacht she'd ever seen (and she'd seen some big ones) when she got Eisheth's distress signal. She was just as glad. The big vessel was as empty as its owner. Perry Simpkins may have been a billionaire, but he had no friends, and his family wanted nothing to do with him—which was quite an accomplishment when you considered the billions that the man would someday pass on to his heirs.

Agrat Bat had thought about trying for that winning lottery ticket, but after a week on the choppy water listening to the inane prattling of a man who had probably lucked into his money, she decided against it. He'd gotten drunk one night and hit her, and she decided no amount of money was worth putting up with that. Besides, money came and went, but the life force was precious.

She was beginning to suspect that when it came to the consummation, the payoff would be as empty as the man's heart. He'd picked her up in Cannes, and his money, if not his charm, had dazzled her at first.

"I thought Grace Kelly was dead," he'd said as a come-on. She'd heard the comparison before, though not so crassly put. "Hamburger in a can, old Grace," he finished, making it worse.

Her then-companion, a jaded movie star with a declining career, knew Agrat Bat for the shallow gold digger she pretended to be. Not necessarily a promising quality in a Cull, but he helpfully whispered in her ear, "That's the man who owns that gossip site, *Private*

Matters...he's the one you want," thereby confirming for Agrat Bat that the actor was too cynical to fall in love or give all of himself to *anyone*.

So Agrat Bat abandoned her fading movie star and joined up with the billionaire. Big mistake. The movie star was at least entertaining. He didn't take offense at her abandoning him in the least. "You go, girl," he'd said, grinning, and she considered returning to him for round two later on.

Private Matters had started off as a gossip magazine—well, it still was, only online now instead of on paper. Simpkins managed to leverage it into a multimedia empire with a conservative agenda. Agrat Bat didn't care about politics, but she thought any man who caused that much controversy must be interesting. It just went to show, you can't always tell by the trappings.

Her biggest coup in recent years had been a computer tycoon. She'd taken him slowly, savoring his essence, as he became thinner with every public appearance. Finally, she couldn't resist his delectable taste any longer, and she took all of him, and it filled her so that she hadn't had to take another life for years. She was amazed at the outpouring of grief that greeted his demise, the glowing biographies. Admittedly, his life force was strong, but far darker than anyone suspected. She happened to like the spice of a dark soul once in a while; actually, she preferred it.

And yet, Agrat Bat was bored with the men who took and took and took from the world, having to be taught to give to their partners. The females were another flavor altogether. Belinda....

Agrat Bat smiled at the memory. It had been far too long.

Belinda lived in the America now, and she must be...what, ninety? Really? Had it been that long? But it didn't matter—if she were still alive, a few drops of Blood would take care of that.

Belinda hadn't been happy with Agrat Bat the last time they'd met, but that didn't matter either—the Blood would take care of that too. They could satisfy each other all day and all night, and no harm would come to either of them.

If only the Daughters of Lilith could regenerate through the female life force, instead of just the male life force. That would have been heaven.

After Eisheth's call, Agrat Bat decided to end her dalliance with the billionaire that very night. Too bad, really. Simpkins was in Cannes because he was thinking of starting a movie company. It was easy to implant the idea in his head that his first movie should be about a Succubus. Dangerous, perhaps, but the temptation was nearly irresistible.

"You could call it *The Daughters of Lilith*," she had said.

"I like it," he'd said, lying on his back in bed like a beached whale. "No, I *love* it. I see the lead actress looking something like you. Have you done any acting?"

"I've acted my whole life, darling," she had purred. "But never in front of a camera." It was never going to happen, no matter how much she liked the idea. Cameras couldn't pick up the sexual allure of the Succubae. Indeed, their image barely registered.

"Get in bed, bitch," Simpkins had said. His tone was playful, but they were the same words he'd used a couple of nights before when he was drunk, and that hadn't been playful at all. When she'd hesitated in bed—not because she wasn't going to have sex with him, but because she was trying to figure out how to satisfy him without letting him penetrate her—he had slapped her. It had taken all her willpower not to tear his head off.

Agrat Bat was quite skilled, as were her sisters, at satisfying men, making them fall for her, without actually having intercourse. They used sex of every kind and description, but saved that one act for special occasions—Culls, for example. It wasn't hard to pull off, usually. For most men, it only heightened anticipation for the final consummation.

Now Agrat Bat went down on the billionaire, as she had on all the nights before. He was at a fever pitch, begging to be released, but she sensed when he was about to unload and backed away each time.

She was a couple of days early, but it wasn't easy to fend off the selfish, narcissistic types who were used to getting their way.

He was begging now, muttering, "Please…please…fuck me."

She maneuvered herself down past his belly and onto his cock, and started rocking gently. Simpkins came within seconds, bellowing, nearly bucking her off.

"Best damn sex I've ever had," he muttered. He made a motion as if he wanted to roll over and go to sleep.

"Not so fast," she said. "I'm not done."

"I don't think..." he started to say. Then, "Oh, wow."

This time, she slammed up and down on him until he was practically whimpering, but she didn't hold him off; she made him come as soon as possible.

His belly was flattening, his cock growing larger, and he was suddenly energetic, which was a nice surprise.

"Didn't think I could still do that," he muttered, grinning up at her. Then his grin faltered as he glimpsed her face, her *true face*. It always happened in the end, partly because Agrat Bat couldn't be bothered to hide herself any longer, but mostly because nature demanded it: *This creature is taking your soul, killing you, and you must look upon it, you must know it is happening; you, human, must despair as the last of you is drained.*

Simpkins didn't last long after that. He was wheezing by the fourth climax, too weakened to push her off. "My heart..." he gasped. "Stop, my heart can't take it."

"It isn't your heart," Agrat Bat laughed, her voice guttural. Her blonde hair was a scraggly mess of grey; her blue eyes were black, and her chin came to a point so sharp it could cut. "It's all of you. I'm taking you into me, every little last bit."

His eyes bulged out, and he came one last time, and with that last tiny spurt, more air than liquid, his tiny little soul moved into her.

But Agrat Bat was far from satiated. She threw his body over the side of the yacht, bathed, and then Culled the three crewmen she had been cultivating on the side. One was surprising full of life force, a young man who was moonlighting for the summer. She wondered briefly about him. What secrets in his life gave him stature in his society?

She left the captain alive, letting him believe he was the exception, until they were just outside of port, then drained him. She put on her white one-piece bathing suit, looking more like Grace Kelly than ever, dove overboard, and swam to shore.

Laughing, she slicked her hair back as she left the water, ignoring the pathetic humans who stared at her, open-mouthed, men and women alike. She smiled. None could resist her.

Over the centuries, she'd ignored Eisheth's cries for help more often than not, but this time she thought she could risk helping her, especially if Naamah came also. The Daughters of Lilith were long overdue for another Summer of Love. She laughed softly. That *was* fun. Interesting things happened when they were together, for their powers multiplied and expanded, and their appetites grew. They were the party girls from hell, and men everywhere desired them, and at the same time, they feared them for the ball-busters they were.

Naamah loved a conquest, the hotter the better. Unlike her sisters, Naamah enjoyed sex, especially the final round, which she often delayed as long as possible, enjoying it while she could. It seemed a shame to take a man during their first time together, before he learned her rhythms and preferences, giving her the exquisite pleasure that usually accompanied repeat lovers.

This was true with Pietro.

Naamah was enjoying her latest conquest. (She didn't like to say victim.) He was cute, dumb, and sweet natured, with a body to die for (him, of course, not her), and she enjoyed having him around.

Pietro and his friends had been scrambling around the ruins of a crusader fort on the island of Malta, ignoring all the off-limits signs. The boys spotted her and came bounding over the stones, gathering around her like puppies anticipating a snack.

She looked them over carefully, raising her finger as she recited the children's rhyme, running a hand over the bronze skin of each boy as she passed, counting them off. "Eeny, meenie, miney, moe, catch a monkey by the toe…"

She only regretted she wasn't able to take them all, but that many missing boys would be noticed.

She knew which one she wanted already, of course, and her finger landed on the biggest, most vibrant of them, a lithe boy tanned dark brown, with startling blue eyes and sun-bleached hair.

Naamah took him back to her "primitive" hut on the beach, which was incredibly expensive on account of the Wi-Fi and air-conditioning. She wore a bright yellow sundress with nothing underneath. "Slinky" was the way she'd heard herself described (often followed by words like "slut" or "whore," but she didn't really care). She and Pietro were like mirror images of each other: small and brown and vibrant, except for the fact that she had black hair to his blond and brown eyes to his blue—and the fact that she would soon swallow his soul.

The usual preliminaries ensued, up to and including anal sex, but on the second night, Naamah lay on her back and let him enter her. Pietro was a vigorous lover, almost too vigorous, and he prided himself on his stamina. She tired eventually, so she rolled on top of him, doing her little tricks, and he came with a howl that echoed down the beach. The neighbors shouted back with good humor.

Pietro quickly regained his energy, and this time didn't hold back but went straight for the orgasm. He ground into her, paused, then shuddered. He laid his head on her shoulder.

Ordinarily, Naamah wouldn't have let him rest. Once she'd started, it was nearly impossible for her to stop until she had totally drained her conquests.

But then she did something that the Daughters of Lilith had agreed not to do. She bit into her finger and let a drop of Blood form, then she stuck the finger into his mouth. She let him rest before twitching her vaginal muscles just enough to get him going again. He started with micromovements that were so sexy she almost came herself, which rarely happened before the final draining.

Pietro came for the fourth time that night. He was becoming lethargic as his fat was drained away (and he'd never had much fat on him to begin with). His muscles were taken next, all but the heart. Naamah had learned early to keep the heart muscle pumping till the last and the brain going even beyond that, for maximum pleasure.

Pietro was powerless now, unable to move, though his cock was bigger than ever.

"What are you?" he asked in Italian.

"Your lover," she said, trying to sound sexy, but her true nature had manifested and it came out as a snarl, and her tongue forked between her lips and lapped against his cheek.

It was time. His eyes had rolled back in his head; his thoughts were dissipating and unfocused. His final climax approached.

Naamah's hands were claws now, her fingernails long and pointed. She aimed at her chest and stabbed down, and Blood trickled into the valley between her breasts. She flicked some of the Blood into her man's mouth just as he came.

"Oh, God!" he cried. His body filled out again, and his eyes popped open. "More!" he demanded.

She flicked a second drop into his mouth, curious. No man had survived more than one resuscitation before, but Pietro was young and vigorous, and he not only survived but slammed into her, making her gasp, and she screwed him like a dying, heaving beast late into the night, until the neighbors howled—not in good humor now, but in anger—at the noises coming from the hut.

Finally, Naamah disengaged from her conquest, and was amazed to find them both alive and complete. It was almost, but not quite, as good taking him completely.

When Pietro awoke, his eyes were filled with fear, as though he had endured nightmares all night long. But Naamah was so cheerful, so solicitous, sashaying around the hut naked, dancing over to him and giving him long, loving kisses, that the nightmares were soon forgotten.

She didn't let him regain his equilibrium. When he tried to get up, she came over and pushed him down again. When he tried to sleep, she awoke him. And always there was sex, whether consummated or not, and he finally gave up trying to do anything else and just lay in bed as his big, sad eyes followed her.

The nightmare in his eyes lingered on the second morning, then on the third, no matter what Naamah did. But she liked him too much to let him go, so she gave him a good sucking and the tiniest bit of Blood, and he stayed, entranced, captivated, unable to move except for his eyes, watching her cook, listening as she sang. His eyes were filled with death already, though his cock was ready for the taking.

She intended to keep him alive for a long time.

Naamah was annoyed when Eisheth's summons came. She was going to ignore it as she always did and continue her prolonged pleasure with Pietro, but then Agrat Bat's response came.

She sighed regretfully as she trailed her fingers over him.

"Sorry, my lovely boy," she said as she mounted him. "I must be going."

Chapter 34

Serena awoke in Cary's arms. She untangled herself and went to the bathroom. As she headed back to bed, she caught a glimpse of herself in the mirror. For a moment, she didn't think anything of it; it was her inner image of herself, after all, the way she had looked in her early twenties.

Then she stopped in midstep, turned on her toes, and gasped. She had never looked *this* good. There was not a single blemish on her. There was not an ounce of flab on her, either. She looked as if she ran marathons, slept nine hours a night, and ate nothing but fruits and vegetables. Her eyes were bright; her slightly offset nose—broken in a long-ago skiing accident—was perfectly straight. She ran her hands over her body, cupping her perky breasts, gaping in disbelief. They were firm and high, as they hadn't been in years.

"Admiring yourself?" she heard a voice say.

She turned, embarrassed.

"You should," Cary said. "I've never seen a more beautiful woman, not in life, not in the movies. Frankly, you look eight years younger than me, instead of the other way around. Not that you ever looked that old."

"It's the Blood of the Succubus," Serena said. "I'm not sure I really believed the legends until now. I was in such a fight for my life last night, and biting her was a last resort. But I couldn't believe how strong it made me."

He came up behind her, but stayed a polite distance away. She grabbed a towel and wrapped it around herself, then turned to face him. They were eye to eye, and Serena was suddenly aware of her morning breath.

Cary seemed to know what she was thinking. "Even your breath is fresh, though I'm not so sure about mine." He pushed past her. "I'm going to take a shower," he said. "Be out in a minute."

"OK." Serena felt vaguely disappointed. She'd been trying not to stare at his lean body, not letting her eyes drop below his neckline. He'd been clutching his clothes at his waist.

As the water started running in the bathroom, she resisted the urge to join him. Instead, she booted up her laptop.

Serena: *I was attacked last night by Eisheth.*

Rick: *Are you OK?*

Serena: *I used her own Blood against her.*

Rick: *Good for you. I'm on my way. Stay in the hotel with your friends. Stay together. Unless I miss my guess, Eisheth will call for her sisters. We may finally have them all in one place.*

Serena: *Anything we can do?*

Rick: *Barricade yourselves in your rooms. They will be coming for you.*

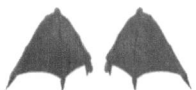

When Cary emerged from the bathroom, he was dressed. He was glad he'd thought to grab his clothes on the way in. The sexual tension was so intense that he couldn't hide his erection.

Serena hurried past him, and he heard the water start up. It was her turn to take a cold shower. She stayed in there a long time.

When she came out, she quickly and efficiently dropped the towel she'd wrapped around herself and started dressing, her back to him. Cary watched her, admiring her movements. Serena never seemed to give a thought to what she wore or how she looked, but everything she did oozed style and class. He looked down at his T-shirt and faded jeans. What chance did he have with a woman like her?

They didn't look each other in the eyes, both ashamed of their dreams, unaware that their dreams were the same.

"Did you sleep well?" he asked. The question was fraught with implications. Did she sleep well next to him? Because he was near?

She was brushing her hair. Her hand froze for a just a moment. "Thank you, Cary, for being so understanding. It must have been…difficult."

He walked over and stood behind her. He didn't touch her, though he wanted to take her in his arms. "Absolutely. You needed to feel safe, I get it."

"I want you to know that I like you." She said it brusquely, the way you might say, "I like bagels."

"I like you too," he said, and his voice quavered. "I like you a lot." It sounded lame to him, but also simple and true.

Serena finished putting in an earring and turned abruptly, somehow managing to get past Cary without brushing up against him.

In the ensuing silence, Cary turned on the TV news. News of the massacre at Howard's Bar blared from the screen.

They sat down at the end of the bed and watched, and Serena's hand reached over and clutched his. When the reporters started repeating information they'd already reported several times, Cary muted the TV.

"It's her," he said.

"Of course it's her," Serena said. "It's how she gained enough glamour to impersonate me."

"Will she try again?"

"She's wounded," Serena said, taking the newscast off mute. "Besides, everyone is on the alert now."

They watched TV for a while longer, but there was no new news about the massacre.

The others were waiting for them in the restaurant.

Food and newspapers covered the table, all of them emblazoned with headlines about the massacre at Howard's Bar. Someone had spilled a cup of coffee and tried to mop it up with the ad section of the paper. Serena caught the waitress's eye and smiled, as if to promise a big tip. The waitress nodded back.

Serena grinned at how relaxed her young charges looked, despite the traumatic events of the previous night. Apparently, there was a lot of sexual healing going on. Jeremy and Lucinda were holding hands and giving each other puppy-love eyes.

Though Serena hadn't specified a time, they had all showed up just as the breakfast crowd was clearing out.

"I'm hungry enough to eat a porcupine," Bobbie Jo proclaimed.

"Me too," Adam said, grabbing a roll and eating it plain.

They ordered huge breakfasts, and were soon laughing and talking as if they were old friends. The waitress came over to refill their coffee. "Newlyweds?" she asked.

Again, they broke into laughter. "Newly something," Jeremy said, finally.

"Yeah, you could say that," Lucinda giggled.

When they were finished eating, Serena added a big tip for the waitress onto the bill. "Would it be all right if we stay for awhile?" she asked.

"Stay as long as you want," the girl said. "There's a doughnut shop next door. We get them for free. Want some?"

"Yes!" Bobbie Jo cried.

"Doughnuts! Doughnuts!" Jeremy chanted.

"So now we know which ones get hungry and which ones get sleepy," Serena said.

"I get both," Bobbie Jo said. "After fucking, I usually fall asleep with a sandwich in my mouth."

Serena was a little shocked by such language so early in the morning. Then she smiled ruefully. *Yeah, a real proper lady I am, contemplating robbing the cradle.*

Cary watched Serena's face. The sexual tension hadn't dissipated one iota, despite being out in public. She was flushed. She glanced at him, and he saw in her eyes the same desire he was feeling.

"Rick thinks that all three Succubae are coming here," she said. "He said we should barricade ourselves in our rooms and…"

Adam broke in. "We need more guns. We have Serena's Glock, but that's not enough."

"Has everyone handled weapons before?" Cary asked. "I mean, do you know how to load them, take the safety off, and all that?"

Cary had seen Serena handle the Glock, so he knew she was up to the challenge, but he wasn't so sure about everyone else having a gun, including himself. Cary had subscribed to the rule: don't keep a gun in the house, but don't tell anyone you don't. But that had been before he knew Succubae were a thing.

It was getting hard to concentrate on the conversation. He felt his jism rising in his groin, wanting out. Just a touch from Serena and he'd explode.

Cary noticed that Lucinda's eyes were following Jeremy's every movement. Cary smiled. *Young love*, he thought. Every once in a while, Jeremy would look at Lucinda and give her a shy smile. They were so in love, and trying so hard to hide it that it made it all the more obvious. Cary's eyes wandered back to the woman beside him. He felt the same way about Serena. He'd just had more practice hiding his true feelings.

"It's too late to get guns," Serena said. "We'll just have to hope for the best…" He voice drifted off, as if her heart wasn't really in the conversation.

Cary jumped as Serena's hand landed on his lap and then playfully approached his crotch. *What are you doing?* he wanted to say.

Meanwhile, across the table from them, Bobbie Jo and Adam couldn't keep their hands off each other. It was almost embarrassing. At one point, Adam let out an involuntary screech. Bobbie Jo smiled maniacally. The newspaper draped over the table near their laps was flapping suspiciously.

Cary cleared his throat loudly, and Bobbie Jo looked up, startled. The newspaper stopped rustling. Cary frowned and looked around to see if anyone else in the restaurant had noticed.

"You look...different," Jeremy said.

Cary realized he was talking to Serena. The young man was looking at her appreciatively. Cary shot a glance at Lucinda to see what her reaction would be.

But Lucinda was also examining Serena. "Yeah," she said, with narrowed eyes. "You're looking very nice."

Serena was at a loss. "I...ah..."

"It's the Blood of the Succubus," Cary said. "It heals you, gives you energy."

"No shit?" Bobbie Jo said, elbowing Adam gently. "Extra energy?"

Adam nodded, a big grin on his face.

"I wonder..." Lucinda said. They all looked at her.

"I mean...I wonder if that's why she is the way she is. The Succubus. I'll bet you anything people have hunted her for her Blood."

"There are stories," Serena admitted. "Some not very nice. But that doesn't excuse her. You must understand: she has taken many, many more lives over the years than can ever be justified, no matter how horrendously she was treated. Whatever her reasons, she's dangerous and must be stopped."

"I know, I know," Lucinda said. "But...I...I feel sorry for her."

"Don't." Serena said firmly. "When the time comes, don't hesitate. She must be stopped."

Plates crashed to the floor behind them. Cary looked back to see the waitress pressed against the doorway between the kitchen and the dining room. The cook was standing behind her with his hand up her dress.

What the hell is going on?

Cary expected the girl to slap the cook, who looked twenty years older than her, but instead, she was laughing, leaning into him.

Cary frowned again and looked away. Serena's hand landed on his erect cock, and he restrained a shout. Almost to his surprise, he didn't climax right then and there.

Out the window, he caught a glimpse of motion on the sidewalk. An older man and woman were in each other's arms, kissing furiously, and the woman had her hands wrapped around the man's ass. As he watched, Serena's hand suddenly shot down inside his pants, grabbing his cock.

"What are you doing?" he gasped.

Serena snatched her hand away as if burned. "I...I'm sorry. I don't know what...why I did that."

He stared at her. *God, she's beautiful! Why did I stop her?*

Lucinda and Jeremy were kissing passionately, oblivious to everything else. The newspaper was flapping over Adam's lap again, and Bobbie Jo was staring intently into her boyfriend's eyes.

What's happening? Cary wondered, beginning to freak out.

The previous night's dreams came back to him, and as he remembered the vivid details, he realized that these weren't normal dreams.

There was an apartment building across from the restaurant. Cary glanced over and noticed that, in front of the building, the older couple was now making love on an old rickety lawn chair like teenagers.

What the...?

Serena spoke up, interrupting the goings on. "If you guys can manage to take your hands off each other for a moment, you need to hear this."

The other two couples reluctantly broke apart and stared at her.

"We're in trouble, big trouble," she said. "The Daughters of Lilith are here."

As soon as she said it, she forgot why it had seemed so important. Cary was close. She could smell him, the Cary-smell that she found on his shirts, a whiff of which gave her a serene feeling.

"Trouble?" Bobbie Jo responded, as if from a distance.

"When the Three Daughters of Lilith appear in the same place, the erotic energy is multiplied," Serena managed to say. "People lose control."

"No shit," Bobbie Jo said. "I'm horny all the time, but I ain't *this* horny!"

"What do we do?" Adam asked, the newspaper over his lap rattling with unprecedented speed.

Serena had been planning to say something, but she forgot what it was. The only thing that mattered right now was the man sitting beside her, who was kissing her neck. She tilted her head up to give him access. He started unbuttoning her blouse, right there in the restaurant.

She managed to push his hand away. "Our room," she said. "*Now.*"

They hurried away, barely making it to their room before tearing off their clothes. It felt so wonderful to finally give in to her desires that Serena didn't question it. Cary was the man she'd been waiting for her entire life—and it was this knowledge that had scared her. But all fear was gone, and now she saw only his handsome face and his confident smile. He loved her just as much as she loved him.

They nearly tore off their cloths, wanting them to just be gone, to be skin to skin. As they embraced, Serena's body filled with a soothing mixture of comfort and pleasure. She sighed deeply as Cary tilted her head up and kissed her.

No foreplay was needed. She was as ready as she had ever been.

She spread her legs, and as Cary entered her, Serena had a passing thought. *Aren't we supposed to be doing something else?*

Then Cary was kissing her breasts, and the question vanished from her mind.

Chapter 35

Serena awoke to the sound of the shower. Cary wasn't in bed, and the bed felt empty. The room felt empty, the world felt empty. She couldn't stand to be separated from him for even a moment. She got out of the bed, which was a sticky mess.

Her midsection and lower places were sore from the vigorous pounding Cary had given her. Despite the pain, she almost went to him for another go at it.

It was her fault—she'd urged him on. Now she could barely walk. What had gotten into her? Usually she didn't like rough sex. She searched her heart for guilt, but it wasn't there. She had told herself she would never again have a relationship until her son's murderer was brought to justice. But it had felt so good that the moment she'd succumbed, she known it was right.

She decided to join him in the shower after all.

He was leaning into the shower to test the spray, and she admired his backside for a moment. He turned with a smile and a full erection.

"Want to join me?" he asked.

Serena peeled off the long T-shirt she'd worn to sleep in. Cary soaped up first, and she washed him off slowly, touching every part of his body. Then he returned the favor, and they both rinsed off together, clutched in each other's arms under the showerhead.

In the middle of it, Cary put his hand under her chin and turned her head until he was certain he had her attention. "What about the Succubus?"

"What about her?" Serena asked, then felt vaguely annoyed that he'd brought the subject up, though until this evening it had been something she had never stopped thinking about.

"Shouldn't we be doing something?"

Should we? With relief, Serena remembered what Rick had told her. "Rick said to stay put."

Cary looked into her eyes and smiled, accepting her explanation. Then the smile vanished and he frowned as if he'd just thought of something. "You don't suppose that we...I mean, that we are..."

"In love because of her?" Serena finished. She laughed. "I don't think it makes the slightest difference, do you?"

"No, I suppose not. I mean, how could we tell?"

It was her turn to be serious. "Don't doubt this, Cary. Never doubt this."

She felt him growing between them. She reached down and put her hand around his cock, then raised her leg, propping it on the edge of the shower stall.

"A little awkward," she murmured.

"When we're an old couple, we won't be doing this anymore," Cary said. "We'll be properly in bed, but for now..."

He slipped into her, and she closed her eyes, feeling him move slowly against her. Then he stopped.

"Hey, don't stop!" Serena said, laughing. She slipped on the wet floor, and he caught her before she toppled over.

"How do I know you're you?" he asked, teasingly.

She looked back into his eyes. "Because I'm a klutz. I bet *she* wasn't a klutz."

"No," Cary admitted.

She could feel him drawing away, and she grabbed his head in her hands. "Look at me, Cary. I'm Serena. I'm...I'm yours."

They made love, taking their time, completely unaware of what was happening in the world outside.

Outside the hotel, the media was descending on the town. The massacre at Howard's Bar was the headline story. Twenty-eight men and nine women had been killed in a horrible way.

It wasn't your run-of-the-mill American mass shooting. The experts were stymied by the oddities of the case. Whoever had torn the victims apart had used a weapon that was sharp and deadly, and it had taken time to kill them all, enough time for most of the victims to know what was happening and to try to escape.

The town was rife with speculation. Howard's Bar was the base for a local motorcycle club, the Hawks. Was this the work of a rival gang? But as far as anyone knew, the Hawks were mostly wannabe biker types, with the leather jackets and the tattoos but without the bellicosity and criminal history. The bar was a dive, and the police found illegal drugs on many of the corpses. Half the men were naked and had been emasculated. Used condoms filled the trash cans in the bathrooms and littered the floor around the pool table.

There was speculation about jealous lovers, but that seemed unlikely. Both men and women had been killed. Some experts suggested it was the work of a mentally unbalanced moral crusader of some kind, or simply a lunatic. Why else would a killer decapitate thirty-seven bodies and line them up on the bar?

Into this already boiling sexual maelstrom came Naamah and Agrat Bat, and the night exploded into a sexual frenzy.

As the other two Daughters of Lilith converged on Bend, Oregon, they became stronger with every mile. Old men who hadn't approached their wives in years were suddenly frisky. Grandmothers were stalking the outnumbered men in their retirement homes. Teenagers who had vowed to wait until marriage gave in to carnal temptation at last. Casual first dates became torrid one-night stands.

At first, it wasn't so bad. Wives and girlfriends watched their men with worry, either because the men were being uncharacteristically amorous or because they seemed to be trying to get away. Then women began to be affected too. Stay-at-home moms headed for the bars, still wearing their everyday clothes.

"I'm going to the..." It didn't matter what they used as an excuse— the tavern, the bowling alley, the theater, the concert—it was obvious some men and women wanted to go out, and both men and women knew why, if not consciously.

Porn sites lit up with traffic from this small section of the country, and Web administrators tried to make sense of it. The few stores in town selling pornography, even the relatively tame *Playboy*, were sold out. Erotica sections were cleaned out in every bookstore. In locked rooms, men and boys masturbated to visions of Goddesses.

Each person felt the change individually, unaware what was happening. The authorities could tell something was going on, but it was too early to gather statistics, and each department thought that it was just because of a strong confluence of factors. "A full moon," one dispatcher commented. "The crazies are out."

His two coworkers, who were making out in the next cubicle, ignored the statement.

As night fell, men and women stopped asking for permission. They didn't bother to seduce their partners, but forced themselves on the first vulnerable man or woman they found. The police were inundated with reports of rape; the hospital emergency rooms ran out of rape kits.

Whether they succeeded in their goal or not, the affected men and women fell into a deep lassitude soon afterward. When morning came, they could not be awakened, no matter how vigorously shaken or how loud their alarms were. In many cases, the women of the household were content to let the men sleep, the aggressive advances of the night before still a fresh and often traumatic memory. People who never missed a day of work, students who never missed a day of school, slept on.

By midafternoon, some of the spouses and significant others became concerned, and once again the hospital emergency rooms were packed. Cars spilled out of the parking lot and into the highway as people slept in passenger seats and backseats. The phone lines were jammed.

It didn't matter. The doctors and nurses who made it to work had no idea what was happening, or how to revive the comatose people.

The affected men and women, meanwhile, weren't aware of being asleep. Their dreams were so vivid and real that it seemed they were carrying on with their lives. The closer the Daughters of Lilith came, the more the bacchanalia expanded. Men and women dreamed of partners so perfect, so alluring, that they seemed bigger than the biggest movie stars, flawless and enthralling. The Succubae offered carnal satisfaction more desirable than any porn star, more than any masturbatory dream the dreamers had ever concocted.

For the men especially, the temptation was too great. In their minds, Goddesses were available, to them and them alone, or so it seemed. No questions, no rejection, only open arms, and, no matter how faithful the man had been to his significant other in the days before, they all gave into temptation eventually. The Goddesses took them and fulfilled their every desire, no matter how strange or perverted, no matter how long or short, how nasty or prim. It was as if these Goddesses read their minds, their every impulse.

Some men chose the blonde one, the statuesque beauty who in real life was unattainable, a myth; the kind of woman who married kings or bedded presidents. Some men chose the slinky, slutty brunette, who wrapped herself around them like a snake. Some men chose the wholesome one, the girl next door, the manic pixie dream girl who always seemed just out of reach, but who could conceivably be captured by personality or humor, who loved the nerdy, dorky, geeky boy-men for what they were.

Some chose them all, or combinations thereof.

Whatever they wanted, in these dreams, was granted, fulfilled to a glorious climax. With unbelievable speed, the men recovered their vigor. The dreams played out again and again, and none wanted to willingly awaken from them.

The women watching these slumbering men couldn't help but notice their hardness and their orgasms, and stood back from the beds and couches and car seats, half repelled, half drawn by the sight. What was clear to all the female partners was that it wasn't them that the men were dreaming about. They muttered names aloud, strange names that made no sense.

"Agrat Bat!" some men cried as they came. "Naamah!' shouted others. "Eisheth!" groaned still others.

And then the men awoke, and it was worse. Again, there was no asking and no coaxing, much less seduction. The men demanded sex then and there, using the most foul and offensive language, no matter how measured and controlled they were in normal life. "Bitch, get on your knees," snarled mild-mannered men who normally gave in to their wives' every demand. "Spread your legs, whore."

Some of the women gave in, others fought back, and some tried to flee. But the sexual tension and violence rose and rose as the Daughters of Lilith grew ever nearer.

By then, some of the women had armed themselves, and the overtaxed emergency rooms started seeing an influx of wounded men, shot or stabbed or bludgeoned.

"It's a modern Sodom and Gomorrah," said the mayor on that night's newscast, but then he was accustomed to a politician's hypocrisy and was already planning a visit to his mistress as soon as he could get out of there. The broadcast was cut off abruptly when the weatherman and the anchorwoman started making out on the air.

Cameras were everywhere, and reporters interviewed anyone who stopped screwing long enough to talk to them. Every time the reporters turned around, someone was getting it on in the backseat of a car or a broom closet, or even in a booth in the local coffee shop.

They tried to be professional and ignore it at first, but the drive was so strong that soon they had great difficulty focusing on anything else. Finally, they turned the cameras on what they were seeing. The national newscasts were filled with blurred footage of couples copulating.

The national anchors were shocked and irritated at first, not recognizing the scope of the horniness problem in Bend, Oregon, but as they witnessed the progressive decline in their associates' professional focus, they sent in backup sexperts and quit showing footage live, as they couldn't trust their Bend counterparts to blur all the necessary body parts or keep the broadcast on the subject at hand.

On the top floor of the Cambridge Hotel, the three couples who were ensconced there didn't notice anything different, for they were already deeply in love, already sexually fulfilled. They fell asleep, still horny but knowing their loved one would be there in the morning.

Chapter 36

The town was theirs for the taking.

Naamah showed up first, arriving at Redmond airport by commercial jet. She looked tan and rested, with long black hair, wearing little green short shorts and a tight black T-shirt: Angelina Jolie, only sexier. "I hope this is worth it," she said by way of response when Eisheth, who'd met her at the airport, asked about luggage. "I've been living in paradise. I spend most of my time naked."

Naamah gave Eisheth a hug with a look of distaste. Eisheth was healing faster in the proximity of her sisters—merely having them turn their conscious attention in her direction was enough to get her started—but she was still a long way from the way she wanted to look.

Naamah radiated sex, available and free, and arbitrarily so, giving every man a chance, or so they thought. The airport lobby seemed to constrict around the two of them as they sat near the big windows and men gathered closer and closer while women stared from outside the masculine circle.

"Are they movie stars?" a little girl asked loudly, and was shushed by her mother.

Agrat Bat arrived at the Redmond Airport in a private jet. Two men came down the steps before her and nearly bowed to the ground as she descended. She was blonde and refined: Grace Kelly, only sexier.

Agrat Bat had reserved the best limousine in Central Oregon, and they rode the twenty miles to Bend behind tinted glass, measuring each other. Men turned their heads as the long car passed, even though they couldn't see inside. They left the limo parked outside an upscale restaurant, the driver still sitting with his pants undone, drained by Naamah's blowjob.

"You really do need our help," Agrat Bat said to Eisheth once they were seated at their table. "Who are you supposed to be?"

Zooey Deschanel, Eisheth thought with a smile.

"If you're trying for a Zooey Deschanel look, you're not quite getting there," Agrat Bat said.

Eisheth's smile disappeared. *Damn her!* Not for the first time, she wondered if her older sister had read her mind.

"Zooey Deschanel?" Eisheth scoffed. "Is she even an ingénue anymore?"

"Since when are we bound by history?" Agrat Bat said.

"Would you prefer Cleopatra, Helen of Troy, and Princess Diana?" Eisheth asked.

"As long as I'm Helen of Troy," Agrat Bat said, laughing.

"And I'm Cleopatra," Naamah joined in.

"So that would make you poor doomed Diana," Agrat Bat said to Eisheth. "Don't worry, darling, we'll get you up to speed in no time. In fact, we'll bring back a couple of men primed and ready to fall in love with you at first sight. They'll think they're screwing me and Naamah, of course, but you'll still take their life force."

Eisheth did not argue. It was what she wanted, after all. Let her sisters do the seducing and she the reaping. As soon as she was stronger, they could leave.

Although…now that her sisters were actually here, she found she was enjoying the sybaritic festival their presence provoked. She didn't have to do all the work herself; indeed, she didn't have to do *anything*. The entire town awaited them, waiting for release.

They left the restaurant and managed to revive the driver enough to take them to an expensive B & B, which they completely commandeered. Within minutes, the male owner was prostrate on the bed, nearly paralyzed by the ecstasy of being pleasured by three impossibly beautiful women…at least, in his dreams.

The Daughters of Lilith had the run of the place. It was theirs, and they intended to make the rest of the town theirs as well. The sisters' first order of business was to restore Eisheth to her full powers, and then the three of them could do as they pleased, for as long as they pleased.

Inevitably, there would be a fight between the sisters over some man two of them wanted, or over the fact that one of them would eventually want to slow down while the others wanted more. But until that happened, it would be as in days of old, when Roman senators groveled at their feet, and 1920s gangsters stole for them, and 1960s revolutionaries bombed buildings for them. They could and would do anything they pleased to men.

As Naamah said to Agrat Bat later, "You take them high, I'll take them low, and Eisheth can have the middle."

Agrat Bat didn't turn away from the mirror, though not one hair was out of place. Her skin was flawless, without a single wrinkle. Her clothing also was without a wrinkle, despite just coming out of a suitcase. Her nails were perfect, her teeth blindingly white.

Eisheth suddenly remembered why she hated her.

Meanwhile, Naamah looked as though she resented having to get dressed at all. She wore a pullover dress with no bra and no panties, and was barefoot: instantly available.

A horny whore, Eisheth thought derisively, despite having had sex with and then savaging an entire bar full of men herself a few nights earlier.

"I don't know," Agrat Bat answered. "I feel like slumming. Care to switch, Naamah? I'll let you borrow some clothes."

Naamah considered it. "No. I don't feel like being the highborn bitch tonight."

"You never do," Agrat Bat grumbled.

"Let's slum together," Naamah proposed.

Slumming? Eisheth thought. *To hell with both of them. They have no idea.*

"What do you think, Eisheth?" Naamah asked.

It was the first time they had asked her opinion about anything since they'd arrived.

"I'm staying this way, if you don't mind," she said. "I've had enough of this rotten town." She didn't have quite the appetite that her sisters did, though she felt stronger with every hour that went by. With every sexual coupling, with every erotic dream, her powers grew. The Three Daughters of Lilith were suffusing the town with their sexual energies. Adult humans in their proximity were paralyzed by lust, able to accomplish little aside from fornication.

"Trouble with you, Eisheth, is that you kill them too fast," Agrat Bat said in a smug voice.

It was that tone that had driven Eisheth away in the first place. But she kept her irritation to herself. She needed her sisters.

Agrat Bat continued. "Keep one around, Cull him until he can't move, find another, use him up, go back to the first one, and so on. But always have more than one in play, and keep them alive for as long as possible."

"Personally, I prefer finding one nice guy and keeping him going," Naamah said.

"Oh, and how do you get enough life force *that* way?" Agrat Bat said with an arched eyebrow.

Naamah looked uneasy and turned away. "That's for me to know…"

"You aren't giving them your Blood, are you?" Agrat Bat said. "I thought we agreed to never do that."

She was taking on her big sister persona, and both Eisheth and Naamah sat up straight.

"Well…I don't see the harm," Naamah said.

"It gives men a *taste*." Eisheth spoke up, surprising herself with her vehemence. "They must never know, never trap us again. Kill them, fuck them, play with them, but never give men the idea that they can use us!"

"Dear Eisheth is right for once," Agrat Bat said. "It's a bad idea. Please don't do it again, sister."

"Or what?" Naamah asked.

Agrat Bat towered over them. She was a blonde Goddess, several inches taller than her sisters, curvier, and physically stronger. Eisheth felt something pass between her sisters. The languid sexiness of the atmosphere turned suddenly cold and gritty, as if they were back in the cave of their imprisonment. Naamah cried out, clutching her head, then fell to the carpeted floor and writhed, hands between her legs.

Agrat Bat turned away, giving Eisheth a glance that said, *I could do this to you, too, anytime I wish.*

"As for you, Eisheth, as I said, you kill far too often, drawing attention to yourself." She gave a low chuckle. "Besides, it's so much sweeter when you have them in your thrall for a long time. Believe me, it's all worth it." She eyed Eisheth disapprovingly. Eisheth had stuck to her hippie look but updated her wardrobe with the help of Agrat Bat's credit card. "If you insist on looking like the girl next door, you're never going to keep them long enough to enjoy them. They'll get bored, and you'll lose them to a Madonna or a whore." A smug smile curled over her face. "Naamah and I never have that problem."

"Two-hour workouts three days a week, plus two hours in the spa every week…no thanks," Eisheth said. *Find 'em, fuck 'em, and leave 'em dead is so much easier. Minimal upkeep.*

Naamah nodded agreement. Of course, all she had to do was let her naturally slutty, lustful nature take over. To Eisheth, that was almost as exhausting as Agrat Bat's routine. No, Eisheth was sure she had arrived at the best method for herself, despite the occasional setbacks. Take only as long as it took for her victim to fall in love, then use him up and toss him away like a used condom.

Agrat Bat held up a finger, and the sisters stopped bickering. They all sensed it at the same moment. Armed men were coming for them. They were driving down the road in front of the B & B, then stopping, then piling out of their SUVs.

"This ought to be fun," Naamah said.

Chapter 37

As the Guardians drew nearer to Bend, they could feel the latent sexual tension rising higher and higher. As Harrison nervously peered out the window of the SUV, everything began to remind him of sex. Trees wrapped around each other, rocks resembled women, and clouds combined and twirled as if embracing each other. It was like a mad Freudian dream.

The men in the SUVs were gripping their rifles tightly. They weren't looking at each other, weren't talking. Every once in a while, one of them would adjust his position to make room for a growing erection. No one commented, and no one teased anyone else, for they were all feeling it. The steady hum of the engines, the bumps in the road; all of it took on a rhythm that was strangely stirring.

Even Harrison was feeling it, and he'd lost interest in sex long ago, after his daughter Abigail was born and his wife left him. Most of the rest of the crew were young men, who had joined the Guardians because they liked the secretive nature of the organization, the cool guns, and the military-style training and camps, but most of all because Harrison was generous with his money.

Three black SUVs each held five men, the best and the most committed Guardians he had.

He'd weeded out the weakest, the most venal over the years, but he wasn't sure the survivors understood the seriousness of the enterprise. Most of them probably didn't believe the Succubae even existed. They probably thought Harrison had some weird sexual kink that was making him want to kidnap three women.

One thing was for sure: he ask them to do the Cutting. Even he couldn't face that.

Heinrich Gerhard is the true Guardian, he thought with a sudden moment of clarity. *We're all play-actors compared to him and his level of commitment.*

He thought about Gerhard's warning. Could he be right? Were they walking into a trap?

The rifle in his hands and the pistol at his hip reassured him. They were well armed and trained. The Guardians who had tried to confront the Daughters of Lilith in the past had had knives and swords. Modern weaponry ought to level the playing field. The backs of the vehicles were filled with every manner of nonlethal weapon: canisters of sleeping gas (and gas masks, of course), pepper spray, tranquilizer guns with enough juice to down a lion, nets, stun guns, and rubber bullets.

"Remember," Harrison said to his men, even though he'd told them the same thing a hundred times before, "don't shoot unless you have to. Even then, fire to incapacitate, if possible. We need to take at least one of the Succubae alive at all costs."

Maybe they heard me this time, he thought. *By now, they are all feeling it.*

Even he was taking it more seriously, now that the moment had come. Gerhard's warning had gotten through to him. Despite what he'd said to his men, if worse came to worst, he'd shoot the monsters in the head himself, Blood or no Blood.

It was their last chance to accomplish their goal. The money Harrison's father had made was almost gone. The younger men were losing interest in the quest, even those who were the sons of other Guardians.

Harrison was the last of the true believers. It was only his willpower and the power of his money that kept the Guardians going.

He checked his cellphone again. Frank should have called back by now. The last message had been that he'd tracked the Eisheth-Succubus to a bed and breakfast. "The sisters have arrived," the voicemail had said, and then it had been cut off, and there had been nothing since.

It was a rare occurrence for the Daughters of Lilith to all be in one place, something that seemed to happen only once a generation. It was fortunate that the Guardians been tracking Serena Carlton, or they might not have located the Succubae in time. Ever since the Guardians had realized she and Heinrich Gerhard were in communication, they'd been constantly monitoring them.

The SUVs reached the outskirts of town, and Harrison glanced out the window again. There was a shopping mall packed with cars, but there was no one in sight. Except...he lowered his eyes to sidewalk level and saw undulating movements, as if there were people on the ground twisting about.

Then it struck him what they were doing.

"God, I'm horny," one of the men in the backseat said.

"Shut up," Harrison snapped. "It's *them*. Don't let the Succubae get to you."

"Hell, I thought it would be like, you know, a really good porno movie or something," the man continued. "I mean, I've managed not to beat off to that. I've held off...but my God."

"You heard the boss, Jerry. Shut up," another man said. "I'm already having enough trouble without you talking about it."

"Focus," Harrison said. "You knew what you were in for."

No one answered, but he knew what they were thinking. None of them had known what they were in for.

They pulled up in front of the B & B.

It looked so harmless: an old Victorian, with a rose garden and a deep green lawn. And yet the wave of sexual energy emanating from the building was enough to make some of the men reach down unconsciously and begin to stroke themselves.

"Out of the car," Harrison commanded. "Remember your training. Concentrate on what you're doing. Whatever you do, don't give in to them, or it will be the last thing you do!"

They stumbled out of the vehicles and went through the motions they'd been trained in. Harrison could barely concentrate himself. If not for the constant practice, he doubted anything would have been accomplished at all.

The three teams of five men were supposed to select one of the Succubae each. Two men in each team were armed with stun guns and tranquilizer darts, two others were to handle the nets, and one man—the best shot—was to cover the others with an automatic rifle. All had pistols on their belts, but were to use them only in a life-or-death situation.

"Let's go!" Harrison shouted. "Once you have them in the nets, you should be safe." *Once you have them in the nets, you can beat off all you want,* he thought but didn't say.

They trotted up the sidewalk and into the B & B. Harrison directed one team upstairs and another down the hallway, and pointed his own team toward a giant sitting room just off the entrance.

He heard the soft thud of tranquilizer guns being fired, saw the sparking of the stun guns. A single shot rang out. He turned into the sitting room.

Two of his men were on the floor, their heads nearly detached. The men with the nets were standing there, nets hanging uselessly in their hands. A single Succubus stood in the center of the room, a blonde Goddess, the image of every sexual fantasy Harrison had ever had. She was naked, and her voluptuous body was beckoning, ready for him, ready to fulfill any desire.

"Stay back!" he managed to shout to his surviving men, but they weren't listening. Instead, they were listening to the same siren song he was hearing.

He lifted the rifle and took aim.

Pull the trigger. God…pull the trigger.

He dropped the gun to the floor and stepped forward. One of his men had already stripped, and the Goddess had mounted him standing up. He stood there grunting as she swayed up and down on him until he cried out, his legs buckling. He was not the strong young man he'd been when he entered the room, but looked as though he was a hundred years old, wrinkled, with scrawny limbs and mottled skin.

The victim fell backward, landing with a soft plop, as if he weighed nothing. A second man had his pants down, and the Goddess pushed him to the floor and mounted him. She took him twice while Harrison watched helplessly. The man kept crying out, and it sounded like both "yes" and "no" at the same time. Then there were just helpless sounds as the last of his life drained out of him.

Despite all this, if anything, the Goddess's sexual allure only grew.

Harrison couldn't move, except to move his hand down to his cock and start stroking it. After the Succubus finished with the second man, she stood and walked toward him, her hips swaying seductively. She wasn't bothering to hide her real features now, the sharp nose and chin, the pointed ears, and the long, sharp fangs.

It didn't matter. Her body held him hypnotized. She clutched him in what seemed a gentle manner and pulled him down on top of her as she landed on the couch. He began pushing into her, and it was the sweetest sensation he'd ever felt, sweeter than his first time with Virginia when he thought that he could die then and be happy.

I'm going to die now, Harrison thought. And the fear almost made him stop for a second, but the Goddess hissed, and he felt desire completely blank his mind.

His last thought was of the nets.

I thought we could catch them with nets, he thought. *How messed up is that?*

And then he thought no more.

Chapter 38

"So you're staying here?" Naamah asked that night, sounding disappointed.

They'd left the bodies of the Guardians lying on the floor, no more consequential than the furniture. Eisheth had gotten a good workout, but she still didn't feel quite back to normal. She had felt the shock of the stun gun one of the men had managed to fire, whereas she knew her sisters probably hadn't felt a thing.

"I'm not ready," Eisheth answered. If she'd been alone, she probably would have gone out, but she didn't want her sisters judging her.

"We don't need her," Agrat Bat said to Naamah. "Let's see if there is anyone else in this town worth taking to bed."

"Who needs a bed?" Naamah smirked, following her out the door.

Her sisters were as good as their word. Later that night, they brought two handsome specimens back to Eisheth. Both men fell in love with her instantly.

She drained them of their life force in ten minutes flat.

Eisheth felt her body mending at last. She dropped the second man to the floor, turned to her sisters, and raised her arms in triumph.

"We are together at last!" Naamah cried out, delighted.

Agrat Bat said, "Yes, the Daughters of Lilith are as one. Let no man escape our wiles!"

"We'll take them all," Naamah said. "We'll Cull every man in this godforsaken town."

"Sure." Agrat Bat's nose wrinkled in distaste. "As soon as we dispose of the bodies."

"Why bother?" Eisheth said. "We'll be out of here before anyone finds them. Besides, we're going to do worse."

Agrat Bat lightened up for once. "You're right. This town needs a good screwing."

They left the B & B and started walking, and it seemed like everywhere they went, men were waiting. But after several hours of prowling the streets, Eisheth realized her heart wasn't in it.

"I don't want *these* men," she complained to Naamah, dropping a man into the gutter after she'd drained him. A few days before, it would have been life restoring; now it was little more than an appetizer. "I want the Culls who escaped. I want *them*."

"Escaped?" Agrat Bat cried in mock horror. "You let *men* escape, little sister?"

Eisheth winced. She had thought her older sister was busy, Culling two men at the same time in the alley around the corner, or she wouldn't have said anything.

"How did you manage to fall so far, so fast, little sister?" Agrat Bat said pityingly.

"How many escaped?" Naamah asked, her eyes wide with curiosity.

"Four," Eisheth muttered.

"Speak up, sister!" Agrat Bat said, but Naamah had heard her.

"Four?" Naamah breathed. "How is that possible?"

Eisheth was embarrassed, but she was also revived enough to be indignant at being questioned. "The fates conspired," Eisheth said. "A wild animal attacked me and killed my first Cull before I was finished. I was wounded, badly."

"And the second one?" Naamah asked.

"I was unaware that he'd just fallen in love," Eisheth said in a low voice, as if hoping they wouldn't hear her. It was something they would tease her about for a thousand years. Letting a virile male get away was rare. It had happened only a few times to any of them.

"And the third?" Agrat Bat was aghast.

"There wasn't enough privacy," Eisheth said defensively. "His girlfriend found us."

"And you let her live?"

"I was weakened by the first two Culls," Eisheth mumbled.

"Who was the fourth?" Naamah asked, sounding slightly more sympathetic than her older sister.

"We were interrupted…" She stopped, trying to explain to herself as well to her sisters what had happened. "A woman attacked me…she bit me while we fought and took my Blood."

"She *took* your *Blood*?" Naamah repeated. "How did she know to do that?"

Eisheth tried to shrug it off. "She's the mother of a Cull I took a while back. She's been tracking me, but I didn't think she could actually *find* me. She must have been talking to the Guardian."

"You've been sloppy, Eisheth," Agrat Bat said angrily. "You know the rules. Any man who finds out who we are can't be allowed to live."

"Yes, but you're the one who wanted to keep the Guardian alive," Eisheth said. "That was a mistake."

Naamah didn't speak, but it was clear she agreed.

"Besides, it wasn't a man who stopped me," Eisheth said. "It was a woman."

Agrat Bat looked angry enough to spit. "Any *human*; it goes without saying."

Eisheth flushed. Her big sister's superior tone was unendurable. *Screw this. I've had enough.* She felt well enough to move on, though not completely recovered. She decided then and there that as soon as this night was over, she was getting out of town. Let her two interfering sisters deal with the wreckage.

"But I think you're right about one thing, dear sister," Agrat Bat said after a few moments. "No man can be allowed to live to tell the tale."

Naamah nodded her agreement. "Or woman?"

"Or woman," Agrat Bat nodded decisively. "Where do we find them?"

Chapter 39

Serena awoke in darkness. Someone was pounding at the door. She groaned and stumbled out of bed. Cary was beside her but didn't stir.

Bobbie Jo was standing in the hallway, looking distraught. "I can't wake Adam up!" she said.

"What do you mean?" Serena looked back over her shoulder at Cary. She was suddenly certain something was wrong. Cary hadn't budged despite the loud noise.

She went over and shook him gently. She leaned down and whispered in his ear, "Wake up, Cary, my dear."

She shook harder: no response. Then something compelled her to pinch his arm, so hard he should have leapt out of bed cursing. Nothing. His cock was rampant however; it seemed to be twitching. She put out her hand to touch it, then withdrew. Something was happening here that she didn't understand.

Lucinda hurried into the room, and Serena knew the instant she saw the girl's panicked expression that Jeremy was in the same comatose state.

"What's happened to them?" Lucinda asked.

"I don't know," Serena said. "But I know this much: it's because of them, the Daughters of Lilith."

"The Daughters?" Bobbie Jo said, emphasizing the s at the end. "I still can't get over the idea that there's more than one of these horrible Succubitches in town."

Cary stirred behind them, sitting up and glaring at them. His eyes glinted in the moonlight, and he made no effort to hide his raging hard-on. Serena wanted to drape a blanket over him.

Without giving them so much as a glance, he walked toward the door, naked.

"Cary?" Serena said. "Where are you going?"

He ignored her. She ran to the doorway, blocking his way.

He slapped her across the face. "Out of my way, bitch," he snarled.

Serena was too stunned to do anything. She backed up and sat on the bed, dazed.

Cary opened the door and went into the hallway just as Adam, naked and hard, was going by. Bobbie Jo rushed after him, grabbing him by the arm. "Wait just one minute, buster," she said. Adam whirled around, swinging his fist and striking her in the chin. Bobbie Jo fell backward, cursing.

Serena watched Cary leave as if in a dream. Adam and Jeremy, both also nude, joined him in the hallway. All three headed for the exit.

The Daughters of Lilith waited on the sidewalk outside the Cambridge Hotel, jeering and laughing as three men emerged, fully erect. There was no one on the street to notice their nudity, and if there had been any observers, they wouldn't have thought it strange. Such a state was the rule rather than the exception by now in Bend.

The men fondled their erections as they approached the sisters. Agrat Bat stroked Cary's member and started leading him away. "I see what you mean," she said appreciatively to Eisheth. "A nice, strong life force."

Naamah walked over to Adam and took him by the cock, smiling.

Eisheth followed their example and grabbed Jeremy. "Remember," Eisheth hissed. "They're *mine*. You can't have them."

"Of course, little sister," Agrat Bat said. "We'll take them back to our place. You can have them all to yourself. Plenty of other men to go around."

"What about the woman?" Eisheth asked.

"We'll get to her soon enough," Agrat Bat said.

Chapter 40

R ick felt them growing ever stronger.

The Daughters of Lilith were going to be at their most powerful when he confronted them, but he was ready. The hate for the Succubae burned within him, never diminishing no matter how many years passed. He concentrated on the rage within, fanning it to a fiery, unquenchable ball within his chest.

Just over the summit of Santiam Pass in the Cascades, he got a short, stark text.

Serena: *They've taken him.*

Rick wasn't sure who "him" was, but he immediately texted back.

Rick: *Stay put. I'll be there in minutes.*

He started passing cars, dangerously, barely avoiding a head-on crash more than once. He sped through the town of Sisters, dodging pedestrians, blaring his horn to get people off the road. He made it to the outskirts of Bend in record time.

A car blew through a red light, just missing him and smashing into the side of a pickup. The driver flew through the windshield and onto the road, his pants around his knees. The woman servicing him was smashed against the dashboard and fell, unmoving, to the floor of the cab.

Rick barely missed being hit several more times, the drivers clearly incapacitated by their lust. In another time and place, he would have suspected drugs or alcohol, but here, now, with acts of public lewdness on every corner, more even than Haight Ashbury at its height, there could be only one source. The three sisters were in full bloom, and their sexual desires had awoken a sleepy town.

He stopped a block away from the hotel. The two Harleys that had followed him closely all the way to town pulled up behind him.

"Wow," Abigail said. "If I had any doubt *they* were here, getting off on my bike's vibrations put an end to that."

Brittany laughed. "Yeah, I'm wet all over."

Rick frowned. He waited for their smiles to fade. "This is no laughing matter."

"All right, old man," Brittany said. "Just trying to take the edge off."

"Keep that edge," he said. "You'll need it."

"What do you want us to do?" Abigail said, all business.

Rick had been mulling that over for the last fifty miles. "I need you to keep them from killing me the moment I walk in the door. I want them to *try* to seduce me."

Brittany turned her head a little quizzically. "You ready for that?"

He didn't hesitate. "I'm ready. I've been ready for decades. You do not know how much I hate them."

"So we keep them from physically slaughtering you, what else?" Brittany said.

"Nothing. I am the one who has to finish it. I must drink the Blood, and I must resist their temptation, and I must squeeze the life from them. There is nothing you can do to help me once that begins."

"Don't they weaken if they are rejected?" Abigail asked. When Rick nodded, she turned to her sister and nodded. "Then we can help."

"What do you mean?…Oh."

Both women were grinning at him. "Didn't the black leather and the Harleys give you a clue?" Abigail said teasingly. "We're such stereotypes."

"I thought…I thought you were sisters!"

They both laughed, as if delighted with the idea.

"Mr. Harrison is Abigail's dad," Brittany said. "I'm the neglected neighbor kid who always lived at their house. He's a bit like a dad to me, but…" She shrugged.

Rick shook his head ruefully. "I am a man of the last century, obviously. But this changes things. I don't want you anywhere near them."

Their grins dropped away.

"What?" Abigail said.

"You have no idea how powerful their attraction is," Rick said. "No man *or woman* who is sexually attracted to them has ever resisted them for long. I've been preparing myself for this from the time I was a very young man, which was longer ago than you think, even if you think I'm an 'old man.'"

Abigail was having none of it. "Yeah, well, how are you going to stop us?"

Rick got back in the van and poked his head out the window. "Just stay away. Believe me, you aren't ready."

He drove away, and the Harleys didn't follow.

He pulled up in front of the hotel alone.

"Who the hell does he think he is?" Brittany said, glaring at the van as Rick drove off.

"No...I think he might be right," Abigail said.

Brittany began to turn, an objection on her lips, but Abigail had come up behind her and was reaching around her waist, pulling her into her embrace and nuzzling her neck.

"That's the one disadvantage of bikes," Abigail said when they finally broke apart, still holding hands. "No backseat."

"What do we do?" Brittany said, her mind still on Rick. "We can't let him do it alone."

"But we might do more harm than good. What if *they*...if they turn us? What if we can't resist them? God knows, I'm ready to do it here in the street."

"We should follow him, at least," Brittany insisted.

Abigail nodded, then reluctantly let go of her lover's hand. "We'll see. But follow my lead, OK lover?"

Harley-Davidsons roared, the sound of their engines filling the empty street. The women cruised off, side by side. Abigail was concentrating on looking for Rick's distinctive van when she realized that Brittany had stopped. She circled back.

"What is it?" she yelled over the engines.

"Look!" Brittany was pointing down a side street. Parked in front of a large Victorian house were the three black SUVs that the Guardians had driven, their doors wide open. Brittany started down the street, but Abigail speeded up and blocked her.

"What are you doing?" Brittany demanded when she turned off her bike.

"Rick isn't there yet," Abigail said. "We can't do anything without him. He's right: as backward as it seems, only a man can kill them."

"But maybe your Daddy's already captured them," Brittany said.

Abigail didn't answer. She'd had a terrible feeling the moment she'd seen the vehicles looking abandoned that the mission had probably ended in disaster. It was an awful feeling, but there wasn't anything they could do now to help. Either the Guardians had failed or they had succeeded, but blundering in now wouldn't help matters. What made the sinking feeling worse was that she was hornier than ever.

"We'll wait for Rick," she said. There was a "For Sale" sign in the yard of a neighboring house, and Abigail pulled her Harley into the driveway. She got off and went to the side door where she couldn't be seen—not that anyone looked in shape to stop them—and broke one of the glass panes in the door. She reached in and unlocked it.

Brittany was standing beside her by then. Abigail took her hand.

"I have an idea of how we can spend our time while we're waiting," Abigail said.

"God, yes," Brittany replied.

Rick parked near the entrance of the Cambridge Hotel, leaving the rear of the van halfway in the street. He wasn't worried about a ticket. The police were either too busy to pay attention to his parking job, or (more likely) were fornicating with each other. The hippie van's eagle and peace sign were barely discernable, but the old vehicle was still a solid piece of machinery. He ran his hand along the faded image as he walked by. He was quite fond of the van, though he could have easily afforded something better. Besides, it held all the gear he needed.

The lobby was empty, though judging by the loud grunting, someone was going at it hard in the office. Rick went behind the counter. The computer displayed the registration page, and he saw that Serena Carlton had booked the top floor. He took the stairs.

The doors of all the rooms were wide open, and the first three he passed were empty. He found three women in the third. He took another look—*they're barely more than girls*, he thought. They looked to be in their late teens, or early twenties at most, and the woman he sought was at least thirty-eight years old.

"Pardon me, but I'm looking for Serena Carlton," he said.

Two of the young women turned to the third, who appeared no older than they were. She was holding a wet towel to her face, and as she turned, ice cubes fell out of the folds.

"Serena?" It was obvious that she'd partaken of the Blood. *Am I too late?*

Serena didn't even look up when Rick said her name. She appeared to be in a daze. He knelt in front of her and took her hands. She jumped at the touch and gave him a panicked look.

"It's Rick," he said softly.

She focused on him, and he realized her stupor was not from the sexual miasma, but from grief. She reached out with trembling arms and hugged him.

"Thank God you're here," she said.

"What happened?" he asked.

"They took Cary," she said dully. Then she looked at the other two women. "They took *all* of them," she clarified.

Rick examined the three young women with growing excitement. *Can it be? Three women in love with the three current victims of the Succubae?*

"You can get them back," he said. "I can show you how."

None of them responded at first. The shorter, plumper woman looked away in disgust. A recent bruise around her eye was purpling. "Who wants them?" she said bitterly. "If Adam dares to come back, he's getting a knee to his pecker."

Serena had pulled an icepack away from her face, revealing a darkening bruise.

The third woman stepped forward with her hand out. "I'm Lucinda. That's Bobbie Jo, and that's Serena. Who you already know, I guess."

"I'm most happy to meet you all," Rick said.

"Is that a German accent?" Lucinda asked.

"I…yes. I thought I was hiding it well."

"Not bad," Lucinda said. "But you sound like my German teacher." She looked him up and down. "How come you aren't affected by those bitches?"

"I was injured in the war," Rick said, not specifying which war. "I was made…impotent."

"Lucky you," Bobbie Jo said. "Men are dicks."

"I see that I must explain something to you," Rick said as all three young women nodded in agreement that men were indeed dicks. "What you saw in your men was not them. They are being controlled. If they were violent toward you, it was not of their own free will."

"Isn't that just the kind of thing you always say?" Bobbie Jo scoffed. "'It isn't me, honey: you know I'm not like that. I promise it'll never happen again, baby.'"

"In this case, it is true," Rick said. "Let me ask you: have the men you fell in love with done anything like this before?"

"There's always a first time," Bobbie Jo said grimly.

Serena rose and faced her friends. She looked calm and focused. "He's right," she said. "That wasn't them. It was the Succubae. And if we don't do something fast, they'll die."

Rick had to tamp down his excitement. Here was young love, and not only that, but the first blush of young love, the most passionate kind. There was a chance his plan might succeed. If not, he'd go down trying. But there was zero chance he'd ever be given an opportunity like this again, no matter how long he lived.

"I swear to you," he said, "you can get them back."

This time, the women appeared to be listening.

"I have a single question," he said.

He waited until they all nodded.

"The question is this: Do your men love you as much as you love them?"

Lucinda was nodding emphatically before he even stopped speaking.

"Up until today, I thought so," Bobbie Jo said slowly.

Only Serena hesitated. Then she shook her head at the look of dismay on Rick's face. "It isn't that he doesn't love me; it's that I haven't let myself love him. But I do."

Rick listened for a false note, for any sign of doubt, but these three women were certain of their love and secure in the fact that that love was returned. "Good," Rick said. "Then we have a chance. Sit down, the three of you, and let me explain things."

"Well, don't take too long about it. Our guys could croak while you're shootin' your mouth off," Bobbie Jo interjected, her arms crossed formidably. "They'll screw them to death, right?"

"In a word, yes," Rick said. "But they won't be in a hurry. They'll want to build the desire to a fever pitch. Only then will they take them."

"What do we do, Rick?" Serena asked.

He started to tell them the history of the Succubae, but Serena interrupted him. "They already know this. I've told them everything you told me."

"Sorry," he said. "Well, here's something that I didn't know until a few days ago; or rather, I knew, but didn't think they had any chance to succeed. There are other people after the Succubae, but they want to capture them, not kill them. This would be a terrible mistake. These shadow Guardians may already be here."

"We heard gunfire not long ago," Lucinda said. "Like there was a war going on."

Rick nodded. "Then the shadow Guardians are probably already dead. I don't think it's possible to capture the Daughters of Lilith. It has only happened once, long ago, and only then by trickery. My ancestors tried many times to put the genie back in the bottle, so to speak, but never came close. I think they always made a fundamental mistake.

"They were of the belief that only men could defeat the Daughters of Lilith. But I think they had it all wrong. Men were never going to control or defeat the Succubae without the help of women. We're too weak, too prone to temptation. Men are made, in other words, of the very flesh the Succubae were created to subjugate.

"But we—men—have been blind to this fact. In our culture, we have always held the political power, the social power. In our arrogance, it never occurred to us that the answer was right beside us.

"If she is given the Blood of the Succubus, a woman is just as strong as a man, but immune to the Succubae's sexual allure...well, most of them are," he grimaced. "These modern times are so complicated."

"Right, because there were no lesbians in the ancient world," Lucinda said drily.

Rick just looked at her, at a loss for words.

"You're saying that *we* should fight them?" Serena asked, rising. She didn't appear to be dismayed by this thought; in fact, she seemed eager.

"Not physically," Rick said quickly. "The only way a Succubus can be destroyed is by a man. A fully virile man who resists her temptation. If such a man can withstand them, approach them, and kill them with his bare hands, the Succubae will be destroyed forever."

"Then why the hell haven't you assholes done it?" Bobbie Jo demanded.

"Many have tried. Innumerable times. No one has had the strength, the willpower to resist them."

"You seem to be doing pretty well," Lucinda observed.

Rick hesitated. It would probably be too dramatic to drop his pants and show them. He was surprised to discover that he still felt embarrassed, like the fifteen-year-old boy who had defied his father.

"I'm not just impotent. I've been…neutered," he said. *Neutered a thousand times.*

"How?" Serena asked.

"We do it to ourselves. We call it the Cutting."

Bobbie Jo's mouth dropped open. "Wow. Normally I'd say that takes balls."

No one laughed.

"What exactly do you want us to do?" Serena asked.

Rick didn't answer for a moment. He waited until they were all looking at him. Then said, "This is key. Nothing weakens them like the rejection of their prey. If your men can be lured away, the Succubae will be vulnerable. *Then* I can destroy them."

His announcement was greeted with silence.

"Why wouldn't they just kill us?" Bobbie Jo demanded. "And our boyfriends?"

"They might, if all is lost. But to do so would be to admit defeat. They will try to show you that they have power over your men and that there is nothing you can do about it."

He ran a hand through his hair and tried again. "The Succubae must be weakened, so that when I face them, I will have a chance."

"I thought you were…you know…missing your naughty bits," Bobbie Jo said.

"The Blood of the Succubae," Serena said. "It will restore you. Am I right?"

"Yes."

"And you think you're ready. That you will be the first man in history to resist them long enough to kill them."

"Yes."

Serena frowned. "I'm sorry, I don't mean to knock your intentions, but have you ever been with a woman? Have you experienced what they will tempt you with? Do you have *any idea* what you are up against?"

"I have loved more than one woman," Rick said. "And it is the memory of this love that will give me the strength. Ms. Carlton—Serena—Bobbie Jo, Lucinda…this is the *only* chance to save your men. If we fail, we will probably die with them."

"We'll do it," Serena said, turning to the others, who nodded their agreement.

Rick fought his elation. He might be leading these women to their deaths. But for the first time in his long life, he thought they had a chance.

Chapter 41

Serena raised her eyebrows at her first sight of the van. There'd still been a few of these love vans floating around when she was in high school, with their shag carpets, groddy pillows, and cassette tape decks blasting '70s-style stadium rock. She remembered thinking the men driving them, usually balding on top and wearing ponytails and beards, were old lechers, and stayed far, far away.

Rick looked to be in his late sixties, and Serena wondered why he didn't drink some of the Blood himself. But he'd implied that he had in the past. When he had described the Cutting, Serena had caught a glimpse of Bobbie Jo pointing a finger at her open mouth and then pretending to vomit.

But Serena was amazed by the bravery and the self-sacrifice it must take to do such a thing. She couldn't imagine doing it once, much less over and over again. These Guardians were truly dedicated to their cause. But Serena also thought she saw a defeated man in Rick. This was his last, all-or-nothing attempt, and it troubled her.

Are we on a suicide mission? she wondered.

"How much do you love your men?" he'd asked, and all three women had declared a love stronger than life itself.

Serena looked inside herself. Was her love enough? Was she really willing to sacrifice herself for Cary? Would she weaken at the last moment?

The inside of the van wasn't what she expected. It was bare metal, with racks along the sides full of weapons, blades as well as firearms. There was a large wooden box behind the driver's seat, and after motioning them in, Rick unlocked the box and pulled out a backpack. He sat on the box, undid the backpack's straps, and pulled out three bags, each of them with a carefully wrapped bottle inside.

The women crouched down at first, and then Bobbie Jo sat on the metal floor in an ungainly sprawl, and Lucinda and Serena followed her example. They stared up into the grim face of the Guardian.

"Each of you must drink of the Blood of the Succubus," he said. He removed a glass bottle filled with a thick red liquid from its enfolding towel. It was an old-fashioned Coca-Cola bottle, and for a moment Serena saw the ludicrousness of the situation. She wanted to say, *Come on, it's all a joke, right?*

There was no humor in Rick's face. He held up the bottle.

"This will not make you equal to the Succubae, for they are the vessels from which these potions were harvested. The Succubae are alive and at the height of their powers. This Blood was taken in a time long before time was counted in years or centuries.

"It is powerful. You will feel younger, more vibrant than ever before. It will make you strong, but don't be fooled. The Goddesses live every day with this same Blood coursing through their bodies. They know how to seduce a man, how to dominate him and bend him to their will. You cannot defeat them that way."

"Then why the hell are we trying?" Bobbie Jo asked.

"Because it isn't sex that will win your men back," Rick said. "Only love can do that. It isn't seduction that will draw them back to you, but tenderness and compassion. It will be the empathy you have for each other, the connections you have nurtured, the kindness you have shown each other, that will make all the difference.

"It is these simple things that you must use: the joys you have shared, the little jokes, the soft entreaties and endearments. There is no trick to this. It is a simple choice. It is you or the Succubae, and your men must pick. As powerful as the sex drive is, it is but a superficial thing, a bodily urge, though love can be expressed through sex.

"You have the advantage, though it may not seem so. If your men truly love you and you truly love them, you will have a chance. If you have any doubt of this, you must withdraw now. Facing the Daughters of Lilith without love on your side will be fatal to both you and your…partner.

"But if you believe, truly believe in each other, you can win."

Rick paused, giving each of them a chance to back out. No one said a word.

"I want to speak to you as a man, now," he continued. "Half a man, maybe, but I have my memories, and I've thought long and hard about this."

"Emphasis on *hard,*" Bobbie Jo muttered to Serena.

"These creatures you face, they were once Goddesses," Rick continued. "Their outward aspect is perfection, but they are elemental powers beneath. But remember—men do not love Goddesses, they worship them; men don't live their day-to-day lives with Goddesses; they put them on pedestals.

"The Succubae are the ideal, but you are the reality. Whatever attracted your men to you in the first place wasn't perfection—perhaps, even, the imperfections *were* the attraction. Let your men see you as you truly are. Help remind them why they love you."

No one said anything for a moment; then Serena spoke for all of them. "We understand."

Rick nodded and crawled into the driver's seat. The van's gears ground as he set off.

"Come on, baby, hang in there," he muttered, patting the dashboard. "Just one last trip."

Those words hung in the air on the drive across town. *Just one last trip.*

Rick hadn't told them everything, Serena could tell. But the fundamental truth of his words came through.

It was to be a test of her love for Cary and Cary's love for her.

Serena had no illusions about the danger they faced. If the destruction of the Daughters of Lilith could be easily accomplished, they would have been killed long ago. No doubt it had been attempted many times before—which meant that all previous efforts had failed.

What makes me think I'm different?

Serena drew in a deep breath. She *wasn't.* There was nothing special about her except that she had loved her son and had lost him to the

Succubae. Now she would lose Cary if she failed in her task. These Goddesses could kill her in the space it took to draw a breath. The love she felt for Cary was deep and strong. But so was her love for her son, and that hadn't saved him from being taken. She glanced over at Lucinda and Bobbie Jo and saw no doubt in their faces. For some reason, it gave her courage.

Rick yelled over his shoulder, "We're almost there. Drink the Blood, ladies. Don't worry, the taste is masked by the honey. Just think of it as a very sweet juice."

Bobbie Jo went first, popping off the top. "Bottoms up!" she said, saluting the others. She guzzled down the contents and made a face. "Yuck."

Both Lucinda and Serena paused, their Coke bottles frozen halfway to their mouths.

Bobbie Jo had nice features, but she was stocky, and her face showed the hard life she'd lived in the tight skin around her eyes and the wrinkles around her mouth. All these blemishes instantly disappeared. Her short, sandy hair became longer and shinier, each strand thicker than before and almost glowing. Though she was still heftier than modern tastes might deem desirable, she turned into a knockout before their very eyes.

Bobbie Jo looked from one to the other. "What?"

Lucinda grinned and emptied her own bottle. She was very pretty, a little round, with unruly hair that she'd given up trying to straighten. She also had a big butt, which she was skilled at disguising. All these features diminished. She was still the same Lucinda, but somehow a Lucinda with Photoshop improvements.

Serena downed her own bottle.

She saw her transformation reflected in the eyes of the others. She'd already had a taste of the Blood, but this was ten times more, and it was as if every part of her began to operate at full capacity: heart, body, mind, and spirit.

"Wow," Lucinda breathed. "You are so gorgeous."

Bobbie Jo grinned at her. "I'm glad you have Cary," she said. "Otherwise I'd knock your block off, just in case."

The van slowed, pulling up to a large Victorian house across from downtown's Drake Park. A sign hung outside: *Bend Bed and Breakfast*.

Rick climbed over the seat and into the back of the van. His eyes widened at the sight of the women. "I do believe I feel a tingle, as impossible as that is," he said, smiling. Then he dropped his smile. "I didn't give you the Blood of the Succubae for your looks. Not matter how beautiful you think you are, the Daughters of Lilith are more so. Don't try to complete with their beauty. Love is the answer. This just gives you a chance, a little bit of a lever to gain your man's attention.

"So remember, it is your love that will win them back. Don't try to use sex appeal unless you can show the caring beneath it." He stared at Bobbie Jo until she nodded.

"I got it, I got it already," she said.

"Don't try to fight the Succubae physically," Rick warned. "The vigor you feel is something they have lived with every day. You can't win. Remember, the battleground is the men you love."

Serena sighed. "Like we're going to forget that."

He crawled past them to the van's back door and put his hand on the handle. "Ready?"

Serena felt a moment of doubt. *What if Cary doesn't love me as much as I think?*

"Let me at them Succubitches," Bobbie Jo said. Lucinda laughed, and all of Serena's doubt disappeared.

"They're waiting for you," Rick said. "They know you are coming, but they aren't concerned. They are supremely confident. They might kill you immediately, but I doubt it. If they kill you, the conquest of your men won't mean anything. So I think they'll let you try to win them back. They won't believe you can do it."

"What about you?" Lucinda asked.

Rick looked up at the weapons on the racks. "I'll be waiting. If you defeat them—that is, *when* you bring your guys out, it will be my chance. Best of luck."

He threw open the van's door. "Have at them, ladies."

Chapter 42

Despite their promises, Agrat Bat took Cary to one bed and Naamah took Adam to another. Eisheth was left with Jeremy, which wasn't enough. She wanted them all. They were *her* Cullings. Her sisters had no right to them.

"We need to show you how to milk these humans, Eisheth, dear," Agrat Bat said. "Like this…" She straddled Cary's neck and chin, allowing him to pleasure her. He licked and kissed her until she bucked in orgasm. "See, little sister?" she panted, smiling. "I've already reaped satisfaction without even beginning the Cull."

In the next bed over, Naamah brought Adam closer and closer to a climax without letting him go over the top. She ground into him slowly, stopping whenever he started to grunt. It was all so familiar. They'd once spent centuries together in one small cave; instinctively, they'd moved their beds into the same room. To them, sex was a public thing, something to be displayed, a show of dominance.

Eisheth knew how to do all these things, of course. She was just as old and experienced as her sisters. She simply didn't see the point of drawing it out.

She mounted Jeremy, put her talons on his neck, and used all her abilities to make him come. Then she started again, and he quickly approached another orgasm. Between her regained powers and his youthful virility, he was probably good for another half-dozen climaxes before he was dead.

Suddenly she felt a void, a suction as she was lifted straight into the air. Agrat Bat had pulled her off in the middle of the act.

"You are not listening to me, sister," Agrat Bat said. "Let him recover. Make it last. I don't want a dead man lying around, nor am I inclined to help you dispose of him when you've drained him, Eisheth. Just take what you need. "

The lecture was one too many. Eisheth didn't consciously decide to attack: she simply transformed into her natural form before she could stop herself. Long talons appeared on the ends of her hands and feet, her teeth elongated into fangs, and her soft body became dry and hard, the muscles taut and tough. She looked like the creature that mankind called a harpy, a Gorgon, or a dragon.

A Succubus.

She slashed the blonde Goddess across her torso, tearing her abdomen wide open. Blood sprayed out, and some of Agrat Bat's organs protruded, but the damage repaired itself in seconds. Eisheth knew she'd made a mistake. Her sister transformed instantly, and dimly, through her fury, Eisheth recalled that Agrat Bat was not only bigger and stronger than her, but that her teeth and claws were longer and far more deadly.

In a heartbeat, Eisheth was lying on her back with Agrat Bat pounding down on her, each blow cutting more skin and smashing more bone. Eisheth couldn't repair herself as quickly as Agrat Bat could. She felt her strength ebbing. Naamah tried to pull Agrat Bat off her, but their older sister lashed out, cutting Naamah's neck in her rage.

All their wounds healed almost instantly, but each of them felt weaker. It didn't worry them. This little fight between sisters was almost inevitable. This type of thing had happened many times before—that's why they had separated in the first place. They had a whole town with which to restore their strength.

Agrat Bat raised her talons again, and then stopped. She rose, shifting back into her blonde Goddess form.

"They're coming," she said.

Cary came back to himself lying naked on a bed, unable to move, while monsters grappled with each other just feet away. One of these monsters had been draining him only moments before. *Where am I?* he wondered. *What are those things?* He tried to sit up but couldn't move.

The last thing he remembered was spending hours in bed with Serena. He closed his eyes at the memory, trying to recall the peace he'd felt.

One of the creatures hissed, "They're coming."

Serena was coming for him; somehow he knew this. He gasped for breath and tried to rise on one elbow, but fell back with a groan. He felt as though he was drugged, his thoughts sluggish under a layer of thick confusion, all meanings blurred. But his love for Serena cut through the miasma, and fear for her accelerated his awakening.

When the monsters flashed back into women, they looked strangely familiar. The one who been on top of him before he came back put her hand firmly and possessively on his chest, pushing him down, and at her touch, his memory began to fade again.

Cary reached out to Serena with his mind.

Go back, Serena. Go back! They'll kill you. Don't let them…not for me…go back…

Blood called to Blood, leading Serena directly to the Succubae. Cary was there, perhaps even now being drained by one of the monsters she'd sworn to destroy.

She led her friends to the second floor and down the hall to the master suite at the end. The door was open, and she didn't hesitate to enter.

Cary lay on his back, staring at her, begging her with his expression…then the Succubus stepped up next to him, sliding her hand over his chest and then down around his engorged and glistening cock. Cary closed his eyes and moaned.

The Succubus captured Serena's gaze, and her heart sank. The woman was impossibly beautiful, as if all the blonde movie stars of old had been melded into one irresistible creature.

She isn't a woman, Serena thought. *She's only a wet dream, nothing more.*

She was the *Other*, wanting the person Serena loved, trying to steal what was hers, the man who had come out of nowhere long after she'd given up on love. This thought gave Serena resolve beyond the justice she once craved. Rick was right. Revenge was not enough. She had to fight for love, love for a young man who had joined her crusade without complaint, who had comforted her when she asked for comfort and hadn't taken advantage of her.

She would give him more in return, every day of his life, if she could but save him.

One of the same monsters who had taken her son was now destroying her hopes for the future. It was only now, after just one night with Cary, that she realized she'd been a fool. She loved Cary, and had loved him from the start, but had come up with excuse after excuse to deny her love. She could not let him down now.

This thing who confronted her, who had stolen Cary away, this wasn't a woman. This was a creature from the subterranean depths of man's hatred and fears, the enemy of love and life.

It was the sight of Cary, so pitifully trapped by his own desires, ensnared behind this monster, that gave Serena the strength to go on. The sexual allure of the Succubae suddenly struck her as tawdry, demeaning. Lust had trapped Cary, but love would free him.

She heard Bobbie Jo's voice. "Get your ass over here, Adam."

It was quickly followed by Lucinda's softer voice. "Jeremy?"

When she heard the fragile human voices of her friends, all the love she felt for Cary flowed out of her.

"Cary," Serena said. "I love you. Come back to me."

Cathy was everything Jeremy desired and more. How could he have ever left her? She was the girl he'd pined for in every nerdy movie and TV show he ever watched, who paid attention only to him, no matter who else was around, who actually liked his weird interests. And most of all, she *wanted* him, *wanted* to have sex.

She walked toward him, and his heart skipped with each little bounce of her mischievous step.

When Lucinda came through the door, he barely paid her any attention.

"Jeremy?"

Then Lucinda's soft voice called his name, and he glanced over curiously. It was that girl, the cheerleader who had somehow latched onto him—after embarrassing him for years. Why would he ever go back to that? He stared up at Cathy, at her perfect face, the face of a thousand dreams before he'd even met her.

And yet…

"Jeremy."

Lucinda repeated his name, and the memory of them playing on the beach came back to him, and he suddenly recalled how her image had also filled a thousand nights, how he'd longed for her from across crowded classrooms, and the high school football games where his only objective was to watch her, the lead cheerleader, being acrobatically tossed into the air and landing gracefully.

He remembered the quiet times, too, studying together and going for walks, laughing about mundane things, things only they understood as funny.

"Jeremy," she said, her whisper soft and filled with a longing that suffused his heart.

Confused, he glanced at Cathy and saw not the manic pixie dream girl, but the Succubus: evil, superficially beautiful, and empty. Worse, he saw that she hated him, hated *all* men, and all of humanity. He saw that now. She would use him up until there was nothing left.

"Come back to me," Lucinda whispered, stretching out her hand toward him.

To his own surprise, Jeremy rose from the bed.

Agrat Bat struggled to keep her unease from showing on her face. She rarely felt fear. Once she'd been unchained, few men had ever resisted her charms, and physically, she was far stronger than any human.

But she sensed her own Blood coursing through the dark woman facing her. Not Naamah's nor Eisheth's, but her own. Worse, across from Naamah stood a woman with *her* Blood, and the same was true of Eisheth's adversary. The coincidence of this, almost as if it were destined, gave the Succubus pause. Whether she was an instrument of God's justice or Satan's capriciousness, she neither knew nor cared, but this...this was unnerving.

But she'd learned that her path often skewed in mysterious ways. She'd often believed she had Culled at her own choosing, only to discover a deeper meaning behind the selection of her victims.

This Blood was taken from us, millennia ago, when we were mankind's prisoners, when they tortured us, year after year, century after century. This Blood came from our torture.

It was the unfairness of this that enraged her. That her own Blood, the very thing that gave her strength and power, should be used against her struck her like a blade to her heart. This woman had had but a tiny portion of it, and it was old; ancient, even. The rest—the real Blood—coursed through Agrat Bat's own veins, multitudes stronger.

I can kill her with a single blow, she thought.

And yet she hesitated, knowing that something would be lost, that to do so would be to admit that the other woman's appeal was stronger. That would be a defeat. She sensed, though it had never happened, that it would be a weakening she would never recover from. It was a law that had never been stated aloud, never written down, the essence of the war between the Three Daughters of Lilith and humanity. She must win through her wiles, not her strength, or she would be diminished, perhaps fatally.

"Stay right there, Cary," she purred in her most seductive voice. She put her hand on his forehead and stroked his hair, then ran her fingers down his chest and stomach. His cock quivered at her touch.

It was a mistake. Her voice betrayed her fear and doubt.

"Cary, she doesn't love you," said the human woman, Serena. "Remember what my hand feels like. Remember the love and gentleness we shared. That's not what this creature is doing to you. She appeals only to your body. Remember our love, the bond of heart and mind we have."

Agrat Bat could scarcely believe it. The man's erection was starting to deflate, self-awareness lighting up in his eyes. She dropped to her knees and gave his cock a soft lick. It sprang upward again, and a small bit of pre-come leaked out. She could think of no words to help her cause, and with that realization, she lowered her mouth onto his member, and he moaned.

"Don't be fooled, Cary," the woman continued. Her voice trembled, but with resolve, not fear. "She hates you. She will kill you when she is finished with you. If you let her have her way, we will never be together again."

Serena came nearer. Agrat Bat was so enraged that she wanted to tear the woman's head off.

I'm weaker than I thought. I can't allow her such a cheap victory. I must defeat her as I have every other human, by being more desirable.

She turned Cary's face toward her and put on her most beguiling smile. She leaned down to kiss him. He lifted his face, eager.

"Cary," Serena said softly.

At the last moment, he turned his head, and the kiss became a hard peck on the cheek. Agrat Bat could tell it meant nothing to him. He was feeling disgust, with himself for falling for such a creature and at her for using him.

Agrat Bat hissed, and whatever allure she still held disappeared completely.

The human female stood on the other side of the bed, maddeningly ignoring Agrat Bat's presence, smiling down on her man. She held out her hand, and Cary moved to take it. Agrat Bat's talon sank into his arm and he cried out, staring up at her in horror.

And the Succubus knew she had lost.

She looked to her sisters. Naamah was on her knees, her head down, as her Cull was led away. Eisheth was slashing at the pillows and mattresses of her bed. Her Cull was in the arms of his woman.

The Goddesses had lost...to mere mortal women.

But there was no reason to leave the humans alive now. Agrat Bat saw the same thought bloom in the eyes of her sisters, and they began to transform.

Surprisingly, it was Naamah who struck first. She scuttled across the floor, catching Adam just as he was nearing Bobbie Jo. Naamah swiped at his neck, and his head flopped to one side, blood fountaining over Bobbie Jo.

Bobbie Jo screamed, "You bitch!" and launched herself at Naamah, who extended a single, long talon, which punctured the girl in the chest. The human looked down with a puzzled expression. "Oh, shit," she said.

Naamah lifted the girl into the air and watched as she shuddered a couple of times and then died.

With a terrifying scream, Agrat Bat launched herself at Serena and Cary, intending to follow her sister's example. They would be weakened, but at least they would have the satisfaction of destroying their enemies. They had all the time in the world to become Goddesses again.

She felt something hard slam into her chest, and a part of her scalp flew off her head. Suddenly, she was falling backward. The pain hit as she landed, as bullets slapped against the wall behind her.

"Hurry!" a man shouted from the doorway. "Take your loved ones and get out. I will end this."

Agrat Bat got to her feet, the Blood streaming down her face and neck, confused and disoriented. Cary's rejection had taken its toll, even more than the bullets. She could barely summon the strength to stand.

She hadn't been defied in centuries, and in one day, not only had she lost a Cull, but here came someone challenging her face to face. He was a handsome man, naked, his huge member engorged. He had a pistol in his hand, and he was grinning defiantly at the Succubae.

It was a Guardian. No, it was *the* Guardian, the last of his kind, the one who had been hunting them for decades. She had convinced her sisters to let him live so that they might torture him and take revenge. He had partaken of the Blood. His cock was rampant, and she could feel his desire.

Agrat Bat was enraged. This mortal thought he could withstand the wiles of all Three Daughters of Lilith. She gave a low laugh and used the last of her strength. She sealed her wounds and covered her bloody countenance with her best illusion.

Beside her, she saw Eisheth transforming the opposite way, turning into her eternal form and running toward the Guardian, her talons out stretched.

Agrat Bat cried out, "No, sister!"

The Guardian didn't see her coming.

The door flew open and two human women burst into the room, dressed in the same battle gear as the men who'd been killed earlier. But the sisters hadn't sensed these women coming.

The women riddled Eisheth with bullets, shredding flesh and bone. Eisheth suddenly shrank. The bullets couldn't kill her, but she now looked more like an animal than a woman. Her face flickered as she tried to take a pleasing shape, but she remained broken and bleeding.

"Finish it, Guardian!" one of the women shouted. "We'll cover you."

Chapter 43

Newspapers and mail were piled high in the hall near the front door of the house that Abigail had broken into, so they weren't worried about being discovered. There was a bedroom on the second floor that looked out over the street.

They fell into bed, undressing each other awkwardly while kissing, and started to make love. The erotic atmosphere was overwhelming, and soon both women were crying out from their repeated orgasms.

Despite it all, Abigail was apparently keeping watch, because she suddenly reared up and stared out the window.

"Rick's van just went by," she said. She got out of bed and quickly started dressing.

Brittany followed more reluctantly. "What are we going to do?" she asked.

"I don't care what he says," Abigail answered. "Rick needs our help."

"But...are we ready?"

Abigail stopped and stared at Brittany.

"I mean...the Succubae are apparently irresistible," Brittany continued. "I love you, babe, but I'm a horny bitch, you know that."

Abigail started to protest, then stopped. "Remember Florence," she said simply.

The beach at Florence, Oregon, was where they had first made love, after dancing around the subject for years. They'd never been apart since.

"Safeword?" Brittany said.

Abigail grinned. "Safeword."

Abigail dug into their backpacks and pulled out the two bottles of Blood. "Are you ready?"

Brittany hid her uncertainty and put out her hand. She popped the lid and drank. It tasted like one of the smoothies her mother insisted on making for her, with vegetables and fruit and only God knew what else. She'd learned to drink them fast and smile.

Abigail was still choking down her drink when Brittany finished hers, but managed to get it all down.

They walked to the bed and breakfast, since it was so close, leaving their Harleys in the driveway of the house they'd broken into. With every step, Brittany felt stronger, more alive than she'd ever felt. She felt as if she could leap into the air and start flying.

So this is the Blood, she thought. *No wonder men desire it.*

The door of the B & B was wide open. The first room they passed had a pile of clothing in the middle of it. Brittany took a second look and gasped. There were bodies—or parts of bodies—within those piles of cloth. The cloth was the remnants of black fatigues, just like the ones Brittany and Abigail were wearing.

"Don't go in there..." she started to say, but Abigail had already brushed by her. She looked down and let out a small cry. Brittany didn't want to get any closer to the carnage, but it looked like Abigail had recognized her father. She stood silently for a moment, then hoisted her rifle and marched past Brittany, her jaw set.

Well, now Abigail will stay resolute, Brittany thought.

They were on their way up the stairs when they heard people descending. They both took aim. It was two young couples. The women were supporting the men, who looked dazed.

"Rick?" Abigail asked.

One of the women, who seemed slightly older than the rest, answered, "He's inside. You'd better hurry. He'll need help."

Abigail pushed past them and Brittany followed, trying to give the escapees a brave smile. Brittany met the older woman's eyes, and a shock of recognition went through her.

Blood calls to Blood.

Can I do this? she wondered, one last time.

Abigail opened the door without hesitation, and Brittany hurried to catch up. They entered the room just as a wild creature was leaping toward Rick. He had his back to his attacker and didn't see the thing coming.

Abigail fired, and the creature, who had the shape of a woman but wasn't, fell to the floor, shredded by the bullets. Brittany swung her gun around to cover her, and that's when she saw the vision at the center of the room.

Abigail told her that the Succubae once were Goddesses, but Brittany had assumed it was a figure of speech. But the apparition before her was no mere mortal woman, but someone from a higher plane, tall and blonde, her body well proportioned, her face so beautiful that Brittany couldn't take her eyes off her.

She dropped her gun without realizing it and fell to her knees in front of the Goddess, reaching up to touch her.

Women had never before defied Agrat Bat. Men had always been her enemy, but she'd felt nothing but contempt for the women. Yet...there was something here. As she gazed upon the humans, she saw one of the women looking at her perfect nude body in appreciation. Agrat Bat turned every ounce of her glamour on the mortal.

The woman dropped her weapon.

"Brittany," the other woman said. "What are you doing?"

As if pulled by a string, Brittany went to Agrat Bat and fell to her knees. Agrat Bat felt her energy returning.

We can still win this, she thought.

"Come back to me, Brittany," the other woman said. "Remember Florence."

The girl at Agrat Bat's feet looked up, seeming confused. "Abigail?" She tried to rise.

Agrat Bat put out her hand to keep her new admirer on her knees.

"Are you going to let this bitch dominate you?" Abigail's sharp voice made Brittany lift her head, as if she suddenly realized where she was.

Brittany rose suddenly and scrambled away from Agrat Bat, snatching up her gun. "Sorry, Abigail," she muttered.

Agrat Bat was too stunned to move. She felt her knees buckle as the rejection took hold. Too many rejections, too quickly. Both the Guardian and the women now had guns pointed at her.

"Do what you have to do, Rick," Abigail said.

Amazed by the events, Rick quickly strode to Eisheth's battered body and grabbed her by the neck.

"Try to seduce me now," he said. His hands tightened on her neck, turning white with the tremendous pressure as Eisheth's face darkened, her eyes becoming huge. Blood poured from her mouth and eyes. He leaned over and took a lick.

"So much stronger than the bottled stuff," he said.

Agrat Bat gathered herself to leap. It would be better to be physically destroyed than to let the psychic damage continue. On the other side of her, she saw Naamah preparing to do the same thing.

Naamah jumped first, but bullets struck her in midair, nearly cutting her in half, sending her sideways and into the wall.

Agrat Bat froze. Both her sisters were injured, but Rick was concentrating on Eisheth. Her sister struggled against the Guardian, but it was not a battle she could win. He had rejected her advances, and she was too weak physically to shake him off.

"Stop," Eisheth pleaded. "I will be yours…"

She took the form of a woman for a moment, and then a small animal. Human and animal forms alike flickered desperately, a Proteus dying. Then she stopped moving altogether.

It took only a few moments, but to Agrat Bat, it was an eternity. *I'm the strong one*, she thought. *I must save her.*

And yet she did nothing. She watched Eisheth die, unable to move: Eisheth, who as a Goddess had wanted only peace and harmony with mankind, who had fallen in love with the Storm King and thus doomed them all. Eisheth didn't even struggle at the end.

The Guardian dropped Eisheth's remains to the floor. She was a shriveled and broken husk, her Blood congealed as if frozen by the air, then turned to dust.

Heinrich Gerhard turned his gaze on Naamah and Agrat Bat with a triumphant shout of joy. "Gone! I've killed one of you at last. And now you are all going to die."

He looked older now, not quite as handsome, and Agrat Bat sensed the Blood thinning in his body.

Naamah managed to get to her feet. She somehow still had the strength to heal herself and to take on an attractive form. She approached Rick slowly, swaying. The human women's fingers tightened on the triggers of their guns, but they didn't fire.

"Can you do it?" the taller of the women asked. "Can you resist her?"

"Stay back," the Guardian said.

Naamah looked softer and more vulnerable than Agrat Bat had ever seen. "Please," she said, reaching for the Guardian. She rested her hand on his arm. "There is no need for this. We can have each other, forever."

The man's cock returned to its former glory. He reached out for her. Her soft belly pushed his cock up between them, and she gently rubbed up and down on it, staring adoringly up at his face.

"Claresa," he whispered, his eyes widening in surprise.

For the first time, the man seemed to feel doubt. Even though he knew it was an illusion, that didn't lessen its force. Whoever this Claresa had been, she was important to him.

Then he shook himself, gripped Naamah's neck, and choked the life from her.

Scarcely had Naamah's body thudded to the floor when the Guardian turned to Agrat Bat. The two women had moved to his side and were holding their guns on her. But Agrat Bat simply stood there, unable to summon any emotion whatsoever.

Her sisters were gone. She was alone for the first time. A vast sense of loss and emptiness filled her, but she consoled herself with the thought that she wouldn't have to be alone for long.

So this is how it ends, she thought.

The Guardian came toward her, reaching for her neck.

Self-preservation finally kicked in. She screeched her defiance, ready to tear him apart.

"Not going to play fair?" one of the women asked, and calmly lifted her gun and shot Agrat Bat in the gut.

She fell to the floor, unable to move. The man lay on top of her, his cock still hard, but he didn't enter her.

Like the sun passing behind a cloud, the light dimmed. Agrat Bat looked up at her lover—her killer—and she saw the rough face of Moros the blacksmith, the human she'd most liked, a human who had worshipped her and who had sacrificed himself for her.

He smiled welcomingly.

She was going to die, but she would live on. For the Goddesses were eternal, and as long as man existed, he would need them. And as the light dimmed, Agrat Bat remembered the benediction she hadn't thought of in millennia.

"We are here. Your prayers have moved us, and we will give you succor. For we are the natural mothers of all things, the powers of life, in our form, the Three…"

Epilogue

When Rick emerged from the Bend Bed & Breakfast, he was no longer the young, vibrant man who had burst naked into the suite to confront the Three Daughters of Lilith. Serena blushed at the memory of his rampant appendage, huge and red.

I can still be embarrassed, she thought in wonderment.

Rick appeared older now, in his mid-thirties or so. He looked tired, but serene. He was dressed in an ill-fitting shirt and pants, and was barefoot. Two women in black leather followed him. They ignored the others and kept walking, then started up two Harley-Davidsons in a nearby driveway with a roar and drove away.

Cary and Jeremy's nakedness was hidden in the back of the van. The town's inhabitants were awakening from their sexual abandon as the carnal energy dissipated like a cloud dispersing. Half-dressed people on the street stopped what they were doing, staring shame-faced about them before scurrying for cover instead of completing their carnal relations with total strangers.

Rick took a gas can out of the back of the van and went back into the Victorian building. When he returned, flames were already flickering behind the gabled windows.

"What about the owner?" Lucinda asked.

Rick simply shook his head.

No one spoke on the drive back to the Cambridge Hotel. Rick pulled up in front, allowing the engine to idle while Lucinda wrapped Jeremy and Cary in sheets and hurried them upstairs.

"Why don't you come in and rest?" Serena suggested. "We have an extra room. I'll buy you lunch. It's the very least I could do."

"No, thank you," Rick said. "I kind of want to start my new life as soon as possible. Something simple, not too exciting." He started up the van. Serena hesitated at the driver's-side window.

"The Blood will wear off after a while," Rick said. "Enjoy it while you can. There is no more Blood of the Succubus to be had. Ever."

"Hooray!" Serena said, and he chuckled.

"Thank you," she began, then hesitated, wanting to say what was impossible to put into words.

"Thank *you*," he responded. "I could not have accomplished this without you. Truly."

She stepped back, and the van lurched its way down the street, backfiring and belching black smoke as it went.

Only then did Serena finally relax. She fell slightly backward, knowing Cary had returned, dressed now, and would catch her, and as his arms enveloped her, she closed her eyes, and for the first time since his death, Serena was able to cry for her son.

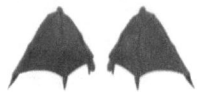

Brittany cheated on Abigail for the first time only a few weeks later. Worse, it was with a man, not a woman. They'd talked about the possibility of her straying, because she truly was a "horny bitch," as she'd said, but it was always assumed by both of them that it would be with a woman.

Even stranger, she thoroughly enjoyed it, though a penis had never held much interest for her before. She had so much energy after the affair that she immediately went to another bar and picked up another man, and instead of it tiring her, she came home jazzed.

She waited for Abigail to get home from work, wondering whether to confess. When Abigail walked in the door, more cheerful and talkative than usual, Brittany recognized the signs. Abigail had gotten laid too. It had probably been a man, since she had that predilection.

What's happening to us? Brittany asked herself.

Neither woman said anything to the other.

Serena waited for the Blood to wear off, and took advantage of its effects as much as she could until Cary begged for relief, laughing. She often joked about him robbing the cradle, and new acquaintances were puzzled at the laughter it provoked in Serena, because to outward appearances, she looked a good decade younger than him, instead of the other way around.

"You're wearing me out," he said a few months later, after they had made love for most of the evening. He said it as if he was joking, but there was an element of grumbling beneath it.

Serena had no patience for it. She wanted more.

She swung over onto him, and when he didn't respond, she started to gently stroke his cock.

"I think I'm done," he said.

She ignored him.

Serena felt something stir inside her, a desire so strong that it seemed to pour out of her, and sure enough, his erection returned, harder than ever.

She positioned herself on top of him and started grinding.

"Enough, Serena," he pleaded. "I need some rest."

She paid no attention and kept going until he grunted, almost in pain, and came for the third time that evening.

Serena still didn't feel satisfied, and she went down on him, licking and sucking him until he was hard once again, ignoring his protestations.

She'd felt something the last time he had climaxed. It was as if a part of him had entered her, giving her a euphoric energy. Surely that couldn't be a bad thing? Cary was being childish, denying her this pleasure. She knew that deep down he was enjoying it too; why else would he orgasm?

She rode him, eyes closed, not noticing the look of fear that came over her lover's face.

She just wanted a little more.

About the Author

Duncan grew up and spent most of his life in Central Oregon, the dry side of the Cascades, and whose terrain is featured in many of his books. He wrote several books out of college, including the heroic fantasy novels *Star Axe*, *Snowcastles*, and *Icetowers*. In 1984, he and his wife Linda bought Pegasus Books in downtown Bend, Oregon, which they still own and operate. They also ran a used bookstore, the Bookmark, for 15 years.

In the last five years, he's been able to get back to writing again, and found that he has a lot of pent-up creative energy. He's written numerous books for several different publishers, mostly in the horror or dark fantasy genres, though recently has been branching out into fantasy again, as well as thrillers.

BIBLIOGRAPHY

The Tuskers Series

Tuskers I: Wild Pig Apocalypse

Tuskers II: Day of the Long Pig

Tuskers III: Omnivore Wars

Tuskers IV: Rise of the Cloven

The Vampire Evolution Trilogy

Book I: Death of an Immortal

Book II: Rule of Vampire

Book III: Blood of Gold

The Virginia Reed Adventures

Led to the Slaughter

The Dead Spend No Gold

The Darkness You Fear

Other books

Star Axe

Snowcastles & Icetowers

Blood of the Succubus

Castle La Magie

Deadfall Ridge

Eden's Return

Faerie Punk

Freedy Filkins

Gargoyle Dreams

I Live Among You

Shadows over Summer House

Snaked

Takeover

Curious about other Crossroad Press books? Stop by our website:
http://crossroadpress.com
We offer quality writing
in digital, audio, and print formats.

Subscribe to our newsletter on the website homepage and receive a
free eBook.

www.ingramcontent.com/pod-product-compliance
Lightning Source LLC
Chambersburg PA
CBHW031555240626
47153CB00002B/519